Books by Nancy Hale

DEAR BEAST

DEAR BEAST

by
Nancy Hale

Little, Brown and Company
Boston . Toronto

H163dε

Alas, thought the merchant, if my daughter Beauty could only know into what danger her rose has brought me!

— THE BROTHERS GRIMM

Part One

1

I DEALT with the young person from *Life* on the long distance telephone," Mrs. B. D. Starkey said. She set her teacup down and assembled a number of crumbs by touching her finger to her tongue and rapidly tapping the top of her round dining-room table. Then she put the collection into her mouth and continued. "I informed her that, since I had agreed to this photographing performance, I would certainly keep my word. But, I added, it is no treat at all to Starkeyville to come before the public eye. It should hardly be necessary to bring to your recollection, I said, First Starkeyville, that crucial battle; General Starkey of the Fifth Virginia; Birdsong Delaunay who was Lee's scout, and other facts and figures too numerous to mention."

"And what did she say, Miss Grace?" Annette Barr asked in a low voice. Rushton Barr had married her straight out of North Carolina, and Annette wavered between keeping her Tarheel accent subdued to spare the Virginians, and spurts of open rebellion. "Didn't she comprehend the trouble she was putting you to?"

3

"I trust she came to do so. I explained, more than once, that Cousin Lucinda Delaunay is not expected to live, and that, for us, a funeral in the Tidewater must always come first."

Little Abby Daniel, whom Mrs. Starkey counted on to help out at parties since, having no children, she had nothing better to do, abstracted the teacups that had been left by two departing ladies and slipped with them out into the kitchen. Her voice could be heard through the swinging door, asking Mattie, the cook, for more Sally Lunn. In a moment more she had slipped back into the dining room and into her place at the table, smiling.

Mrs. Starkey's tea had reached the stage where it would soon merge pleasantly into a cocktail party when the men arrived after half past five from their law offices, their shops, and the Merchants National Bank. Presently the ladies would wander across the broad hall to await the gentlemen in the living room; but now they sat on, relaxed, chairs pushed back from the table. The highly varnished portraits of Mrs. Starkey's ancestors hung — gray-fleshed faces tipped forward — against satin-striped, dark red wallpaper that had peeled away from the wall at the top. But the gilt cornices over the windows were still imposingly bright, and the heavy folds of garnet brocade that they overlapped, unfaded.

Since it was June and hot, a smell of mildew pervaded the old town house. It emanated from the plaster. It drifted down from the closed wardrobes in the upstairs bedrooms, and from the trunks in the attic where the dresses of four generations lay packed — with a revolver or two, bought for visits to country houses, tucked away in the layers. But nobody minded the smell. It was associated with indoor

4

coolness in hot weather, and spoke of green light sifting in through closed blinds, and the tinkle of iced drinks.

"I said to myself, We must move with the times," Mrs. Starkey said, though without conviction. Her large, military-looking face was flushed from the hot tea; her white hair mounted into a pile which, as a lady, she made it a point never to touch after she had once erected it in the morning. "I said to myself, Think of the pleasure we will be giving others."

There was a general murmur of gratification.

"My cousin Sally Wilson," Mrs. Armistead Nash put in, "kin to us through the Bowker connection, says that an architect she met in New York at a dinner, when she was sailing on the *Mauretania* last fall, the time they went to Italy and the Greek Islands, and continued on to visit the Holy Land — a most rewarding trip, both Sally Wilson *and* Gordon reported; they brought back a supply of water from the Jordan for the family baptisms, just in time; all that our great-grandfather brought back has been used up; this architect," said Amelie Nash, emerging triumphant from her struggle with syntax, "told Sally Wilson he considered Azalea unquestionably the most beautiful plantation house in Virginia."

Mrs. Starkey smiled coldly. Mrs. Fred Whiting raised graying eyebrows. "Well!" Miss Lilybud Carter exclaimed, with die-away inflection.

"To say the very least." It was Abby Daniel who voiced the general reaction.

Mrs. Starkey let her smile, grown warmer, drift on to Abby. Abby smiled back, shyly and appreciatively. Everybody in Starkeyville was devoted to Abby. She was just the sort of girl it might have been hoped Boogher Daniel would

5

marry. Boogher was right difficult — all the Daniels were difficult. But Abby handled him perfectly. You would hardly have known she was a Yankee.

"I wrote a poem about Azalea after first seeing it," Annette Barr said. "It got printed in the *Brambler,* at Sweet Briar. The place made such an impression on me! I could just see them, stepping down the slope to the river in their hoopskirts."

"Azalea is an evocation of all that was best in the past," declared Miss Lilybud Carter.

Mrs. Starkey, as the closest representative of the family who had originally owned Azalea, accepted the compliments with a comfortable nod.

"I assume *Life* will photograph every angle of the old place," Amelie Nash said. "As you pointed out, Miss Grace, it helps to think of the pleasure it will give. But little do they realize!" Mrs. Nash raised lovely, bovine eyes toward the flaking ceiling. Her listeners realized that she had paused to allow the vision of Reconstruction, hard times, and the sale of the great houses to Yankees, to appear: a familiar apostrophe. Mrs. Nash's face — feminine, luscious — was well suited to such upward glances. Army Nash was fond of declaiming, with a gesture toward his wife's dramatic postures, "Mrs. Armistead Nash as the Tragic Muse." Amelie's eyes suddenly descended with a jerk from the ceiling. "I didn't realize that you wrote," she said to Annette.

Several speculative glances were thrown toward young Mrs. Barr. But everybody was too polite to pursue this clue more overtly. Instead, the conversation returned to the photographer whom *Life* was sending to Starkeyville.

6

"He'll take this house too, I trust, Miss Grace?" Mrs. Cary Scott inquired. She was Mrs. Fred Whiting's house guest from Richmond. "It's so typical of the Southern, small-town residence. So, well, so homey." They all knew that she meant dowdy, and it smarted. Richmonders could always be counted on to say something snippy. "And Starkeyville is characteristic of just the sort of little town *The Rose That Died* describes," Mrs. Scott went on. "Didn't you say they plan to use the photographs like they were illustrations to the actual scenes in the novel?"

"I reckon so," Mrs. Starkey replied with her own share of hauteur. "I really have not inquired into every detail of their plans. This is, after all, a Starkey house, and I have no objection to their photographing it as long as it is done with dignity — They say they want to take the outside kitchen," she added with sudden enthusiasm. It was too boring to stay haughty. Only Richmond people could keep it up for hours on end.

"But honey! You haven't used the outside kitchen for thirty, forty years," objected her old and privileged friend Lucy Whiting.

"Honey, you think that matters?" Mrs. Starkey retorted. "I'm just trying to be accommodating, is all."

"I wonder who *did* write the book," put in Mrs. Nash, who had been brooding. Everyone looked at her, and there was a silence. Then Mrs. Nash put into words one other thought which they all shared. "I wonder if it *is* supposed to be Starkeyville?"

Mrs. Starkey, as hostess, rallied them. "I think not," she said decidedly. "It's just a pretty, charming Southern town, written about by somebody with quite a flair; quite a gift.

7

A Southerner. You can see that. Some lady or gentleman, I reckon, with a sense of delicacy about seeing their name on the cover of a book."

"Especially of a successful book," Mrs. Whiting amended. She was forever qualifying Mrs. Starkey's remarks; she had been doing it since they were six.

"Especially of a successful book," Mrs. Starkey echoed irritably. It was the easiest way to shut Lucy Whiting up. She returned to her main point. "It is for once, praise the Lord, a fair picture of the South. With so much filth going around under the name of literature, I declare it's a joy to read something pleasant for a change. Cousin Rosalie Delaunay, in Charlottesville, did write that Mr. Faulkner, when he was at the University, turned out to be a real sweet little man, if he *did* write those dreadful books . . . But the characters in *The Rose That Died* are people I'd be pleased to know. However," she went on, "I don't. Don't recognize a soul. Unless it is that fat man, always going on so about his ancestors. What was his name? It could be old Charlie Delaunay down in the Tidewater, Lucinda's brother. You reckon?"

"I, for one, can't think of a single town in the Tidewater to fit the book," Miss Lilybud Carter declared — a mouse making a major pronouncement.

"It wouldn't have to be exact," Mrs. Scott explained to her. "Authors make some of it up."

"I reckon I know that," the mouse retorted, sniffing.

"Grace," Lucy Whiting said, wiping her chin with her tea napkin and pushing her chair back with a loud scraping sound, "what are you going to do if your Cousin Lucinda decides to die just as that young man arrives to take pictures and you're not here to explain to him what's what?"

8

"Let him worry about that," Mrs. Starkey said grandly. "I explained over and over about Cousin Lucinda, but they would go on with their plans. He can just wait, that's what he can just do, until I get back and see about tending to him." Then she decided to be a little more realistic. Her voice dropped a key. "Abby can drive him around and show him where everything is," she said. "Can't you, Abby, child? Around Courthouse Square and into the law offices, and out to Azalea, and stay with him to see he doesn't break china or steal anything?"

"I'll be glad to," Abby Daniel said. She smiled her willing smile.

"Annette, you can conduct him through your mother-in-law's place, can't you, honey? And Lucy, you certainly know this house as well as you do your own," Mrs. Starkey finished, not wholly pleasantly.

Lucy Whiting threw her friend a look. "Grace," she said, "have you asked Lady Barbara yet about photographing Azalea? You said they'd left making the appointments to you."

Mrs. Starkey concealed a slight start. And at that moment a masculine voice broke in, from the doorway: "Well, well! So much pulchritude, and unattended! I see I am needed here." The owner of the voice, a tall thin man with sleek, orange-red hair, eased himself into the dining room, flashing his eyes at his hostess.

Abby Daniel looked up eagerly as her husband entered. Her hand went to adjust the black velvet ribbon that held her dark straight hair back from her forehead. Boogher Daniel threw her a smile and she subsided.

Mrs. Starkey rose. "We were just about to go into the living room for a little tetch. The bourbon is in the side-

9

board; bring two bottles, will you, Boogher?" She gave the name its Virginian pronunciation of "Booker." "Abby, tell Mattie to get out some ice. Lucy, the Parkinsons are coming this afternoon and I can speak to Lady Barbara then." Having disposed her troops, Mrs. Starkey marched off into the living room.

Boogher Daniel straightened up, with a bottle from the sideboard cupboard in each hand, as the ladies began to stray out of the dining room. He caught Mrs. Nash's handsome eye and lifted his brows.

"Stay me with flagons, and comfort me with apples," he declared, waving one of the bottles. "For I am sick of love!"

"Oh, *Boogher!*" she cried, with the arch look for which, as one of the beauties at the Hot in years gone by, she had been much admired. "You're so *literary!*"

2

Don't you once in a while long for a Martini?" Abby Daniel asked Rushton Barr, sitting beside her on a love seat. "I've gotten accustomed to bourbon in seven years, but doesn't anybody ever want some variety?"

"No, why should they?" Rushton replied. He had the handsome, spoiled face of the young man raised by adoring women; he was vice-president of the bank, hunted, and played golf at the country club. "Give me drinkin' whisky and branch water every time," he added ritualistically.

"Yes, I know; but just to enhance it by change?" Abby persisted. She smiled at Rushton coaxingly. Her lips trembled with the amused response she would have liked him to make; but to no avail. She could never seem to interest the Starkeyville men.

"Why should I change when I've got what I like?" Rushton said.

Abby gave up, on the subject of Martinis. "The first sip is the only thing that matters," she went on. "Sometimes I

11

think I'd give up the whole rest of the drink for that first wonderful sip."

Rushton stared blankly. He turned to his hostess, on his other side, who was deep in a discussion of South Carolinians with Armistead Nash, Rushton's superior at the bank. "Gaillards come into the Barr connection by way of Honora Gaillard, who married my great-uncle Percy Barr," Rushton contributed.

Abby sighed. Getting up, she took two of the Medallion china saucers that were being used as ashtrays and emptied them into the fireplace.

Mrs. Starkey's living room was less grandiose, more contemporary, than her dining room. The armchairs and the large, lumpy sofa were covered in a pale cabbage-rose chintz. Rose-colored broadloom carpeting was on the floor. Small tables stood about next to the chairs in the modern fashion of arranging furniture, most of them marked by alcohol rings, since Mrs. Starkey considered coasters vulgar, and Mattie never got around to removing the rings with oil and salt as she had been told to. The lower sashes of the three long windows on the garden side had been raised and a late afternoon breeze from across the rosebushes trickled in to stir the ladies' light dresses and the hair at the nape of their necks.

Over the mantel, with its plaster life-and-death frieze of ox skulls and bambinos, hung a St. Memin portrait of the Revolutionary War General Starkey. On the mantel stood two Wedgwood Portland vases that had come down through a Delaunay aunt. The china cabinet in the corner, however, displayed among Royal Worcester, Sèvres, and Crown Derby, some imitation Dresden, a number of hand-painted souvenirs of the 1907 Jamestown Exposition, and several pieces of blue willowware out of the five-and-dime store. The contents of the cabinet had been selected on no more involved a principle than that they were all Starkey possessions, and consequently of interest. Most of the objects included had sentimental associations with particular members of the connection. The Canton bowl at the top was that into which the Confederate General Starkey had bled to death from his Chancellorsville wound. The pink china vase shaped like a pair of baby boots had been presented, filled with sweetheart roses and forgetmenots, to Mrs. Starkey on the advent of her first-born, Elizabeth, who had later died from the strain of being married to a Yankee. The Benares brass bell had once been the property of poor May Beth Starkey, now a patient at DeJarnette Sanitarium.

On a black teak table inlaid with mother-of-pearl, in the bay window on the street side, stood the bottles of bourbon together with a silver pitcher of water and a kitchen mixing bowl filled with ice. One of the bottles was already empty.

"Come on, Boogher, bwah!" cried old Fred Whiting, who had just arrived from his law office. He accepted a drink from Abby Daniel and stepped forward, a small, withered, white-haired man who made a specialty of being forthright. He took a sip of bourbon. "*You* wrote this alleged work of fiction, did you not? Come clean, bwah! A literary fellow like you, dash a thing like that off in a week, I reckon."

"If he did, he'll soon be rolling in the long green," Rushton Barr remarked sourly to Mrs. Starkey. He looked with aversion toward Boogher where he sat leaning attentively toward lovely Mrs. Nash and gazing at pretty Mrs. Barr. "My good wife tells me it's gotten on the best-seller list,"

Rushton added, anxious lest anyone should imagine he read novels.

Boogher looked away from the ladies. He smoothed his red hair in a gesture he had, as if of recollecting its presence, and flashed a roguish smile at the faces turned toward him.

"That would be telling!" he said, shaking a forefinger. "Anonymous authors wouldn't *be* anonymous if their identity were revealed!"

"That's practically admitting you did write it, Boogher," Mrs. Nash rallied him.

"Far from it, dear lady," he replied. "I am only respecting the author's wish for privacy. As one with a vested interest in the literary world, I am loyal to the whims and reticences of its members."

"I b'lieve Boogher knows who wrote it and won't tell," Army Nash said as he sweetened his drink at the teakwood table. "Come on, now, boy," he said, turning. "*Is* this novel about Starkeyville?"

"Ah, ah," Boogher chided him. "Ask me no questions and I'll tell you no lies."

"Infuriating creature!" cried Mrs. Nash.

"Boogher is just trying to whet our curiosity," Annette Barr said from the sofa where she sat, looking pretty as a Jacqueminot rose.

"Curiosity is the lice of spife," Boogher retorted. He caught Abby's eye and his hand flew to smooth his hair. He was aware that he was talking ridiculously, but he could not stop. Like a child being naughty at a party, he could only go on and on. "My better half is looking at us," he murmured to Amelie Nash. "I fear she is either angry at me — for what, I can't imagine — or jealous of you. Which any woman might be forgiven for being," he said gallantly.

14

"I can't imagine Abby angry," Amelie said. "She's always so quiet."

"She *is* a quiet little thing," Boogher said. "But underneath, sometimes, I suspect she is criticizing us, if only in her diary. My honor as a gentleman, however, won't allow me to verify it," he added laughing. He shot his cuffs, and rested his hands on his thighs.

"I don't consider that being very loyal," Amelie said with traces of loftiness. "I feel a lady doesn't keep a diary after her courting days are over. Yankees may feel differently about it."

"Yankees are raised to be right critical," he agreed. "That's why they seem so cold."

People paused in their conversations, for a moment, as Peter and Lady Barbara Parkinson walked in, he ruddy and stolid, she wiry, voluble, and shrill. The Parkinsons were the present owners of Azalea. Peter Parkinson flew his private plane to the Washington airport every Sunday night, enroute to his New York brokerage office, and returned Thursday evenings to William and Mary County, of which Starkeyville was the seat. He was thus in time to ride to hounds on Fridays in winter, and for a weekend of polo in warm weather. The Parkinsons had altered Azalea out of all recognition — for the worse, in the eyes of the Delaunay connection. Their dinners were, however, delicious, and the contents of their stables admirable.

"So frightfully kind of you to ask us, Mrs. Starkey," piped Lady Barbara. "We *would* have been in time for tea, but I did have to fetch Pe-tah from the plane."

"Won't you have some tea now?" Mrs. Starkey asked, looking vaguely about for Abby.

"I *don't* think I will ectually; I've had my tea," Lady

Barbara said. She gave a high laugh that petered out into a whinny. The years, residence in many parts of the globe, and the unusual number of wars which her travels had exposed her to had left Lady Barbara virtually unmarked. It was impossible to imagine her, at any age, different from her present self — tanned, bony, and as though made of a tough bisque. "How *do* you do, Mr. Daniel," she said, advancing upon Boogher, who rose. "I hope you didn't think me too frightfully intellec-tual, ordering those eight books from England at one go; but you see I did rather have to have them, ectually. So kind of you to go to all the trouble," she went on. "My friends at home *keep* writing me 'What, you haven't read this or that new novel? Bubs dear, what is to become of you?' Ectually, I do like a bit of a read in the evening, especially when Pe-tah is in New York — p'raps you'll think it very booksy of me."

Mrs. Whiting was explaining Lady Barbara to her guest from Richmond. "Such good family," she said. "Barnabas d'Ives — a Norman name, of course. Lady Barbara is most appreciative of Starkeyville and the county; most appreciative. Grace doesn't like what she's done to Azalea — so fixed up, you know; but I tell Grace one never does like what outsiders do to one's own house."

Mrs. Scott nodded. "She must find the life here in William and Mary so interesting," she said. "So quaint. It's still just the way life used to be, when I was a girl and visited about. Y'all have managed to keep everything exactly the same."

Richmonders were too exasperating. Mrs. Whiting dealt a wrist slap. "Yes, up here we haven't been overtaken by commercialism and vulgarity. Not that I don't feel an occasional trip to Richmond keeps one in step with the times.

One mustn't get moss-grown, pleasant though it may be."

"The Prime Minister . . ." observed Mrs. Scott, who could change a subject as well as the next one. ". . . Didn't he marry a Barnabas d'Ives?"

"I b'lieve so; a cousin of Lady Barbara's, she would be."

"It *is* so satisfactory, I think," Mrs. Scott said, "the way the great British families manage to stick together, no matter how hard the times."

"They're *all* connected." Mrs. Whiting sighed with pleasure. "It's a bond, isn't it? It's just like Virginia."

"Exactly," Mrs. Scott agreed. The two ladies beamed at each other and held their glasses out to Abby for another drink.

". . . To tell the honest truth, Lydia Warren is *not* one of the Pocahontas Warrens," Mrs. Starkey was saying. She was still talking genealogy, but in so doing she was not neglecting her duties as hostess; from time to time a guest had attached himself to her group until now it constituted the principal conversation in the room. "She is, rather, a Roanoke Warren. She always claims kin with the Pocahontas Warrens, but I have yet to see the connection established to my satisfaction. I have never been a snob; nobody could claim kin more freely than I; but . . ." Mrs. Starkey gestured with one hand to express the helplessness of the position in which Lydia Warren put her.

"Did you ever hear Dan Faubiere's story about Miss Virgie Warren, Grace?" Fred Whiting asked.

"Many times," Mrs. Starkey replied.

Fred continued regardless; no female was going to put him off telling a story.

"Virgie was, as usual, carrying on and holding forth about the Pocahontas Warrens, as though no other family on God's green earth could hold a candle to them, until finally old Dan got plain disgusted and said, 'I know, Virgie; but on your mother's side, at least, you are white.' "

"Just *like* Dan," Mrs. Starkey commented automatically. Miss Lilybud Carter, as usual, seized upon anything that could lead into her favorite subject of contumely, integration.

"We won't *have* it," she chattered; they all knew what. "Never! We do *not* approve. What, mix our beautiful pure little darlin' children with that element? Even to *think* of those big, coarse niggra boys makes me shudder. Let them in Tennessee have it, if they wish. Let them have it in Kentucky. But we of the Tidewater will never . . . *never* . . . We just won't, that's all."

"But then, Lilybud dear, you're not *of* the Tidewater, are you?" Lucy Whiting inquired gently. She spoke from a position of security. She and her forebears had all been born into this world at Greenleaf Plantation, which, if not in the Tidewater, was on the right side of the Blue Ridge, here in William and Mary. In her family, there had been no accidents of the sort that had precipitated an infant Lilybud into the Valley of Virginia; all Mrs. Whiting's ancestresses had got back from places like North Carolina or West Virginia in time.

"I am in spirit," Miss Lilybud answered reproachfully. It was so unkind of Lucy, always throwing Harrisonburg up at her.

Boogher had deserted Amelie Nash's side for pretty Mrs. Barr. He sat with her on the sofa, one elbow propped up on the sofa back to give him a good view athwart her. His face was flushed, his smile fixed, and he was spouting puns like a geyser.

18

Mrs. Nash had gone to pour herself another little snort, and then joined the genealogical conversation. Lady Barbara Parkinson stood near the drink table, one foot up on the seat of a chair, talking to Armistead Nash.

"Mr. Daniel seems such a cur-ious man for a bookseller," she was saying. "Not that I know what a bookseller *ought* to seem . . . But does he always give one those *bold* glances? I *quite* blush," she said. "*Does* it help to increase sales, do you suppose, ectually?"

Army Nash laughed.

"I went to the University with Boogher," he said. "There isn't a particle of harm in him."

"He *is* a bit of what poor Mummy would have called a hand with the ladies."

"He'd be the first to agree," Army said. "At the University he and I courted the same girl for a while there, and one night when I was doing my courtin', what did Boogher have to do but hang around outside her house until I came out, and then haul off and swat me one. I was right put out with old Boogher," Army said. "Next day I asked him, I said, 'What in the name of the merciful heavens had I done to you, Boogher Daniel?' He put his hand up to that red hair of his, way he does, and said in the toploftiest voice, 'I've got the Daniel temper,' said. 'When I get worked up about a girl,' said, 'like I'm worked up about Linda, I just can't control myself, that's all.'"

"Oh, de-ar," Lady Barbara said sympathetically. "How too dreary of him! I do detest men who will come over all carnal, *don't* you? How is your roan mare?"

"Got a fistula and I had to shoot her," Army said.

Abby Daniel was trying to have a conversation with Peter Parkinson. While it had gone well enough at the beginning, it had steadily sagged since the moment Abby began telling how she first met Boogher, at a booksellers' convention in New York.

Peter's eyes had glazed; "Is that so?" he said. He sought about for the hard, animated face of his wife, talking sensibly about horses to a chap on the other side of the room.

"Yes," Abby said; smiling, trying to be entertaining. "I'd never heard an authentic Southern accent before, I can't tell you how taken I was with his!"

Peter had not come to the party to hear about how women without sex appeal had met their husbands; women, moreover, who appeared not to be interested in horses. "Do you go out with the William and Mary?" he asked, just in case he were mistaken. "Or with the Fairfax?"

"Go out? Oh, you mean hunt. I've never dared!" she said. "When I'm on a horse I always feel the reason it keeps looking over its shoulder is that it's plotting against me."

"Do you?" Peter said coldly. In his world, a horse was not called *it*.

"Let me put a little more in your glass," Abby offered in desperation.

"About to here," he agreed, marking the place on the glass with his finger. The woman appeared to be some sort of factotum around the place. He wished, when she hurried back with his glass and continued to talk animatedly to him, that she would simply stick to her duties.

He had not long to wait for an excuse to leave her. Everyone had had several drinks and gradually, inevitably, the party began to separate like curds and whey. The men stood in knots over by the long windows, talking law, banking, and horses; Peter joined the latter group. The ladies were left to their own devices in the vicinity of the sofa, where Mrs. Starkey still held forth. Abby Daniel, abandoned, gathered up some soiled glasses, misplaced by guests who had subsequently started over with fresh ones, and carried them out to the kitchen.

"Who is that woman?" Peter Parkinson inquired of Fred Whiting, beside whom he found himself standing. "The scrawny one, leaving the room."

"That's Abby Daniel," Fred said. "Boogher Daniel's wife."

"Great one to talk," Peter said.

"She's a nice little thing," Fred said. "Seen any good horses lately, Parkinson?"

"No. Seen any?"

Ensconced deep in the middle of the vast sofa, Mrs. Starkey was equally deep in genealogical considerations. "My Aunt Rosalie," she was explaining to Lady Barbara, "on the Delaunay side — that is, she married a Delaunay — was, herself, English. A Chiverton. Of Kent. Their place is called Taunton Wells. I have an engraving of it in the library."

"Really?" Lady Barbara said. "How love-ly." She sounded doubtful.

"Yes. The families have always remained in touch."

"Miss Grace!" Abby Daniel leaned over Mrs. Starkey from behind the sofa. "Mattie says there's no more ice. What would you like me to do?"

"Abby, honey," Mrs. Starkey said, distracted. "I don't know what in the world to tell you. Deal with the situation, hear? You've got so much sense."

"Shall I run home and get a tray or two of our ice?"

Abby was tired, she did not want to run home at all,

but since the offer had suggested itself to her she could not see how to avoid making it.

"Oh, yes." Mrs. Starkey cried, relieved.

Abby stood alone, irresolute, trying to gauge the party — how much longer it would last; how much more ice was likely to be required.

On the sofa, Miss Lilybud Carter gave a little shiver of pure delight. "Oh, Grace!" she cried. "It's such fun talking kin! I don't see how people stand it who haven't got any!"

Boogher Daniel, who alone had not joined the other gentlemen but had been replenishing his glass, came sliding across the room toward the ladies. Abby's face lighted up as he approached her.

"Abby," Boogher said. "Don't forget poor Miss Grace's party, child. There's not a smidgin of ice left in the bucket."

"I know," she said. "I was just considering running home to get some." She hoped Boogher would offer to go instead; she felt perhaps he might.

"Well, run, then, darlin'," he urged. "And bring me back some of my cigarettes when you come."

Since he had not offered to, there was nothing left to do but go herself.

3

By nine o'clock, soft warm darkness had fallen over the streets that crawled up over the hill of Starkeyville and down the other side. On Main Street newsstand, bowling alley, and drugstore were wide open and brightly lighted. Girls and young men came out from bowling a string and strolled over to catch a dope at the drugstore. "Ha, Bitsy!" they called into the mild night. "Ha, Gooper! Ha yew?"

Just above them on the crest of Starkeyville's hill stood the templelike courthouse, with a lone bronze Confederate soldier in front of it, leaning upon his bronze rifle in the darkness. A gleam from the street light twinkled, unobserved, upon the rim of his forage cap.

Down the west side of the hill ran the residential streets — Cary, Starkey, Bolling Avenue, Buford Row. Along them, Victorian brick or frame houses showed here and there the hint of dignified life within — a family around a late supper table, a lady watering a plant in the window — before the shade was drawn, the curtain jerked across, and life continued within unseen, open only to conjecture.

Far down the west side of the hill, below the shopping streets, lay the jumble of shacks that made up Brownsville: dark brown ruins, weathered board lean-tos, and an occasional, more prosperous stucco house. Down there a guitar was being strummed faster and faster and faster. Life boiled, in that darkness, and out of it voices called vibrantly, "Booker T., you gimme that . . ." and "Take *care* you'se'f, Sugar . . ."

Around the base of the hill, in a broad curve, swept the lights of the cars, following the cut-off on Route 43 from Washington to Richmond that left Starkeyville moldering upon the foundations of its past.

The last guests had just departed Mrs. Starkey's house on Armistead Street — the Nashes and the Barrs and the Daniels all together — in the rush of nostalgia for the University that always struck them along with the fifth drink. "Sweet Sue . . . It's you . . ." sang Army and Boogher and Rushton in close harmony as they went slowly down Miss Grace's steps and out of the circle of radiance cast by the veranda light. Followed by their wives they passed down to the corner of Cropp Street, waving their arms to conduct the music they were singing to. As they reached the corner they began a fresh tune. "Come, fill your glasses up," they sang under the winking light, standing in a huddle, bodies jerking up and down together in time to the rhythm. "For Tilka . . . For Tilka . . . For Til-ka . . ."

Mrs. Starkey closed her front door and went back into the house, turning out lights. She moved on to the kitchen, where Mattie had left a covered plate of supper in the refrigerator and gone home. Mrs. Starkey lifted the inverted soup bowl off the plate and peered at what lay underneath. Cold lamb and mint jelly, sliced cucumber and cold fried tomatoes. "Pooh," said Mrs. Starkey, disappointed. She carried the plate back into the living room on a tray set with silver and a napkin, and sat down on the sofa with her supper on the low table in front, to eat it like a lady.

Her eye strayed. When she had eaten about half her supper, she put down fork and knife with decision and crossed the room to fetch the third bottle of bourbon, standing on the disordered drink table.

She puffed ineffectually at some cigarette ash that had been spilled on the mother-of-pearl inlayed surface. But Mattie could clean it all up tomorrow. Mrs. Starkey carried the bottle back to the sofa, poured some of its contents into the half-full glass of water on her tray, and sat down. After a few moments, still dissatisfied, she picked up the glass, and with it and the bottle, leaving the food behind, she went off to find snugger comforts in her downstairs bedroom.

There, loving faces within photograph frames — Cousin Lula Delaunay; Aunt Mary Stuart Starkey; Cousin Willie Starkey posed with his wife, poor May Beth; Mamma; Mrs. Starkey's own darling dead daughter Elizabeth, who married the Yankee; Grandfather Delaunay on the porch at Azalea with Papa and all the uncles — gazed at Mrs. Starkey night after night with the old approbation and encouragement. It was the easiest thing in the world to let them come alive — to let Elizabeth sit here beside her on the bed while Mrs. Starkey went into detail about what she thought of a man who would just plain kill his wife with his neglect and his scoffing, and his staying out all night when the baby was coming — that poor little baby that never saw the light of day. Wit and intellect were all

25

very well, she would declare, but they didn't begin to compare with an honest heart and a kind tongue when it came to dealing with the prettiest girl in Starkeyville, who could have had anybody, but had to fall in love with a Yankee, when all that came of it was sorrow, and tragedy, and a poor little dead baby, and a broken heart, and death . . . "No indeed, Elizabeth," she would declare, "I have no use for him."

She could relive the day when May Beth Starkey took the knife from the kitchen in this very house, the biggest knife, and went in the yard — to kill whippoorwills down at the foot of the garden, May Beth had explained over her shoulder as she went down the steps . . . She could sit among the uncles on the hot dry brick of the porch at Azalea, lazily admiring the crape myrtles blossoming on either side of the white steps in the August sun, while Uncle Cecil rocked in the rocker he had lifted from the lawn of the University when he was graduated twenty years before, and Uncle Jay, the one who married Cleo Woodbine from down in the Hollow — only he hadn't got drunk and married her yet — told about finding panther tracks in the bottom land, the part they kept in corn; it was the year of the bad drought, when the panthers came down from the mountains for water . . . And all the time Grandfather sat there, not talking, just being Grandfather, until he made up his mind he *would* say something, and then it was, "Grace. Where the hell is my toddy? Sun's directly overhead."

Oh, far away and long ago, sweet gold Virginia days! Memory clothed them in garments of rose and of azure, swathed them in veils of glory — memory, that soil of one's whole proper being.

26

After a pick-up supper, the Nashes sat in the living room. Amelie read the William and Mary *Messenger,* while Army, who had always cared for history, followed the campaigns of Stonewall Jackson with book, map, and contemporary letter.

"Old Miss May Gunn is sailing for Europe Tuesday from New York, on an extended tour," Amelie reported.

"You swear," Army replied.

"Did you consider my flowered pink successful?" she inquired, turning over a page of the paper.

"You looked fascinating," he said, one finger on the line marking the Union supply route at the First Battle of Manassas.

"I wasn't quite sure," Amelie said, after several minutes had passed.

Army had not lost track. "You're too modest," he said "Every eye was upon you."

"Whose?" she asked.

"Well," he said, finger still holding the line a little further on, "Mistoo, Mistoo, arrah, arrah . . ." He sought about for a name in the Virginian fashion. "Mistoo Parkinson. You seem to have made right much of an impression on Parkinson."

"What makes you think so?"

"He showed it."

"Who else?"

"Well, Rushton as usual. Old Fred. And Boogher, if you want to count Boogher."

"Why do you always take that tone about Boogher?"

"I don't like him."

"Jealous?" she rallied him.

But his finger had stolen still further along the line toward Bull Run. There was a silence while Amelie scanned the paper further.

"Who else?" she asked.

"Wasn't anybody else there," he said.

"Boogher is ardent," she observed. "Like a European."

Army nodded and bent over the map. From time to time he glanced in reference into the volume lying open on the table beside him.

"Women like ardor," Amelie said.

Army lifted his face and threw her a warm, mechanical smile. "How does it feel to be just as fascinating at forty," he asked, "as at twenty? Or even more so? You now add the charm of maturity." He returned to his map.

Amelie continued ruffling through the newspaper, her eye catching a paragraph here, an advertisement there. Occasionally she readjusted her attitude so as to recline more gracefully upon the cushioned sofa. She read all over again, from the beginning, the column headed COUNTY SOCIALS.

Then she picked up, from the coffee table before the sofa, the novel everyone was talking about, *The Rose That Died,* and opened to where she had left a book mark on page 32. It had taken her two weeks to get that far. She began, conscientiously, to read.

"There is *not* all the time in the world!" Eugenia exclaimed. Turning away from Mary Lou she stared down past the barns to the winter-bare woods. The seasons intermesh, she continued, silently, within her mind; already in January I can feel the spring — in the light, the thrush this morning. The seasons intermesh, and are gone in their very beginning.

Mary Lou, beside her, was looking down the hill also; what could she possibly see there? The barns, the woods, the road, was that all? Mary Lou was as obedient as a sheep; she could be counted on to go to the dance at Oaklands, to engage herself to Arthur Carrington, to have seven — no, six — children; seven would too nearly approach a rebellion from something, from having six, perhaps. And all the time the world would be there, beyond, with the diamonds gradually dimming and the music fading, while Mary Lou completed the delivery of a sixth child to her satisfaction. "Oh!" Eugenia cried; she turned on her heel to walk back to the house.

"What's the matter?" Mary Lou asked, startled.

"I said, there is *not* all the time in the world," Eugenia repeated, but in a quieter voice. For it had occurred to her that, although she could imagine such a fate for Mary Lou, it might be she herself who would inherit it; that is, unless instead of anger she could contrive action.

But how was action contrived?

Amelie laid the novel down again. It was very deep. The characters seemed all to be people who did a great deal of thinking. She picked up the *Messenger* again, and tried to find in it something she had not already read.

Then she looked across the room at her husband's bent head, yawned loudly with her chin tipped far back, and let the newspaper fall with a crash under her hands. "Damn your old Stonewall Jackson," she said.

Army put down the map he had been studying, turned, and stared at his beautiful, full-blown wife.

"You better be still," he said. "Unless you want to talk about Hugh Warren. Unless you want to talk about the time with Carter Williams. I know plenty about you."

Amelie jerked her shoulders and picked up the paper again. "I'm sorry," she said fretfully, from behind it. Armistead scared her to death when he talked like that. She always had the instant vision of an enormous filing cabinet full of data about her. Carter Williams . . . Hugh Warren . . . Did Armistead know about the night she had kissed Rushton Barr out in his Pontiac convertible? What *did* he know?

Sometimes the vague feeling reached her consciousness that perhaps she had not really done anything so awful, on those occasions she visualized as filed away under names and dates. Was kissing grounds for divorce? — for of course she had always been a *lady*. What, the vague feeling went on, did Armistead actually know? What was there *for* him to know? The feeling was very vague — too vague to compete with the terror that took over when Armistead spoke threateningly. He was a man, he knew things. Amelie's whole irrational feminine nature reacted so as to bring her at once to heel.

After a moment Army removed his stare from her and looked back at the map. In another moment he stretched his left leg out; then his right leg. Then he stretched his neck, twisting it from side to side.

"Wear your flowered pink again," Army said, after some time had passed. "It shows your figure off to perfection." Humming almost inaudibly and holding his finger to a point on the map, he flipped over some pages in the volume beside him.

Mrs. Cary Scott, in the guest room at the Fred Whitings', sat writing a letter to her friend Virgilia Harrison in Richmond. She was aware that what she wrote would be read aloud to the members of the Tuesday Afternoon Bridge Club, and so she was endeavoring to be both newsy and guarded.

Just the same old Starkeyville [she wrote in a flowing hand]. Countrified. Remember how we used to call Beady Starkey "Stark," just because he looked as juicy as a ripe cornfield melon dancing at the Germans? How we did giggle! And he never caught on.

Everyone here, of course, is talking about *The Rose That Died,* especially since *Life* is sending somebody down to take pictures of Starkeyville, to show the kind of small-town life the novel describes. I don't know whether Starkeyvillians are most stuck up about getting photographed, or scared for fear the book is really about them! Have you heard any more theories as to who wrote it? My hunch has been all along it is a Richmonder. All Virginia authors are Richmonders. Besides, the novel shows the influence of Miss Ellen's style . . .

Mrs. Scott paused, shook her head, smiled, and allowed an inner dialogue to develop between Virgilia Harrison and herself. It was a frequent occupation of Mrs. Scott's to hold conversations with people not present, including many of the deceased; she was able to hear the very tone of their voices. "Why, Mary Stuart Scott!" Virgilia was exclaiming, "It does *not* show the influence of Miss Ellen or anything like it! Miss Ellen never wrote about anybody except Richmonders or either poor whites, one. This *Rose* book is about the pokiest kind of people. Miss Ellen wouldn't any more have fooled with it than fly to the moon."

"That's what you think, Virgilia," Mrs. Scott retorted. "But you never did follow literature very closely, did you? I realize I myself enjoyed exceptional advantages, having Papa for a father and him being editor of the *Newsleader* so long and all; so I don't expect others to have the same background, or literary judgment. I'm just informing you,

31

honey, that the style of this novel shows it is written by somebody who sat at Miss Ellen's own knee."

"Speaking of knees," Virgilia interrupted, "I ought to tell you that several of us at the Tuesday Afternoon Bridge Club think you honestly are wearing your skirts too short for your age, honey. We wouldn't want you to be laughed at by outsiders, so we decided one of us ought to take it upon herself to tell you, as a friend. We wouldn't wound you for the world."

"Virgilia, honey, far from wounding me you make me shake my head in wonder, at how far behind the times in fashion Richmond can get when it really puts its mind to it, and it most always *is* putting its mind to it just as hard as . . ." But the conversation seemed to Mrs. Scott to be getting both trivial and out of hand. She turned her attention away from the curious life of its own which such a conversation seemed always to take on, back to her letter.

— You ask after my host and hostess. Poor Fred! Lucy has about as much consideration as a hoot owl. Fred is the greatest possible sufferer from sciatica and you'd think Lucy hadn't even been informed of the fact, the way she's always after him to do something and go somewhere. She's the kind of woman who will push her husband straight into the grave if she doesn't pay him more mind. Once her children were born and raised Lucy saw no further purpose to Fred. There's the Virginia woman for you — sweet and loving on the surface and underneath a manager. I don't mean to say for a moment Lucy is *hypocritical*.

A party this afternoon at Grace Starkey's. Remember Grace? Beady Starkey's wife. Beady had quite a case on me at the White, years ago. Don't you know Grace still holds it up against me? It's the Delaunay revengefulness. She hardly spoke to me once the men started coming in. Grace always was man-crazy, but nobody ever looked at her but Beady, and he didn't look at her much, if the truth must be told. — Sometimes I get the feeling that with all I know about the ins and outs of people here in Virginia I could just burst.

Mrs. Scott paused, and then drew a line through her last sentence. Virgilia's own past was on the colorful side. Dissatisfied with the adequacy of the scratching out, Mrs. Scott wrote the word "Baby" over and over on top of the words until they were quite undecipherable.

Miss Lilybud Carter lifted the kettle off the hot plate and poured its boiling water over the tea leaves, chuckling quietly to herself as the pleasant aroma rose to meet her nostrils. Delicious! There were so many little innocent pleasures that the hard in heart, the jeering and the worldly-wise of Starkeyville wotted not of, she reflected. With a teapot and cup and saucer, she retired to her tiny bedchamber, curtained off from the main room which she rented from Mrs. Harper Reaves on Cropp Street. Plain people, the Reaveses, but clean and honest.

Snugly in bed, Miss Lilybud sipped her tea while continuing to write and draw diligently on an old cutting board that had been used in her childhood by visiting dressmakers. Miss Lilybud was designing a family tree. She had been drawing them for years, and each one was more elaborate than the last. This one had beautiful, realistic bark shaded in on the trunk and branches, and little veined leaves which Miss Lilybud drew with infinite care. On each leaf was inscribed somebody's name. Sue Ann Blythe, said the one Miss Lilybud had just finished. Its tip pointed, as though in accusation, straight at George Ster-

33

ling Blythe. As in life, so on the family tree, Miss Lilybud reflected, chuckling. Sue Ann never could abide George Joseph.

Mary Frances Blythe married Alonza Carter III, June, 1892. Issue: Alonza IV, David Dancer, Mary Frances, Elizabeth Blythe. Tears came to Miss Lilybud's eyes, and a sob to her throat, for Elizabeth Blythe Carter was none other than herself, born sixty years ago in the Valley of Virginia by mismanagement. Pluckily she swallowed her tears and sketched away at her own little leaf. It was going to be beautiful, this tree, and when it was done she would give it to Cousin Lulie Stokes Blythe to show her that she bore no hard feelings for anything Cousin Lulie Stokes might have said about origins. Christian forgiveness was what Miss Lilybud clung to. Between Christian forgiveness and drawing family trees she managed to keep busy every hour of the day. And besides, with a blot like Harrisonburg on her past, it was important to keep a clear idea of her own identity.

"I want to finish turning this heel," Annette Barr protested. "I've just started. I always lose count if I stop in the middle."

"You've always just started something," Rushton exclaimed. He stood with his hands in his pockets; his soft handsome face rebuffed, offended.

"No I haven't either. Just right now."

"You seem to think knitting is more important than your husband. Some women wouldn't."

"Wouldn't think knitting is more important than you? Am I supposed to get jealous?"

"It's perfectly simple, what I meant. I meant it's not

natural and normal, the way you always let something stand in the way of our going upstairs."

"It's not natural and normal the way you always want to go upstairs," Annette retorted. "You can't seem to get it off your mind."

"You should be pleased. You should be glad I'm so in love with my pretty wife."

"I should weep with delight when you give me a smile and tremble with fear at your frown. Like Abby Daniel and Boogher."

"You know that's not what I mean," Rushton said, outdone. Annette for some time had been turning everything into a tangle of talk this way. "I mean plain old let's go upstairs."

"Well, I mean plain old let's don't."

"When *are* we going to? Are you always going to be turning a heel or too tired?"

"Don't be silly. Don't exaggerate. I just happen not to think sex is every single thing in life, that's all. The way you do."

"I do not!" he shouted, outraged. "I just want to lead a natural, normal life and have natural, normal —"

"*Now* we're getting down to it," she said. "Now we have it. You just want some normal, natural little Barrs, don't you — whole litters of them?"

"What in the world is the matter with that, darling? Of course I want babies. I thought you did too."

"Maybe I would," she cried, tears starting from her eyes. "If they were just going to be nice little children of my own. But *oh* no! They have to be William and Mary Barrs, Oak Hill Barrs. Bred for like you'd breed horses. I *won't* be a brood mare for Barrs!"

"Honey *lamb*," he said, getting down on his knees beside the arm of her chair, "nobody in the wide world would let you do any such thing. Darling child, don't you know it's you I love? Babies would only be an expression of how much we love each other, I sincerely hope and trust —"

"That's what you say," she said, wet-cheeked, pulling away from him to the further side of her chair. "But it isn't really so. You don't — *nobody* pays any attention to the real me. Everybody laughs at me for being from the wrong state. *I* know they hate me! Nobody in the world but my Daddy cares whether the *Johnson* line is going to be continued. Because the Johnsons are common. They're from North Carolina."

"Honey, that's not one word of it true."

"Forgiving, aren't you? Willing to overlook the fact I'm only a Virginian by marriage. Lucky me; just so I strain every nerve to cover up the fact I'm some little old Tarheel nobody ever heard of. Well, I don't care! I *like* being a Tarheel! I'm *used* to it! I'll fix those old Virginians! I'll — I'll write them up in a poem!"

"There, love; there now," Rushton gentled her. "There, my darling. Some of the *old* girls can be right stiff-necked, for a fact. But most of what you've said is your own imagination. And you ought to know *I'm* not living in the past. I wouldn't have married you if I didn't want you exactly the way you are."

"Oh, Rushton . . ." she wailed. Putting her head on his shoulder, she wept.

"There . . ." he soothed her. After a moment he said, "Let's go upstairs."

She raised a tearstained face.

"Rush."

"Yes, love."

"Just one thing."

"Anything."

"If we had a baby — if it was a boy — I want to name him after Daddy. Alfred Johnson Barr. I think it sounds nice."

Rushton sat back on his heels, still patting his wife's shoulder.

"I think it does too," he said slowly. "And naturally we'll name a son after Mr. Johnson. Only for a first son, darling — don't you think the normal, natural way is to . . ."

"I don't see why nobody will ever listen when I talk," Abby Daniel said. She and Boogher sat in their sitting room on the third floor of the Robert E. Lee Apartments. "I try so hard to be nice, and be funny, but nobody talks to me, and nobody ever laughs at my jokes."

"Your passion for attention seems insatiable," Boogher ejaculated, interrupted in his reading. He smoothed his light red hair and laid the copy of *Theocritus* down on his knee. "With a devoted husband, a host of distinguished friends, in beautiful surroundings, one might suppose you could be content. Not so. Your nature appears to cry out for endless notice."

"Boogher!" Abby cried. She could never get used to his rages. "It does not! It's only I sometimes wish people talked to me at parties —"

"Perhaps people feel you are critical," he said.

"But I'm not critical!" she wailed.

His eyes lit up with a fanatic fire. "You're a hard little Yankee Puritan, sitting in judgment."

"How can you *say* that! I do everything I can to make

37

you happy, and to make people love me . . ." Her heart beat painfully.

"You have no love. No pity," he said.

"I love *you*," she said.

"Actions speak louder than words."

"I never criticize . . ."

"You don't need to voice criticism. I see it in your eyes. Don't you suppose *I* ever need sympathy?" he said, his voice swelling richly. "Do you suppose *I* can exist on a cold, rational relationship?"

"I'm not cold!"

"Do you suppose any husband likes being relegated to second place? Don't you suppose I realize I am not your central concern?"

"Yes, you are!"

"Oh no. *Oh* no. You yourself are. You have to take *everything*, in this marriage," he said.

"I don't know what you mean."

"You know well enough what I mean," he said.

"But I've done everything you asked me to," she said in despair.

"Done what I asked," he said, "but at the same time sat in judgment. Loved me, but with your mind on something else. You're tough, Abby. Tough and hard."

She gazed up at him helplessly where he stood before her, face dark, hands clasped behind his back.

"I wish I could make you understand me," she said. "I'm not tough and hard. Really I'm not."

"I wish I could make you understand *me*," he replied. "It's pleasant, in a marriage, when the wife understands the husband . . . But you've never thought about my

38

problems. You've never tried to. You've been too wrapped up in your own little Yankee concerns."

Abby burst into tears.

"Bravo!" Boogher said. "A certain type of woman, pushed into a logical corner, tends to resort to tears. Are you trying to make me sorry for you, perhaps?"

"No," she said. "It's only that I'm *always* trying to do what you want . . . I'm always trying not to be egotistical . . ."

"It might be more appropriate to the facts if you felt sorry for *me*," he continued. "I can't see that you need pity. You have everything you've ever gone out to get. Me, for instance. I sometimes wonder what it is you want of me. Or do I just go along with being a married woman?"

"How can you say such things?" she cried, beside herself.

"Do I?" he persisted.

Abby dried her eyes hurriedly and put her hand out to touch Boogher's.

"Boogher," she murmured.

"Yes?" he replied.

"You *know* how I feel about you."

"How do you feel?" he asked.

"I love you," she said. "I'm crazy about you."

"Yes?" he said, sitting down on the arm of her chair. "Tell me."

"I want you," she said.

He put his cheek beside her thin one, laid his hand on her lap, and said, "Go on."

Abby drew a long shuddering sigh. *"Why* do you always have to get so angry with me?" she murmured as he kissed her.

39

He straightened up, surprised. His hand went to smooth his hair. "Honey, you know I can't control my temper," he protested.

At Azalea, the Parkinsons had gone to bed. The windows stood open to the warm, singing night, the fields of darkness stretching for acres over Azalea land. Their chamber was a large one, one of two on the front that overlooked the box-encircled lawn. They occupied twin beds. They were reading — Peter a copy of *Sports Illustrated*, Lady Barbara a novel.

"I say Pe-tah," she said.

"What?" he murmured.

"I say *did* you hear that fearful woman ask me if I'd allow the house to be photographed on Tuesday next? Only she didn't *ask*, ectually, I should say she rather *told* me, the bloody impertinence of it. *Do* you think I should get my back up, Pe-tah? I mean to say, I did write that editor or whoever he was that he might, but now if I chose I could simply write again and say I *don't* think I want pictures of the place in their filthy magazine, thank you very much. Mummy would never allow d'Ives Abbey photographed, not even by silly old Beaton. Why the hell should *I*, ectually? *Shall* we be frightfully difficult, darling?"

"Oh, God," Peter said. "What do we care? As for the Widow Starkey commandeering the place for Tuesday, she thinks it still belongs to her, you know."

"Well, it doesn't, as she'll soon see. Nothing of it is hers but the wretched graveyard."

"It's just the way things are in Virginia, my dear. Have to put up with it."

"I don't have to put up with a bloody bit more than I

bloody well choose," Lady Barbara said. She glanced down under the lower rims of her spectacles and smoothed the lapels of her tailored satin bedjacket. "What bliss it would be to properly do the Virginians in."

"Have to keep the good will of the countryside, you know, Bubs. We hunt over their land — or their cousins' cousins' land, same thing," Peter said. He went back to his journal.

Lady Bubs sighed and let her eyes return to her novel. It was not very amusing. She wriggled her thin buttocks more comfortably down into the bed, snatched her pillows about into different positions, and gave a hitch to her bedjacket. Then she reached for the handkerchief on her bed table, and blew her nose irritably.

"This is such a filthy book," she complained out loud. "*The Rose That Died* was ectually a fearfully amusing job of work, *didn't* you think?"

Peter did not reply. Lady Bubs gave him a furious look.

4

You mean the photograph of the cavalry officer in the parlor is a likeness of Mrs. Starkey herself?" Tommy Hume asked Abby Daniel a week later. They stood on the gingerbread-railinged porch after closing the front door of Mrs. Starkey's house after them. They had already made two trips to carry Tommy's camera equipment out and pile it in the drive-it-yourself car again.

"That was Miss Grace in her mauve," Abby said, nodding.

"How perfectly darling, to surround yourself with pictures of yourself," Tommy said, lighting a cigarette. "So homey. I'd love to see Miss Grace in her gun-metal. And in her steel-gray. I bet she looks like a meat cleaver."

Abby giggled. Tommy ran down the front steps with a loose-ankled clatter of heels, Abby following. They got into the car. When he was behind the wheel Tommy consulted a letter that he took from his breast pocket. With a pencil he crossed off one line in it.

"Azalea next?" he asked, starting up the motor.

"Courthouse Square would be nearer," Abby said. "Then we could drive out to Azalea. In between we'll go home while I get you a bite of lunch." Tommy seemed like an old friend, she reflected; such a friend as she had never in fact had.

He shook his head. "*You* have lunch with *me*," he said. "In some local *patisserie*. There's all that money of Mr. Luce's I have to spend. And eating at home gets to be so deadly monotonous in a small town."

"How did you know?"

"I come from one."

"Southern?"

"No, Middle Western. But if you overlook the Middle Western passion for two Cadillacs in every garage and having supper at half past five, I begin to fear it's not so very different. *The Rose That Died* sounds like home. My old Middle Western home, with some white columns pasted up in front."

"The Southerners would die if they heard you."

"It's a nice theory, though," he said. "And that would be why the columns in the South look so insistent. You don't knock yourself out insisting you're something that you indisputably are. Just if you're scared you might not be. Then the abyss yawns."

"What would happen if the white columns were taken away?" she said, turning in the front seat to look at him. "— You turn left here."

"If they were a real part of the house, it would then fall down," he said. "If you weren't, you'd have a house left. Goodness, how I do love to be profound."

"Do you want to look at the courthouse first? The law offices are in the same neighborhood."

43

"Courthouse first, law offices afterwards," Tommy decided. "And one law office ought to be plenty. Benson's letter says, 'Humphrey Deane's law office' in the singular. Can you pick me out one that'll be like Humphrey Deane's law office?"

"Down here you pronounce it 'Umphrey," Abby said, "I can show you just the one."

They parked the car at the foot of the rise crowned by the courthouse, and walked in the June sunshine up worn marble steps toward the Confederate statue.

"He's all over the South," Abby said, nodding at that solitary figure. "In every town square and in every cemetery. Just standing there."

"You sound quite moved," he said, looking down at her.

"I always am," she said. "The same thing that can be so exasperating when people fight the War all over again at parties seems suddenly pathetic, when it's reduced to a statue, standing there all alone all night long, in the rain and everything."

He continued to look down at her smooth dark head, six inches lower than his own.

"Well," he remarked, looking up at the courthouse, "that's a mighty fine body of Colonial architecture, ma'am."

"It certainly is," she said.

The pink brick courthouse, pediment supported by slender white pillars, arcades stretching to either side of its central façade, stood in beautiful symmetry overlooking all of Starkeyville.

"They couldn't do anything wrong, in those days," he said.

"The taste of angels," she agreed.

44

"Where did it all go to?" he continued as they entered the dim, damp, central hall of the building. "What went wrong? That house we just cleaned up on — hardly a beautiful thing in it on which to rest the exhausted eye. Anything good was all jumbled up with a lot of garbage. Those oil paintings — Jesus! Doesn't anybody know the difference? What happened?"

"The official answer is that the War did it," Abby said.

"Oh, *the* War," he said. "Do you think that's possible?"

"I don't know," she said, "I can't see how a war would change people's *taste*. Unless the act of engaging in a war is ruinous. Corrupting."

"You think there's some mysterious corruption in war itself?"

"I don't know. But what did happen?" she asked, her cheeks flushed, her eyes shining with the intoxication of being listened to. "Perhaps it isn't defeat that destroys, so much as choosing to fight in the first place — although that doesn't hold water. Because the North's taste would have been lost too, if that were so."

"Besides, Victoria got her finger in the pie in the meantime. And then there's the South's famous poverty . . ."

"I never heard of taste absolutely requiring money," she said. "— This is the courtroom." She led the way through double swinging doors into a big chamber painted light green with white woodwork. Modern varnished chairs were set in rows for the jurors, and a copy of one of the Stuart Washingtons hung behind the judge's bench.

"Okay," Tommy said after looking around a minute in silence. "We'll do some outside shots, and then this, and then the sheriff's office. A quickie of the sheriff's office, just enough to show what kind of a place Howard P. Custard would work in. In the novel. — What a name, Howard P. Custard."

"*Holland* P. Custard," Abby corrected him.

"That's right," he said.

Outside again, Tommy interrupted the game, that used pebbles for marbles, of two little colored boys at the foot of the courthouse steps, and gave them quarters to carry his equipment up to the broad marble plaza at the top. Half an hour went to photographing the outside of the building, and nearly an hour to the inside. For the pictures of the interior of the courtroom and the sheriff's office, Tommy got Abby to wave a large sheet of white paper slowly back and forth in front of the light, diffusing it, while he counted the minutes of exposure on his wrist watch.

"Ba, Miz Daniel," Sheriff Crown said as they left his office at length. "Tell Boogher hello for me. Ba, sir."

The two little colored boys had long ago lost interest and disappeared. Tommy hired fresh ones to take his equipment back to the car again. As he walked with Abby down the long flight of marble steps, now shining in noonday sunlight, he said, "But perhaps the War *did* have that effect on the North too, bearing out your theory of corruption of taste lying in the act of turning from peace to war. You don't find anything as nice as Greek Revival in New England again, after 1865."

"I suppose the taste was so superlative down here that its loss shows up more," Abby said.

"And of course now, in the North, you find the modern — Gropius — all sorts of new taste," Tommy said. "Taste that looks outwards, I mean reaches for new forms instead of crawling around in the old ones. It's as though after the

War the South's licking the wound of defeat withdrew its taste, so that it could no longer look out, only in; back. As a matter of fact, that's what this novel, *The Rose That Died,* is about, how the past can be like a false center — give the illusion of being a center, but can't hold up in a pinch, so the rose, whose center it is, dies."

"Yes, I know," Abby said.

"What gets me is that a hundred years pass and Victoria's dead and the poverty *can't* be from the same cause, and yet it's still the War's fault and Sherman's fault etcetera that the Southerners can't select anything to put in their houses you'd give henhouse room to."

"They can't let go," Abby said.

"Of the past?"

Abby nodded. "What *is* it about that war?" she said. "They're not the only ones who brood about it. Northerners brood about it. We're brooding about it now."

"I had a friend," Tommy said, "a guy in New York who died of cancer last year. When he was delirious at the end, guess what he raved about? His wife told me afterwards. The Civil War. He fought its battles over and over and over, she said. I happen to know that Halloran had never given history a thought since he left P.S. 28."

"How strange," Abby said, entranced.

They had reached the halfway point in the steps, where a wide marble landing had a bronze plaque set into it to commemorate Starkeyville's Revolutionary soldiers. Tommy and Abby walked around it looking at the names — Starkey, Nash, Armistead, Cropp, Rushton, Whiting; and Starkey again and again. Tommy looked away from it, rested one elbow on his hip, and gestured with the hand as he continued to theorize.

47

"Nobody can drop that war," he said. "The South's unable, apparently, to accept defeat, and the North can't seem to feel sure it even won. So I guess it *didn't* win; or win something about it, anyway."

"Something they feel they should have won," Abby agreed. "It's as if there were something in there — something nobody can see, that's like a festering sore. Everybody keeps picking at it, can't leave it alone."

"Why does everybody get so angry, for instance?" Tommy said. "I suppose it all boils down to the Negro. I mean, nothing makes any sense unless you grasp the idea that the South doesn't really view the Negro as human. Nice, yes; lovable, yes; human — not quite. And the North gets just as angry about the Negro, because for the North he's gotten to be sort of superhuman — a symbol of something. And of course the being *less* than human is that too — I mean a symbol."

"They're really awfully kind to the Negro," Abby said. "Boogher is wonderful. It's the way you're kind to animals, as a point of pride."

"And of course the trouble with confusing people with animals — whether it's the Negro, or women, or children, as it has been in the past — is that you punish them to teach them, not believing in their reason. Not realizing that you don't teach them what you're trying to teach them. All we teach them is how to punish, thus perpetuating the punitive impulse which is at the root of all our troubles — Boy, when I get to using the pronoun we, I'm *really* in the groove."

"So the Negro is really the blind spot," Abby said, unwilling to relinquish this delicious heady conversation. "The thing that can't be, and has to be, assimilated."

48

"Wouldn't it be awful," Tommy said, beginning to descend the steps again, "if the Negro turned out to be the soul of the South, or something? Its true psychic identity, never recognized as such? Would that cause a stink! Let's have lunch."

"You've thought an awful lot about the South," Abby said admiringly, following him.

"Oh, everyone I know has some kind of theory," he said. "It's an amazing thing, have you ever noticed that every country has a South, even Alaska? And all those Souths, no matter whether they're in Italy, England, India — to say nothing of the South in one's own insides — seem to be exactly alike and have the same characteristics. So everybody's theorizing about himself. Where shall we go?"

"Where would you like to go?" Abby asked politely. "— The country club's supposed to have the best food."

"*You* don't want to," Tommy declared. "I want to go where you want — 'I want to *go* where you *go,*'" he sang, clattering down the last few steps with that loose-limbed flopping of his that was almost falling.

"I'd like to go to Reidecker's," she said after a moment. "I don't believe the food is so terribly good — no Starkeyville restaurants have good food — but I've always wanted to see what it was like. Men go there."

"Women are going there now," he said, helping her into the car.

From the sidewalk outside Reidecker's which had SALOON in brass letters imbedded in it, that Abby explained were left from the days before Bishop Cannon, they went down four steps and through glass doors into a crowded dining room. A hostess greeted them "Ha!" and showed them to a booth which was just being vacated.

49

"Could we have something to drink?" Tommy asked the hostess as she pulled the table out; he gazed up at her with piteous eyes.

"Beer," she suggested.

"Two Schlitzes," Tommy said, and sat down. Folding his hands on the tablecloth he looked across at Abby. "What the hell are you doing, down here?" he said.

"I live here," she said.

"Why do you live here?"

"Well, I'm married to a Starkeyvillian," she said.

"But why are you married to a Starkeyvillian?"

"I just am," she said. A waitress, hurrying past, thrust a basket of biscuits onto the table. Abby took two, split and buttered them. "I *like* to be married to him," she said, looking anxious.

"Okay," Tommy said. "I'm sorry. Don't look so harassed. Let's talk about the Civil War some more. Probably everybody here is, too. Tell me, how do you know so much about it?"

"But I don't!" she exclaimed. *"You* do."

"Why, no," Tommy said. "Those ideas you have about the War as our national psychic conflict — I was impressed."

"But that was you!" she said.

"No, it wasn't," he said. "Don't be modest. It was you." He looked at her, his boyish face puzzled.

Abby felt puzzled, too. Who, actually, had propounded the theory? Perhaps, after all, it was herself . . . "That's General Starkey," she said, nodding to a framed colored chromo on the opposite wall of the restaurant. "The Revolutionary one."

"The same as the St. Memin one we saw this morning."

"Yes."

"How have the mighty got themselves vulgarized," Tommy said.

They were eating an indifferent oyster omelet and drinking beer when Abby, looking up, saw Boogher coming toward them between the crowded tables. Close-shaven, vigorous, his orange hair sleek, he approached their table smiling.

"Well, Abby!" he said. "And this must be Mistoo — Mistoo — oh; Hume. How do you do, sir? I saw you lunching and thought I'd join you for coffee. Well, Abby! This is quite a spree for you! — Mrs. Starkey was to have taken you about, Hume, but was, as you may have heard, called away by the death of a relative. My wife was asked to make herself useful."

"Mrs. Daniel has been very useful indeed," Tommy said.

"I trust she will continue to prove so," Boogher said. "I am aware that you must have a very great deal of business to transact while you are in Starkeyville."

Tommy looked back at him. "Not a God-damned bit," he said.

Boogher smiled. Lifting his fingers to his lips, he coughed. "I beg your pardon," he said. "I see that I have offended you. I should, perhaps, have used the word compositions. You must have a very great many compositions to photograph during your stay in Starkeyville."

"That's right," Tommy said.

"So you finally came to Reidecker's," Boogher said, turning and smiling at Abby. "Women!" he exclaimed, shaking his head. "They get their own way infallibly, don't they, Hume? Perhaps you are a married man?"

"Yes," Tommy said. "I am. Why?"

Boogher shrugged his shoulders. "All Starkeyville is taking the liveliest interest in you," he said. "As the merest hamlet, off the beaten track entirely, we are agog. Your coming seems a fitting climax to the general hooraw that has gone on over *The Rose That Died*. I must have sold thirty copies," he said. "For a town that lends books unto the third and fourth recipient, that is unheard of. Abby has probably told you I operate the local bookshop. A small concern, but fascinating work. My tastes have always been literary."

"Then you have read the novel?" Tommy asked. He looked down into the bottom of his beer glass, and licked the rim of it with the tip of his tongue.

"My dear Hume! I strive to keep abreast, even of popular fiction," Boogher said lightly. But Tommy, looking up, saw that Boogher's lips were closed in a narrow line. His face seemed swollen, empurpled. As Tommy looked, Boogher ran a hand over his red hair. "There is not much in modern fiction worth admiring," he said. "But if we waited until what is worthy of our love came along, our love would rust away."

Tommy drew a long breath. Then he let it out again. "You are a philosopher, sir," he said.

Boogher smiled. "When I was at the University," he said, "my professor of philosophy, old Septimus Gale, he of the Platonic *Commentaries* — but perhaps you are too young, Hume, to have conned your Plato? — dear old Gale would sometimes say to me — I was only a whippersnapper at the time — 'Daniel, you have your grandfather's feeling for logic.' "

"It would be a part of the overall picture, sir," Tommy said.

Boogher smiled and wet his lips. "I try," he admitted. His hand went out to cover Abby's where it lay on the table-cloth. "It is essential someone preserve the tradition of harmony. In a day when technology would seem to constitute the whole of education, we of the South must remember the meaning of the phrase, 'the liberal mind.' Who else will?"

"Who else indeed?" Tommy said, lighting a cigarette.

"What was your university, Hume, if I may inquire?" Boogher said.

"Me? Oh, I'm not in the same class," Tommy said. "Winonia's my alma mater."

Boogher's eyes narrowed. "I don't believe I've heard of it," he said.

"You wouldn't have, sir," Tommy said reassuringly. "It's in the Middle West."

Boogher's face cleared. "While you are in Virginia, I hope you will avail yourself of the opportunity to visit the University at Charlottesville," he said courteously. "You will find it amply repays your effort. It is not only a beautiful, it is a dedicated institution." His eyes lit up.

5

N o, I don't want to go to Mr. Whiting's law office!"
Tommy exclaimed. He and Abby stood on the sidewalk outside Reidecker's, after Boogher, with a bow, had walked
away. "The hell with Mr. Whiting. Let's go to Azalea
next."

"But I'm afraid I did notify Mr. Whiting —" Abby said,
worriedly.

Tommy looked down at her.

"I'll un-notify him," he said. "When we get out to the
country. I trust they do have a telephone?"

"Oh, the Parkinsons have lots of telephones," Abby
said. "Only I don't think we should keep Mr. Whiting waiting."

"Mr. Whiting has an eternity to wait," Tommy said. "I
have two days. Let's go."

Driving into the country Tommy was silent. They
stopped at the red STOP sign on the outskirts of Starkeyville, crossed the bypass, and entered a narrow road that
ran past summery fields. Horses grazed, ankles slender, coats

shining; black Angus cattle stood stolidly in the shade of the willows that grew by grassy springs.

"Turn right," Abby said at a crossroads where a paintless board shack sold gasoline from a single pump and several battered enamel signs advertised Black Draught, 7-Up, and Dr. Pepper. Turning, they rolled into a red clay road that led straight on between white board fences.

"I don't know how to go on with our conversation," Tommy said at last, "Unless you will let me say that I think your husband is a son of a bitch."

"Oh, no!" Abby exclaimed, shocked.

"I am aware," Tommy continued, "there are women who love, devotedly, men who are bastards, and who seem to love them more the more bastardly they get." Tommy slowed the car down as he spoke. He leaned forward with his folded arms on the wheel, staring ahead down the road. "There seems to be something in such women that drives them to be that way. It just doesn't seem to fit with *you*."

"Boogher is really a very sweet person," Abby said.

"Sweet," Tommy said. "Sweet!"

"He wasn't at his best at lunch."

Tommy laughed shortly. "I gather he was favoring me with his jealousy," he said.

"He really loves me. No matter how he acts," Abby said.

"The kind of terrific person you are ought to have something better than — well, let's call it simply, that."

"I'm not terrific. You've got some snap impression," Abby said. "I'm mousy. I even used to be called 'Mouse.' I look like a mouse."

"All right, you look like a mouse. What's the matter with looking like a mouse? Mice are important. They're terrific," he said.

55

She laughed.

"That doesn't mean you *are* mousy," he went on. "With your wonderful inside life and private opinions — you're crazy if you think you're mousy."

"I guess I have got an inside life," she said slowly. "All sorts of things seem to go churning around in my mind — But it doesn't do me any good in a roomful of people."

"I suppose that preposterous charlatan you married put this idea you're mousy into your head."

"No," she said. "I've told you. At home I always used to be called —"

"All right, all right," he interrupted. "Where *are* you from, incidentally?"

"Vermont," she said. "We turn into that drive on your right."

They drove between tall black cedars up to a circular lawn, around which they swept. Tree box lined the drive so thickly as to make almost a tunnel. The house stood at the far side of the approach; of pale, rosy brick, with a small, templelike façade in the center, its low wings had long French windows. On either side of the front steps grew crape myrtle bushes. To the right, behind the mass of the house, could be glimpsed whitewashed outbuildings. To the left the land fell in terraces to a cluster of stables gleaming fresh white in the June afternoon sun. From the branches of the shade trees circling the lawn moaned mourning doves.

Tommy looked all about him as, slowly, they crossed the drive, went up the steps, and rang the doorbell. "Never a single mistake," he said, shaking his head.

A middle-aged colored man came to the wide screen door. "*Good* evenin'," he said. "Y'all come to take the pitchers?"

"That's right," Tommy said.

"Is Lady Barbara at home?" Abby asked.

"No ma'am, Miz Daniel. Lady Barber say tell you come on in and take the pitchers. Just don't move nothin' round, she say. She say she want everthin' like she got it. She don't want nothin' no different."

"All right, Stanley," Abby said. "Thank you."

Stanley squirmed in his starched white coat. "An' Lady Barber say," he went on, "she be mighty tickled if y'all don't break nothin'. She say, don't go smashin' nothin' and she be right proud."

"Which, being translated," Tommy murmured, "means Lady Barber's a bitch."

"All right, Stanley," Abby said. "We won't. Thank you." She passed in through the door the colored man held open.

"And Stanley," Tommy said. "Go out to the car there. Get all the camera equipment you'll find in the back seat and bring it in here. And don't break anything."

"No, *sir*," the man said in relieved tones.

Tommy set up lights in the blue dining room first and took several pictures of the long, shining Sheraton table and of the mantelpiece with its blue and white Wedgwood medallions. Then he moved into the drawing room and shot the four matching lyre-based card tables that stood in a polished row, alternating with the four long windows overlooking the lawn. He turned his lights round to bear upon the fireplace.

"*That's* no Southern product," he said, nodding at the Reynolds over the mantel.

"No, that's something Lady Barbara brought from England," Abby said. "It's a d'Ives."

"It's a dwhat?"

"One of her ancestors."

"Oh."

"What's the matter with ancestors?" Abby asked. "I wish *I* had any. I don't see why you say 'Oh.' "

"Because I meant 'Oh,' " Tommy replied. "Ancestors are all right in their place, just they're so dead. Wave that sheet."

Abby let the sheet that Stanley had got for them sway slowly back and forth to one side of the lights, while Tommy stood watching the time.

"That last shot's beautiful, with the portrait, but I don't know if it's appropriate," Tommy said. "I don't remember anything in *Rose* about portraits by Reynolds."

"Don't you remember Eugenia's portraits of her ancestors at Waverley?" Abby asked. "For all I know, some of them were English."

"A great artist seems to me too important for this setting," Tommy said. "But I guess it's all right."

Abby stared.

After he had finished views of the library, Tommy took out his handkerchief and wiped his forehead. "That's all *I'm* going to do," he said. "Such toil is beyond my frail strength. Stanley?"

The colored man popped up instantly out of the shadows of the central hall. "Yessir," he said.

"Stanley, Mrs. Daniel and I are worn to the bone. We're going out into the garden to rest. And, Stanley, we need refreshment. Bring us something."

"Yes *sir!*" The man bustled away.

"Don't sit on the grass," Abby told Tommy when they had reached the shade of a big oak, at the far end of a rectangular box garden, where there was a view of the river.

"You'll get ticks. Sit on the bench beside me — I do hope Lady Barbara won't mind our taking time off this way, in her garden."

"You make me weep with exasperation," Tommy said, sitting down. "What's Lady Barbara got to do with it? Why do you care what *she* minds? *I* mind being tired. What do *you* mind?"

"I guess I don't mind anything," Abby said reflectively. "Not really."

"So I've noticed," he said. "What's your name — your own name?"

"Abigail Woodbury — Daniel," she added.

"Okay, you've got a name. Q.E.D., you exist. You *must* mind things. Now tell me about Vermont."

The sound of ice tinkling came drifting down the red dirt path from the house, and Stanley rounded a big box bush, carrying a tray on which stood two silver tumblers. "Yes, sir!" he said, gratified, handling the tray.

"Very nice, Stanley," Tommy said. "We'll call you when we want some more. I know you'll hear."

"Yes, sir, Mr. Hume."

"How'd he know my name?" Tommy asked when Stanley had gone.

"Everyone in Starkeyville knew you were coming, and Brownsville knows more than the rest of Starkeyville put together," Abby said. "Stanley is the brother of Mrs. Starkey's Mattie, so anything Mrs. Starkey knows he knows."

"You have such feeling for social functioning," Tommy said. "Now about Vermont."

"What do you want to know about Vermont?"

"What have you got, about Vermont?"

59

"It wasn't a bit the way you think," Abby said. "We didn't live in a beautiful, bare old farmhouse or anything. We lived in a village called Cubbage."

"What happened?"

"Nothing. I played with the other children on Mountain Street, and went to public school, and then went away to New York and got a job with Terhune and Jason, the publishers. That's all there is to tell about me."

"I mean what were your father and mother like?"

She gave him a shrewd look. "All right," she said. "I know what you mean. My father was a drunk, as a matter of fact. A morose one. My mother hated him. She used to lock herself in the spare bedroom. But that hasn't got anything to do with me. Boogher isn't a drunk, and I love him. Now, where do *you* come from?"

"I told you practically the minute we met. From the Middle West. If I said Ukiah, would that mean anything? No. It isn't even a Middle Western name. Ukiah was named after a town in California, of all places, about fifty years ago. Ukiah barely exists at all. *I* exist, though."

"Cubbage is nice," Abby said defensively. "It's in the mountains, and it has two church spires, a Methodist one and a Congregational one. The main street runs straight uphill. If you go over to Burley, on the next mountain, you can see the spires and the dome on top of the Public Library, sticking up through the woods."

"You spent a lot of time in that Public Library," he remarked.

She laughed. "I used to go there most afternoons, after school," she said. "The reading room got the direct sun from the west. I always remember it with the sun shining on those long golden-oak tables, and how the air smelled of soiled books — But I was never intellectual," she hastened to say. "I wasn't there to read the great works of literature or anything. I used to sit and study the articles in the women's magazines, and think how glamorous it must be to write them. I loved reading the cake recipes, and the tips on how to give a teen-age get-together — Mostly I used to read Rider Haggard, and Conan Doyle, and Eulalie Hobson Howe, and the Little Colonel books."

"What would have happened if you *had* tried to give a party?" Tommy asked.

"I would have worried myself sick, about how Dadda might take it into his head to get sore at somebody at the party. And about how Mother didn't believe God wants us to seek selfish pleasures. It just wasn't worth trying. I never even considered it. I guess I'm a coward."

"You sure as hell say everything you can think of against yourself," he said.

"I'm just telling you the way it was. I used to dread even being in the same room with Dadda and Mother when they were together. I could feel the hate they had between them, twanging. I used to go back to the Public Library to get away. If it was light enough to. Mother didn't want me out after dark."

"Rape, you mean? The dangers of rape in Cubbage, Vermont?"

"Yes," she said. "— So after I graduated from high school with a secretarial course I went to New York and got a job as a typist. After a while I got to work for Mr. Jason himself. I did all sorts of other things besides shorthand, too. It was at a booksellers' convention where Mr. Jason sent me that I met Boogher."

"Big thrill," Tommy said.

61

"Well, it was," she said. "I never had any beaux. And he was a Southerner. I always thought the South must be wonderful."

"In God's name why?"

"It sounded so wonderful in the Little Colonel books," Abby said. "And it really *is* wonderful," she added anxiously. "Really it is. It's warm, and hospitable, with parties all the time . . . And then Southern courtesy . . . It all appeals to me emotionally, the way Boogher does, I suppose. I'm rather a cold person myself, I'm afraid."

"What gives you the idea you're cold?" he said.

"Oh, I'm supposed to be very cold," she said.

"I suppose you know your husband bullies you," he said.

"Oh, no!" she said. "He's a terribly courteous person. I wish I could tell you how old his family is. The Daniels were Cavaliers."

"Not one of these local characters has any idea of your real quality," he continued, impervious.

Abby looked startled. "I haven't any special quality," she protested.

"Okay," Tommy said. "So you're nobody. There's something awfully fishy about all this. You couldn't be all that humble."

"I'm just telling you the way things are."

"You're so overwhelmingly fair to everybody else that by rights you should be dead," he said. "The human organism has to have *some* self-protective reactions — Shall I shout for another drink?"

"Have you finished photographing the house?"

"Not quite. I've got to try to get something that looks like Eugenia's bedroom at Waverley," he said. "Feminine.

Fluffy. Like in the scene where she has the long midnight talk with Mary Lou."

"I'm afraid Lady Barbara is not very feminine," Abby said doubtfully. "But we could look upstairs and see what there is."

"Let us first have another the hell drink."

"I don't want Lady Barbara to come back and think all we've been doing is sitting out here drinking," Abby said.

"*All* right," Tommy said, getting up. "I have become the slave of the slave. It occurs to me," he went on as they walked slowly up the red dirt path, "just as it also fortunately occurred to me barely in time at lunch, that it's possible you may have to answer to that ghastly husband of yours for everything you do and say. Have to get forgiven for living, or some such. Am I miles off the track?"

Abby did not reply.

As they were putting their silver tumblers down on a table in the central hall, Tommy turned his over and squinted at its bottom in the dim green light. He read the inscription aloud: *Made to Replace One Stolen by a Yankee Officer During the Second Battle of Starkeyville,* 1863.

"That would have been when the house was looted," Abby said. "Mrs. Starkey's father sold the tumblers when he sold Azalea, and they've gone along with the house whenever it's changed hands."

"Makes one feel welcome, doesn't it?" Tommy said. He began to collect his paraphernalia in preparation for climbing the stairs.

6

UPSTAIRS, they traversed the broad central hall from back to front of the lovely old house, looking into the bedrooms and discussing the suitability of each for purposes of illustration. The right-hand front chamber appeared to be the principal bedroom, with a large dressing room opening off one end of the long side, balanced by an equally large bathroom at the other end.

"I see what you mean about hardly fluffy," Tommy said as they stood in the doorway between bedroom and bath, viewing the black-and-white tiling, the big white towels with square black monograms, and the row of square, silver-topped bottles on the white marble slab alongside the basin.

"I told you she wasn't feminine," Abby said.

"What *is* she?"

Abby hesitated. "A horse," she said. "With nostrils dilated."

Tommy began to laugh. "You're breaking down," he said. "That's the first time I've got you to criticize anybody."

"Oh, but I'm much *too* critical," she said, surprised.

"Who says so?"

"My husband."

"It becomes gradually apparent," Tommy said, "that your husband is not married to you. Everything you tell me leads me to conclude that, as far as he is concerned, he is married to, maybe, William Tecumseh Sherman; and is making a damned good stab at redressing the South's wrongs."

Abby laughed. "I really *am* much too critical," she insisted. "You don't know. You don't really know me at all."

"I realize that," he said. "I realize I know only what you've chosen to tell me — a carefully selected body of self-castigation. I have eyes and ears, however, and none of what you've said about yourself makes any sense. You are not critical. Neither are you a dreary little mouse who has hospitably been allowed into the inner circles of Southern aristocracy." Tommy leaned against the bathroom door and lighted a cigarette with some deliberation. "Likewise, you seem to me not to be General Sherman. I'm not sure who you are. Who are you?"

Abby looked out of the bathroom window, across the long stretch of gardens that led around to the back of the house and thence down to the river. "Nobody much," she said.

"That I doubt," he said. "I've been reading Yeats's *Autobiography,* and in it he says something about, it is only from rich and varied minds that the expression of extreme opinions offends the sense of probability."

"My mind isn't rich and varied," Abby said faintly.

"No, dear," Tommy said. "Disclaimer number one thousand two hundred and twelve. You haven't got a rich and varied mind, you haven't got good sense, but, baby, you got rhythm."

65

Abby started back into the bedroom.

"Don't be scared," Tommy said. "I wasn't going to attack you. That is, I don't believe so."

"I didn't think you were," she said quickly. "You're married."

"That's right," he said, smiling kindly at her. "Married. Not in jail."

"This bedroom looks as if it were a man's, doesn't it?" she said, walking around. "Mr. Parkinson must sleep in the other bed, so in a way it is a man's room. But you'd never think a woman lived in it at all, would you?"

Tommy shook his head in agreement, peered out of a window, stood back to look at a pastel portrait of Peter Parkinson hanging on the wall, and bent to look at a photograph in a silver frame standing on the Queen Anne bureau, of a lady dressed for presentation at court. "That Lady B.?" he asked. "Is it Starkeyville's invariable custom to keep pictures of yourself around for yourself to look at?"

"It isn't Lady Barbara," Abby said, looking over his shoulder. "Though there's a resemblance. It must be Poor Mummy."

Tommy glanced at her, and strolled toward the hall door. Together he and Abby crossed the hall to look at the other front bedroom, also large.

"Cold," he commented. "Cold and expensive. Lady Barbara must be a real gone ice cube."

"I don't believe she thinks how it looks," Abby said. "I think she arranges a house according to some idea built into her of how you do arrange a house. Like, you have to have a sofa on each side of the fireplace. You have to have chintz. You have to have silver cigarette boxes. You don't think about it, you just have it."

66

"I see," he said.

"What I *don't* understand," she went on, "is how people like this never have anything personal showing in the bedrooms. I mean, across the hall there where they sleep there isn't a book, or a package of cigarettes, or a powder puff, or anything. Where do they put things? I can't figure it out. Do they stuff it all away in bureau drawers?"

"Let's go look," Tommy suggested.

"It seems to be only rich people that do that way," she went on. "— Though it can't be because of their having servants; because how would the servants know where they want the things put each time, specially new things? The people must do it themselves. But when?"

"I wonder," he said.

"Most Starkeyvillians don't," she said. "They keep their books and cigarettes and papers all piled on their bedside tables the way I do. Do you suppose it's money that causes it, or does it involve belonging to a grand social class too?"

"You might write a thesis on it," Tommy said.

Abby stopped short.

"Let's go back and look again at that bedroom in the back," Tommy said after a pause. "The pink one. It's the most feminine."

They passed down the hall, which was hung with groups of framed sporting prints, to a small room looking over the back lawn and, past the whitewashed outbuildings, down to the softly flowing river.

"These places were like towns," Abby said as they stood looking out of the window. "There was a laundry, and a cobbler's, and a carpenter's, and lots of other kinds of shops, out there, and then there were the places around the stables and the barns — the blacksmith's, and the dairy, and I don't know what all. Like a big, thriving village."

"Only in this kind of village one family owned everybody else," Tommy said.

"It *was* unjust, but the plantation owners took their responsibilities very seriously, most of them. The mistress would get up in the middle of the night to go down and care for somebody sick in the quarters."

"I can withhold my tears," Tommy said. "If I owned a dog, I'd feel responsible for him, too. If I owned a cow, Heaven forfend, it would be to my advantage to keep her a fine, upstanding cow able to do her own work."

"I feel such pity for the South," Abby said.

"You want to watch that," Tommy said. He stepped back from the window, where she still leaned. "You want to look out for pity. It's one hell of a lousy emotion."

"But people are so touching!" Abby said. "They act so big and tough, and try so hard to cover up, but underneath they're all full of desires and longings and disappointments and things."

"How about you?" Tommy asked. "You all full of disappointments, hm?"

"I wasn't talking about me," she said. "I was thinking how sorry I feel for everybody."

Tommy gazed at her with his chin propped in his hand. "I seem to be behaving like the portable *Bartlett's Quotaions*," he said. "But may I remind you of something somebody said about Gandhi after he had been killed. They said, 'He taught us to be just, when it is so much easier to be generous.' Don't you go being too God-damned generous, Miz Daniel, honey."

"Sometimes I feel as if I would burst with pity," she said.

68

He looked down at her small white pointed face for a moment longer. Then he began to move about the bedroom — standing off to view an old engraving of a country house in a park, hanging over the bed; looking critically at the little fireplace with its pretty, painted paneling. "We'll go back and take the front room," he decided at length. "This room isn't effective. Got your sheet to wave?"

"But this seems just right for Eugenia's bedroom!" Abby protested.

"The front room will photograph better."

Tommy started up the hall again energetically. Abby only caught up to him as he was going into Lady Barbara's black-and-white bathroom.

"*Please* don't do this room," she begged. "It's so austere. It looks like Lady Barbara, not like Eugenia."

He leaned as before against the bathroom door and lighted a cigarette, squinting through its smoke at the interior of the bathroom. Then he turned and viewed the bedroom on his other side.

"We'll begin with a shot of the wall where the beds are," he said.

"Eugenia didn't *have* twin beds!" Abby said. "She had one bed!"

"She did?" he said. "Well, I can take it so you don't see but one bed. You'll see part of the other wall there, with that wonderful hunk of antique bureau."

"But it's all wrong in here!" Abby insisted. "Eugenia's room was pink and fluffy and feminine. If you photograph *this* cold room, you won't be illustrating *The Rose That Died* at all!"

"What's it to you?" he asked, turning and looking with curiosity at Abby.

"I wrote it," she said.

Tommy kept on staring at her through the rising smoke of his cigarette. Then he took the cigarette out of his mouth, laid it on the edge of the marble slab, and salaamed, with arms outstretched. When he straightened up he saw that Abby's face was flushed and alarmed. He reached out; pulling her to him, he kissed her on the mouth.

"If you have to report this back, you can say I attacked you," he said.

She did not move.

"— baby," he added, and kissed her again.

Part Two

1

WELL!" exclaimed Boogher Daniel, coming well pleased to the breakfast table. He wore a foulard dressing gown over his white shirt and cord trousers. His ruddy cheeks were closely shaven, his orange hair parted and brushed meticulously. "How is my little fuzzy-wuzzy wish-wash?" he continued, giving an imitation of W. C. Fields that had been much in vogue during his years at the University. Boogher was an excellent mimic. His shining morning face assumed a raffish air, and an astral cigar seemed to protrude from his lips.

Abby laughed unresistingly at this ghost of a buffoon whom she could not herself remember. She was not as fully recovered from the previous night as her robust mate and she felt the heat; but she did feel much relieved after her confession, and as anxious as ever to be a good wife.

"My favorite breakfast!" Boogher declared as he accepted a plateful of country sausage, fried apples, and grits. "Hand me down my walking cane," he sang, attacking the food.

When Boogher was in good spirits, such tended to be the sentiments and tags which erupted from the geyser of his cheerfulness, as though its source lay in deposits of experience twenty years and more deep. As long as he remained in this mood there was really nothing *to* being a good wife, except to laugh at the jokes, appreciate the references, and bear in sympathetic mind the golden aura surrounding undergraduate days at the University — "Where all is bright and gay," as Boogher so often sang. He was likely to be upheld for days by the steady upsurge of his bonhomie. "Butter pass the butter," he chuckled now, and groaned at his own pun.

Abby sat down to her own plate of sausage and apples, without any grits. She felt a strong, lightheaded gratitude to Boogher, for the way he had taken the news of her disobedience. It had taken her weeks to get up her courage to confess what she had disclosed to Tommy; now she had taken her punishment, and felt emotionally poised in a kind of exhausted balance.

"We must begin to plot our campaign for when the dreadful disclosure is made," Boogher said, composing his heavy features into a more serious cast and mashing up hominy grits with his fork. "Have you any idea when the fatal issue of *Life* will appear?"

"Tommy said by the end of this month," Abby said. She experienced a twinge of conscience for that part of the afternoon at Azalea which she had failed to confess. "Whatever the date of the last issue in July will be. They wanted to rush it through because novels go so quickly out of the public mind," she added.

"That's not very long. We must calculate how the ire of the community may best be appeased," Boogher said,

74

employing the ornate language which came to his tongue on certain types of occasion.

Abby leaned forward at the small, round mahogany table in the sitting room where they sat at breakfast; there were some corners in modern living that Boogher refused to cut, and eating in the polite part of the house was one of them. She was wearing a fresh pink-and-white cotton housecoat, and a pink ribbon in her smooth dark hair. Propping her chin in her fists and looking earnest, she said, "Maybe there isn't going to be any ire."

Boogher's brow darkened. Fearing a repetition of last night's tirades, Abby added hastily, "Of course there very well *may* be. I was just thinking that, public opinion being so unpredictable, people might just possibly be pleased instead."

Boogher's look changed from anger to his patient, explaining expression. "Virginians do not like to be written about," he said. "They are extremely jealous of their privacy. Anything that suggests they might have been observed, spied upon, judged, is anathema to them. We must expect to weather a very considerable storm," he said, not without satisfaction.

"They seem to have loved *The Rose* so far," Abby said in a small voice.

Boogher's irritation returned. "Must we go through all this again?" he demanded. "I thought I'd made it clear that the atmosphere of approval now obtaining results from the anonymity in which the author's identity has hitherto been cloaked. Which, you will remember, I advised. And which that same author has now chosen to rupture," he added reproachfully. "A book by nobody is a very different kettle of fish from a book by somebody everybody knows."

75

"Is it really?" Abby asked dolefully.

"A different book entirely," Boogher insisted. "If you had remained loyal to your word," he went on in the tones of magnanimity he had adopted toward the end of last evening, "— if you had continued to follow my advice, you might have avoided the unpleasant consequences we now face. But since, succumbing to the importunings of an itinerant photographer who guessed the secret of your identity, you did consent to this public broadcasting of your connection with the novel, we must brace ourselves for ostracism. I have been calculating how much I am likely to lose in custom at the shop, and for how long."

"Oh, Boogher!" Abby cried. "Surely it won't have to affect *you!* Even if you're right about people getting mad, they'll just be sorry for you being married to me. Won't they just buy all the more books, to show how they commiserate with you?"

"Dear Abby," Boogher said angrily. "You have not grasped the situation at all. Listen to me. People are going to be outraged, hear? They are going to ostracize us — not just you, *us!* I know of one Virginia author who returned to his home — quite a long time after his novel about Virginia came out, too — and people wouldn't even call on his wife. You have trespassed, Abby, hear? Trespassed on the privacy of Southerners. That, Southerners will not countenance. You and me they will not countenance, either."

"I haven't trespassed on anybody's privacy," Abby said. "I made it all up."

Geniality had entirely vanished from Boogher's face; the Daniel darkness had taken its place.

"What do you take me for?" he asked. "You forget that I have considerable knowledge of literature. More, I venture to add, than yourself, for all this work of fiction about which you have become so megalomaniac. Listen here. Characters are composed of bits and pieces of real people, are they not? Obviously! I did not suggest you painted portraits of individual Starkeyvillians in your novel; I am stating the truth that there are traits in all your characters recognizable to any Virginian. Can you deny it?"

"But that's what they like about it!" Abby protested.

"Permit me to know a little more about my own kind than you possibly can," he said stiffly. "Just because you did turn out a very nice little *tour de force* — you see, I use Charles Poore's phrase for it — doesn't entitle you to set up as the authority on the South in this family. You must grant me that position, Abby — unless, of course, you wish to annex all distinction for yourself."

"Of course I don't, darling," Abby said soothingly. "You ought to know I want you to be the boss."

"Why do you pronounce it 'Bahss'? he inquired. "The word is 'bawss.' "

"You are the bawss, bawss," she said, smiling at him coaxingly. But he would not smile back.

"Sometimes I think you actually court trouble," he said. "What is it about Yankees that won't let them leave things alone? If you'd lived in Virginia in the twenties and seen the to-do when *Boojum* came out — and *it* was by a Southerner — you wouldn't have been so anxious to stir up a hornet's nest."

"But *Boojum* criticized the South! My book doesn't criticize anybody!" she cried. "Ellen Glasgow was far more critical of the South than I've been, and goodness knows they accepted Miss Ellen."

"She was one of us," Boogher said. He ran his hand over

77

his smooth red hair. "And, although you married me, you're not. You can't sail into the South and expect to be accepted as a Southerner just because you drop a few patronizing compliments here and there like largesse."

"I'm not patronizing!" she protested. "I love the South! You know I love it. And it shows in my book. That's why I say maybe nobody will be angry when they find I wrote it. People *like* it because it's true to life."

Boogher stood up from the table and hurled his napkin on his soiled plate. "This is the limit!" he exclaimed, "I've accepted your going against my wishes in the matter of preserving anonymity. I've forgiven you, I've stepped forward to face the music by your side, yet you go right on flouting my judgment, asserting your ignorant opinion, and making a fool of yourself. You give me no reason to suppose you entertain the slightest respect or love for me. There's a limit to what I can put up with — My life is at no time easy," he added, and left the room, slamming the bedroom door behind him.

"Boogher!" Abby cried. After putting the sausage meat back into the refrigerator, in view of the day's heat, she followed Boogher into the bedroom.

The Robert E. Lee Apartments, where the Daniels lived, were actually nothing in the world but Miss Clara Harrison's old house grown too big and expensive for Miss Clara to keep up. On the ground floor lived the Travers Keiths, an elderly couple who played a great deal of duplicate bridge. General Larrimore, kin to the Starkeys, the Barrs, and hence to the Harrisons, kept widower's hall on the second story. The Daniels, who were thought of as young and strong, occupied the premises at the top, where the ceilings of all the rooms slanted to the eaves, and even such insulation as Miss Clara had introduced failed to keep the rooms cool after eleven o'clock in the morning.

The apartment was divided into four nearly equal-sized rooms — a sitting room into which the caller entered, where the round dining table was set; Boogher's study; a kitchen behind the sitting room, and the bedroom. In the study Boogher kept his large collection of silver cups, won in University days for tennis; his framed photograph of the Rotunda with old Fishwick and old De Butts and old Watters sitting on the steps; of the Phi Psi house; of President Newcomb, and of the Virginia–North Carolina game that Virginia won 20–0. The study was lined with books. Almost the entire library of Boogher's grandfather, also a Boogher Daniel, was there: Tacitus, Horace, the Greek Anthology, Lucretius in half-leather, Virgil. From Boogher's father's day had come down bound sets of Tennyson, Meredith, and George Gissing. Besides these were present-day works which Boogher considered worthy of preservation: Jules Romain, Charles Morgan, James Branch Cabell, Ellen Glasgow, and Mazo de la Roche.

The kitchen was, perforce, modern, having been installed at the time the house was divided up into flats. But Miss Clara had economized to the hilt on the quality of the fixtures with the result that the sink was too shallow, the refrigerator and the stove too small, the capacity of the cupboards hopelessly inadequate.

In the sitting room, however, Miss Clara, who could never be accused of economizing on important things, had installed Venetian blinds and opened up an old, sealed-off grate, so that in winter the young Daniels could sit by open fires. The impoverished and unconnected Abby had brought with her to the marriage neither furniture nor any other worldly goods, but a number of Daniel and Whiting aunts had made contributions out of their own houses, so that now a small carved Victorian sofa, two comfortable armchairs which Abby had herself covered with dark red corduroy, two marble-topped tables, a marble-topped chest of drawers, and a large, not unbeautiful Oriental rug now furnished the square room to which Abby and Boogher presently returned, in a better humor than that in which they left it. Boogher had exchanged his dressing gown for the cord jacket that matched his trousers.

Abby passed directly through the sitting room and out to the kitchen to make a pot of fresh coffee. As she left the room, Boogher, who had reseated himself at the breakfast table, had all at once the not unfamiliar sensation of being left stripped of comfort and self-esteem. It was as if, with Abby's passing, the warm emotional bath water in which he had been sitting suddenly ran out. He was abandoned to the obscure and pernicious feeling he had behaved badly. As usual his mind began casting about to find the flaw it sensed, searching like a scurrying rat among the pronouncements, the denunciations, and the sounding periods he had uttered in the past several hours, sniffing among the rejections, the dominations, and the embraces.

Boogher was forty-one, and he had never before in his life had to face a situation so complicated or so unsettling as the present one, into which Abby had, by revealing her authorship of *The Rose That Died*, plunged him and herself. No satisfactory attitude toward it had risen to Boogher's consciousness out of the reservoir of his raising, down in King and Queen County. He had to piece together an attitude, out of bits and pieces of what he knew and could believe in. Jealousy, hurt pride, envy burned in him; he had tried to do his best, be a man, and consign them to the realm of the baser emotions, while he struggled to crystallize a more acceptable approach than any of them offered.

A Yankee wife, as a phenomenon, had already taken skill to arrange for, as an element in his life picture. But a Yankee wife who had written a novel, a novel concerning a small Southern town similar to that in which he and she lived — houseroom for this image called upon the untapped strata lying close to the fundament of his being. The rat of doubt in him continued to scurry frantically about in his recent behavior, but he was unable to discover any flaw. The rhetoric and the syntax he had employed had been his father's; the moral principles upon which his diatribes had been based had been those of his mother, a Hollingshead from Gloucester County. All were irreproachable.

His inner being, however, shivered still. Seeking deeper in the caves of consciousness, his mind suddenly presented him with an irrelevant scene from his childhood. For a moment which seemed timeless, he was back at Danielstown, climbing the front steps laboriously. He could not have been more than four, from the effort it took. With him was his friend Pie, Aunt Annie the cook's child. Pie was probably four too. His round black woolly head was dusty from the dried clay they had been playing in, but Boogher's hair, the red of the clay, did not show the dust.

"I goin' show you somethin'," Boogher promised as they climbed between the flowering crape myrtle bushes by the steps. With the first warm sensations of proprietorship Boogher led Pie down the long central hall, past mildewed full-length mirrors in chipped gilt frames. At the door to the dining room they paused; heavy silver bowls sweated upon the marble-topped sideboard. It was not necessary to point out to Pie the dining room's glories, they were evident. The two children stood side by side, soft little elbows touching, staring at the silver tea service on its ornate tray, the hurricane lamps, the faded pink-and-white-striped satin chair seats; the long table, the polished surface of which reflected a tear-drop chandelier. Both boys were barefoot. They stared, breathing intently and audibly.

"C'mawn, Pa," Boogher said. He led his playmate up the stairs, that curved slightly as they mounted through the upper reaches of the high-ceilinged hall.

The children went noiselessly along the upstairs hall on their dirty little feet, peering into such doors as stood open. There was Granny's bedroom, and Cousin Lucy Langford's, and the upstairs sitting room, and the room that Boogher shared with his brothers Hubert and Henry Davis. In the nursery at the end of the hall they found what Boogher had been searching for and paused, side by side on the threshold.

"Look," Boogher whispered to Pie. Mother sat on the nursery sofa, her starched shirtwaist unbuttoned partway down the front, holding little Lucy Langford to her breast. Pride, love, and alumniship pulsed in Boogher as he gazed at the loveliest and dearest of all sights; the heaven from which only Lucy Langford had evicted him. He looked at Pie's face, six inches from his, to see if Pie was appreciating perfection.

The door that connected Mother's bedroom with the nursery opened, and red-haired Daddy walked in, in pants and shirt, with his braces hanging down over his backside. "Lucy, honey," he began. Then he saw Boogher and Pie. Boogher saw the very instant when Daddy's face turned dark.

"Get on down to your mammy, boy," he ordered Pie, not unkindly. He turned Pie round by the shoulder and gave him a little shove down the hall. Boogher he commanded to "Come in yere!" and led the way back into the big bedroom.

Boogher, following Daddy, threw an imploring look where Mother sat enthroned. She, who had not spoken, gave back a gentle and abstracted smile to this youngest of her boys, now of an age to be in his father's province and charge.

Daddy laid a heavy hand on Boogher's shoulder and steered him into the bathroom opening off the high, dim room with its big old-fashioned walnut furniture and broad bed. In the bathroom all was white, and pitilessly bright with sunshine. Daddy sat down on the toilet seat and pulled the little boy between his long legs, facing him. "Now sir," he began. "Now sir! What you were displayin' to that niggra boy is sacred, hear? Your mother and her baby. It's a sacred sight, sir. Remember that."

The child, full of fear and doom, cried out in despair, "I didn't mean to, Daddy. Daddy!"

"I propose to instruct you, boy," his father said. "That's what you're here for; instruction." He reached up to where the strop for his straight razor hung on the wall by the basin, and flipped it off its hook. With the other hand he took down the child's insignificant breeches and, holding Boogher out at arm's length to give himself room, whipped him briefly. "Stop screaming, sir!" he ordered, raising his voice to be heard. "You're a man, not a baby!"

Boogher, who would have preferred to be a baby, faced reality; screamed once more and was still.

"Now sir," Daddy said. "Never forget who you are."

83

Boogher shook his head; tears and snot ran into his mouth.

Daddy looked at him doubtfully and added, "You're a Virginian. A gentleman. And white."

Boogher nodded.

Daddy laid on one more lick with the razor strop still hanging from his hand. Boogher screamed with the shock and surprise.

"Say 'Yes, sir' when you answer me," Daddy explained.

"Yes, *sir*," Boogher said fervently, backing away.

But Daddy had not finished yet. He drew his son to him — short pants still hobbling his ankles — and kissed the child upon the lips, as was the Daniel family custom. "All over now," he said. "Daddy's little man. Never do it again?"

"No, *sir!*"

Up from this scene as from the deep, the grown-up Boogher's consciousness rose wonderingly as the sound of coffee cups rattling in the kitchen recalled him to Abby and the present. Here, now, in the sitting room of his apartment in Starkeyville, he felt calm and restored to his proper identity; reconciled with his actions. A sadness, however, still shadowed his mind, that it should have been again his fate to suffer the self-criticism proved in the end to have been for nothing. He was never able to find the slightest fault.

Rapping impatiently with his fingertips upon the top of the breakfast table he said to himself that the scene he had just relived with such mysterious urgency was simply a reminder that feelings of flaw, a sense of sin, must ever follow if he forgot for a moment who — as he had been properly taught so long ago — he was. "Abby!" he called irritably. "Do you propose to take forever?" The words, spoken, made him feel better. And when Abby entered, bearing a tray of fresh cups and the percolator, her face wreathed in placatory smiles, Boogher felt suddenly all right again. The sustaining fluid seemed once more to cushion his loneliness. He relaxed, inwardly, and stretched his being. "Sugar," he demanded; Abby had forgotten it again. "— It's on the side table," he added as she started to hurry out to the kitchen, for he did not care to have her leave the room. "Thank you," he said, when she handed him the silver sugar bowl which had belonged to old Cousin Lucy Langford.

Abby sat down facing Boogher and held her coffee cup cradled in both hands as she gazed peacefully at her husband's ruddy face. She sipped her coffee in the ensuing silence and reflected that Boogher's rages were always followed by this sort of fatigued peace — a peace which could apparently be achieved, with Boogher, in no other way.

There was another factor, not good to contemplate, rather to be glanced at hurriedly and pushed out of mind, which contributed to her present satisfaction. That was the sense of guilt. She knew she had done wrong in letting Tommy kiss her, and she had not yet confessed it to Boogher. There was no doubt about it, feelings of being in the wrong seemed very stimulating to love. It was a reprehensible reaction, and one which was surely peculiar to herself, and to be condemned. She threw Boogher a smile across the table.

"What?" he asked, surprised.

"Nothing," she said. "Just I love you."

Boogher lifted his chin up out of his collar. He raised his brows. "Upun my word," he observed. "The woman has taken leave of her wits."

"Because I admire your masculine beauty?" she asked.

"Jest in fun," he replied hastily, stroking her hand as it lay on the table. "Just being very punny."

Abby began to laugh. Boogher cleared his throat; his jokes were a success. But Abby was laughing too hard and too long. Uneasiness attacked him such as he felt late at night when he came upon his wife writing in her mysterious diary.

"I do enjoy a good laugh," he said, nervously.

Abby dried her eyes. "So do I, darling," she said.

Boogher stood up while he drank the rest of his coffee, napkin still in hand. He set the cup down, wiped his lips, cast his napkin into his soiled plate, and went to kiss Abby. "I'm late already," he said.

"Good-by," Abby said, embracing him as though for the last time.

"Pshaw," Boogher said.

Soon after Boogher had left, the telephone rang. When Abby answered it a woman's voice said, "Is Mr. Daniel there?"

"Mr. Daniel has just left for the store," Abby said, through the crashing and booming of the connection.

"Oh, well, I'll call him there," the woman's voice said, and the telephone clicked off.

It sounded like Amelie Nash, Abby thought as she hung up and began carrying the breakfast dishes to the kitchen. Amelie was certainly after Boogher, she continued to exclaim mentally, with a vast expense of indignant energy.

2

Toward the middle of the morning Clifford Joy came to wash the windows. He stood at the top of the stairs as Abby opened the apartment door to his knock, tall, pitch-black, greenish old hat in hand, loose limbs flopping every which way. He grinned. "Mownin'," he said.

"Oh, Clifford!" Abby cried. "I thought you weren't coming! You said you'd be here at nine, and it must be — why, it must be —"

"Yes, *ma'am*," Clifford agreed heartily. "It's right late. I was detained. I had a regagement down yonder on Parson's Hill." Parson's Hill was the darkest and most lurid section of Brownsville. "Occupied considerable of my mownin'," Clifford explained. He ambled into the apartment, stuffing the moldy hat into the pocket of his brown, ragged jacket, which was so greasy as to seem hardly to be made of cloth at all.

Clifford was Abby's despair. Surely such a fine young man, who had never had opportunities or backing, and only an elementary-school education! Eminently an object for her respect, encouragement and interest, he continued to display what she was sure was only the result of generations of discrimination, and was completely unreliable. It was demonstrably not his own fault, but society's, for example, that he spilled window-washing water on the sofa, wasted the polishing wax, and once simply fell down, tripped by his own large feet — breaking, as he did so, the marble top of a table.

Abby could not decide what was the constructive attitude to be taken in dealing with Clifford. If she smiled and asked him about his family he relaxed entirely, laid down the waxing mop, and, weight on one hip, talked for hours, at a dollar an hour. If she buttoned up her lip, gave some brisk orders, and withdrew, in a moment or two she could hear ominous noises — squeaks, scrapings, crashes; and, such was Clifford's irresistible attraction for disaster, when she rushed back into the room it would be to come upon some fresh accident for which not Clifford, really, but Fate was responsible.

Yet it was wrong not to trust Clifford. Trust was the very element he stood in need of. Trust was an essential to the improvement of his status; what he and his race had been starving for all along. Sometimes Abby took herself firmly by the principles and went outdoors for an hour while Clifford was at work in the apartment, just in order to show him that she did trust him. Perhaps her principles were not strong enough, though, for she could never, upon her return, resist eyeing the whisky bottle, which she had had too much respect for Clifford to lock up, and which, alas, did always seem reduced in contents. Poor Clifford! was all she could think at such times; he didn't even have the guile to fill the whiskey's level up with water.

Sometimes she was on the point of telling Clifford she

could not employ him any longer, for it was too exhausting nervously to sit waiting for the next vase to get broken. But Boogher always stayed her. "Quit picking at him," he would advise. "He does the best he can. His best ain't much, I grant you, but he's better than most niggras today. Knows his place, old Clifford. I've known Clifford since he was knee-high, when I'd come up yere and stay with my Hungerford kin; he's all right. I wouldn't trust some niggras to work for a lady alone. Not that they'd *do* anything," he hastened to add. "Just wouldn't know how to act around a lady."

"I could wash the windows so easily myself," Abby would wail.

"My wife wash windows? No indeed! That's man's work. Why can't you just leave old Clifford be, honey? Take him like he is. You get all worn out worrying."

But to accept a thing, when that thing had something the matter with it, seemed to Abby wrong. It was wrong not to worry; one ought to worry. If there was something the matter with a thing, one ought to worry until one had changed it. As a result, Clifford continued to come to work at the wildly irregular intervals dictated by his complicated Brownsville social life, and Abby's heart continued to bleed for him.

"This morning we have to wash windows," she began efficiently. "I had hoped you could get them all done before I have to go out to lunch."

"You goin partyin', Miz Daniel?" Clifford inquired with interest.

"I'm going to a lunch party that Mrs. Robbie Fenn is giving for Mrs. George Boogher — she's Mr. Daniel's cousin's wife," she explained.

89

"Oh yes ma'am!" Clifford agreed enthusiastically. "I know Miss Mary Adelaide Boogher good. Miss Mary Adelaide, she Miss Fanny Buxton's daughter, and Miss Fanny, she had me down there scrubbin' that old basement *all* the time. Miss Mary Adelaide went on up to New York, that right? How she likin' it up there, Miz Daniel?"

The colored people with whom Abby came into contact always called her by her married name and title. It was a sizing-up of her difference in quality which Abby accepted humbly.

"I don't know, Clifford," she replied. "I expect she'll tell us at luncheon." If she was not careful they would be embarked on a long conversation about the Booghers, the Buxtons, and all their kindred. "Now, Clifford, if you feel you won't be able to finish the windows by one o'clock, I want you to tell me. You see I'd planned on your being here at nine. Perhaps the best thing would be for you to wash a few of the windows this time, and come back tomorrow to finish up."

"Yes, ma'am," he agreed.

"But Clifford, if that is the way you would like to do it, you *will* come back and finish, won't you? It wouldn't look nice if some of the windows were clean and some not, would it?"

"Oh, no ma'am, Miz Daniel!"

"Do them slowly and carefully, won't you? — Since there isn't time to do them all," she repeated anxiously. "I'd rather get only two windows done thoroughly and nicely than have you try to do them all and hurry through the job. Something might get broken."

"Yes ma'am. You want for me to wash two winders. That right?"

"No, Clifford. I want you to wash as many windows as you can do thoroughly, before I have to pay you and go out to lunch."

"Yes ma'am."

Abby sighed. She helped him to get his bucket of water with vinegar in it, his wet cloths, and his dry cloths. Water with vinegar in it was apparently an approach to window-washing taught Clifford early in life and the only one he felt comfortable with. It had proved wiser and safer to indulge him in it.

By the time Abby at length left Clifford alone in the sitting room with the windows, their curtains draped up to be out of his devastating way, she was trembling with strain. She retired to the bedroom to continue writing in her diary; Clifford's arrival had interrupted her in it. Gradually, as she wrote, she relaxed. Within these pages was the only place in the apartment where she knew complete privacy.

Of course I couldn't have gone to New York, as Tommy wanted me to. I've done quite enough as it is! But it comes over me sometimes, like being swallowed by a dream, what it might have been like if I had. I imagine it as like what I used to see at Jason & Terhune, when authors of new books would come in and Miss Lear in Publicity would take them to radio and TV appointments, and Mr. Raymond would take them out to lunch with reviewers. If it was a big book J & T used to give a party for it. I remember how the authors all wore a certain expression — even if they looked scared and lost at first; they got a radiant look, as though they were wandering in a land of heart's desire; you got the feeling that the fuss being made over them corresponded to some private fairyland they had already.

Back in those days I never dreamed of such a thing as writing a book — no; don't say that; you know you always wanted to write a book. [Abby wrote severely, bearing on hard with her pencil.] But my life was so different from all that — how we used to peer out the glass sides of the cubicles at J & T to see the authors going down the corridor! Anyway, I never dreamed a fuss like that could be made about me, and it's *not* going to be made about me, either. I've put it out of my mind. Actually I never thought of *Rose* as something I could parade behind the way some of the authors used to, like a parent pushing a perambulator, collecting compliments on a baby.

I wrote *Rose* because I could see it so clearly — because it was there to write, the way they say about climbing a mountain. It was as if it already existed before I wrote any of it down; as if it were a real rose that I was only telling about. I still see it as a real rose. I wonder if I will feel any different when the *Life* article announces my writing it? Will I really feel vain and egotistical and self-centered and conceited the way B. says I am? Am I already?

I keep thinking perhaps it will make people love me, not ostracize me at all, as B. predicts. People seem to love *Rose,* just as if they saw the thing I saw — the turned-in preoccupation of the South with the past, like a rose with a worm in it. Hugging itself, finding its only sun inside, never opening out until at last the petals are old and simply begin to fall, one by one, thick and white. People seem to feel that. Some of the letters, like the Georgia one, surprised me, they were so enthusiastic. They seemed to think I got it right. And it *is* right. I still feel it is, the way I did when I wrote the chapter about Eugenia, sitting up in bed writing the night B. went to Lynchburg, with tears running down my cheeks. Maybe when the news comes out people here will say, "Abby, you are the only one who has understood. We never meant to hate, we only wanted to love. But we were hurt, ourselves, hurt so deep that the rose couldn't open. Only you have seen that."

Oh, what rubbish! How fatuous can I get?

But people *do* write that kind of letter to the author, from other places.

"Between the essence and the dissent/Falls the shadow."

I ought to be satisfied with poetry. And novels. And with becoming thirty-two in good health. Having B. And a nice apartment. B. says I don't appreciate my life and I guess I don't, or I couldn't have ever told Tommy I wrote the book. I could have been serene and detached. And I wouldn't have let him kiss me. The shadow!

Perhaps I really had better confess. I'm scared to. But B. always does forgive me in the end.

Abby paused and gazed off unseeing at the opposite wall of the bedroom. Then she wrote,

"Perfect love casteth out fear." B. says my love is flawed. I know I *don't* love the way I ought to, without any thought of self. Tommy was so fascinated to hear about Mother and Dadda. I suppose that's the modern psychological interest people have, in the North. But Tommy didn't seem to be able to understand that Mother wasn't the only abused one; she never gave any love to Dadda either, she never gave him anything. She was stingy with that kind of love, and I must try not to be like her. I remember her sitting on the settee at the foot of her bed, sewing; looking up from her work to answer me; I must have asked her something about sex. "Sex is necessary to animal existence," Mother said. What a thing to tell a little girl!

People used to bring girls up to be so completely girls they were almost cripples — half-people; as though one could stand on only one foot. I ought to appreciate more being married; with a husband, you find your other foot. Think of all the poor unmarried women — Miss Lilybud;

93

Miss Grace Starkey now her husband is dead. No, Miss Grace stands on two feet of her own! Well, me, then, before I met B. Sometimes the memory comes over me in a wave, of how lonely I was in New York, after work. How helpless. I didn't know how to go about making a life.

It *could* be today that the *Life* comes out, I didn't tell B. because I wanted to get off the subject. But it *could* be.

Having come back to her starting point in the loop of associated ideas that she was recording as they came to her, Abby glanced back over what she had written; she felt dissatisfied, as usual, with its unlikeness to the journals of Katherine Mansfield or Virginia Woolf, and sighed.

There was no sound at all from the sitting room. Abby thrust her diary back into the drawer in the table on her side of the bed, closed the drawer tightly, and went in there.

Clifford sat on one of the dining-table chairs, like a pile of bones heaped on the seat. With long black fingers thrust into the heel of one of his broken shoes, he was dreamily scratching his foot.

"Clifford!" Abby cried. "What's holding you up? You aren't anywhere near finished!"

"Yes ma'am, I is, Miz Daniel," he replied, standing up. Miraculously the pile of bones fell into some kind of order, as though strung on an elastic band. "I was just fixin' to come tell you I through."

"But look! You haven't done this window! Or this!"

"No ma'am, I ain't done them winders. You tell me wash two winders and that's all. I done washed the two winders over by the do', see, Miz Daniel?"

"Oh, Clifford!" Abby wailed. "I didn't say to only wash two windows, I said . . ." But there was no use going on. Clifford, as Boogher always insisted, did his best. Unquestionably stunted by lack of opportunities, Clifford's best just wasn't very good.

Abby pushed down the rage that rose in her at the morning wasted, and the windows dirty. It was ignoble to be angry at a poor colored man, and materialistic to let things like dirty windows disturb your composure.

"I'll give you your money," she said, resignedly. Going to the sitting-room desk she wrote out a check for two hours' work, although Clifford could not actually have worked more than three quarters of one. "You *will* come back and finish the windows tomorrow, won't you, Clifford?" she asked, holding out the slip of paper and gazing at him earnestly. The thing about Negro faces was that it was so hard to find in them such nuances of expression as might possibly convey something important. You were able to trace the basic expressions — the grin, the bashful smirk. But beyond that the dark countenances swam as though upon a film negative; mysterious, evasive. They were conveying something, but what?

"Oh, yes ma'am, Miz Daniel," Clifford promised — agreeable, conciliatory, as ever anxious to please. "I come back anytime."

"Will you come tomorrow, Clifford?"

But you could not possess them or confine them. Poor things, Abby thought, it was the only freedom they knew, the freedom not to commit themselves, not to keep promises, not to meet obligations; the freedom to slide out from under.

"I'll see y'all," Clifford said in reply. He ambled out through the front door, check in hand, ankles cracking.

95

3

Mrs. Robbie Fenn's house represented quite a different aspect of Starkeyville from Mrs. Starkey's, Abby thought, climbing its neatly brushed new concrete steps. There was no money to be made anywhere within Starkeyville, but Robbie Fenn ran the plow-and-tractor concern twenty miles up Route 43, and could keep his wife in style. Abby often saw Robbie driving home from work in the late afternoons — fat, flabby, leaning back masterfully behind the wheel of his cream Buick convertible. He looked like a movie actor typed for gangster parts, but he was a Delaunay, a Nash, and hence related to half the families in the county.

Abby was met with outstretched hands at the door by her hostess, as plump and inviting as a well-corseted pink marshmallow. Aurelia Fenn could afford to buy her clothes at Montaldo's in Richmond, and to send away for her foundations to a wonderful woman at Saks who had her measurements. Today her body appeared as though poured into sheer pink-and-mauve print, conspicuous for its elegance against the simpler summer dresses of the other ladies gathered in the living room — Miss Lilybud and Annette Barr and Amelie Nash and Mrs. Fred Whiting. Only the dress of the guest of honor could outshine Relia's. Mary Adelaide Boogher wore a beautifully cut white linen sheath; her gay, rosy face, piquant even in middle age, was surmounted by hundreds of tiny graying curls. It was some comfort to the other ladies to realize that Miss Dorothy down at the Kubla Khan Beauty Box would never in this world be able to reproduce that effect for anybody.

Relia Fenn, leading Abby up to Mary Adelaide, said, "Honey, will you have whisky or whisky?" It was a favorite joke, and everybody laughed.

"How's my old stinkin' cousin Boogher?" Mary Adelaide inquired, kissing Abby and taking a sip from her own long drink.

"He sent you his love," Abby said.

"Abby, talk back at her, hear?" Amelie urged. "Ask her how's her own stinkin' husband Georgie, why don't you? Old money-grubber!"

Just then Mrs. B. D. Starkey marched into the living room, flinging aside the scarf which had protected her skin from the sun out in the street. "Why, Mary Adelaide! Bet your Mama's glad you're home!" she exclaimed, and accepted a drink from her hostess. "Where *is* your Mama today, Mary Adelaide?"

"Her bay mare's poorly," Mary Adelaide said.

Mrs. Starkey nodded. With her old friend Fanny Buxton, out in the county, horses took precedence of people and always had.

"Tell us, Mary Adelaide," Mrs. Fred Whiting said,

tasting the fresh whisky in her glass, "I want to hear all about New York. Is it just horrid?"

Smiling, feeling the iced whisky slip down, enjoying to the full the luxury of the cool room, where Venetian blinds were drawn against July heat, the ladies seated themselves in Relia Fenn's expensive chairs from Sloane's and prepared to savor the worst.

"Well, there's always the Blue Ridge Ball to work for if you get homesick," Mary Adelaide began.

"You look pretty as a fashion plate, honey," Mrs. Starkey interrupted. "Like you just stepped off Fifth Avenue."

"Thank you, Miss Grace!" Mary Adelaide said, dimpling.

"You just know you couldn't get a dress like that in plain old Miller and Rhoads' — or in Thalhimer's, either," Annette Barr said.

"Right pretty," Mrs. Whiting granted.

"Y'all really think so?" Mary Adelaide asked.

"New York's got some uses, I reckon," Mrs. Starkey remarked. "Old Yankeeland."

"Hush, Miss Grace! Abby Daniel here's a Yankee," her hostess admonished her.

"Pshaw, Abby knows how I talk, don't you, Abby?" Mrs. Starkey asserted. "Abby's taken to our ways — Look so sweet and pretty this mownin', Abby!" she continued. "In your pretty pink dress!"

"This old thing?" Abby said, blushing. "I had this dress before I was married."

Mrs. Starkey and her old friend Mrs. Whiting exchanged glances. Trust a Yankee to reject any compliment you might pay her. It got to be almost like a game of wits, with the Yankee trying to block you from saying anything nice.

Everybody accepted a second drink and leaned back

98

against the crackling glazed-chintz sofa cushions, the blistered-satin upholstered chairs. There was no tiresome inherited furniture in this house, to protest pride over. Relia's living room was done in pale gray and rose — the most perishable colors to which one could aspire — with swag curtain of pale gray satin, draped with a dash no Starkeyville seamstress could have approximated. The whole room smacked of decorator — not inconceivably New York decorator; although everybody knew it had really been nobody in the world but Hattie Martin in Richmond — kin to the Lynchburg Martins. But Hattie Martin's prices were not to be sneezed at either; people were known to have sent for her from as far away as Charleston, West Virginia, out where they had nothing and were nobody.

Old Mrs. Fred Whiting kicked her white kid pumps off and wriggled her toes in the pale gray carpet. Nobody minded; they all felt the same way, sybaritic, and besides, this was a ladies' lunch party. Mrs. Fenn's guests could relax for two or three hours as if nothing had changed for the past fifty years, as if all were well as in their heart of hearts they defined well. What could be pleasanter than to sit with a silver tumbler — a *new* silver tumbler, from Kirk's in Baltimore, filled with Robbie Fenn's Jack Daniel — among friends, with the men home eating the sandwiches one had left for them on the dining-room table, discussing the people one liked and the people one didn't like?

After they had finished their drinks at leisure the ladies strolled out, chattering like a flight of birds and taking a good five minutes for the passage between living room and dining room, to seat themselves around a table set with appliqued organdie mats, cut-glass water goblets, unchipped

99

china, and new flat silver. Nobody in Starkeyville except Relia Fenn and Doris Taliaferro had bought a new piece of silver in their whole lives. Silver was something to be inherited or received as a wedding present. To buy new silver was a delicious, risky vision, not even to be contemplated unless one's pedigree were so water-tight that it would be obvious that one possessed ancestral silver; had merely chosen to buy new. Doris Taliaferro's good luck had been to have a sister in Roanoke to whom the family flat silver went when she was married; far from feeling discriminated against, Doris, with a clear conscience coupled with Jim Taliaferro's salary as vice-president of the bank, went off joyfully to Washington and purchased a whole new set for herself at Galt's.

Such reflections about possessions as these had been flitting through the mind of Miss Lilybud, who, with her unfortunate origin, would not have dared, even if she could have afforded it, to buy so much as a silver teaspoon. She had always, in fact, to make a point of wearing the topazes which William Byrd had given to one of her Blythe ancestors, unbecoming as they were to her sallow skin. "Mary Adelaide," she said, raising her voice to the conventionally high, questioning pitch, "tell us all about your lovely apartment in New York?"

"Well," Mary Adelaide said. "Y'all wouldn't think it was so big. Space costs its weight in diamonds in New York."

"I just know you've put your own individual touch on it, honey," Relia said. "I just know you've shown those Yankees how a lady fixes her living quarters. Your mother says you've taken the Buxton portraits up."

"Yes, they look real nice, one each side of the fireplace. And the fireplace, ladies, works," Mary Adelaide said, dimpling. "The same can't be said of all New York fireplaces."

"Always said the North was cold and frozen!" said Mrs. Starkey, throwing back her head and roaring at her own joke.

"It's not as cold as we like to tell ourselves," Mary Adelaide said. "There's some right warmhearted people, same as there are anywhere else."

"That's *your* warm heart, always finding the good," Mrs. Starkey retorted. "Don't take away the only thing I've got to hate!"

Mary Adelaide showed her dimples again.

"No question but what it's just wonderful to be down home!" she said. "George keeps saying 'Where else you going to make real money but right here in New York?' but it's nice to be back where we're not in such a tearing hurry. Where we know about the little amenities. Where we use finger bowls, for instance." Mary Adelaide lifted the finger bowl, with its filmy lace doily, off her dessert plate, and laid the silver fork and spoon to either side.

Little Abby Daniel, down the table, followed suit in silence. She knew that the assertion about finger bowls being a Southern institution was not true, but she would never have dreamed of contradicting it. It was as if there existed two truths — the truth, and the truth as it was for Starkeyville. Like accepting the rules of a game she had been allowed to play in, Abby felt it would be impossible to live in Starkeyville without agreeing with everything. She knew from experience that it was impossible to live with Boogher without agreeing with him about everything, and Starkeyville and Boogher, she felt, were quite a lot alike.

She looked up and down the long, oval table, with its centerpiece of white July roses, surrounded by women who had been brought up that it was bad manners ever to allow a silence. Not one of them but was imbedded in layer after layer of relationships — relationships with connections of their husbands, with friends, with friends of friends, with servants, with the families of servants, with their own families stretching back generation behind generation. The life they led consisted of people; people in all colors and degrees, people loved, hated, dealt with, people on terms of familiarity and people held at arm's length. Tradespeople, servants, cousins, children, spouses, friends by the dozen depended from each of these women, as from the myriad udders of an Oriental animal goddess. They moved and breathed within relationships; they never stirred unaccompanied; even their thoughts were group thoughts, family thoughts; they were region thoughts, race thoughts.

The life was a rich one, Abby reflected, as she had so many times before sitting, silent and meager, at one of these bountiful luncheons. A friendship with one of these women did not mean only friendship with an individual, but with a whole family, a whole section of society which was surmounted by the woman as if she were the finial on an amorphous pyramid of people.

When she had lived in Cubbage, and later in New York, Abby had been conscious of nobody so much as of her own dismal, skinny, chilly self. How cold had been those winters in Cubbage snow! How dirty the newspapers that blew across the street at dusk when she would come home after work to a solitary apartment in New York! In the North everyone was an individual, or tried to be. People asserted individual opinions, striving to make them original. People moved through crowds, solitary. If they felt impinged upon, they said they were tired, and went home to be alone.

When you made a friend in New York, she was likely to be all you would ever know of the complex of her life; you might never meet her sister or her best beau, let alone her mother or father. People moved through life by ones and Abby's own threadlike oneness had been so tenuous as to seem always at the point of breaking entirely. But in Starkeyville she could go for days without being aware of being herself at all. Will-less, possessed, sometimes when she opened her diary it was with the sensation of coming to from an anesthetic that she wrote the opening word, "I . . ."

The lunch-table conversation had meanwhile proceeded without a moment's break. A kind of continual interrupting existed in Starkeyville that was the best of manners, that was a part of people's not expecting to exist alone and un-assisted. "Honey," Relia was saying to Mary Adelaide over her tall sherbet glass of whipped-cream dessert, "you find yourself taking part in any of those society doings we read about in the New York *Times?*"

"All those pictures of women, lookin' right haggard?" Miss Lilybud amplified.

"You *are* a Buxton, child." Mrs. Starkey contributed another angle to the question. "A Derby. And I believe a Barr, too, if I am not mistaken."

"Yes, you're Rushton's second cousin once removed," Annette Barr said.

"I was just wondering if you ever fooled with those balls they always seem to be getting up, sitting together at those coffee tables to get their pictures taken, chairman of this and on the board of that," Relia said.

The question, as put by the collective woman present, was now complete.

"Unh-hunh," Mary Adelaide replied. "Once in a while

— mostly on account of George's position in General Foods, of course — I get asked to be on charity committees. There's right much done for charity, in New York. I'm on one committee now, for a theater benefit in the fall."

There was a flaw in the logic of what Mary Adelaide had said.

"General Foods, stuff, child," Mrs. Whiting observed, to mend the flaw. "With all that Boogher and Buxton blood?"

"Oh, Miss Lucy! Up there in New York nobody ever heard of a Boogher or a Buxton!" Mary Adelaide said, dimpling at the elderly lady. She added, "This particular benefit is for International Orphans Incorporated — a charity that brings children over here from Europe."

. There was a moment's pause. Then Mrs. Starkey said indignantly, "Got plenty of orphans right here in these U-nited States. Just *like* Yankees! Can't stay home where they b'long, always pokin' in where they're not wanted . . ."

"But it's a great big important organization, Miss Grace," Mary Adelaide explained. "They've brought over more than three thousand orphans, I understand."

"Charity begins at home, *I* say," Relia Fenn put in. She rang the tiny silver bell, at her right hand, and the two Negro maids, in gray uniforms with organdie aprons, reappeared and began to clear away the dessert plates. "I truly do. You can spend your millions of dollars all over the globe on your stark heathen and your coal-black, and it won't do one particle of good if there isn't charity in your heart." Her words were swallowed up in the torrent of generally voiced agreement.

Abby's eyes followed the colored maids as they passed silently in and out through the swinging door to the pantry.

Her eyes returned to the tableful of ladies. By some association of ideas, she visualized her diary, lying in its drawer beside the bed, at home. Then she allowed herself to be swept on again by the avalanche of opinion around her.

"— Like the way the Northern newspapers talk so big about integration," Mrs. Whiting was saying with heat. "You think for one moment those Northern parents send *their* children to public school along with niggras? You can bet not." Mrs. Whiting gave her dessert plate a push, so that the maid could more easily reach it. "They send them to private schools; that's where they *send* them. That's why the North *has* all those private schools!"

"I call it plain old hypocrisy," Mrs. Starkey declared, and everybody beamed. "And covering up the fact of the matter, which is that as usual the North is trying to make it just as hard as possible for the South."

"One thing I have no use for, it's hypocrisy," Miss Lilybud said.

"I have *never* approved," Mrs. Fenn said.

"If they had any real concern for the niggra," Mrs. Whiting continued. "But they haven't. We've got more real love for the niggra down here in our little finger! Love isn't making up theories, love is doing for! You take my Phil St. Clair, I've been keeping Phil in shoes and square meals for thirty years. He hasn't got good sense, he's just a poor old niggra who can't read or write, but I've always had Phil's interests at heart."

"And take my Rosalie . . ." Amelie Nash chimed in, eagerly.

The maids brought in the coffee, on two big silver salvers which they placed at either end of the table. Mrs. Fenn and, at the other end, Mrs. Whiting, poured out into tiny red-and-gold cups.

"Trouble with New York is, it's *hard*hearted," Mrs. Starkey announced. "Seems like they don't *know* anything. Why, when I went on up there the time Mary Alice Delaunay married the Yankee, that old *mill*ionaire from Long Island, I went to the wedding and it was all mighty fancy, mighty shiny, but mighty cold and impersonal, too. I didn't get introduced to hardly a soul. Seems like those New York women don't know how to behave."

"I know," Relia Fenn nodded. "We just don't *do* that way."

"The South's just naturally as hospitable as it can be," Mrs. Whiting began. "We're just naturally kind, and loving, and outgoing to the outsider and the stranger."

"And not a speck of hypocrisy," Mrs. Starkey agreed heartily. "When we take somebody to our hearts you can count on it."

"Instead of puttin' on, and coverin' up, and spendin' millions on some old orphans nobody ever even heard of!" Mrs. Whiting concluded. "Reckon they just don't know any better."

"And what are your views on hypocrisy, Abby?" Mrs. Starkey asked. "You haven't said boo-turkey in half an hour."

Abby swallowed. "I worry a lot about hypocrisy," she said. "I don't know — things seem to backfire so on me. Sometimes I get the feeling I don't dare do anything, for fear it might turn out to be hypocritical. If one could only see the whole of a thing all at the same time . . ."

Mrs. Starkey stared. "Mercy!" she said.

Amelie Nash had been the first to drop the subject of

hypocrisy. "Mary Adelaide," she was saying, "How 'bout that book? *The Rose That Died?* Who do people up there in New York think wrote it? Hm?"

Mrs. Starkey, turning away from Abby, hastened to augment the question. "Gives the first recognizable picture of the South in years and *years,*" she said.

"Right pleasant. Right acceptable," Lucy Whiting added, running her tongue around her vertically wrinkled old lips, to catch any bit of dessert that might remain before beginning on her coffee.

"Why!" Mary Adelaide replied, all laughter and dimples. "I was sure y'all would be full of ideas about the authorship! I thought surely y'all would have the author pinned down and labeled by the time I got down home!"

"Has your Mama told you about the pictures, going to be in *Life?*" Miss Lilybud asked.

Mary Adelaide nodded. "Trust dear old Starkeyville," she said. "Always right up there in the forefront."

"Abby can tell you about the pictures," Mrs. Starkey said. "Abby took the photographer all around town to see he didn't burn holes in the upholstery and so forth and so on. Abby can tell you when the pictures are scheduled to appear. When is it, Abby?"

"I'm not sure," Abby replied. "I haven't heard from Mr. Hume since he left. He said sometime the end of this month." Her heart began to pound.

Mrs. Robbie Fenn stood up and brushed the crumbs off her sleekly tubular torso. "Shall we go into the livin' room?" she proposed.

The ladies began the long trek back, with sudden halts in the hall for the revelation, with hands laid detainingly on sleeves, of suddenly remembered news; with pauses for viewing Mrs. Fenn's new inlaid console table in the hall, and for gazing up the broad front stairs. Two ladies had to go to the powder room; they backed and filled for some time in deference to each other. Ten minutes later the company had reassembled in the living room.

"Mint?" asked Mrs. Fenn. She passed a silver filigree basket filled with pink and white candies. The candies were delicious — sweet and not too sharp. A sense of luxury prevailed, and of being ladies who knew how to do everything but needed to do nothing; of a beautiful afternoon pleasantly passing and a delicious meal digesting.

At length Mrs. Whiting rose reluctantly. "It's been sweet, Relia," she said. "But I've got to go look in on old Mr. Buck Whitehall. My cross. My year-round Lenten penance."

"I don't see why you fool with that old billy goat, Lucy," Mrs. Starkey said. "I see him prancin' down Boogher Street wavin' his cane like he thought he was General Beauregard."

"He does think he's General Beauregard," Mrs. Whiting said. "And sometimes he thinks he's General Pickett."

"Don't let him charge *you*, Miss Lucy," Relia Fenn said, laughing. "You're too kind to him. He's got a perfectly good colored woman to look after him, has he not?"

"She's crazy and she drinks," Mrs. Whiting said. "I only *go* once a week. I inherited Mr. Buck Whitehall from my sister Amelia, and *somebody* has to see whether he's waked up dead or alive."

All the ladies had risen and were gathering up their summer purses, their white mesh gloves. They moved slowly in the direction of the front door, shooting off appreciative remarks about the lunch party as they went, like sparklers.

Mrs. Starkey had to go straight home to supervise Mattie, or the house would be in ruins. Annette Barr had an appointment with Miss Dorothy at the Kubla Khan for a shampoo and set. Amelie Nash and Miss Lilybud had had a date for days to go see the movie at the Orpheum together.

"Come on go, Abby," Amelie urged. "It's so nice and cool in there with the air-conditioning. Any old movie would seem just fine, and this is Gary Cooper!"

"Come on go," echoed Miss Lilybud, civilly. Actually she was not eager for Abby's company. She could hardly afford to associate on intimate terms with a Yankee.

In the end Abby found herself walking home alone by way of Armistead Street, Boogher Street, and Buford Row. She passed the fire station on Boogher, and the four or five shops that served this part of town. In front of the newsstand she hesitated; on a wire rack copies of the Richmond *News Leader,* the William and Mary *Messenger,* and the New York *Times* flapped in the hot breeze. She went into the dark interior of the store where a big circular fan on the ceiling agitated the air. "Has the new *Life* come?" she asked fat old Mr. Harper.

"I'm gettin' 'em out as fast as I kin," he replied irritably, tugging at the fuzzy string that bound a big brown-paper package. The string broke, and the glossy magazines with their red-bordered covers spilled out. "Here you are, Miz Daniel," Mr. Harper said, sounding abused.

Abby started to look, to make sure whether this was the issue; then she had the sense that, with Mr. Harper there, the place was too public. She handed him the money for the magazine and walked out into the broiling midafternoon sun on Boogher Street.

It was hard to tell whether it was the heat of the day, or her agitation, that made her heart pound so. She rounded the corner into Starkey Street. Unable to wait till she had climbed the two flights of stairs to the apartment, she sat down on the neatly mortared stone wall that bordered the Harrisons' place and opened the copy of *Life*.

4

IN the middle of that night, Abby woke Boogher by suddenly throwing her arms around his neck and pressing her face against his shoulder.

" 'Smatter?" he ejaculated quickly. He threw himself over on his back, raising himself on his elbows.

"I had such a terrible dream! I was so scared . . ."

"Oh, for God's sake." Boogher lay back and jerked his head from side to side, waking up.

"But it was so real! It was right in this room! I was lying in bed, just as I *am* lying here. And the door to the hall was open. And all of a sudden, as I was looking in that direction, a tiger came walking in! Oh, *Boogher!*"

Boogher lay still. He was almost fully awake now. He slid his hand under Abby's shoulders and patted her further arm. "Don't be foolish. It was only a dream," he said.

"But it was so real! It's still real! The tiger was so huge. And its face was so serious and deadly . . . It came walking over here to the bed, just looking at me, steadily. When it got to this side of the bed I woke up."

"Poor little child," Boogher said, patting her.

"I wish I could stop seeing that terrible, serious face, coming toward me!"

"There . . ." Boogher turned over on his side and put both arms around his wife. Now that he was awake, this was the way he loved her to be. Fanciful, swayed by dreams and portents, she was plainly in need of his reason, balance, and objectivity. "It's only a dream," he repeated.

"I know . . ." She wept against him. "I just keep seeing that face . . ."

"It'll stop. It'll go," he said, holding her closer.

She put her arms around his neck.

"Who's a foolish little child who gets scared by dreams?" he demanded softly. "Who's a little silly?"

She gave a convulsive sob.

"Who is my silly baby?" he insisted.

Grateful for his comforting, eager to be convinced of her own foolishness, she clung to him who was real, and alive, and no dream.

"Boogher. I love you."

"Damn right you do."

In the dark he need no longer feel the eternal pricking of self-doubt. His face was wholly hidden. He was, perhaps, beautiful; or huge, or stalwart, or relentless, or insistent, or importunate, or ruthless, or dominating. He had a thousand faces.

Abby too, in the darkness, could be the wife of these. She too could have a thousand forms, soft, luscious, abundant and desirable; dark as a cloud or blazing golden.

The bitter recriminations that Boogher's daytime self had hurled at Abby's daytime person in the earlier part of this night were forgotten by these two immortal beings.

5

NEXT morning, with a sense of girding herself for whatever shock she might encounter, Abby prepared to walk downtown to market. Would she meet turned backs? Direct insults? Furious denunciations? — Or, possibly, delighted recognition; praise; amazement; pride; pleasure; invitations; tributes . . .

In any case her hour had struck, her time had come. The identity of the author of *The Rose That Died* was now an open book, she thought as she locked the apartment door after her and prepared to descend the stairs. On the landing she came upon General Larrimore, the door of his apartment standing open behind him, picking leaves off the large cactus on the landing window sill. For a mad instant it occurred to Abby that the General had arranged this meeting especially to congratulate her upon her achievement.

"Good morning, General," she said, demurely.

He shot her a suspicious glance. "What's that?"

"I said, good morning, sir."

"Oh. Morning. What's the matter with this thing? Need water?"

"I don't think cactuses are supposed to get water, are they?"

"How do I know? Asked you. Looks dead."

"No, see, there's a little green at the tips. Is it your plant?"

"What?"

"I suppose if it is out in the hall it must be Miss Clara's," Abby answered herself.

"Can't hear you when you mumble. Speak up. You're Boogher Daniel's wife, are you not?"

"Yes, sir." Abby besought herself to feel compassion for the elderly; the mislayers of their memories; the no-longer-growing.

"Well . . ." the General muttered, irritated. He continued picking brown, spiny leaves off the wretched plant. Abby passed down the second flight of stairs and out into the hot morning sun.

She reflected that it was most unlikely that General Larrimore ever read anything, even on *Life*'s level. Old army reports, perhaps? What *did* retired Generals read? What, indeed, did retired Generals do?

She walked on down Starkey Street. It was still early enough in the day for the air to seem fresh. When the overwhelming heat of noon arrived, the day would be flattened out into a relentless, steady glare, until at last, at dusk, an evening breeze sprang up and the town fell exhausted into the arms of night. But at this hour the birds still dared speak up, in the sycamores bordering Starkey Street.

Old Miss Firth was out watering her front flower bed. Everybody else had given up on gardening a month ago, for there was nothing much that could be done while the ground was as hard as a brick — was, in fact, a brick; made of William and Mary County clay. But Miss Firth had made up her mind, laid out her money, and was going to see it through. She watered every morning with an old hose, and the water trickled around the bases of the zinnia stalks and ran down the myriad tiny gulleys in the hard earth.

"Good morning, Miss Firth," Abby said as she passed, wondering nervously how Miss Firth had spent the previous evening.

Miss Firth peered to make sure who it was, before she would speak. Satisfied, she replied, "Good morning, Mrs. Daniel."

"What a hot day!"

Miss Firth peered again at the maker of this supererogatory remark. Swinging her hose over toward another section of the flower bed, she turned her back.

Had she been snubbed? Abby wondered.

When she turned in to Bolling Avenue, she could see at intervals down its length ladies out to do their morning errands before the heat grew too intense. They were taking their time. They strolled along the tree-shaded sidewalks very, very slowly, so as not to get into a perspiration. Some of the ladies carried parasols; they looked like red or gray mushrooms floating down the street. Miss Lilybud Carter came toward Abby, a pink parasol tipped back over her skinny shoulder that was perhaps designed to throw becoming lights.

"Morning, Miss Lilybud," Abby said, trying to act as

usual; trying not to look eager or anxious; trying to keep herself from stopping dead on the sidewalk to implore a reaction to the great news.

"Morning, Abby," Miss Lilybud replied. She visibly shrank, and hurried on.

There! She *was* trying to get away from me, Abby thought — But then she always hurries by me.

She continued along Bolling Avenue to the next corner, where she turned into the unshaded, glaring heat of Main Street. Cars came thicker here, and the traffic lights, here and further down at the corner where Carver Drive led down the hill into Brownsville, flicked with a tiny click — red — green; red — green — like alternating raspberry and lime drops melting in the sunshine. Tradesmen sauntered along the sidewalks in their shirt-sleeves, on their way to pay a call on old Pete at the newsstand, or to catch a dope, or just to stand outside the drugstore for a little bit. Abby nodded to Mr. Wilson of the shoe store and to Mr. Jewell of Jewell's Drugstore.

In the Piggly-Wiggly it was cooler; not air-conditioned but swept by breezes from huge ceiling fans that whirled round and round horizontally. Abby bought ground meat and then went to pick out her vegetables. In the state she was in, it was only upon reaching the checker's counter that she realized she had selected but one artichoke. She had to hurry back for a second, while the checker totted up her coffee, butter, and bread.

The brown paper bag was heavy. Abby walked in the direction of home, weighed down by it and by a sensation of disappointment and frustration. Outside Jewell's Drugstore on the corner of Main and Bolling, she hesitated. Would a Coca-Cola make me feel a little bit better? she wondered. Or perhaps ice cream, even at this hour of the morning? Recklessly, she went in and gave her order to the slatternly fifteen-year-old girl with a dirty towel tied around her waist as an apron, who stood behind the counter washing glasses. The interior of the drugstore was dark; its electric fan hummed steadily; Abby sat down in the end booth, sniffing the special drugstore smell compounded of candy, medicine, and soda water.

"Why, Abby Daniel, you bad girl!" a voice exclaimed. Amelie Nash, fresh and ripe as a peach about to burst its skin, stood before her. "I'm going to sit down yere with you for a little bit. I'm hot," she complained. She raised her chin at the slatternly girl and called, "*Bring* me a Coke?" in a tone that obviated the need of the word "please." "Why Abby!" she continued. "Did you write the story in that book sure 'nough?"

Abby was experiencing the greatest difficulty in speaking at all. She nodded and smiled. The counter girl came sauntering over with a metal, footed cup of pink ice cream in one hand, and the short, dark drink crammed with shaved ice in the other. She set them down and waited, looking away, for payment.

"*I'm* treating *you*," Amelie declared. "To celebrate you being so smart. Here!" she said to the girl, handing her change. "Sure 'nough!" she repeated, turning her attention back to Abby and gazing at her, chin propped in hand.

Abby bent her eyes modestly on her ice cream and ate a spoonful.

"What I liked was the picture of the bedroom out at Azalea," Amelie continued. "I used to sleep in that bedroom, when I was a child and visited out in the county. The Mansfields owned Azalea then. My father used to handle

117

their law business. But I can't see why you took that picture of Miss Grace's living room. You know there's nothing *to* that poky old living room, pore old Miss Grace! Relia Fenn's would have been more representative of a real nice Starkeyville home."

Abby hardly knew where to begin to answer.

"I didn't take the pictures," she said. Then, as Amelie looked blank, she went on, "The pictures were taken of the places *Life* picked out, to illustrate the kind of life the characters led in *The Rose That Died*. Relia's house wouldn't have been like anything in the book, you see."

"Is that right?" Amelie asked. With the menu card she fanned her neck and plump, pretty shoulders. "Anyway, I like your Courthouse Square pictures, a whole lot. Real picturesque. Daddy used to practice in Fred Whiting's office, did you know that? I thought that one was a *real* good picture. And I liked the one of the courthouse."

Abby was aware that in Amelie's words existed an element of the complimentary. "I didn't have anything to do with the pictures," she explained again. "Tommy Hume — he was the photographer — took the pictures *Life* wanted; I just showed him around."

Amelie's lovely face wore an expression of bewilderment even more marked than usual.

"But you *wrote* it," she objected. "It's meant to be pictures of your own story — you know it is, Abby Daniel," she chided; clinging, apparently, to what for Amelie felt like reason.

"Nobody knew I had written the book at the time the pictures were taken," Abby said. She drew a long, quivering breath. "The book's authorship had not yet been revealed," she said, striving to speak with formality and distinctness.

"Now, Abby." Amelie spoke severely. "You mustn't keep trying to fool people all the time. It says right there in *Life*, it *says* you wrote the story. You go and look yourself and see if it doesn't."

"I know. You see, I told Mr. Hume . . ."

"That's what I'm saying! It's right there that you wrote it, in black and white. I certainly never knew before that you *wrote*," Amelie said, her eyes large, clear, and innocent of understanding. "Except in your diary, that is; Boogher told me you keep a diary. But he didn't tell me it was *stories* that you write in your diary."

"It isn't."

"Well, but . . ." Amelie stopped, outdone. "Abby, honey, you don't make any sense," she said earnestly. "You honestly don't. You keep contradicting yourself."

Abby smiled helplessly.

"Darlin', I've got just loads to do," Amelie said, tipping her Coke glass back and letting a mouthful of shaved ice slip into her mouth. "If I ever expect to get home by lunchtime, that is. 'Bye, honey — I thought what it said under the pictures was *real* pretty," she said, making a last effort to be appreciative. "I just loved what it said about the courtly, charming life lived in the old town houses of Starkeyville. That was just fine, Abby, I thought. You wrote that just sweetly."

"But I didn't *write* it!" Abby cried. "*Life* wrote the captions! I didn't have a thing to *do* with the pictures!"

"Now, Abby Daniel!" Amelie smiled chidingly and shook her head. She rose and clasped her paper bag from Reaves's store to her deliciously curving bosom. "See you!" She strolled out of the drugstore.

Abby resisted an impulse to put her head down in her

arms in public. But after a moment the realization came to her that the whirling hodgepodge inside Amelie's head was a concoction uniquely Amelie's own. No one else on earth was quite the bit of delectable, unreasoning flesh that Amelie was; and if Heaven only knew what report Amelie would pass on to her friends of this morning's conversation, Heaven also knew that people were well aware of the total unreliability of all Amelie's reports. "Batbrained" was Starkeyville's word for Amelie. The town did not expect good sense from her.

Abby got up to go home, telling herself that Amelie had, at least, been far from offended. Then, as she pushed open the heavy glass door and drew her first lungful of burning heat, the thought struck her, as if it were part of the breath-catching blast — But why should Boogher have been telling Amelie about my diary?

6

WHEN Abby reached home the mail had already come. She opened the box marked DANIEL, fastened outside the door of the Robert E. Lee Apartments, and drew forth a handful of envelopes: bills, something from the Merchants National Bank for Boogher, two letters for herself — one from Jason & Terhune and one from Tommy Hume.

She climbed the stairs, feeling as if she held live flesh-and-blood in her hands. Boogher was not coming home for lunch; a book salesman was taking him out to Reidecker's. Abby put the groceries away with care, to prolong her pleasure, and at length sat down on the sitting-room sofa to read her letters.

Mr. Jason, her old boss, wrote in his usual, old-school way.

DEAR ABBY,
The decision you had written me of earlier, to reveal your authorship of *Rose* via the *Life* article, strikes me as

characteristic of your reserve in the whole matter. Naturally, as your publisher, I wish you had acceded to our entreaties to make yourself known at the beginning, when there would have been, of course, considerable fanfare in connection with the publication of the book. However, speaking not as publisher but as friend, I can appreciate the dignity inherent in revealing your literary identity only now, when attention has somewhat died down. I may say that never in my entire publishing experience have I encountered quite such modesty on the part of an author.

Jason & Terhune has all along been proud of publishing your book. Now, of course, we can express our pride, not only of *Rose* but of Abigail Woodbury Daniel! I am writing today to ask if you won't reconsider your inclination to have nothing to do with the promotion of the novel. If you would come to New York at once, in the wake of the *Life* pictures, interest might be renewed by means of interviews, TV and radio appearances, together with the increase in sales which we anticipate. I can promise you that Jason & Terhune would strive to protect you from any undue notoriety. I am not the only member of the firm who feels your shrinking from publicity is not only unusual in this day and age but is part of the reason why you are the writer you are.

I hope you are working on a second novel. There is no question in my mind but that your very remarkable gifts are those of a romantic writer. There is little of the cold or the classic in your work. If anyone had asked me two or three years ago, I would have said it was impossible for a good romantic novel to be written in America today; and I think I would have added, particularly a good romantic novel about the South, already so overromanticized both in its glamorous and its corrupt aspects. It only goes to prove, of course, the old publishing truism about making categorical predictions. Anything can be done, in the novel, if it is done well.

Do write me you will come to New York. We can see to it that you have a little whirl. I must emphasize that the time for this must be now, for, as I am sure you remember, the life of even a successful novel is brief.

Yours ever faithfully,
HORACE F. JASON

Abby, without pausing, tore open Tommy's letter.

DEAR ABBY,

Or at least I certainly do hope it is dear Abby and not dear Stink-Puss that is contemplating these lines.

How did you like the pictures? And how does it feel to exist? I'm sorry I couldn't get more of a play in the magazine for your authorship of *Rose* — those two lines buried in a caption were inadequate, to say the least. If you had let me take that picture of you, it might have helped out in the space situation. But now, baby, you are a living author instead of a ghost or some such. You can never again attempt to kid itinerant photographers into believing you are nobody. They would laugh in your face. As, clever me, I did.

How about rising from your ashes like a good phoenix, and coming the hell up here while the coming's good, which won't be long? You could have a ball. I seem to recall they don't give no balls down yonder in Starkeyville, whereas we-all's just pinin' to. Authors, I hope you realize, don't generally get second chances like this. After the first boom it's phht. If it's the cold frozen North that's scaring you, Elsa and I would just love to have you treat around here like home. Elsa's dying to meet you, I'm dying to see you — why stall? C'est le premier pas qui coute, and the premier pas is already taken, so you might as well relax and take a plane. You're a celebrity, not a housewife.

(Dig that, you old horror.)

Love,
TOMMY

Abby sat quite still on the sofa. She could hear blood pounding in her ears, and began to count her heartbeats as they came tripping after one another: Twenty-two twenty-three twenty-four twenty-five . . . The telephone rang.

Abby sprang to answer it, crying "Hello?" into the receiver.

"Hello." The voice on the other end hesitated. "I'd like to speak to Mrs. Daniel."

"This is Abby, Miss Grace," Abby said, let down.

"Oh, Abby. It didn't sound like you — Abby, I'm expecting you over to help with the party this afternoon, child. Come a little early, will you? I asked people for —" The mysterious crashes and crackles which accompanied all telephone conversations in Starkeyville broke in at that moment; and far, far away, a tiny unknown voice said, "You take your chitlings and fry them good. Then take your —"

"What did you say, Miss Grace?" Abby shouted.

"I said, come at quarter to four, hear?"

"Yes, Miss Grace. Good-by."

Abby went back to the sofa. Did this mean that Miss Grace intended to speak her mind, at a quarter to four, on the subject of novel writing? To rake Abby stem to stern, as Boogher had warned that Starkeyville's old guard would do? Why, then, did she still want Abby to serve at her party? Whatever might be awaiting her at a quarter to four, Abby decided, it could not be complete ostracism.

She returned to the contemplation of her letters. She was much impressed by the sophistication of the language employed in them. It seemed almost unbelievable that it was she, Abby Daniel, who was being addressed both as "baby" and "a celebrity" as well as told that never had such modesty as hers been encountered in a long publishing experience. Perhaps I *am* rather modest, Abby reflected, preening slightly.

Mrs. Starkey met Abby at the gate, to one side of the shabby Victorian house, that led back into the garden. Her handsome face was flushed and a strand of white hair had fallen out of her pompadour. She kept puffing at it to get it out of her eyes, but it would instantly fall down again.

"I thought we'd take tea out under the grape arbor," she explained. "The thermometer says it's two degrees cooler than this morning. Unless it's going to rain, you reckon, Abby? — I've been out pinning those old floppy rosebushes up on stakes. I'm glad you've come, there's right much to attend to. Mattie brought out the tea table, but I'm not going to allow her to lay her hands on my embroidered grass-cloth tea cloth the Bishop's wife brought me; that was when the Bishop was just a plain old missionary to China. *Go* in the house and fetch it, child?"

As Abby stood laying the tea cloth on the drop-leaf table that had been placed inside the dilapidated old arbor just in back of the house, Mrs. Starkey approached her again to ask, "Hasn't Mattie finished making those cress sandwiches yet?" But she did not pause for an answer. "Look yere for a moment. Do these roses look just too stinkin'? Gracious, I should never have left everything to the last moment; I declare, I'm distracted! Run back into the house and tell Mattie hurry up with those sandwiches and get moving putting the cookies out on plates. Then *you* carry out the teacups, hear? The Delaunay ones with gold rims. Use a tray, child, it'll save time. Last time I let Mattie carry cups she broke two. Run."

"Do I look a sight?" Mrs. Starkey demanded when Abby had returned, laden with the china. "Not that I care if I do, really," she continued. "If I haven't reached the age of seventy-two without earning the right to have my nose shiny, I give up — Rouge! Did I remember rouge?"

"Yes, Miss Grace," Abby replied, eying the two round spots of pink the old lady affected.

"That's something. Where's the spoons? Can't take tea without spoons, dear child, what are you thinking of? In the drawer just to the left of the sink you'll find the cheese-cloth covers for the cake plates. The flies are beginning," Mrs. Starkey said, fanning herself violently with one hand and puffing at the loose strand of hair. "Run, now. Is Boogher coming in later?"

"He was, the last I knew," Abby replied.

At that moment the gate creaked on its hinges and Miss Lilybud Carter appeared — the first guest, as usual. " 'Do, Abby," she said, dodging Abby's hand. "Why, Grace, dear! This is mighty pleasant! Your lovely gyarden!"

"Stuff," said Mrs. Starkey. "It's dried up solid. But I thought it would make a change. Abby, *bring* the sandwiches?"

When Abby returned with a cake plate in either hand the two old ladies were talking together in lowered tones. Their heads drew apart as Abby approached. Mrs. Starkey smiled warmly and reached out to take a cake plate. The gate hinge creaked again and a Mr. and Mrs. Carrington came walking down the path. People from Prince William County, well on in years, kin to the Whitings, it appeared that they were passing through Starkeyville on their way to pay a visit in Fredericksburg and had been told by Lucy Whiting — so they explained amid little screams from Mrs. Carrington and bows from Mr. Carrington — to walk into the party.

"I should think so indeed!" Mrs. Starkey said warmly.

126

"Sit right down, yonder in those wicker chairs. Will you take sugar in your tea? We plan to indulge in a little tetch of something, later, when the sun is lower."

The arbor was shaded from the blazing west by the house itself, which at this hour threw a bulky shadow eastward. In the intervals of passing teacups, Abby sat in a corner of the arbor trying to remember not to lean back too hard against a loose cedar crosspiece. Her mind throbbed with the puzzle of her reception. It had become obvious that she was not to be castigated or ostracized for daring to write a book which might conceivably be about Starkeyville. Nobody had criticized her; on the other hand, nobody had praised her either. Nobody had, in fact, spoken of the book at all, since Amelie's remarks in the drugstore this morning.

Abby knew Starkeyville too well to imagine for one moment that news of her authorship had failed to get around. Even if it had not been for the issue of *Life* she had seen lying on the bench beside the telephone in Mrs. Starkey's front hall, she knew from experience that if so much as one person in Starkeyville possessed a piece of news in the morning, it would be shared by everyone in town by night, not forgetting Brownsville. One reason for those unspeakable telephone connections for which Starkeyville was noted was that upon any given conversation at least two to four other subscribers were listening in.

Amelie would have served as Starkeyville's sole informant; but to imagine Amelie that, would be absurd. Everyone saw *Life*. Nobody could have missed those lines, under the photograph of the Robert E. Lee Apartments, which read, "Today Starkeyville is a charming backwater. On Starkey Street (above) lives Mrs. Boogher Ffoulkes Daniel,

Vermont-born, hitherto anonymous author of *Rose*. She and her husband, Starkeyville's bookseller, are representative of Starkeyville's aristocratic younger set, live quietly, drink bourbon, play poker. Sara Lou Starrett, character in the novel, when she married Wingfield Gaines, set up housekeeping in just such an apartment house, lived just such a life." That caption would have been as easy for Starkeyville to miss as a local detonation of the bomb.

So what conferences had been held, for hours, over Starkeyville's telephones today? What debates? What decisions had been come to, and for what reasons? The atmosphere seemed to Abby more than mysterious and ambiguous; it seemed Machiavellian. Was something to be sprung upon her? Some ultimatum, some carefully timed, concerted declaration? She looked from face to face as more guests arrived — Mrs. Whiting, Annette Barr, Relia Fenn, Amelie. . . . All of them spoke to her, calmly; outwardly the same as ever. There was something menacing about such a silence on such a vital matter. Some very unpleasant surprise must be planned.

Meanwhile conversation continued to tumble, spill, gush from the lips of the company. In an effort to quell her nervousness, Abby tipped her chair back against the shaky post and attempted to view it objectively. The scene looked pretty but not entirely real, she thought, as if it were an Impressionist painting of an outdoor fete in the Nineties — Miss Grace in her mauve, light and shade playing on the white pyramid of her hair; Amelie in pink, luscious as strawberries and cream; Annette and Mrs. Whiting both in white. The grape leaves cast flickering blue and purple shadows on the light dresses. Mrs. Carrington, as befitted a traveler, wore navy blue voile; Mr. Carrington sat on the outskirts of the bevy like the male figure wearing a boater hat that may be spied behind the frothy creatures that fill the foreground of a Renoir. Animated yet peaceful, the scene might have belonged to fifty years ago, and been embalmed in the amber of an afternoon's sunshine.

All at once Abby heard Mr. Carrington remark to his hostess, "I trust y'all feel pleased with the very charmin' pictures of Starkeyville appearin' in *Life* this week?"

Abby stiffened. The front legs of her chair came down to the ground.

"Tell me, Miss Grace," Mrs. Carrington added, helping to propound the total question which the Carringtons, as a couple, wished to put. "Am I right in understandin' that that delightful story, *The Rose That Died,* was written by a fellow townswoman of y'all's?"

Mrs. Starkey bowed to Mr. and Mrs. Carrington before casting her eyes toward Abby in the corner.

"Yes," she stated. "Abby Daniel here wrote it. Abby is very clever with her pen. Her husband — Boogher Daniel, my husband's second cousin, you know; a Starkey daughter married a Daniel in the second generation back, so Abby is very close kin — as I say, Boogher keeps our bookstore here in Starkeyville. A most exceptional shop indeed; *most* exceptional. I am told that only three such independent book shops are in operation throughout the entire South."

"Is that a fact?" Mrs. Carrington murmured politely; her eyes kept flickering back and forth between Abby and Mrs. Starkey. "Exceedin'ly interestin'."

"The Daniels are our literary lights," Mrs. Starkey continued. "Known — as I am sure you must realize — far beyond the confines of Starkeyville, indeed of Virginia. I know of no other town this size with a comparable literary distinction. But then, we old Starkeyvillians have always clasped literature to our hearts," she observed, reaching up and breaking off one of the grape leaves just above her head. She crumbled the leaf between her fingers. "My dear father was a very great reader; Dickens was his favorite. How well I remember Papa reading to us children, night after night around the fire in the study at Azalea. *Little Dorrit. Great Expectations.* Dear old *David Copperfield.* Lady Barbara Parkinson, who occupies Azalea at the moment, calls the room the library. But 'study' sounds far more natural to these ears. It *was* a study, Papa's study, so why not call it a study?"

During Mrs. Starkey's speech Mr. Carrington had never lost track of the Carringtons' original question. He turned to Abby.

"You have kept an admirin' public in the dark for some time, as to the authorship of your delightful work," he said.

Mrs. Starkey hastened to reply.

"Abby has always been a selfless child," she informed him, throwing an approving smile at the subject of her compliment. "Remaining anonymous was very ladylike of Abby. Very suitable."

Mr. Carrington made a slight bow, and started to turn aside to speak to Amelie Nash on his other hand. But Mrs. Starkey had not entirely finished with him.

"When all the hooraw was over and done with," she said, raising her voice commandingly, "Abby could, in her modest fashion, allow the authorship of her little story to become known. I approve."

Abby, sitting in the corner, burst into a perspiration.

Mrs. Starkey was pouring a cup of tea for Lucy Whiting. "Abby, child," she said without looking around, "*take this teakettle into the house?* There isn't a smidgin of hot water left."

Abby got up, lifted the teakettle out of its brass framework with one hand, took the china teapot with the other, and went up the rotting old steps that led from the garden into the house. As she entered the indoors after the outdoor sunshine, she felt as though suddenly struck blind. Little story, she thought, the words pounding upon her darkened mind. *Little story!* It isn't a little story, it's a beautiful book . . . Groping around in the dimness of the kitchen, she rinsed the tea leaves from the Staffordshire teapot and put in fresh tea with a silver teaspoon that lay on the grooved board beside the soapstone sink. Steam was gushing steadily from the spout of the enormous teakettle on the stove. Abby seized its handle and poured boiling water into the pot and into the teakettle. One in either hand, she started back out to the garden. Little story, she ejaculated mentally, trembling all over, as she descended the broken steps.

Several men had arrived in her absence, Boogher among them — handsome and full-blooded in the striped shirt with a tab collar that fitted him so well. As Abby looked, she saw him lift his chin up out of the collar and arch his eyebrows roguishly at Amelie Nash. He seemed to throb with vitality; Mr. Carrington, beside him, looked like a poor weak minnow.

Abby slid the hot-water kettle back into its framework over the alcohol flame. She heard Mr. Carrington say,

131

"We've just been sayin' how much we enjoyed your wife's story, *The Dyin' Rose*."

Blood rushed to Abby's head. Her hand jerked away, as though burnt, from the handle of the kettle. She slipped into her original corner of the arbor.

"— *The Rose That Died*, you mean," she heard Boogher reply.

"It don't signify," Mr. Carrington said. "In any case, charmin'."

"Tell me, Boogher," Amelie put in. She raised her face, like a great pink flower, to look into Boogher's. "Wasn't it a surprise to find Abby could write a real sure 'nough *book?*"

Boogher laughed. "Hardly," he replied, flashing his eyes. "Abby's a *smart* little somebody. The only question was, how long we should wait before ejecting the feline from its receptacle."

"Oh, Boogher!" Amelie exclaimed, dismayed by such long words.

Mrs. Starkey turned to them from the tea table. "I much approve of the anonymity with which y'all have veiled the entire affair," Abby heard her say to Boogher. "I have often said there seems something right indelicate about brandishing one's name around publicly. There is, it is true, Miss Ellen's example; still, Richmonders do tend to callousness. You and Abby went about this very properly, Boogher. Your dear father would turn many times in his grave, I am sure, were the name of Daniel to be bandied about on the covers of novels."

"But Miss Grace!" cried Amelie. "Aren't they even going to put Abby's name on the book *now?*"

"Certainly not," Mrs. Starkey declared. "Now, Amelie,

you will kindly hush. We will say no more about it. Remember what I said!"

Time passed. The light failed, and the violet shadows of evening began to lie long across the vivid grass. A whippoorwill called from the marshy ravine that separated the places on Armistead Street from those on Buford Row. Abby, from her seat in the corner of the grape arbor, surveyed the party rattling on, its members talking with one another as excitedly as if they had not met for months and did not expect to meet again. They looked and sounded curiously far away, as though she were seeing them through that end of a telescope which renders the object tiny. She was conscious of a faint ringing in her ears. The breeze which had sprung up felt cool and grateful on her aching head.

Someone, not she, had gone into the house and fetched the whisky bottles; Mattie had come staggering out with a tray of glasses. "Let me fix you a tetch," people said. Peter and Lady Barbara Parkinson walked in, late as usual. Fred Whiting arrived, out of breath; something, he said, had turned up at the courthouse to detain him. He, and all of them, seemed as unreal as figures perceived through the mists of fever. Abby stared down into the dusk-filled hollows of the ravine; it looked no realer there.

"How love-ly to see you!" Lady Barbara's shrill voice cut into Abby's solitude like a knife. "I did *so* hope I would find you here! How too marvelous about your book."

Abby felt as though Lady Barbara were carrying water to her dying thirst. She had always assumed, especially since that day at Azalea when Stanley transmitted the message about not breaking things, that Lady Barbara disliked her. Now she smiled gratefully, glad to have been wrong.

"Pe-tah and I are mad to get you to dine, ectually," Lady Barbara continued. *"Would* Tuesday week do? Or *do* you need to look at your book? I could ring you up."

"No, I'm sure we're free," Abby said to this appreciative person.

"I'm *so* glad!" Lady Barbara spoke in a high but curiously flat voice, as though she were not attending to what she said. "I have some chaps coming over from Middleburg just then, they'll be fascinated meeting you. Ectually," she added, her voice dwindling away.

"We'll look forward to it so much," Abby said shyly.

"As will we. Black tie." Lady Barbara broke into one of her long, inexplicable whinnies.

"Abby!" Mrs. Starkey called from the tea table, which by now had become a bar. "There isn't one particle of ice in this ice bucket, child, not one particle."

"Excuse me," Abby said to Lady Barbara, rising. "I have to help with the drinks."

"Do you re-ally?" asked Lady Barbara. Her eyes, large, blue and cold, were already off in the distance, fixed on a knot of men.

The party was drawing to its close. It was almost dark in the garden, now, and people could not find their glasses if they once set them down. They sipped out of anything they could lay a hand on. There seemed no use in trying to get anybody to go indoors; Mrs. Starkey had tried, and Abby had tried, but nobody would budge. With mob fixity they wished, as a group, to remain where they were.

Cigarette lighters twinkled for an instant and clicked out. The whippoorwill called and called, unattended, but unconsciously registering upon the guests so that they said, into the twilight, "What a lovely evening . . ." The breeze continued to trickle, coolness itself, through the darkened garden, touching the backs of people's necks; then someone began to sing alone, softly: 'Bye . . . bye . . . blackbird . . .' He was joined by two, and by four, and by six others. It would soon be felt, collectively, to be time to go.

"Abby, honey." Boogher put his hand on Abby's elbow. "Let's go on home."

"All right," she said. They moved in the darkness toward the place Mrs. Starkey was likely to be. Boogher's fingers closed about Abby's upper arm.

"Good night . . . Good night . . ." The tune the singers sang had changed, now. In the warm summer evening the strong, round male voices sang, in close harmony, ". . . Like I know Susie! Oh! Oh! Oh, what a girl!" As the Daniels walked across the lawn toward the gate, Boogher sang softly with them.

". . . There's none so classy, As that fair lassy . . ." It seemed a tune of long ago and far away, recalling faces and scenes now gone forever. The Daniels passed through the gate and out into the street-lighted sidewalk as into the real present.

"Well!" Boogher exclaimed, as they walked in step together down Armistead Street. "That wasn't so bad, was it?"

Abby started up out of her haze. "What do you mean?" she said.

"What do you think I mean?" he replied. "I mean nobody was put out with you. Or with me. Everybody seems to have accepted this thing."

She did not speak.

"We may count ourselves lucky," he added.

Abby cleared her throat.

"Lady Barbara asked us for dinner," she said. "A week from Tuesday."

"Oh? Good; good. Wonderful food at Azalea."

Abby was silent.

"Mighty kind of Lady Barbara," Boogher said.

They turned into the entrance of the Robert E. Lee Apartments, and in silence climbed the stairs. On the lighted landing old General Larrimore was out fussing with the half-dead cactus again, picking at its leaves. He held a small glass pitcher in one hand.

"Good evening, General," Abby said as she came up on a level with him.

The General ignored her. "Daniel!" he exclaimed, frowning at Boogher. "What's the matter with this thing? Can you tell me that?"

"I'm afraid I can't, sir," Boogher said.

"I've given it water. Don't know if it was wise. Thing makes me nervous, dying out here. It's criminal. House full of people ought to be taking care of it."

"I'll consult the Encyclopedia," Abby offered, "and see what it has to say about cacti."

She might as well not have spoken; the ancient, eagle eye of the General did not stir from the face of the other male. "Daniel," he said, "what would you say to my calling a florist about this plant? Would that be wise? Hm?"

"I don't see how it could do any harm, sir."

"Mmmm. Don't like it. Don't like it at all," the General muttered. As the Daniels began to mount the second flight of stairs he was still picking at the dry, spiny leaves.

Boogher unlocked the apartment door and let Abby pass through ahead of him. She switched on the light and stood

136

still in the sitting room, shaking. "Good old Southern courtesy," she remarked.

Boogher turned from taking the key out of the latch. "What did you say?" he asked.

"I said, 'Good old Southern courtesy,'" she repeated.

Boogher flushed. "What are you *talking* about?" he demanded.

"General Larrimore," she replied, passing into the kitchen beyond.

7

Abby bounced slightly in the front seat of the Chevrolet as they drove along the cedar-lined road, out into the county, one early evening ten days later. "I just love wearing evening clothes and going to dinner parties!" she exclaimed. "I wish we did it all the time!"

Boogher, in a black dinner jacket, lifted his chin out of his collar and gave Abby's knee three rapid pats. "The country could do with some rain," he observed, eying the acres they drove past with an authoritative eye. "Those thunderstorms just ran right off the top."

Abby subsided into her own thoughts. It was just possible — it was an idea not to be wholly discarded — that the dinner of Lady Barbara's to which they were bound was being given in honor of her. She didn't like to put the idea into words, for fear of sounding ridiculous; or, still more likely, self-centered.

Lady Barbara had certainly said, "These chaps will be fascinated to meet you." That did of course show that the chaps had been invited before Abby had; but on the other hand they were to be at Azalea as house guests. A dinner party might still be planned around her — as local celebrity, as author of *The Rose That Died*. There must be *somebody* in the whole of Starkeyville and William and Mary County who had such a conception of her. Lady Barbara, as a woman of the world, as a great novel reader, might just be that one.

It did not seem to have dawned on anyone else, in the time since the pictures of Starkeyville had appeared in *Life*, that the news about Abby made her any different, to be treated in any different kind of way, from before. Abby found it extremely depressing. The chances were, she felt, that the general indifference to the great news implied something intrinsically the matter with herself. Miss Ellen had been allowed to be a celebrity, Mr. Cabell had insisted upon being a celebrity, but there appeared to be something about Abigail Woodbury Daniel which rendered her a creature not to be considered when the palms were being handed out. At the various luncheons and teas and the supper at the Nashes' that Abby had been to since the pictures appeared, the atmosphere had been indistinguishable from always: relaxed, familiar, joking. At the Nashes' party everybody got pie-eyed after dinner and played the accustomed neighborly poker, with many an affectionately hurled epithet.

Perhaps tonight would be different.

The car turned into the driveway to Azalea, and continued through the tunnel of tree-box bushes that led to the forecourt of the old house. The sun had dropped behind the Blue Ridge, and birds called sleepily from the tops of the big sycamores and oaks bordering the lawn as they got out of the car. A late, ruddy glow hung over the grass, lit up the façade of the house, and dappled the tree trunks.

Stanley came to the screen door at their ring. "Ha yew, Mr. Boogher? Ha yew, Miz Daniel?" he said. "They's out on the ter'ce, doin' they drinkin'."

Abby dropped the triangular shawl she had worn as a wrap into Stanley's outstretched hands and looked anxiously at herself in the large, gilt-framed mirror hanging near the door. She was wearing her one summer evening dress, a blue chiffon. Her dark hair appeared neat, drawn back under its tortoise-shell bandeau. Her face was small, white, triangular, and clean. She looked, she thought, no worse than when she left home.

She walked with Boogher the length of the hall to the other end, where voices could be heard from the terrace beyond. Boogher opened the screen door and they stepped out onto flagged paving. Ten or twelve people in white dinner jackets and sheer, printed cotton evening frocks were sitting about on white iron and red canvas chairs, holding drinks and talking very loud. On a glass-topped, white iron table stood a vast array of bottles and glasses.

When Lady Barbara spied the newcomers she did not stand up but merely screamed. "Divine!" she continued, shrilly, after the scream had died away. "You *must* help yourselves to drink! I *won't* introduce you, *do* you mind, except to say to the rest that this fabulous creature in the *pale* blue dress is Abigail Woodbury Daniel, actually. It *is* so extraordinary she should be living here in our midst and so utterly dear and approachable. I mean to say I was absolutely *bouleversé* when I heard it was she who — Damn you, darling, don't spill your drink on me, *do* you

140

mind?" she cried, turning to the heavy-lidded young man to whom she had previously been talking. "One doesn't like to spoil your fun, but ectually!"

It was all like a play, Abby decided. She took the drink Boogher handed her and stood nervously sipping it, and wondering if Lady Barbara's introduction of her had not gone to an opposite extreme — been too laudatory and scared everyone off. Abby need not have worried. An enormous red-cheeked man came lumbering toward her, beaming.

"I read your book," he said.

After a moment it dawned on Abby that this was tribute. She smiled back. The huge man was joined by a slimmer, shorter man of fifty-odd who looked shrewdly at Abby and said, "I suppose you have the matter of investment covered? You must be absolutely raking it in."

"Well, I —" she began. The man lifted his gray eyebrows humorously at her and interrupted.

"I know what you're going to say! You successful damsels and your do-do-deo-do! Well, I don't blame you for throwing it around, while the stuff is warm off the presses, so to speak. Ha! Pun! I mean to say, it's the book that's warm off the presses, is it not? — In any case, when the excitement subsides you might bear Prentice, Lawson in mind. I'd be glad to arrange a balanced little portfolio for you — I'm Reginald Prentice. Oh, I know what you're going to say, that this is no time for the transaction of business, and you're quite right. Let joy be unconfined or something. May I pep your drink up?"

"I've got quite a lot left," Abby said. She smiled into his friendly face. "Who are all these other people?"

Prentice moved over so as to stand elbow to elbow with

her and the huge man lumbered away. "There's a whole pack here from Middleburg," Prentice said in confidential tones. "The girl in the orange thing is Baby Kilpatrick. Paid the highest price given for a horse this year, at Saratoga this week. The Middleburgers all huddle together so, Lady Bubs says nobody else can understand a word they're saying. Mayo Herps, Gene Balsam, the Cassidy sisters, Norah and Biddy . . . Their brother's the steeplechase jock. The tall man on the end is Royal Drane, the polo player. All the women go for him."

"Oh, yes?" Abby said. "Who was the great big man?"

"Oh, that's Pete Bird, one of those horse-factotum fellers. Breeds 'em, deals in 'em, boards 'em, does anything you might want done with 'em. *Poor* as Job's turkey, naturally. You a great horsewoman?"

"No," she replied, as she had so many, many times before.

"I'm not such great shakes of a horseman myself," he said, smiling. "I just get down from Washington for a couple of days to hounds a week, winters. I first met Lady Bubs out with the William and Mary. What a girl! You know her well?"

"I'm afraid only slightly."

"Of course if you don't hunt . . . Lady Bubs has horse blood; we often tease her about it. Of course you've noticed the resemblance? What a girl!" he exclaimed again, shaking his head. "Stops at nothing. Pops over five-foot post-and-rails as if they weren't there. A real goer. What *do* you do?"

"Well . . ." Faced with the question, Abby for the first time heard herself say, "I'm a writer."

"I know, and a very good and successful one, too. I

meant more in the line of . . . That is to say, what do you . . . How *do* you fill your leisure hours?"

While she was debating how to reply, Abby saw the young woman in the orange cotton, backless evening dress approaching.

"I adore your book," Baby Kilpatrick said, coming to a loose-limbed, graceful halt.

"Thank you," Abby said.

"I don't see how you do it," Miss Kilpatrick continued. "I mean how *do* you? Do you sort of get an idea?"

"Yes," Abby replied happily. "You get a sort of general idea, first. In *The Rose That Died* I was thinking about how a society, like a flower, can turn inwards and cling to its center, as if for safety. Only it isn't safety, and the flower just dies, because by then it is too late for normal blooming."

Miss Kilpatrick said, "Oh." After a moment she added, "But how do you put the people in?"

"I make them up," Abby said.

"How do you mean?" Miss Kilpatrick said. "I'm dying to know who Eugenia is. Is she some girl down here in William and Mary, or did you put her in from somewhere else?"

"I made Eugenia up," Abby said.

Baby Kilpatrick smiled helplessly.

"No, but I mean who were you writing about when you made her up?" she said.

Abby could only smile helplessly back at the face confronting her. The girl was tall and hard as a boy. Her legs were muscular, her cheeks lean, her throat cordy. On this bony frame an expensive and seductive evening dress hung, as from a hanger; loops of pearls, pearl earrings, rows of gold bracelets, scarlet lipstick, and green eye shadow had been added. Her face expressed nothing but good nature, anxiety to please. She sucked at the long gin drink which she carried and looked over its rim at Abby with small, clear, puzzled green eyes.

"Anyway, I think you're marvelous," she said. "I mean I don't see how you do it."

The young man with heavy lids, Mayo Herps, came lounging across the terrace. He looked down out of those sinister-looking eyes at Baby and Abby and said, "Hi. You two having a literary discussion? If so, include me out. I'll just listen."

Once more, Abby and Baby smiled at each other across that barrier, like a post-and-rail fence, separating them.

"When will you be giving us another of your spicy novels?" Herps said to Abby.

Abby tried to see the eyes concealed under those veiling lids. They appeared blue and candid. It struck her that all his menace might perhaps lie in his bone structure.

Lady Barbara uttered another piercing scream. "Dinner, ducks," she lamented when the echo had died away. "*Do* you mind? Bring your wretched drinks with you." She led the way into the house and down the now-lighted hall to that dining room where Abby had once stood with Tommy, waving a white sheet.

People took their time about following. Guests stopped dead in the hall for an argument about the treatment of fistulas; they gesticulated with their drinks, and set them down, empty, on polished side tables as they passed. In the dining room, down the long table were ranged small, gilt-bordered place cards. Abby was on Peter Parkinson's right. So the dinner *had* been given for her, she reflected, slipping into her seat. She gazed up the length of the white cloth, surrendering herself to the delights of the silver, the two flower-laden epergnes, the rows of sparkling wine-glasses.

Mr. Prentice was on her other side. She looked for Boogher, and spied him down at the other end — not on Lady Barbara's right, but on her left. The place of honor by her was occupied by the polo player, Royal Drane. Abby had a moment of anxiety about how Boogher would take such a slight.

"Listen to this one," Prentice exclaimed, turning to Abby from his other dinner partner, one of the Cassidys. "Biddy and I have been having a marvelous conversation about the Civil War, isn't that appropriate of us? Although we're just a couple of rank amateurs at it, actually. Biddy's got the most marvelous story, haven't you, Biddy darling? Go ahead, tell it again. Mrs. Daniel will probably want to put it in her next book."

"But I got it *out* of a book," Miss Cassidy said, looking worried. "And it's not so terribly funny."

By now, mysteriously drawn, everyone at that end of the table was listening.

"Go on, Biddy," Herps, beyond Biddy, insisted. "I can't wait."

"I feel like an absolute, uh, ass," Biddy said. Her pretty blond face flushed. "It's just that in this, uh, book, it said some Northerner was talking to some Negro and he asked him why there hadn't been more Negro, uh, troops, used in the Civil War, and the Negro said, 'When there's a dog fight, the bone doesn't get up and join in.' But I don't know if that's funny," she said worriedly.

"*Prenez-garde, les domestiques,*" said her sister Nora, a few places away.

"I *know*, that's what I *said*, but you all *made* me . . ." Biddy protested.

"Isn't that frightfully amusing?" Prentice asked the table at large.

Stanley, with a second colored man in a white coat, went on setting the flat broad soup plates before the guests, impervious. Abby thought of Relia Fenn's luncheon and the conversation about race carried on before the maids without even the embarrassment that Biddy Cassidy had just displayed. She took a spoonful of the cold soup before her, and found it full of chopped vegetables and herbs; delicious.

"How's the world been treating you?" her host inquired. "A penny for your thoughts."

"I was just thinking about hypocrisy," Abby said. "How hypocritical people can be, even at the moment when they're saying they hate hypocrisy."

Peter Parkinson stared. "Well, now," he remarked judicially; he bent his head forward and pulled in his chin so that it rested in folds on his soft pleated white shirt front.

"There's so much talk in the South about hospitality," Abby amplified. "How the South is so hospitable. Yet the South hasn't been hospitable to the Negro, has it? You might say it hasn't been hospitable to him at all. Or even polite," she added, warming to what seemed like a fruitful subject for a dinner conversation.

"But my dear young lady, the South never set out to be!" Peter said, tasting the fish that had just been set before him.

"Yes, it does, too," Abby said. "Excuse me, but I mean it sets up as a model of hospitality. If you set up to be more hospitable than anybody else in the world, then you have to *be* more hospitable than anybody in the world."

"But Mrs. Daniel! Be reasonable! Nobody is perfect! I mean to say, it's absurd to say anyone in the world can be more hospitable than everybody else!"

"Of course they can't! That's what I say! Of course everybody's about the same. I'm only saying that people shouldn't lay claim to the impossible, since they won't be able to achieve it. That's where the hypocrisy lies. Can't you see?"

"Well, no, I must confess I can't," he said stiffly.

"Mr. Prentice!" she said urgently, touching the sleeve of her other dinner partner. "Don't *you* see what I mean, when I say the South is hypocritical when it boasts of being more hospitable than any other part of the world, and yet isn't a bit hospitable to the Negro?"

"Aren't you being rather starry-eyed?" Reginald Prentice replied. "I see what you mean, of course, but you do have to allow people their little prejudices; their little failings. Don't be too severe."

"I'm not severe," Abby protested. "Just the opposite! Naturally people have their little failings. I'm talking about people claiming not to *have* any failings! Claiming to be more hospitable, for instance, than anybody else."

"Too abstract for me," Peter declared, turning thankfully away to the company of a beautiful girl whose blond hair hung about her shoulders.

"Come now, Mrs. Daniel!" Prentice said. "I'll bet you're a good hostess, but I'll bet you're not the perfect hostess. Who is? *My beef's unseasoned*," he whispered conspiratorially.

"Of course I'm not the perfect hostess!" Abby cried. "Far

from it! I never claimed to be! What I'm objecting to is people's laying claim on supremacy at something when they can't live up to their claims."

By the time dessert was passed, Abby found herself deserted by both dinner partners. A great flat dish of *crème brûlée* was immediately followed by a bowl of raspberries to put on it. Abby continued eating in solitude, her eyes wandering over the decorative and animated company. She looked at the white mantelpiece on the long side of the dining room, with its blue Wedgwood medallions, and thought of Tommy. He had always understood what she was talking about.

She imagined, when he was in Starkeyville, that Tommy with his instant sympathy was unique. But perhaps in New York, she thought, there were other people like him. Perhaps people there would understand what she meant when she said what came into her head; the way Tommy had. It had seemed to be no effort for Tommy. He had simply thought that what she said made sense. If it were not for remembering him, she thought, she would be even more depressed than she was at this dinner given in her honor, after the blankness in Peter Parkinson's eyes, the bored look in Prentice's. Tommy wouldn't have cared whether her notion were right, or true, she thought; but instead of laboring over it, snarling at it and rending it, he would have been able to look at it, give it a toss in the air, catch it again . . . The fact Tommy even existed seemed to Abby to prove that it was possible to play with an idea.

Reginald Prentice turned to her again as the plates were changed and fruit was passed. "You haven't yet revealed what you plan to do with your shekels," he said pleasantly.

"Build a house? Go round the world? I'll bet one thing," he said. "If you don't own a whole batch of mink you soon will. Just as soon as this heat lets up and mink is thinkable about."

Abby stared at him, and then laughed. She scraped a last bit of custard up off her Crown Derby plate.

"My husband runs the bookshop in Starkeyville," she told him. "We're going to add another room off the back of it to make additional storage space. It's badly needed."

"Very praiseworthy," Prentice said. "Very *comme il faut*. Now tell me what you're going to get for yourself."

Abby looked reflectively back at the kind, uncomprehending eyes wreathed in tanned wrinkles. "I think I'll buy a dress from Hattie Carnegie," she said, to her own astonishment. "I've always wanted one."

"Well, I should rather think so," Prentice said. "One at least."

"It hadn't occurred to me before, that now I can," she said.

Prentice looked puzzled. "Don't spend *all* your money," he said. "Bear in mind the rainy day. Bear in mind Prentice, Lawson."

"I used to walk past Hattie Carnegie's every day on my way to work," Abby said dreamily. "When I lived in New York . . . In those wonderful chilly sunny mornings when the whole city seems to sort of *echo*. I'd forgotten. I used to look into the windows, every morning, and decide which things I wanted and which I didn't. And which things I would get to go with which other things. I don't know if you ever noticed the shop; it's got wrought-iron plate-glass doors. Some great big long car would slide up to the curb as I stood there, and some wonderful-looking woman would get out of the door the chauffeur held open, and walk in through those glass doors, into where it was all warm and luxurious, with a thick carpet . . ."

"You ladies are all the same," Prentice remarked. "Clothes stimulate you as nothing else can. Clothes and your looks."

"Not me," Abby said. "I never cared about clothes. And my looks aren't much."

"But you just this minute said . . ."

"I *do* want a dress from Carnegie's," she said. "But that's different. I don't exactly want it to wear."

Prentice, looking bewildered, opened his mouth to reply; but just then Lady Barbara rose to leave the table and the other women followed suit.

During the evening everyone drank bourbon or Scotch and soda, whether playing bridge or Scrabble, or merely sitting on a sofa in the drawing-room. By eleven o'clock Abby was talking to Mayo Herps, who replied to her sallies in stiff, carefully measured phrases, looking back at her with eyes that were now not only hooded, but glazed. Abby left him and went to stand behind Boogher's chair in the library, where he sat telling Baby Kilpatrick the history of William and Mary County.

"I think it's time we went home, darling," she said.

Boogher looked up. With one hand he smoothed his red hair. "Very well," he said. "If we must always be the first to go."

"The others are staying here in the house," she said nervously.

"Oh?" Boogher said, and rose.

Abby went up the broad staircase. As she turned into Lady Barbara's room an extraordinary sight met her eyes.

Biddy and Norah Cassidy were lying wrestling on the nearer of the twin beds. Nora had both hands in Biddy's hair, pulling.

"Pig! Pig!" she was shouting. "Leave Roy alone or I'll kill you!"

"I won't leave him alone! I've *got* him," Biddy chattered. She got her head away from her sister's hands for a moment and struggled to sit up. "Bubs said to me only tonight, 'Biddy, I can see you've got Royal, haven't you?'"

"She did *not!*" Nora said. She slapped Biddy's mouth.

"Oh!" cried Biddy in pain. She began trying to bite Nora's hand. Then she saw Abby, standing aghast in the doorway.

"Excuse me," Abby said inadequately.

"Oh, come in," Nora said, ungraciously. She got up off the bed to her feet, switching her skirts into order around her pretty legs. "We were having a family row. You keep out of my affairs from now on, do you hear?" she said to the girl still lying on the bed, and walked out of the room.

Biddy sprawled, lovely, disheveled, and obviously drunk, on the bed. "Oh," she moaned, eyes shut. "You utter bitch . . ." She turned over on her face and appeared to go to sleep. Abby walked across the room and into the bathroom.

Standing in front of the marble basin with her hands in the clear bluish water, she felt overwhelmingly shaken by the scene of violence she had just witnessed. She stared at the shape of her hands in the wavering water and wished she could go straight home to bed; go right to sleep; die. Everything else before her seemed too much to face — the drive home with Boogher in his present bad temper, her inevitable efforts to placate him, the nature of the efforts, the fatigue in the morning; the morning itself. Tomorrow stood waiting before her, filled with unrewarding encounters, with fruitless speculation as to why Starkeyville ignored her achievement.

She lifted her hands from the water and dried them on a huck towel that had a padded black monogram. Starkeyville had not even paid her the compliment of ostracizing her, she reflected bitterly. Nobody was mad at her, nobody had cut her. Nobody cared at all. She seemed to be unable to move them whether for happiness or hurt; they were simply indifferent to her. Suddenly, in this glacial white bathroom where Tommy had once kissed her, she wanted to burst into tears because it occurred to her suddenly that all she wanted was to be loved.

At such a childish, self-pitying thought she pulled herself together, let the water go gurgling out of the marble basin, and walked briskly back into the bedroom. Biddy still lay sleeping on the bed. Her shoulders had come out of the straps of her evening dress, her skirt was above her knees; she looked the picture of abandon. Staring at her, Abby arranged the triangular shawl, which Stanley had taken upstairs, around her meager shoulders. She felt both fascinated and repelled. She turned and went downstairs to join Boogher.

They drove along the lonely, midnight country roads in silence. As they approached the hill of Starkeyville where a few late lights still burned, and paused at the red Stop sign at the cut-off of Route 43 before crossing to Armistead Street, Boogher said, "I certainly hope you enjoyed yourself."

"Didn't you?" she asked, nervously.

"What was there for me to enjoy?" he said.

"Apparently Lady Barbara is crazy about that Drane man," she said, plunging into what seemed to her the cause of Boogher's anger. "Royal Drane. The polo player. That's why she had him on her right at dinner. All the women seemed to be —"

"It is no concern of mine whom Lady Barbara places beside her," Boogher interrupted. "That is more the kind of consideration which preys upon *your* mind, it would appear. Honors. Distinctions. Adulation . . ."

"Oh, Boogher!"

It was all beginning again.

"Can you deny that you are entirely taken up with your own personal fame, with the attention you do or don't receive? With your own personal celebrity?"

Abby thought longingly of that happy night when Boogher had forgiven her for releasing the news of her authorship of *Rose*. It had seemed, at the time, to have resolved everything.

"I'm really not," she replied apprehensively.

"It revolts me," he continued. "I, myself, was raised with a sense of honor; decency; pride. Not to go around licking boots to get a pat on the head."

"Oh, Boogher!" she cried. "I don't lick boots! How can you say so? Boogher," she continued as he turned into Starkey Street, "wouldn't you like me to go to New York for a while? Now? If you really think I seem publicity-mad, maybe I could get it out of my system by going to New York," she explained.

He did not reply.

"Wouldn't you?" she repeated, as he turned the Chevrolet off the street and ran it into Miss Clara's one-time stable. Harness could be glimpsed still hanging from cobwebby crossbeams, before Boogher switched off the head-lights.

"Wouldn't I what?" he asked. He switched off the ignition. "Wouldn't I like you to go to New York and parade your celebrity up and down the streets as if you were a side-show freak?" He reached for the door handle. "Is that what you're asking me? No, since you ask me, I wouldn't like it."

They walked into the old house, where a central light burned, illuminating the stairwell from bottom to top. In silence they climbed the two flights of stairs. Boogher unlocked the apartment door and walked in ahead of Abby.

A totally unrelated voice inside Abby remarked, "Southern chivalry." She listened to it with astonishment, and then returned to her anxiety over Boogher's anger.

He walked straight over to the door to the bedroom and said, "Good night."

"Boogher! Aren't you going to talk this over?" She knew that she was in the right; she knew that she was being reasonable in this matter that they were once more tearing apart between them. But not to have a chance to state her position once more gave her the feeling of being thrown off balance, put in the wrong. "Please let me explain how I feel," she heard herself plead.

Boogher stood in the bedroom door looking at her with a tortured expression.

"I love you," Abby added.

Boogher gave a short, offended laugh.

"I do, darling," she insisted, coming over to him. "You upset me so . . . I won't go to New York."

Boogher put one hand on her arm with its little finger held stiffly out as if he held a cup of tea.

"I don't even want to go to New York, since you feel that way about it," she added.

"The way *you* feel about it makes me ill," he remarked.

She buried her face in the sleeve of his dinner coat, and had the flash of insight that it had been the only black one at the dinner party which now seemed so long ago. "I do love you," she said into the cloth.

Boogher took his other hand off the knob of the door and turned directly to Abby. Lifting her face from his sleeve, he held his hand under her chin, looking at her as intently as if he were searching for something. "Why are you so damned calm about it, then?" he said.

"Calm?" She laughed, shakily. "I'm not calm."

"It seems to me you get excited about everything in the world except me," he said in a low, troubled voice. "Why does it take so much to penetrate your damned calm?"

"Kiss me," she said, realizing that the log jam of his rage was broken.

But as he pressed his mouth to hers she could only think how tired she was.

8

At the breakfast table next morning Boogher's face was shining. "Roll the rolls down here and quit muffin around," he chuckled.

Abby passed him the biscuits that she had made from a ready-mix. It had no doubt been silly to get up earlier than necessary when she had gone to bed so late, but she had felt she wanted to leave no stone unturned in her efforts to be a good wife.

"Well, I must be gone. *Scram,* in the popular vernacular," Boogher declared, getting up and wiping his mouth. He cast the napkin into his soiled plate. Then he walked around the table and kissed Abby tenderly. "Dear wife," he said. "Dear, sweet little wife. You look tired."

"I am, rather," she said.

"Go back to bed, why don't you? Catch a little snooze! Be a lady of leisure! After all, we kept late hours last night," he said.

"I may do that," she agreed.

"Well . . . good-by . . ." he said again, the mysterious dissatisfaction starting up again in him. Snatching his cord jacket from the chair back where he always hung it as if on a rack, he hurried out.

Abby heard his footsteps go thumping down the stairs. She thought of Tommy Hume's way of half falling down a flight of steps, heels clattering. Then she drew a long breath and got up to clear away breakfast.

The hot dishwater felt good to her tired hands. At the sink she stood facing a window; the August day outside looked cooler than July had, and a small breeze drifted in through the window across her face, refreshing her. When she had finished the glass, the silver, and the china, she decided the tea towels she had dried them with looked gray. She put water on to boil in a big pan and stood facing the stove waiting for it to boil, with a curious sense of tension. At the moment when the water burst into curling, bubbling motion, she felt relieved. She put the tea towels into an enamel basin, poured boiling water over them, and added some Clorox from the half-gallon brown glass jug.

The jug was nearly empty. Abby looked around for something more convenient in which to put the little bit remaining. There was a discarded Listerine bottle in the trash can by the sink, and she fished it out and poured the Clorox in. Then she threw away the jug and looked about for a pencil to write "Clorox" on the white edging to the Listerine label. She found one, and interrupting herself wrote "Clorox" on the marketing list that she had already taken down from the peg on the wall where a pad of paper always hung. She set the basin of towels at the far end of the working surface, and began to put the silver away, when the front-door buzzer sounded.

She opened the door, to be confronted by Clifford. "I come back to do them winders you said," he explained, beaming.

"Oh, Clifford! If you could ever give me some idea of when you are coming! I was just going marketing."

"Mus' I go way?" he asked.

"No . . . no . . ." she said. "Now you're here, you'd better stay. I'll attend to something else, while you work. You'd better start right in where you left off, on the windows in the living room. I'll help you fix your bucket."

Once she had Clifford started on the job she retired to the bedroom and, sitting down on the edge of the bed, took out her diary from the bedside stand. But, pencil in hand, she found it impossible to think of last night's party in any terms she could express. The whole of it seemed too violent, too disorganized; inchoate; a medley of loud voices, bright-colored dresses, food, money, passion, anger. She wrote in an unnaturally small hand, "Dined at Lady B's. Fourteen at table." Then she stopped.

Her mind went groping back, step by step, through the scenes, last night, between herself and Boogher, to the scene just before that — the scene of the Cassidy sisters sprawling on the bed. She saw them, in her mind's eye, wrestling there, with their bared thighs: spread-eagled, grasping at each other's hair and flesh. Suddenly she jumped up and let her diary fall on the floor; she picked it up and stuffed it back into the drawer, which she closed. Clifford or no Clifford, she had to get outdoors at once and let the fresh air soothe her mind, so disordered with fatigue.

She entered the living room with her handbag hanging from her arm. "I have to go out now for a little while," she said, looking severely toward where Clifford's long form was balanced upon the kitchen step-ladder. "I want you to keep busy while I'm gone."

"Yes, *ma'am!* Mus' I wash the other winders too?"

"Of course," she said impatiently. "That's what you're here for. Do the bedroom windows next, and then the kitchen. I'll probably be back by then anyway. — I may be back much sooner than I expect," she added warningly.

As she went downstairs she wondered what disaster would befall the apartment while she was gone, under Clifford's kindly tutelage. A vase, a table? Something was bound to go. Clifford might try to read her diary while he was in the bedroom, she reflected. Then she brushed the thought aside. He would not be able to understand a word of it if he did. It was, she thought, all rather like going off and leaving a tiger cub to roam the premises. But she still felt she needed to get outdoors.

The brown paper bag of groceries which she presently purchased weighed so heavily on her arm that she stopped at Jewell's Drugstore on the way home, to seek rest and refreshment. Her head ached from the sun. Sinking into a wire-backed chair at one of the tables, she asked for a Coca-Cola.

As she was taking the first sip a man's voice said, "Mownin', Abby." Old Fred Whiting was standing over her. "Mind if I join you?" he continued. "I'm just catchin' a little break from the arduous labor which the practice of law imposes upon me."

Abby looked her limp acceptance, and he sat down.

"What you drinkin', child, a dope? Pshaw, I'm plumb sick of dopes. I think I'll have me an *ice* cream. Allie!" he called to the waitress in her dirty towel apron. *"Bring* me a strawberry *ice* cream? . . . And how is our lady authoress today?"

Abby smiled painfully. "I —" she began.

"I'm forgettin'," old Fred interrupted her. "I didn't intend to refer to it. Miss Grace Starkey would snatch me baldheaded did she know I brought the subject up. Let's us converse upon other topics. How's old Boogher?"

After what she had heard, Abby's very eyes felt hard, swollen, and as if they were forcing themselves from their sockets. "He's all right," she said numbly.

"Saw old Boogher, already this mownin'," Fred went on. "Drivin' up Armistead Street like he was his own grandfather, just as leisurely! I reckon he must have left poor old Ginnie Harmon to tend shop."

"I suppose so," Abby said through stiff lips.

"Poor old Ginnie! She's about ready to drop in harness one of these days. It's *real* charitable in Boogher, employin' her. Can't be of too much use or value to him, dodderin' round like Ginnie does . . ." Fred went chattering on.

"I'm sorry. I've got to go." Abby got to her feet and lifted the bag of groceries from the chair beside her.

Old Fred looked up, surprised but smiling. "Well, don't walk too fast," he said. "Wait till it gets to be September."

She stared back at him as he sat there, smiling, in his chair. "Courtesy!" she ejaculated. "Chivalry! It's all a lot of talk."

"What in the *world* you ravin' about, child?" old Fred began. But Abby had gone out of the door.

She stalked up Bolling Avenue with short, stabbing steps, her rage boiling higher and higher. Mrs. Starkey! For years, Abby thought, Mrs. Starkey had used her as a convenience — a sort of slave; and now she had arranged this conspiracy of silence to deprive Abby of the praise and honor that was her due. Fred Whiting! An old boor who didn't get up when a lady left a table. Miss Lilybud Carter! Obsessed with the importance of being a lady but was not enough of a lady to be even polite. How many times had she failed to return Abby's direct greeting?

"Mownin', Abby," said Rushton Barr, passing her on the corner of Armistead Street. His head, in its Panama hat, was bowed as he lighted a cigarette and he was peering at her as he spoke from under his hatbrim. Abby nodded brusquely, and walked on without speaking. Rushton, that flower of Southern aristocracy, had not moved a finger toward his hat. Everybody seemed to be rude at the same time, she thought, and then realized that it had all happened many times before.

She continued her furious march up Armistead Street, name by name and face by face disposing of her acquaintance. Fakes, she thought; claims to perfection was all they had to show.

She softened her step as she approached the top of the apartment stairs; it might be interesting to find what Clifford was up to . . . But when she had opened the door, gone in, and heard the stepladder creak, from the kitchen, as Clifford shifted his weight on it, and the sound of his voice singing, "*Over* in Jordan a milk-white horse . . ." she suddenly felt she could not cope with him now. She set the paper bag down on the side table by the front door. What she wanted, above all things, was to be alone and burst into tears.

The bedroom door was closed. She opened it, stepped over the threshold, and found Boogher sitting on the edge of the bed.

He glanced up, startled, from her diary, which lay open on his lap. "Clifford said you'd gone out," he said, shutting the notebook.

She stared at him. "So you read people's diaries," she said bitterly. "Good old honor! Good old holier than thou."

"I've been so unhappy and worried, Abby," Boogher began, shoving the diary back into the drawer of the bedside table. "I know it wasn't very . . . But if you knew the way I've been feeling — so cut off from you — you might understand how I could —"

"Oh, *I!*" she interrupted, her voice shaking with fury, "*I* might have done anything! But *I* never pretended to anything! *I* don't have to be honorable!"

Part Three

1

Tommy hume sat sidewise in the big chair under the great north window of the Humes' studio on East Fifty-Seventh Street. His legs hung over the arm of the chair. He held the telephone against his ear with one hunched-up shoulder, knocking the rims of his shoe soles together as he talked.

"No, but truly," he said to his friend Harriet Walters, literary critic of *Lady*, who had just returned from a vacation, "you'd be doing us the most enormous favor by giving a party for Abby. I can promise you that."

A muted gabble came from the other end of the instrument; Tommy listened to it and said, "Of *course* she'd love it. The thing you have to understand is, she's absolutely insatiable. Poor darling. Elsa and I are exhausted feeding her appetite for recognition and you've got to help. It's so understandable, of course. It's as if the poor child had never gotten anything to eat. If you tell her you loved her book, or you're so interested to meet her, she positively inhales it. You can see her pores take it up. Old

Jason takes her out to lunch about three times a week, at assorted expensive caravanserais with anybody he can dredge up at this time of year who ever wrote a word. And Elsa and I have been literally scraping the bottom of the barrel every afternoon for drinks here; anybody we can find with a name, or people with names passing through town on their way to somewhere else. How Abby does love a name! It's as if hearing a recognized name makes her realize all over again that she has one too. It's touching, like watching somebody asleep come awake; or a butterfly inching out of its dreary old chrysalis. Do they inch, Harriet? Or simply burst? — But the awful truth is —"

Metallic chatter at the other end of the wire took over, and Tommy listened for a few seconds, reflecting that he spent most of his life in talk.

"The awful truth is," he resumed, when Miss Walters stopped, "it's too late. One can't tell her that, naturally; but even with the *Life* piece to revive it the book is, actually, six months old. After all . . . Oh, people recognize her name, I know, and that's fine. But the thing is, by now there are so many newer names. It's only to Abby that *The Rose That Died* is a recent event. You know, darling, it's not true that in small towns the time passes slowly. It absolutely whizzes by. A whole summer will be gone in an instant, without one single thing happening. It's only here, or at least in big cities, that you get the value out of minutes and seconds. My God, it feels like years since I left *Life* . . . But poor Abby is absolutely glued to something that happened a half a year ago."

Miss Walters had something to say about that. Then Tommy went on.

"What Elsa and I have actually been doing, ever since

Abby got here three interminable weeks ago, is to try to fan into life something that in the ordinary way would be dead. We *are* so fond of her. We *do* think it's a shame the way she's been buried. But I promise you, we ache in every muscle. If she'd only come in the beginning, when she should have!"

"— No, her old horror of a husband wouldn't let her come," he replied in answer to a question from the other end. "And yes, she is finished with him; or so I hope and pray. At least, she shows no signs of going home. If she could just pull herself together, now, hole up somewhere, and write a book — a new book — we'd have something to put the flags out about. All that talent . . . Elsa and I keep suggesting it to her. Because she has this good running start with *Rose*, and Jason & Terhune are definitely behind her — they'd advance her anything she needed. Though, actually, she must have made quite a little from *Rose* . . . Everything is fine. All she needs is to the hell do something."

The other voice took over.

"She won't!" Tommy cried. "She won't do a thing! All she wants apparently is to hear her own name spoken, over and over and over! So anyway. Give her this party, won't you? I keep thinking, every time we get something like this organized, that this will be the clincher. Her ego will finally get its thirst quenched and move on to, for God's sake, getting some work done. Harriet, darling, you've got an ax to grind in getting good writers started, so you will, won't you? Friday? . . . Bless you . . . Whatever you like . . . Any time you like . . . But can you *get* anybody that soon? Oh . . . Oh . . . I see, just slide her in as guest of honor . . . Fine . . . Good . . . We'll have her there at six. For God's sake, darling, do invite any-body even resembling a celebrity from now till then, won't you? We will too. If we may. Listen, I hear somebody coming in. 'By."

But it was Elsa, after all; back from making studies of the animals in the Central Park Zoo for the bas-relief she was working on for the façade of the new South Africa Building, which needed zebra forms, giraffe shapes, to peer out of its jungle depths of frond and leaf.

"I left Abby looking at the elephants," she said, throw-ing her things on a chair. "I thought she might just pos-sibly be getting an idea. So I said 'See you later' and slipped away." Elsa sat down, on the sofa directly under the big window, and threw her strong white arms, in their short sleeves, out to either side of the sofa back. The milky, freckled skin of her neck, fronds of red hair springing from the nape, rose from a dark green-and-blue plaid dress. She had a wide square face, faintly freckled and flat-nosed, and the pale eyebrows of the redhead. "Whooo!" she said. "I'm bushed. Who's coming? Anybody?"

"James Coughlin? Eli? I don't know . . . *Somebody*'ll be along. Listen, Harriet was having some people to cock-tails Friday, and she's turning it into a party for Abby," Tommy said.

"Oh, good!"

Their eyes met. Elsa sighed.

"She's in a condition of stasis," she complained. "Alive, but barely; as if she were hibernating, sort of." She reached for the sketch pad that she had thrown on the chair with her purse and gloves. With a pencil she took from the mug of pencils, on the low table by her knee, she drew rapidly a furry little animal, an otter or muskrat, rolled up into a ball, head tucked nearly into its tail to make a complete circle. "See?" she said, handing it to Tommy.

"I don't agree," Tommy said. "I see her as a plant, more. One that's been on its last legs for want of rain, and, now that it's raining, can't do anything else but drink." On the same page with the picture of hibernation he sketched in a cactuslike growth, with great spiky leaves ending in points that stood apart from each other in pairs, like gaping mouths. Rain slashed across the page.

"That's ghastly," Elsa said when he handed it to her. "You don't really think of her that way, do you?"

"Let me see again." He took the sketch pad back. "I suppose it does look rather rapacious," he said. "That's because I don't know how to draw as well as you do. My nature isn't as sweet as yours, either, I don't seem to see dear furry little balls, I see monstrous cacti, it seems. Something the matter with my God-damned psyche."

Elsa glanced at him. "How *are* you, darling?" she asked.

"I'm all right." Tommy hurled his legs up and over the chair arm and lit a cigarette. "Don't you think it's late enough to start drinking?" he asked. He got up and walked across the studio to the little kitchen under the balcony. In a moment tinkling sounds, of a Martini being made, were to be heard.

Elsa leaned her head back and stretched out her round arms. She drew a long breath and her eyes sought a cloth-covered shape on a stand, which was the head, in clay, of an archbishop, that she was currently working on.

Abby was standing viewing a camel, who looked back at her down its Roman nose; tall, saturnine, rotating its jaw slowly. Patches of mangy fur hung in mats from its back, and it smelled. But its proud and independent air was impressive. To be a camel, Abby felt, was to be self-contained. But could a camel be said to have a self? If you did not know you were alive, had you a self? Perhaps camels *did* know they were alive. But, if on the other hand they did not know they were alive, could they then contain the selves which they did not know they possessed? How, otherwise, could one account for a camel's unmistakable air of being self-contained?

She passed on, to a pair of antelopes from Africa. Delicate, faintly spotted, with pointed horns, they seemed like figures in the prehistoric cave drawings — timeless, eternal; with their slender legs for running and the wild look in their eyes that disregarded the bars that confined them. Lay a field out in front, take away the bars, and they would be off like arrows from a dead stop. Their very bodies spoke of speed.

Abby came at length to the terrace at the end of the Zoo, where people, most of them Negro, sat about at tables in the September afternoon, sipping from straws. The tables were all taken. Abby bought herself a cup of coffee inside and carried it out to where a fat white woman sat alone reading a book. She said, "May I sit here?"

"Sure," the woman said, glancing up. She hitched her chair accommodatingly to one side and reached toward the chair which she had loaded with parcels, as if to move them.

"Don't bother," Abby said, slipping into still a third chair.

She noticed at once that the book the woman was reading, which wore a plastic lending library cover, was *The*

Rose That Died. Instantly — as ever — Abby seemed si multaneously to freeze and to burn.

The sunshine of the late New York day fell in watery yellow floods over the terrace. The woman beside her went on reading. She was somewhere in the middle of the book.

Abby's spoon made a clatter in the saucer and the woman, her attention distracted, glanced up. She looked at the coffee cup and then at Abby, and yawned.

"You read this story?" she inquired, holding the book so as to expose its title.

"Yes." Abby stirred the cream she had put in her coffee round and round.

"Say." The woman let the book flip open again, and rested it against the rim of the table. "It's the darnedest. There's this Southern belle, like, this Eugenia . . . You say you've read it?"

The temptation Abby felt was insuperable. "I wrote it," she said.

"Well, say." The fat woman shut the book and laid it down on the table. "Well, what do you know. Pleased to meet you. You see all kinds in this city, don't you?" She reached a large, blubbery hand across the table. Abby took it and shook it. "I saw Leo Durocher coming out of the City Center the other day."

Abby took a sip of coffee. It dawned upon her that now she never would know what the woman had been going to say about the novel.

The woman had placed both huge elbows on the table-top and was leaning forward on them, gazing greedily at Abby. "Say, it's something to tell my husband, all right," she said, shaking her head. "Right here in the Zoo, who do

I meet —" She glanced down at the book's cover. "What *is* the name?" she asked. "It don't say here." She picked up the novel and began flipping through its pages.

"I know," Abby said. "I wrote it anonymously."

"You wrote it which?" the woman murmured. She leafed through the front of the book. "You wrote it . . ." She set the book down again. "You say you wrote it . . . Oh. Anonymously."

"Yes." Abby had the familiar sense of speaking a truth that sounded like a lie.

"If I may ask," the woman said, "why did you want to write like a story anonymously? Hm?"

"My husband didn't want me to sign it," Abby explained.

"Is *that* right?" The woman paused to consider. "Why wouldn't he want you to sign it, though? Gee, I can see my husband. If I was to decide to write a book one of these fine days, he'd be all for my signing it all over the place."

"My husband didn't want me to get any attention," Abby said. She could feel the blood beginning to mount to her face. "He didn't want me to get any praise. He was sadistic. You know, he liked to hurt me."

The fat woman appeared to rear back for a moment and blink. Then she lowered her chin into her fists. "Yeah?" she prompted.

A sense of freedom, of knowing that she would never again see this woman, spurred Abby on. "He was trying to make a slave of me," she continued. "He never wanted me to have anything for myself. He always had to be the one to have everything."

"Beat you up much?" the woman suggested with interest.

"Oh, no, I mean mentally. Mental cruelty . . . He

was always running me down. I had to submit to him in everything. He couldn't stand to have me write a book and sign it, because he hadn't done it himself. He was a bully," Abby confided.

"Well. Gee. Why didn't you give him back as good as you got? I would of," the woman said.

Abby stared back at her. There they sat, two wildly mismated table companions, talking intimately of matters about which Abby had hitherto been able to speak to nobody. "I guess I didn't have the courage," she replied. "I don't know. I guess I was cowed. I never said anything back at him."

"You know what I think?" A shrewd expression came over the woman's fat features. "I figure deep down you love him. Some women just like getting beat up. You liked him doing you that way."

"I hate him!" Abby replied. As soon as she had said it, she knew it was true. "I hate everything about him! I never want to see him again."

"So you got a divorce, hm?"

"No." Abby's angry flood was checked. "No. I'm just not living with him right now, that's all."

"You better get rid of him, if you hate him that bad."

"I don't know . . ."

"Well . . ."

After a minute more of silence, the woman began to make tentative and ineffectual moves toward departure. She picked up some of the parcels from the chair and dropped them all upon the terrace paving again. She bent down and, panting, began to pick them up. Abby bent to help her.

As they straightened up in their chairs simultaneously,

their faces suddenly confronted each other, not six inches apart.

"No kidding. Did you write that book?" the woman asked.

"Honestly I did." Once more, the truth sounded like a lie.

The fat woman did not reply. Opening her elaborate, imitation tapestry handbag, she took out a compact and a lipstick, both encrusted with jewels, and began to do her face. As she applied a neat outline to her lips, mouthing awry, she looked over the top of the mirror at Abby. Her eyes were unimpressed, skeptical. Over the face of this woman, so lately Abby's closest confidante on earth, could be seen to descend a standard, suspicious face, one designed to fit stylish stout features. "Well," she said, rising. "It's been interesting to meet you, Miss . . . Mrs. . . ." She waited for Abby to supply the name.

Suddenly it seemed important that she not know. As long as the fat woman did not know who she had been talking to, she could not repeat any confidences. "Good-by," Abby said, smiling apologetically.

Standing, arms filled with parcels, the woman shook out her skirts by switching her mammoth hips. "Well!" she said. "You surely meet all types in this city." She moved off, a moment later throwing one backward glance, as if perhaps she were expecting Abby to come running after her with apologies or confessions. Lumbering, deliberate, she disappeared.

Abby finished her coffee and walked away toward the animal cages. She stopped once more before that self-contained creature, the camel, who gazed back at her with detachment and contempt. As she passed on, Abby reflected that it was curious what peace, what quiet, she felt in proximity to animals. They seemed to transfer to her a thought-free, trust-enclosed, voidlike state of consciousness. The animal side of one's nature, she had always been taught, was something violent, excited, passionate. Yet if she in any sense faithfully reflected the tempo of these creatures, to be an animal was to be calm and still. It was not with animals that the mind became flooded with struggling thoughts, conflicting feelings, she thought; it was with people.

She looked at her watch and saw it was time for the daily party at the Humes' studio to begin. Every afternoon people stopped in to drink with that warm and always-available couple. Painters and photographers, writers, musicians, publishers blossomed under the kind of interest and affection the Humes dispensed. Abby began to wander back along Fifty-seventh Street, looking up at where the sun from behind her striped the tops of the high buildings with golden streamers. People were hurrying home from their offices. The great shops between Fifth Avenue and Lexington were locking their bronze doors. Abby looked with appreciation toward the beautiful furs, pictures, hats, furniture, in the shop windows that she passed. She had a right, now, to go in and buy any of them.

2

As Abby let herself into the studio with her latchkey, the sound of voices came to her and Tommy called, "Abby? Come and see the Rassermans, they're dying to meet you. They've just left John Huston on location."

"As soon as I wash my face," Abby said. "I've been looking at camels."

There was a burst of laughter from the studio. Everything Abby said these days — the same sort of thing she had always said — made people laugh. What had never worked in Starkeyville worked in New York. Could it be, she wondered, rubbing pink soap between her palms, that New York was easier to please? It was all very mysterious.

When Abby walked into the studio, dark hair freshly brushed and a black velvet ribbon tied around it, she was at once drawn by affectionate hands, by eager and interested smiles, into the group of people sitting under the great window.

"How lovely to meet you," said a Mrs. Fellowes. She had a thin face, an arched nose, and intelligent eyes. "I feel as if I'd known you for a long time. I was an only child, so the only childhood I can ever share with anybody is in books. I have one friend, Herbert Maygold — perhaps you know him? — with whom I can walk around in *Swann's Way* for hours. It's like having a brother, only much nicer. No dichotomy whatever."

Abby, sitting beside her, smiled back and wriggled with pleasure. Everybody in New York said "dichotomy." She had looked it up in Tommy's Webster, and all it meant was "division into two parts" but why say "division" when you could say "dichotomy"? It seemed beyond words worldly.

"Now I have the joy of realizing," Mrs. Fellowes continued, "that I can share *The Rose That Died* with you, because after all you created it! Let's be in the field full of daisies where Eugenia lay on her back when she was ten and looked up at the sky. You know, I feel as if I'd *done* that, myself. Do we go back to the big house for lunch afterwards?"

"I think we would," Abby said, joining in the game. "We'd walk along the road through the woods — woods with vines hanging down from the trees — in all that heat. The vines are honeysuckle. Then we come out of the dim woods into the sunshine."

"The barnyard?"

"Yes. And go past whitewashed stables, and a great many rather tumble-down outhouses, also whitewashed, where tools and plows are kept. One of them is the springhouse and another the smokehouse. You climb a slope past the gardens over on your right, bordered beyond with cedar trees."

"Yes. You know I can see the bark, raveled and hanging off in shreds. How do I know that?"

Abby smiled directly back into the clear brown eyes, with their expression of enthusiasm. "Then you go into the house out of the heat — it's really hot, with bees humming everywhere, all over the gardens and in the crape myrtles, one on either side of the front steps. Four white stone steps, stained with red clay, with a big scraper for boots on one side. You go into the house where it's all cool and dim. The shutters have been closed since early morning."

"How nice!" Their eyes met again.

Tommy was having his third Martini. "Where is Huston *now?*" he asked Eph Rasserman, a heavy man who worked on story treatments for various of the studios. He looked like a stevedore except for small, restless eyes that flickered and lit up behind their black-rimmed glasses, or turned shrewd and concentrated. His wife, Marian, was a beautiful Jewess dressed in high fashion; her head was as neatly perfect as something carved of basalt. She was leaning forward intently and telling Elsa, and Andrew Fellowes, who was an Englishman, about her analysis. Over their heads the white fluorescent bar of light burned on the ceiling, mixing with light from the early evening that still came in through the vast window. "He's not still in Arizona?" Tommy persisted. "He hasn't fought with Harry?" The doorbell rang. Still looking back, not cutting the conversational cord with Rasserman, Tommy went to answer it. His attention never swerved till the moment Rasserman answered.

"No, he sails on Monday week from San Francisco," Rasserman said; and Tommy opened the door. Several people swarmed in — two painters, a composer, and a young woman who was a singer.

"Darling!" Tommy's voice could be heard from across the

room. The new guests began trickling across the room to meet Abby. "Our darling Abby Daniel, whom we love," Tommy said as he performed the introductions. "Godfrey . . . Liz . . . Howard Turner . . . of course you know Abby's beautiful book. I don't need to tell *you* . . . Our little friend," he recommenced, "whom we rescued from a chain gang . . ." People laughed. "No, but truly," Tommy said. "She's our debutante. We're giving her a coming-out party — several coming-out parties, aren't we, darling? James! James, come here. I want you to meet Abby Daniel, who wrote *The Rose That Died.*"

"Why, Abigail Woodbury Daniel!" cried Mr. James, one of the painters. "Not the Madame X of the literary world!" He sat down sidewise on the sofa on Abby's other side; knees tight together, he leaned confidingly toward her. "But all last spring we were but frantic to know who had written it. It couldn't have been more frustrating. Carson, I could have sworn. But no! Howie said to me — Howie Turner, you just met him, the tall, aggressive-looking one — he said, 'Carson would never in this world have written about those upper-class Southerners.' "

People began sorting themselves out. They groped for chairs with one hand while continuing to talk. They fell into separate, intimate conversations.

"Howie insisted it was Truman," Mr. James continued, clasping his hands together and inserting them between his clenched knees. "But I said to him, 'Howie, you're mad! This isn't in the least Truman's kind of thing.' As of course it wasn't. How too fascinating to meet you in the flesh, like meeting one of the world's great mysteries! My dear, you look like Charlotte Brontë, has anyone told you that?"

Abby smiled blissfully. Then a terrible thought struck her. Surely it was wrong to experience so much undiluted pleasure? To think only of one's own selfish happiness? Her mind rattled on in this vein, effortlessly.

Eph Rasserman, who had been dislocated by the general shift in seating, had strolled up. He looked severely over his black-rimmed glasses at little Mr. James. "The mystery was dispelled by *Life*, several weeks ago," he informed him. "Don't you read *Life*?"

Mr. James met Eph's gaze head on, lifting his chin rebelliously. "Of course I don't read *Life*," he retorted. "Who does?"

On the sofa by the fireplace Marian Rasserman and Liz Cooke, the singer, were having an argument.

"But I don't care if I do sweat in elevators," Liz was insisting. "It would be worse to be analyzed. I happen to know it takes away your creative power and when they get through you're nothing but one great mass of adjustments."

"Jung is different," Howard Turner interrupted, squeezing in between the two women on the sofa and licking his bright red lips. He was very swarthy.

"I've been in analysis for nine years," Marian Rasserman said, talking right across, over, and through Howard. "And I can feel myself slowly coming to life, like a statue that's being chiseled out of, I swear to you, granite. My analyst can see the real me in there and he just helps me, thing by thing, to cast off all the things that have . . . I mean, I'm a regular Galatea."

"But I don't want to be Galatea!" Liz wailed. "I want to be creative! I want —"

"Jung bases his approach on the creative aspect," Howard

180

began again, looking from one tense face into the other and moistening his lips with the tip of his tongue. "Jung says —"

"Take sex," Marian said, impervious. "I hate to tell you what sex used to mean to me. If I told you the symbols I had for Eph in my dreams, you'd die. I am only just now beginning to see that, in sex, fear is unnecessary."

"But the artist needs fear!" Liz cried. "You take away the artist's fear, and you take away the artist. He wouldn't *be* an artist if he was adjusted, for God's sake. Your old Freud. He views art as just another neurosis. I shudder when I think of all the artists that have been ruined — Take Moss Hart," she produced, triumphant.

"Jung says —" said Howard, urgently, patiently. No one paid the slightest attention to him. He looked as if he might be going to cry. Elsa passed the sofa carrying a drink, and Howard caught hold of her free hand. "Elsa!" he cried. "*Isn't* Jung better than Freud?"

Elsa leaned down to him, her serene, milk-white face showing concern at the appeal in Howard's voice. "Of course he is, darling," she comforted him. "Come and help me with the blotters. They've all run out."

Relief flooded Howard's face. He sprang to his feet.

"I saw everybody in London," Godfrey Home, the composer, was saying to Mrs. Fellowes. "Nobody stayed in New York this summer. Everybody was there. You should really have come. I saw Percher, even. Britten. And Lenny and Peter and Jeff."

"John Gage?" Mrs. Fellowes suggested, bending upon him her intelligent gaze.

"Yes. And Antheil. Did I say Britten?"

"Park?"

"Dear Edith!" Home looked at her with indignant reproof. "I don't count Park. He's a twelve-tone-scale man. And as if that weren't enough . . ."

Edith Fellowes smiled. It was impossible to be sure whether there was mockery in her smile; of acid there was none. She was married to a correspondent for a large English newspaper syndicate, and with him went everywhere in New York; always smiling, wise, inwardly reserved, outwardly responsive; up late every night. When at last the Felloweses returned home to their apartment in the East Sixties of an evening, Edith would go straight to her narrow, white bed, turn on the bedside light, and shut the door. She would read for hour after hour, until the window she had opened turned to a white square in the wall instead of a black square.

"My analyst says," Home observed after a moment, "that he thinks a twelve-tone-scale man must be in some way off center. It is out of the normal development of the culture of the West. We of the Christian-Judaic tradition must accept our destiny and not go horsing around with the twelve-tone scale. I put my trust in the great tradition of Western music."

"Personally, I can't even begin to understand your music, darling," Edith said.

Home looked offended. "You're teasing me," he said. "I'm in the great tradition. I come directly after Landau. First Antheil, then Perser, then Landau, then me."

"Please, please have another drink," Tommy urged, appearing before them with a Martini pitcher in his hand. He smiled down upon his friends with love. As they held up their glasses, Tommy filled them carefully, wiping the lip of the pitcher with the napkin he carried in his other hand.

"Of course you are right," Edith said penitently to Home.

"About what?" he said, startled.

"About everything. Darling Godfrey, I've been wanting to ask you to explain the difference between tonic and dominant to me, I'm so stupid," Edith said, knowing he would now be happy for some time.

"Have a drink," Tommy was saying a little further along in the ring of chairs. He leaned toward Abby, where she sat with Andrew Fellowes. The pale yellow fluid passed from the larger vessel to the cups held up to receive it. Tommy wiped the lip of the pitcher and passed on.

"*My* theory is this," Andrew Fellowes continued in his light British voice. "Faulkner and Caldwell describe their Southerners as beasts. Now, the beast is very much there, as is also the pervert in Capote, but he is not visible in ordin'ry life. I, myself, don't think life in the South is in the least like that. The beast, I mean to say, is there; but he's not a flesh-and-blood beast. Do you bear me out?"

"I think I do," Abby said, looking at the Englishman's high-colored face.

"I notice that in your own splendid novel you don't show anything but a polite Virginia."

"No."

"But don't you feel that underneath your polite Virginians' skins rages the beast in Faulkner, the pervert in all those dozens of what you call regional novels?"

"I guess I do," Abby said. She hesitated. "I think perhaps

183

the Southern system of bringing up boys to be manly does produce beasts . . . I mean, if the little boy is encouraged to think of tenderness, and pity, and art as effeminate, what can you expect? — But of course the English do that too, in their schools . . ."

"Oh, quite! — Look here," Fellowes said, breaking off the train of conversation and looking appreciatively at Abby. "I wonder if you'd lunch with me one day and we could thrash the matter out in some peaceful spot." He followed the switch of Abby's gaze toward Edith Fellowes. "My intentions are entirely literary," he added, laughing. But his eyes, when Abby's met them again, were bright with admiration.

"It would be fun," she said. She liked his English looks and she liked his accent and she liked his obvious interest in her. But then everyone seemed to be interested in her nowadays. "I suppose it's terribly vain," she said on impulse, "but I can't help liking my book to get all this recognition."

Fellowes lit a cigarette without taking his eyes from her face. "Of course you want it recognized," he said. "Everyone wants recognition."

Abby thought: How reasonable it sounds when he says it!

"My analyst says," Marian Rasserman was saying to Liz, "some people are as good as dead — just walking around dead — and don't know it."

"*My* point is," Liz said; she was getting redder and redder in the face; she knew she ought to go home and gargle and lie down, "if you don't even know it, then how are you as good as dead? Take the artist."

"My analyst says," Mrs. Rasserman interrupted, "the

184

reason artists are so damned egotistical is because they haven't got any egos, that's why."

"That's just silly!" Liz cried.

"You don't understand psychoanalysis," Marian said inexorably. "Artists just talk about their egos, instead of having them. I am the girl to tell you, after twelve years of marriage to Eph Rasserman."

Liz, outraged, rose to go. Tommy suddenly materialized beside her like a young god carrying a flagon. "Darling!" he said. "Please don't go. We need you so."

Liz threw a furious glance over her shoulder at Marian. "I've talked too much," she said. "It's bad for my voice."

"But, lamb!" Tommy said; he rested the bottom of the pitcher on a nearby table. "Of course you must go, if it's for your voice's sake. Even *I* feel that; and God knows I need you here. I was trying to get into position to talk to you about your new recording, but you've been so surrounded . . . We loved it. We were deeply moved, Lizzy dear. Elsa said, 'It's pure as water. A young boy's voice.'"

"Did she really? She thought so?" Liz asked. She settled herself on one hip.

"I myself thought it like Isobel Bailey's; or Melba's . . . Was that Kip accompanying you, darling?"

"Yes. You didn't like him?"

"I didn't think him entirely sensitive to your needs."

"Tommy!" Marian Rasserman called from behind him. "Why are you hanging on to those Martinis? Aren't they meant to drink?"

"They are indeed, darling," Tommy replied. His eyes never moved from Liz's. "Magic," he said. "Your voice. Actual magic." Still gazing at Liz, he slid to one side and began filling Marian's glass. In a second more he glanced down to complete the pouring, and gave Marian a long, searching smile. "Are you all right?" he asked in confidential tones. "Need anything?"

"Not a damned thing," she said. "You know why I didn't ask you to our party Monday? Because I hated you so that day, Tommy. You make me so *mad*."

"You intrigue me," he said. "There's such tension between you and me . . . May I come talk to you in a minute? I've got so many things I've been wanting to ask you about Huston. I'll be right back. Save me the other side of the sofa." Tommy saw Liz to the door, holding her arm as they walked and leaning his head attentively toward hers to catch what she was saying about Hugo Wolf.

Edith Fellowes joined her husband by Abby's side. He and she exchanged the smile of two good friends. Edith leaned forward to the little newcomer with the pointed small face and the ribbon-tied dark hair. "How exciting it must have been for Starkeyville — it's called Starkeyville? — when they found out about you," she said. "Tell me what happened. Fireworks? Champagne?"

As Abby looked back into the kind, civilized eyes, her feelings seemed to come to a head and she cried, "No! Nobody cared! As soon as they found out I wrote it, they stopped mentioning the book at all."

"But my dear," Edith said. "I don't understand. They couldn't possibly have *disliked* you. Nobody could."

"Curious thing about Southerners," Andrew said. He leaned back, stretched his long legs, and prepared to theorize. "Noticed it many a time when I've been off on trips there. They don't care a whit for art. Learning, yes. Journalism, to a certain extent. Art? I don't know why, but they seem almost to hate art, don't you find, Mrs. Daniel? Is it perhaps the contempt for art which the aristocrat has always felt, as Voltaire learned to his rue? Is it perhaps that they realize art though composed out of sheer fancy is, mysteriously, a fact, and one they can do nothing about? Or is it because they do take it all so personally?"

"I was just thinking," Edith added, "that possibly after the people in Starkeyville learned that it was you who wrote the novel, they might have begun to imagine you were holding them up to scrutiny. You do seem to know every facet of the Southern life so intimately."

"Do you ever hunt?" Andrew inquired.

"No, I don't even ride. I always imagine the horse is plotting against me, when he turns his head and takes one of those malign looks at me," Abby replied, as she had so many times before in Starkeyville. This time her audience burst out laughing.

"But how do you fit all the Southern regional writers into your theory, Andrew?" Edith resumed.

"Oh my dear Edith!" he replied. "Don't fancy for one moment those chaps talk art when they are, God save the mark, at home! Good gracious no. Their conversation is concerned entirely with boll weevils; or hookworm; that sort of thing. Your regional writer may write about his home, but I notice he doesn't live there."

Edith Fellowes was watching Abby's strained expression and working lips. "Do you have to live in the South?" she asked gently. "It doesn't seem to me quite suited to your temperament. But perhaps your husband's work requires it?"

For the second time today, Abby heard herself blurt out a confidence to a stranger. "I hate it," she said. "I hate it."

187

"Well." Edith's voice was like that of a mother, one who with quiet hand soothes the aching head. "Then I think you'd better not live there." She seemed to be about to add, There, there . . .

Abby shook her head. She looked mutely at Edith; blocked from expressing herself. "You don't understand," she said.

"I'm sure I don't," Edith said comfortingly. "Perhaps it will all work itself out. I'm sure it will."

Andrew was still leaning back, fingertips pressed together, with an air of thinking profound thoughts. "Toynbee calls it the worship of the ephemeral past," he remarked. "This whoring after one's ancestors that appears to go on in the South. Of course, that would explain why there's so precious little love — so much hate, come to think of it — in the Southern regional novels one reads. The South's not free. They're tied to the past. 'No one can love who is not free, I do not care how brave he be.'"

"But Andrew dear," Edith said. "Warmth — feeling — is the South's great specialty, or so I've always understood. Wouldn't you say the South expresses itself mainly through feeling, Mrs. Daniel?"

Abby looked worried. "I suppose so," she said. Her forehead darkened again and she exclaimed, "No. Mr. Fellowes is right. They do hate. Or rather, they think they are loving, when they only love things connected with their own past. Anything with no connection with it, they hate." She hesitated. "There's a dichotomy there," she ventured to add.

"Quite," Andrew said.

"It doesn't sound to me suited to your temperament," Edith Fellowes said for the second time.

Abby smiled, hesitated, then said in a small voice, "What *is* my temperament?"

"Didn't you know?" Edith said. "Why . . . I'd say . . ." She began to talk to Abby, leaning forward. Andrew looked around the room, spotted somebody, got up, and walked off.

The party was beginning to break up. People stood half-way between studio window and front door, concluding conversations, finishing drinks. Tommy was everywhere, pitcher in hand, pressing last-minute sweeteners on people. Elsa stood with her drink in her hand, tall as a Greek statue, throat strong and upright, pose serene.

"I shall never recover from what I did to Alida," Tommy was saying. "We'd just met for lunch. I threw my arms around her and said, 'Good-by.' A Freudian slip, to say the least. She'll never forgive me."

"Oh, Tommy, don't be silly," Elsa said, just beside him. "Everyone forgives you."

Tommy looked at his wife. "You do," he said. He made a gesture toward her. "Isn't it amazing?" he said. "She loves me. No matter how awful I get, and I can be ghastly, she loves me."

Over beneath the now-darkened studio window Marian Rasserman was explaining the rudiments of depth psychology to Abby.

3

"Look at her! Maybe that old log jam's burst," Tommy said to Elsa, somewhat thickly.

"I should say so," Elsa replied. Her eyes followed Tommy's toward the spectacle of Abby dancing with Andrew Fellowes.

The Humes, the Felloweses, the Rassermans and Abby had, at Eph Rasserman's insistence, gone out to dinner together after the party, about ten o'clock, to a small restaurant around the corner from the Humes' apartment. It had a canopy, the name BLUE ROOSTER in neon lights, a doorman, and an almost pitch-dark interior; it had a four-piece orchestra and a singer with a prominent bosom. But it was not very attractive, and the goulash that they ordered, when it came, consisted of what appeared to be pieces of cardboard floating in what appeared to be dishwater.

"I've always avoided trying this place, and now I tell myself how right I was," Tommy had said, upon giving up trying to cut his meat.

"Oh, come! It isn't such a bad little place. It's not supposed to be the Waldorf," Eph replied, trying, by a genial manner, to make everyone enjoy themselves.

"That's the trouble with it," Tommy said. "It *is* supposed to be the Waldorf."

Abby, at least, was enjoying herself. Her eyes sparkled, the color had risen in her cheeks, and she danced round and round with Andrew to the ragged music of the orchestra. His head was bent to hear what she was saying.

"Then you feel that what you said about Mrs. Woolf's influence is borne out in her Diary?" he said respectfully.

"Yes," she said. "Don't you remember about the fin turning in a waste of waters? Isn't that the same fin Rosamond Lehmann mentions in the beginning of *The Red-haired Miss Daintreys*? It shows she must have been talking to Mrs. Woolf just before she wrote the story."

Abby had suddenly tasted the *eau de vie* of giving her opinion. Nobody had ever asked for it, in Starkeyville, and she had never dreamed of asserting it. Now, quite as freely as she used to write in her private book, she was producing opinions on every sort of matter. It was, to say the least, heady.

The music stopped; the dancers wended their way back to the tables. Abby walked across the floor slowly, with her head slightly turned to hear what Andrew was saying. They sat down with the others at their long table close to the dance floor.

"Abby," Tommy said loudly, "I hope to Christ you don't still think you are nobody."

"No, I don't," Abby said, and laughed.

Andrew looked at her curiously. "But I say," he murmured, crumbling a roll. "Of all people, you! Such an intense and individual person. What on earth can Hume be talking of?"

"Back in Starkeyville I used to get the feeling I did not exist," Abby explained.

"Dear girl! I do hope you will never go back, if it affects you in any such unhappy way."

Abby took a sip of her glass of sweetish wine. She looked back at Andrew. "I'm not going back," she said. Her eyes shone.

The lights in the little night club lowered, a spot was directed on to the dance floor, and the tap man ruffled his drums. But Tommy, who was leaning far across the table towards Abby, insisted loudly, "Tell your old lifeguard. If you aren't nobody, *who* are you, Abby?"

She smiled at his ashen, boy's face. "I'm a writer," she said.

"You're what? I want to hear you say that again."

A waiter stood behind Tommy touching his shoulder. "Please be quiet," he said. "The floor show is about to begin."

Tommy pushed his chair back and stood up. "Well, I'll be a son of a bitch," he said. "What was that you said?"

The waiter backed off a little. "The floor show is about to begin," he repeated.

"The floor show?" Tommy asked. "You mean the crummy floor show in this crummy joint?"

"Tommy," Elsa called softly from across the table. "Forget it."

"You bastard," Tommy said to the waiter.

"Sir!" cried the waiter, who had a Central European accent.

"It's a little late to be saying 'sir,'" Tommy observed. "You should have said it before, when you were telling me to shut up."

Eph Rasserman stood up and put his hand on Tommy's sleeve. "Let it go, kid," he said. "What the hell."

Tommy peered inquisitively into Rasserman's face as if deciphering an inscription there. Then he sat down. Already a chorus of eight girls had come out on the floor and were dancing up and down in a row in soiled-looking pink tulle tutus, with sequins in their spurious auburn and blond hair.

"Oh, no!" they sang shrilly to the music. "Don't say it's so!" Up to one end of the little floor they hitched, then kicked their way down to the other end. "Oh, no!" they insisted. "And so let's go, man, go!" At length they worked over to the end where the exit was and shuffled off to Buffalo, to be succeeded by a young man in a dinner coat, a baritone with an air of wishing to be taken very, very seriously.

"I do not care," he sang, "how long and far you are away, If you, dear heart, remain my own ever and aye . . ."

"Oh, dear," Tommy moaned. "Can't we go home? I want to get in my own little beddy-bye and forget there is such a place as this."

"Hang on, kid," Eph advised. "After that little scene you made I think we ought to stick the floor show out."

"What's it to you?" Tommy asked suspiciously. "Do you own this joint, for God's sake? What gives, you making us stay here all these years and years and years? Hm?"

"Shhhh," Eph said. From across the table both Elsa and Marian Rasserman whispered "Shhhh . . ."

Tommy put his head down into his hands and remained

thus, occasionally peeking out to see what was going on at the microphone. Then he would bury his head again. At last the lights went up in the main night club, to their maximum brilliance of dark blue gloom, and Tommy, peeking out once more to ascertain the reason for the relative silence, emerged from his hiding.

"Can we leave now?" he asked the table at large. The orchestra had begun again, with two stamps from the leader, to play "Go, man, go." "That certainly sends me," Tommy said. "In fact I'm already sent."

"Wait a little, Tommy," Elsa said through the fog of smoke over the table. "I wanted to tell Eph about —"

"I get it," Tommy said. His voice grew loud again. "The artists are having a closed session. Artists International, proud to know you. How do I get my card? Or don't I get my card? A sterile photographer, is that it? No artist, is that the pitch? Then how the hell do you rate your card, Eph, you damned —"

"Don't say it," Rasserman begged. His face loomed mournfully toward Tommy through the gloom.

"Don't say it? I damned well will say it, you —"

"Tommy," Elsa said quietly. "Don't forget about tomorrow."

"For the artist there may be a tomorrow," Tommy declaimed. "For the non-artist, for the non-creator, there can be no tomorrow. It's all one lousy unchanging today. That's what we call reality, kids. So I don't rate with your union, because I can't create anything, is that it? Why, you damned —"

"Don't *say* it," Eph begged again. His face was even more tragic than ever.

"I know, I know," Tommy continued at the top of his

voice. People at other tables were looking. "I know how you see me, useful with the drinks and a good mixer. But create? Brother, don't make me laugh. Who, him? Whom? Hume? Hm. He's a non-artist. A non-creator. A non-Jew. A nonentity."

Eph heaved a great sigh of relief and leaned back in his chair. "What say we think about going, precious?" he said to his wife.

"Why, Eph," Marian said, with dignified surprise, "I suppose so."

With the utmost composure Eph called for and paid the bill, giving a large tip and a significant look to the offended Central European waiter. Marian drew her dark mink cape around her shoulders and stood up, neatly and fashionably. The others struggled out of their chairs as they continued the conversations in which they were already involved. Only Tommy sat still, palms flat on the table.

"Where you all going?" he demanded. "Don't all go off and leave me, for God's sake."

"Tommy, dear, you wanted to go," Elsa reminded him.

"Don't tell me what I want," Tommy said. "You have taken everything else — my pride, my vanity, my . . . You might at least leave me my will. Whatever the hell the will may be said to be."

Elsa came around the table and sat down beside Tommy. "All right, we'll stay," she said.

Tommy shot up from his chair like a released spring. "Oh, no," he said. "*Oh* no. No heroics. No alma martyrdom."

Elsa got up again and followed the others as they straggled into the street. Tommy jammed his hat down on his head and took Abby by the arm. They walked out under the night club's short marquee, which flapped in the chilly breeze of early morning.

"Nice Abby," Tommy said. "Sweet Abby. You want to get rescued from anything, you let me know. Any time. Rescuing you from that Christ-awful little burg on the top of the hill was one of the most satisfying — I may say the most satisfying experience of my mostly pointless life. Let me ask you something."

Abby looked at him expectantly. He did not go on.

"Aren't you going to ask me what it is I want to ask you?" he said as they strolled around the corner behind the others. The night was light and windy.

"I thought you were going to ask me."

"I never push in where I'm not wanted," he said.

Abby laughed. "What do you want to ask me?" she asked obediently.

"That's better. I wanted to ask you this. Just one simple question."

"Yes?"

"Just one simple, fundamental . . . Sorry. So sorry. Slipped my mind."

They all stood in a group in front of the dark studio building, saying their farewells. Eph shook Tommy's hand emotionally. "So glad," he kept saying. "So glad," he kept saying. "So damned glad. Your friendship . . ."

Marian Rasserman shook hands with Edith Fellowes. Andrew Fellowes kissed Abby's hand. "I shall take you up on your promise to lunch with me," he said. "Or perhaps dine?"

Elsa stood leaning against the side of the entrance; her beautiful head rested against the stone.

The others vanished, some into a night-roaming taxi, and

some walking into the westward wastes of Fifty-seventh Street. Tommy, Elsa, and Abby went up in the old elevator run by a half-asleep Negro, and let themselves into the studio.

"Good night," Elsa said. "I'm terribly tired."

"It's not my fault if you will stay out at night clubs all night," Tommy said.

"I didn't say it was your fault," she said.

"Always the last word," he said admiringly.

"Good night," Abby said. She went down the corridor to her little room. It had been intended as a maid's room, and looked out on the alley between the studio and the back of an apartment house on Fifty-sixth Street. As she took off her underclothes, Abby reflected that it seemed to be her fate always to be cast to some degree in the place of a servant, even in New York.

She had been asleep for some time when she was awakened by someone sitting down on the edge of her bed. Her hand went out to fumble for the light; she struggled up out of the pillow.

"Shhh," Tommy whispered. "It's only me. I remembered what it was I wanted to ask you."

As she struggled to pull consciousness around her she heard the ice tinkling in the glass Tommy held in his hand. "Go away," she said urgently. "Suppose Elsa . . ."

"She's asleep," Tommy said. "Dead drunk. I wanted to ask you this."

"Well, what?" Abby said, distracted. Her fingers found the light switch above her head and the light leaped on, revealing Tommy in a pair of blue cotton pajamas, dark-blond hair on end, a wistful expression on his pale face.

"I just wanted to ask you if you are going back to that

dreary spot and that God-damned wife-beater," he said.

"No," Abby said. "No, I'm not . . . Now go away before Elsa comes."

"What *are* you going to do?" he persisted.

"I hadn't thought. Find an apartment. Write a book."

"Alas," Tommy said. "You happy few. Imagine saying 'Write a book' just like that. Self-starting is what you boys are. *You* don't have to wait around for commissions from a magazine. *You* just get the word passed down from Sinai, Write a book."

"You're a sort of artist, too," Abby said.

"That's dear of you. That's kind. The fact remains I am not an artist. I am an artisan. The spark is not in me. I can only worship at your shrine, kid." He bent and kissed Abby lightly on the lips. Then he reared back, squinting at her. "Why are you so afraid of me?" he asked. "If you could just see how scared you look! I wasn't going to bite you, dear."

Abby turned her head aside on the pillow and allowed herself to reflect for a moment. Boogher filled her mind — the vision of Boogher's wrath, indignation and contumely at her allowing a man to kiss her married lips. Resolutely, she lifted her head and of her own accord kissed Tommy back.

"You still look scared," he said disconsolately. "What is it about me that scares you so? Is it my fearful sterility? Does it repel your own fertility?" He got up and began to walk around the tiny room, making small, jerky gestures and speaking with drunken eloquence. "You artist women — you're just too much. You're all creation — the mothers not only of us but of art. You make me feel like a God-damned drone, but you attract me fatally, Queen dear. You just chuck it all away, don't you? After a whole month in New York, you still seem damned near unconscious of what you are. You're an artist, kid. Your mind moves in mysterious ways its wonders to perform. You're *good*. You've got *talent*," he said with enormous emphasis, jabbing with one hand at the air. "You *write* well. It's always said there are no first-rate women writers. That their physical functioning robs them of the first rank. But maybe it's you who'll break the spell. Perhaps you're it. You've only done one book, but it's *good*. It's one of the good novels of our decade," he declaimed, throwing his rumpled head back and talking to the ceiling. "Who knows what may not be cooking in you. Maybe you're the Shakespearia of the twentieth century. Maybe you're the Proustess of our generation."

"Oh, Tommy," Abby protested feebly. "Don't be silly."

He stood by the bed looking down at her with an expression of exaggerated tenderness. "Little Abby," he said. "Little nameless. Wrenching you out of that environment where you were entombed is my one redeeming act in a lifetime of futility. Discovering your name and facing you with its reality. I don't think you even yet appreciate the miracle. It's my aim to make you conscious of it. Don't you get it? You're wonderful!"

She smiled at him and he sat down on the side of the bed again and put his arms around her, burying his head in her neck. "Oh, Abigail Woodbury Daniel, darling," he said. "You're such a fool."

4

I⟶ seemed delightful, and characteristic of Abby's changed life, that when she was called to the telephone next morning by Elsa it proved to be her new friends, Edith and Andrew Fellowes, asking her to lunch the same day at their apartment. Both of them spoke on the wire.

"We thought you might by chance be free," Andrew said. "And if so, did want to catch you. Hold on, Edith is being grasping."

"Dear Abby," Edith's calm voice said. "Could you come at one? Just ourselves. We have such an urge to talk some more."

"One has hardly touched on Faulkner," Andrew's voice broke in. "One does so want to hear your view of —"

"Faulkner my eye," Edith interrupted. There was laughter and scuffling at the other end. "He just wants to gaze at your remarkable and anachronistic face. You know you do look like my idea of Jane Austen — little and quiet and taking in everything everybody says."

"Nons'nse," Andrew said. "You're far too innocent, my

sweet, ever to be old Jane. Charlotte, perhaps. Not Emily, you're prettier than Emily. Emily, I feel, looked like a horse. But then, most great women *have* looked like horses. Can there be more to this than meets the eye? *Are* great women, perhaps, horses? Psychically speaking? Not that I mean to suggest for one moment that you are not a great woman, Mrs. Daniel — Abby — simply because you don't in the least resemble a horse. It's only that —"

"He's got himself all wound up in images," Edith broke in, laughing. "Also with the honey on my breakfast tray, which is being trampled underfoot."

Andrew's voice said, "There's a woman's gratitude for you! I bring the wretched creature her breakfast beautifully arranged on a tray, so that she can eat it in bed, and then in the age-old fashion of women she befouls me with honey of my own supplying. In order to imprison me, I expect. As if I weren't that already, dear God."

Edith's voice took over. "We'll see you at one then? Good. Lovely. One Twenty-three East Sixty-second. Buzz and walk up one flight."

As Abby hung up, Elsa came back into the studio carrying a pot of coffee. She wore a long floating dressing gown made of sari material in brilliant jade-green. Abby kept her eyes bent upon the level of the coffee rising in her coffee cup as Elsa filled it. Tommy had not yet appeared.

Elsa sat down on the opposite side of a low table. "Abby, darling," she said. "We know each other well by now, don't be embarrassed if Tommy made passes at you last night. I assume he did, he always does when he's drunk. Don't let it make you feel funny with me."

Abby looked across at the wide, milk-white face framed in red hair. "Don't you *mind?*" she said.

"You can't mind everything," Elsa said. "You'd go crazy if you did. I try to select the things I'll mind. If I minded Tommy making passes when he drinks, I'd be stirred up too much of the time. It would be awful for my work, too."

"The thing is," Abby said slowly, "I didn't entirely discourage him." Cold sweat broke out on her face.

Elsa smiled at her. "You didn't have to tell me that," she said gently. "Why did you? — Tommy told me your husband treated you dreadfully the time he met him, in Whatyoumaycallit, that town you used to live in. I suppose you must have formed the habit of confessing things to him? How terrible!"

"But I shouldn't have let Tommy kiss me," Abby said in a low voice.

Elsa moved over to sit beside Abby on the sofa. "Darling," she said. "That's entirely your business. I know you, I know you wouldn't try to hurt me. As a matter of fact you haven't hurt me. I suppose this is a Vermont conscience?"

"I suppose so."

"How terrible for you. Against life and *everything*. I mean, of course lust and license and the sort of life people get involved in, in the big cities, is probably excessive too, but Puritanism seems even more of an extreme."

"Oh, dear," Abby began, looking woebegone at Elsa.

"Don't twist that around too," Elsa said laughing. "For Heaven's sake don't let's think about anything that makes us unhappy."

Abby thought of Boogher; of the long evenings spent in tirade and castigation. "But when somebody does hurt you," she ventured, "oughtn't you to do something about it?"

"Forgive it," Elsa said. "Only that's such an awful word. Forget it means the same thing."

"But suppose you're really wounded? In an important way?" Abby persisted, still thinking of Boogher.

"Forget it," Elsa said again. "After all, you can't have the relief of forgetting something unpleasant unless you've got something unpleasant to forget."

"You're wonderful!" Abby exclaimed, putting her hand on Elsa's.

"Don't say it as if it meant you were awful," Elsa said. "Let's all be wonderful."

Abby still felt self-conscious and embarrassed, and it was a relief when Tommy came stalking stiff-legged through the door from the hall. His hair stood wildly on end. "Oh, God," he said as he saw the two women sitting together on the sofa. He put his arm up over his face and turned to start back toward the bedrooms.

"Come back," Elsa called. "All is forgiven."

"God," Tommy said again, blinking. He sank into a chair and accepted the cup of coffee Elsa handed to him. "I don't know which is worse, women's hatred or their God-damned forgiveness."

"Nobody hates you," Elsa said. "We're all being forgiving this morning." She looked up smiling toward the huge studio window, beyond which sunshine could be seen resting on the buildings opposite.

"Don't give me that," Tommy said. He took short sips of coffee between his sentences. "That's just feminine solidarity. If you're trying to say women aren't basically anti-men, you're crazy. Or you think I am. Why wouldn't they be?" he said, setting his cup down and lighting a cigarette. "Let's face it. Men are the destroyers of women and women are the destroyers of men."

"Tommy!" Abby protested. Elsa giggled.

"I'm talking about integrity," he said. "Man destroys woman's integrity every time he gets her pregnant. You can argue it's the life urge, but all I'm saying is it destroys that particular woman as she was. It makes her something different. That's just a fact. God knows a man's integrity gets impinged upon by any woman who gets, in the quaint old folk phrase, under his skin. Love!" Tommy declaimed, gesturing with his cigarette. "I suppose love is what you're going to throw at me now. Well, love is just what makes it possible for men and women to actually like being destroyed by one another. Love may be stronger than hate, but that doesn't mean there isn't any hate. Oh, dear. Oh, dear. I've talked too much, as usual, too early in the day." He looked piteously at Elsa. She got up and went out of the room. "Why do we all have to be so terribly articulate? And at dawn, too?" Tommy said. He squinted at Abby, rearing his head back. "You're not mad at me, are you?"

"No," she said.

Elsa came back, carrying a bottle of aspirin and a glass of water. "Take these," she said, shaking two tablets out of the bottle and giving them to Tommy.

"— And feed upon them in my lousy head," he remarked. He swallowed the pills. "Isn't she wonderful?" he continued, to Abby. "She's given up horseback riding, for her work, and she's given up skating, and she loved to skate. But she hasn't given up me. She loves me."

Elsa tipped her beautiful white chin back and laughed out loud. "I thought you said I hated you," she said.

"You do," he said. " 'The tigers of wrath are wiser than the horses of instruction.' Blake."

5

At one o'clock Abby, wearing her new dark blue dress and hat from Jay Thorpe's — she had not been able to summon the courage to enter Carnegie's — rang a bell in the vestibule of what looked like a white stone private house on Sixty-second Street. She was admitted to an inner hall by the rattling of the latch. An unexpected glimpse of herself in a long mirror startled her as she prepared to climb the staircase.

New clothes, though a satisfaction in the buying, did not seem to make much difference in Abby. With her dark, straight, short hair, her pointed white face, her small and unimposing figure, she looked neither cosmopolitan nor chic. She looked in fact much the same, she reflected, as the old Abby who had stolen dissatisfied glances at herself in middy and blue serge skirt passing the beveled mirror with its golden oak frame in the Cubbage Public Library; or the Abby who cast a last look at her reflection before stepping out on the terrace at Azalea.

Was she, then, the same Abby? She neared the top of the staircase worrying the question. But in the instant that the door off the landing was thrown open, and cries of welcome came from Edith and Andrew standing in the doorway, and Edith held her arms out to embrace her, as in some last instant before sleep or dissolution, Abby thought, No, no, no; she was not the same. Now she was loved.

The Felloweses led her into the sunny, pretty, urbane interior of the flat. Pots of white chrysanthemums stood in the two windows overlooking Sixty-second Street. Edith drew Abby down beside her on the pink-and-beige chintz sofa, while Andrew stirred a pitcher of Martinis. A tiny wood fire was laid in the small marble fireplace on the opposite wall.

Andrew poured cocktails into three footed glasses and handed Abby hers, cold and foggy. "To new friendships," he proposed. They lifted their glasses, exchanging looks of self-mockery at the sentimentality of drinking a toast. Above the heads of the chrysanthemums fluttered streamers of sunshine. Abby had never felt such comfort and pleasure, even with the Humes with all their warmth. She felt not only loved, but as though raised to some more agreeable version of herself.

Andrew sat facing the two women in an armchair, his long legs, in pin-striped dark blue trousers, thrust far out. His graying fair hair was cut long, his narrow, ruddy face was sharply cut in the planes of the Norman, and his eyebrows bushed out over blue eyes. Abby had only to turn her head to see beside her Edith's face, as familiar now as if she had known it for a long time: narrow, nose arched, eyes brown and intelligent. Edith wore a gray wool dress with a lace collar, the sort of dress, Abby felt, that a woman caring more for books than clothes would buy. Her feet, in black kid slippers with cut-steel buckles, were noticeably narrow and long.

They talked about Faulkner, Hemingway, and Forster, and the houses the writers had built, in their books, to house their characters: the house of the Sartorises; Howard's End; the fact that most Hemingway characters lived in hotels or pensions.

"But they always *want* houses of their own," Edith said. "On the other hand your Eugenia, Abby, wanted so dreadfully to stop living in that lovely house and go live in a hotel, didn't she?"

Abby sipped her Martini. The slight shock she still experienced on hearing herself mentioned bracketed with well-known writers quickly diffused itself and disappeared. "Yes," she said. "She felt her house was a tomb."

"How terribly, terribly clever," Andrew said looking at the ceiling, and then bending his head to sip from his drink. "Knowing what sort of house will add something to a character if you put him in it. Thank God I just report what happens, not invent what never did happen."

Abby finished her cocktail.

"A woman writer seems to me to possess some of the same superior assets a woman doctor has," Edith said. "Particularly in regard to what I think of as literary housekeeping. Just as a woman doctor is good at such things as not ordering medicines that a patient won't be able to afford, so a woman writer can also be more practical. Women are always more realistic. A woman writer can make a house in a novel sound the way a house really might be, while men put all the rooms in improbable arrangements and have people sitting talking where they couldn't possibly be."

Andrew jumped up and began to put together and stir another Martini. Abby gazed reflectively into her empty glass. It seemed strange, now, to remember that in Starkeyville she had never been able to take more than one drink of bourbon without feeling it unpleasantly. In New York, on the other hand, she felt as though permanently and agreeably intoxicated, but from another source. Mere alcohol she seemed able to take without any undue reaction whatever.

"I'll be interested to see what you do with the New York scene," Edith said. "When you come to it, as I hope you will, in your artistic development. I keep noticing how you listen, look — always so quiet and observant — and I realize how you take everything in."

"But, I insist, *not* in the manner of old Jane," Andrew put in, filling everyone's glass again. "In the manner of Charlotte, if you will."

"All right, like Charlotte, then. Of course I know you don't realize you're doing it, darling," Edith went on. "You do it as you breathe. But it's exciting for somebody like me, who am not creative at all, who simply reads. To me the artist is a seven-day wonder."

Abby felt obscurely embarrassed. "I can't get used to people feeling that way," she confessed. "Back in Starkeyville it was so different."

Edith looked at her with her reflective gaze, turning the rings on her long fingers. "As I see it," she said, "the artist being endowed with a perhaps abnormal desire for perfection — or an abnormal apprehension of imperfection — creates a better world than the one he is dissatisfied with. But from the point of view of society, naturally, all the artist has done is to attempt to destroy it."

"P'raps that's why Starkeyville behaved so tiresomely," Andrew said, smiling at Abby.

"But don't you see," Edith went on, "society never asked Abby to be an artist. Society asked her to conform. Abby chose to be an artist and judge society, but society doesn't like it, since they never asked to be judged."

"Abby darling, why don't you just stay in New York, where there isn't any society?" Andrew said. But Edith had not finished what she wanted to say. She lifted one thin hand. Andrew looked resigned and shut his mouth.

"Actually it is the artist who rejects society," Edith proceeded. "Even though to him it may seem that society does the rejecting. The trouble is that the artist wants to be accepted on his own mysterious, perfectionist terms. How can society know what those are? Society doesn't want the artist to create something new. Society's satisfied with things as they are. It doesn't in the least share in the impulse to create an imaginary better world. There is this profound and basic dichotomy between artist and society."

Worry pierced through the rosy cloud of Abby's impressed satisfaction at sitting with this kind of people, listening to this kind of talk. "But then who is going to accept the artist and praise him?" she asked.

"Not society, in any case," Edith said. "People like us, who comprehend the miracle? But perhaps you feel there are too few of us."

"In any case, I implore you not to go back to that bloody awful place you come from," Andrew said.

Abby set her half-full glass down on the low table in front of the sofa. "I'm not going to," she said. "I felt for a long time that eventually I ought to go back because of my husband. I've just begun to realize there's no reason why I should. He was always horrible to me, I don't owe him anything at all."

There was a moment's silence. Then Edith said, "No, of course you need never return, dear Abby. Let the South turn into a symbol for you. There is, you know, a deep South of the soul."

But this was not what Abby meant at all. She strove to make herself clearer. "It's hard for me to believe, the things I let him do and say to me," she continued. "Saying I was only seeking publicity! Calling me ego-mad! You know, *he* was why I couldn't sign my name to my own book. He made me publish it anonymously."

"Poor darling Abby," Edith said, adjusting the antique china lamp on the end table beside her. "You're well rid of him."

"He never liked anything I did!" Abby went on. Vistas of realization seemed opening, vast chamber on vast chamber. "Even before the book came out, he used to say I was hard and self-centered. Me! I was so shy and timid that I let him and everybody else order me around. I was practically his slave. And yet he called me selfish, and cold, and critical . . . He never let up."

"Damnable," said Andrew. "Is your Martini all right?"

"No, it's fine," Abby said. She picked it up and drank.

"Never mind, it will all come together into a marvelous novel some day," Edith said briskly. "Everything is grist to your mill. What I might call your internal economy is different from other people's. I've often thought, the artist can't lose."

"Even so, one doesn't blame you for feeling aggrieved," Andrew said. "After all, one's got to grant you human feelings."

"But Abby isn't human," Edith said enthusiastically. "Not entirely. She's a little more than human. She realizes things that are hidden from us others. She operates on a different level. Her sensibility is larger than life-size."

"She looks charmingly life-size to me," Andrew said.

"Children, drink your Martinis," Edith said, getting up, "while I put some lunch on trays. I won't be long."

"Can't I help?" Abby asked.

"No." Edith turned and looked back fondly at Abby. "You've helped people in kitchens quite long enough, I feel sure. From now on I hope you'll do the work only you can do."

Andrew came over and sat down by Abby on the sofa. He picked up one of her hands and played with its fingers. "When will you lunch with me, Abby, love?" he said. "Or dine?"

Abby was torn between pulling her hand away and feeling that to do so would be prudish. "I don't think I should," she said. "How would Edith feel?"

"Edith? Who's Edith? Look here, my dear. One's not asking you to run off, one's merely asking you to lunch."

"I'd just like to be sure Edith wouldn't *mind*," she repeated.

Andrew lifted one of her fingers and let it drop. "Do you know," he said, "I think it would be tiresome to say, 'Look here, Edith, do you mind frightfully if I take Abby to lunch?' I expect there *is* a bit of a thrill about taking a charming, curiously naïve, and most unusual woman to a rest'rant, but the thrill simply wouldn't be there if one had to clear one's decks on every hand. But after all there is a difference between the quite innocent thrill of man and woman talking, and the sort of great lurid boring bit of misbehavior you seem to have in mind. I *do* want it to be just you and me. I *don't* want to ask Nanny first."

"I'd like Edith to be my friend too."

"Abby, dear. Do try to what you Americans call wise up. Edith and I *are* your friends, but we are quite separate people and you'll have to be friends with us in quite separate ways. If you've some dream of us all playing Ring Round Rosy indefinitely, I'm afraid it simply won't do."

"The thing is, you're married . . ." Abby said.

"Quite happily, thank you very much," Andrew said. "But I'm not under lock and key as a consequence. Do you know, I've always found it to be the case that the Devil is never whom one thinks; he's always a surprise. I mean to say, to be puritanical is not in the least to be free of him."

Abby looked back at the sanguine face, doubtfully.

"Moreover," Andrew said, "the worst possible relationship is that of two women and one man. Absolutely everybody feels frustrated."

"It's so hard to choose between you," she said.

"My sweet, why choose? Why not both of us? Surely you must realize you need male companionship quite as much as female? Oh, far more! I'm sorry to say male companionship is quite essential to lady authoresses," he said, laughing.

"Perhaps *I* should just ask Edith if she'd mind my lunching with you."

"I shouldn't," he said, letting go of her hand.

Edith entered with the first of the three trays, and Andrew got up to help place small tables before each of them. For lunch there was curried eggs on toast, peas, and rice, with a roll on each plate. Like Edith's dress, Abby decided, the food was not very interesting. Afterwards they had pale pink cherries in scalloped glass sauce dishes.

"I must be off," Andrew said. He finished the last of his coffee, set the cup down in the saucer, wiped his mouth, and threw the napkin down into the debris of his tray. "Too long have I dallied in sweet slothful ease. Women, who lure the warrior from his rightful bent, Away! false sibyls, with your direful cant. I must be off to do my duty for the silly old paper." He walked out into the little hallway.

"He's talking about his job," Edith remarked to Abby.

"So I gathered. Could he also be talking about us?"

Andrew came back into the room wearing a homburg hat. "You can't imagine what it does to a man, to hear women laughing together in that awful way," he remarked. "Those echoes of ghastly female secrets, childbirth, that sort of thing. It makes one feel so helpless."

"You don't look very helpless," Abby said, looking up at the tall, dashing figure.

"I'm thankful for that. I must say, I feel as if I might be in rompers. Do wipe those dreadful, knowing smiles off your faces."

"Yes, dear," Edith said.

When Andrew had gone the two women turned to face each other on the sofa. Over a second cup of coffee they talked for half an hour, and Abby rose to go.

"I've had a beautiful time," she said.

"We must do this again, almost at once."

"Yes."

They walked into the hall and Edith put an arm around Abby's shoulders. "You don't know what it is for me, to have found a sympathetic woman friend," she said. "Most of the women we know are primarily attracted to Andrew. They keep their eye on him. The instinctive as above the cerebral, of course. One does want a friend for oneself. One does need a confidante. I find you extraordinarily *simpática.*"

Abby blushed. "Where I used to live," she said, "there were dozens of women, but not one I had anything in common with, really."

"You really detested it, didn't you?"

"I suppose I must have."

"And everybody in it."

"Yes."

"You must then have put only the pleasant parts in your book. I don't see how you stuck it so long."

Edith let her arm drop from Abby's shoulder and went back into the sitting room. In a moment she returned slowly, leafing over the pages of *The Rose That Died.* "This, *par exemple,*" she said, and read aloud.

"The seasons intermesh," Eugenia said to Warrington. Instantly she was oppressed by the realization she had said the same thing many, many times before. And to what purpose? Nothing had been helped. Manley had not been kept alive by it, nor Emily saved from the existence she now led. It was one thing to have seen that the seasons did, in fact, intermesh; and another to have acted upon it; moved out; or even moved away.

Eugenia stared past the blossoming crape myrtles, through the interstices of the Chinese Chippendale bench. Once again she had that familiar sense of autumn in July, of winter wrapped in these green veils of summer. She could smell apples already, ripening in the sun in upland orchards. Mares grazed, brown as shelled horse-chestnuts, in the bottomland. Almost she could have got to her feet and set about pruning the spireas bordering the lawn.

"What did you say?" Warrington asked. He bent his head closer; he was certainly getting old.

"I *said,* Once we've had Fourth of July the summer's over," Eugenia replied tartly.

Edith closed the volume upon her thumb. "That sounds to me so much the work of love and longing," she said. "All that part at the end. It's hard to realize you could have written it so lovingly when you really hated the place."

"It never occurred to me that I hated it, when I lived there."

"How very curious!" Edith said.

"Good-by."

"Good-by, my dear . . ." They kissed.

As Abby walked along Sixty-second Street toward the sunny stretches of the Park, her mind dwelt on Edith with her appreciativeness, her calm and cultivated intelligence. She seemed a friend made to order — interested in the same things as Abby, given like her to speculation.

There was nothing Abby could not imagine discussing with Edith except Andrew. As she turned into Fifth Avenue she thought of his good looks and his British dash. He had said to her, "You need male companionship," and Abby felt sure this was true. But she had a premonition that there would be emotional consequences if she went out with Andrew. She had never been in love with an Englishman, she had never even known one; and she found herself wondering what it would be like. Her mind stood, poised, as on a brink.

She walked toward the spires of the lower city in the September afternoon, and her mind went back to Edith, literature, and safety. It flickered back in the other direction again. Then her feelings for Edith and for Andrew seemed to fall neatly apart into two halves, as of an apple.

6

THE Humes got Abby to Harriet Walters' party early, at six, as befitted the guest for whom the party was being given. But already they were too late with their leading light. Since Tommy had talked to her on the telephone, a greater had arisen upon Harriet's horizon.

"Harrington's in the living room — do go and introduce yourselves," she greeted Tommy in the octagonal hall of her Park Avenue apartment. "He doesn't stand on ceremony, as is so often the way with the really great. How d'you do, Mrs. Daniel? I admired your novel. How d'you like my review of it?" Harriet, who was tall, with a large bony frame and straw-colored hair gathered into a literary bun, spoke in the English accent with which she always began a cocktail party. "I felt I went rather off the deep end about it."

Tommy was not to be distracted. "Who did you say is in the living room?" he demanded.

Harriet turned back from greeting two young men in-

216

timates of hers who came bustling in the front door just
then. "Harrington," she replied blandly. "I was awfully
lucky, I ran into him just in front of Tiffany's. He doesn't
go to parties as an ordin'ry thing. He's just up from Dominica for a bit of a siege with the dentist."

Abby and Elsa had drifted away, into the crowd that
milled about the long, white-carpeted, modern living-room.

"You bum," Tommy said to Harriet between his teeth.
"You let me down."

"I can't think what you've in mind, pet," Harriet said.
"— How frightfully nice of you to come, Lizaveta. The butler will bring you anything you like to drink. Do give your
order . . ."

The White Russian lady, wrapped in stone martens, with
an expression of suffering, to whom Harriet had spoken,
said, "I veel have visky vit a rrrock in it."

"You knew I needed this party for Abby," Tommy continued in Harriet's ear, undeflected.

"Darling, it *is* for Mrs. Daniel, as well! Harrington and
Mrs. Daniel, I've been telling everyone. How *do* you do,
Mrs. Carrick, how delightful to see you. Won't you go into
the living room? The butler will take your order. The guest
— that is to say, the guests of honor are in there — Harrington, you know; yes, Harrington. And Abigail Woodbury Daniel."

"I admit it doesn't sound as good. Does it?" Tommy observed.

Harriet turned to greet other guests who were being let
in at the door by a colored maid in a black uniform and organdie apron. The octagonal hall rang with British vowels
and with laughter. The atmosphere this afternoon was on a
very high plane. Women had dressed to the nines for this,

one of the first of the fall's real cocktail parties. Semi-dé-colletages and orchids were everywhere; jewels, and elaborate coiffures topped by fragile cocktail hats. Tommy trickled away into the living room, protecting his drink by cuddling it to his bosom.

Harrington, a small man with a leathery, seamed neck and a black beard, stood in the midst of a pullulating mass of people saying absolutely nothing. He sipped reflectively at the drink he had been given; his eyes wandered over the tops of people's heads. "But Mr. Harrington," one person or another kept beginning. "But I've always wondered how you felt about Joyce." Harrington made no reply. "Mr. Harrington," a young man said eagerly, "I understand you consider Faulkner to be our greatest American novelist in that he fails to accomplish what he undertakes . . ." Harrington's eyes rested briefly on the speaker's face; he took a swallow from his long glass and said nothing. A short woman, stretching her neck up like a hungry baby bird, piped, "You're a legend, did you know it? An absolute legend! Why is it that you never come to New York?" Harrington did not even glance at the speaker. He seemed to have perfected the art of letting people hoist themselves with their own questions.

Throughout the long living room was to be heard the patter of little names dropping. "I understand Harrington's mistress is present," said Eulalie Hobson Howe, dean of lady novelists, who had made several million dollars out of her books; she still, however, made a point of sacrificing every other consideration to what she thought of as her art. She sat ensconced in the center of a white brocade sofa, surrounded by a bevy of young men who carried her things to eat and drink and carried them away again, and took and brought messages like homing pigeons. "Her name is, I believe, Mary Kilpatrick," Mrs. Howe continued. "Bring her to me. I would like to meet her."

One of the young men took off at once on this errand. Mrs. Howe turned to the Ceylonese lady whom another of the young men had just brought up in obedience to an order. A tiny, erect creature in a sari that was candy-pink against her purple skin, she sat with Oriental patience beside the vast bulk of America's favorite author. "Now tell me," Mrs. Howe began with characteristic acumen. "What do you eat for breakfast?"

The Ceylonese lady looked surprised but unruffled. She adjusted the golden edge of her sari. "Uce-ually I have egg-nog," she replied.

"How very interesting," Mrs. Howe said. Her old eyes gleamed at the reportorial haul. "What do you put in it?"

"Eggs," said the Ceylonese lady. "Milk. Brandy."

The Rassermans had just arrived, and were being pounced on by all the people who made it a point to keep track of where John Huston was. "He's leaving on Monday from San Francisco," Eph had to keep repeating. "Yes . . . Yes . . . For the Solomons . . . Yes . . ."

The Felloweses came next. Spying their new friend Abby at the far end of the living room they began, separately, to work their ways toward her through masses of acquaintances who had to be spoken to.

"Ah!" Mrs. Howe exclaimed with satisfaction as the young man brought up Mary Kilpatrick, a beautiful, doe-eyed woman. "I understand you are a friend of Mr. Harrington's," she began.

"What did you say?" Miss Kilpatrick replied coldly.

"I said, I understood you had been visiting Mr. Harrington on his sugar plantation in Dominica," Mrs. Howe said, with an understanding, maternal smile.

"Did you?" Miss Kilpatrick said; and drifted away.

"She is very rash," Mrs. Howe contented herself with saying. "*Very* rash."

"How divine you are, darling!" one of her young men exclaimed. And in a moment more, word had gotten round within the twittering contingent, "Mrs. Howe says Mary Kilpatrick was very rash to have come . . ."

". . . Love," Marian Rasserman was saying, intensely, to Edith Fellowes, halfway down the length of the room. "My analyst says most of us are as starved for love as if we hadn't any air to breathe. That's why I find Elsa so marvelous. Don't you? She gives us all love."

"Certainly she does," Edith replied. She bent her intelligent and well-read gaze upon the chic Mrs. Rasserman. "There is, I am convinced, a great deal of love in the world, if you know where to look for it. And if you will accept it when it is given."

"But Mr. Harrington!" cried a shabby young man with a red mustache, well-nigh frantic with his efforts to get close enough to put his question. "Do you really feel that the artist should be accepted by society? Because lack of acceptance by society is what made the artist an artist in the first place!" Harrington stared without expression at the red mustache. "You imply in *The Wolf* that the artist should make his peace with society," the man continued. "But how *can* he make his peace? He, and he only, cast himself out. Even here in New York, society does not *relate* to the artist; it merely worships him."

Harrington's right eye twitched. "But Mr. Harrington," another, smaller man began. The man with the red mustache seemed to have answered his own question. "As an expatriate, what is your opinion of Hemingway in his role of —"

Harrington reached out his glass to a waiter passing. "Bourbon and water," he said, and broke a personal silence of some three quarters of an hour.

Over at the back of the room, old Herbert Hoskins lurked around the hors d'oeuvre table, assuaging his emotional hunger with caviar and smoked salmon. " 'Do, Herb," kind Eph Rasserman said as he went by. "Doing any work lately?"

"Nope," Hoskins said, helping himself to an egg masked with mayonnaise. Eph hurried on, mentally touching wood. For it was a stint in Hollywood that was said to have caused Hoskins to dry up in the first place.

"He abused me terribly," Abby was saying to a group of new friends over by the long windows that overlooked lower Manhattan. The curtains had not been pulled, and outside the dark city twinkled and sparkled like a cave full of diamonds. "He was cruel to me. He didn't even want me to write!"

"Really? Not *write?* But you're an artist!"

"I know!" Abby said. "And when I did write *Rose,* he wouldn't let me sign my name to it."

"Dig that crazy mixed-up *bas-bleu,*" a young man with golden hair remarked to a friend as they moved away, making room for Tommy, who had been edging his way slowly through the push in the middle of the room, in which the Felloweses were still immersed.

"I never even *loved* him, actually," Abby was observing. "Yet I endured all that awful —"

Tommy took her arm and turned her around toward the

windows. "Take a long breath," he advised. "Stop talking against Daniel. I hate to tell you, it sounds like hell."

They were the first words of criticism that had fallen on Abby's ears for a month.

"*You* always call him the most terrible names," she pointed out, astonished.

"Okay. I'm not his wife. It sounds terrible, from you."

She continued staring at him. "I thought you sympathized with me," she said.

"I do. That's exactly why —"

"Darling!" Edith Fellowes cried, reaching Abby at last. "Gracious, what a noisy party! Let's run away from it; let's hide behind the curtains, or perhaps under the grand piano . . ."

"I am told the author of *The Rose That Died* is present; the one who was at first anonymous," Eulalie Hobson Howe remarked to Andrew Fellowes, who had paused before her sofa to pay his respects.

"She is indeed," he replied. "A charming creature; I know her. Would you care to have me bring her up?"

"Yes," said Mrs. Howe.

"Your wish is my command, dear lady," Andrew said, and continued his progress toward Abby. When at length he reached her, she was giggling with his wife and Tommy Hume over what appeared to be a joke about the cocktail parties mice gave at night with what was left on the floor after occasions such as this one.

"Come," Andrew said to Abby, taking her hand. "I'm under orders to present you to Eulalie Hobson Howe."

"Eulalie Hobson who?"

"No, Howe. Author of *Peregrine Place*. And *Land of Magnolia*."

"I don't want to meet *her!*" Abby cried. "She's a perfectly horrible writer!"

"Come," Andrew said, pulling. "When Mrs. H. says come, we come."

"Why?" Abby protested as they crossed the room. "Why do we?"

"Because we're all afraid of Mrs. H. She's so unmercifully rich, and so damned disagreeable. She can make real trouble, because she never hesitates to make up any story she chooses if she believes God has told her to punish one."

"But how awful!" Abby wailed.

"Mrs. H.'s real talent for fiction finds its home in the stories she spreads about people. Realistic, utterly convincing stories . . . Dear lady," Andrew said, drawing up in front of Mrs. Howe's great bulk, "allow me to present Abigail Woodbury Daniel, author of *The Rose That Died.*"

"How do you do," Mrs. Howe said, extending a fat hand. "Sit down. Not, not there, here beside me, dear. Now, tell me. Why did you see fit to write an anonymous novel?"

"My husband wouldn't let me sign my name to it," Abby replied promptly.

"My dear child." Mrs. Howe drew her frowsty eyebrows together. "How could he stop you? That may be your official reason, but do not try to disguise from an old woman, who has seen a great deal of the world and of men and women, that there must be another, a real answer. What *was* the real reason?" Mrs. Howe demanded, with characteristic forthrightness.

Faced with the question, Abby could only stare. All around her the huge cocktail party racketed, shrieked, and gabbled, but no thought at all passed across the blank mirror of her mind. She felt rocking in a sort of eerie, unnatural calm. Two colored men were passing among the guests, ministering from towering cocktail shakers to their failing glasses. Powdered bare shoulders shrugged. Gloves were drawn off slowly, provocatively. The English accents of earlier in the party had long since worn off. "Hey, Eph!" Harriet Walters shouted across the room to catch Rasserman's attention. "Hey! Looky!" As she continued to call she thrust her Martini glass to one side for a waiter to refill.

Mrs. Howe said gravely to Abby, "I had hoped that we, as literary women, might prove affinities. I had thought well of your little book."

"But I don't know why it had to be anonymous!" Abby cried, as though to a cruel governess. "If it wasn't just because Boogher wouldn't let me . . ."

"I'm grieved that you do not see fit to confide in me."

"It's not that at all . . ."

Andrew caught Abby's anguished look and bent to help her up from the sofa. "Forgive us, dear lady," he said suavely. "I want this little guest of honor to talk to me, now that she has met the real *pièce de résistance* of the party." Under his breath he said to Abby, as they moved off, "Why on earth did you put the old girl's back up?"

"I didn't mean to."

"You should have agreed with everything she said. She's no fool."

"But she asked me a question!"

"Then you should have answered it."

"I couldn't seem to answer it so that she would believe me," Abby said slowly.

"In any case, this is as good a moment as any," Andrews said, "to ask if you'll dine with me Monday night."

"Monday night?"

Harriet Walters zoomed up. "Baby!" she said to Abby. "You haven't met Harrington yet! Come along and I'll meet you to him."

"I'll ring you up," Andrew called after Abby.

Harriet bored relentlessly into the core of the mob surrounding Harrington. "But Mr. Harrington," a newcomer was asking urgently, "don't you feel that as an expatriate you experience values denied to —"

"Harrington," Harriet shouted. "Wanna knock you down to Abigail Woodbury Daniel, who wrote *The Rose That Died.*"

Harrington turned his eyes on Abby's little face. "Never read novels," he said.

"I don't know why you should," Abby said.

They stood together as though within a small bubble of silence. Outside of it, someone else was beginning, "But Mr. Harrington —" A waiter squirmed through between turning backs and pointed elbows to fill everyone's glass from his enormous shaker. He filled Abby's. She took a sip.

"The first sip is the only good one," she said to Harrington. "I'd give up all the rest for the first sip."

Harrington's face altered. "My, yes," he said. "Why, when I come in from ridin' round the plantation down home on Dominica, and pour out and taste my first drink of bourbon for the day . . ."

"Do you ride horseback very much?" she asked wistfully.

"I'd rather ride round on a real old train, any day," he said.

They continued happily to discuss the pleasures of taste, smell, and sound, and the simpler forms of locomotion, until Mary Kilpatrick, across the room, perceived what was happening, bit her beautiful lip, and came to break it up.

7

By ten o'clock next morning, neither of the Humes had shown any sign of putting in an appearance. They had gone on with Abby from the Walters party to dinner with the Rassermans and some people named Fish from the Coast, at an Italian restaurant on Third Avenue, one of three within two blocks that were called The Original Joe's. Everyone was feeling broke and unwilling to spend much money on food. After a dinner of spaghetti that took a long time to order, to get, and to eat, they had all come back to the Humes' studio and talked till three.

Abby, who had waked, tired, at nine and made herself coffee and toast, dressed and went out into the September sunshine. She did not dare stay in the studio any longer, without some intermediary between herself and the telephone. She was afraid Andrew would call up to ask her about having dinner with him on Monday, and she had not been able to decide what she was going to say to him.

The warm, sunny morning air met Abby's face like a refreshing lotion. She walked up to Fifty-ninth Street and across to Central Park. Without hesitation she once more sought the Zoo, and with a sense of relief came to a halt in front of the saturnine camel. His very smell seemed simple and direct; a naïve, uncomplicated smell. Abby allowed her feeling to move out and to play upon the camel's reassuringly mangy coat. The tied-up nerves in her head relaxed. She became less a person who had stayed up too late talking too much, and more somebody just standing and looking. It was some time before her soothed fancy caught upon balloons — red, blue, orange, and green — floating on the other side of the animal cages.

She abandoned the camel, and walked around the cage block to where the balloon man stood in the morning sun with his bunch of bobbing bubbles. She purchased a red balloon on a long string and walked away past a long row of cages containing various species of deer from Africa and from Asia. For some time she was able to forget her inner worries by watching the bubble leaping at the end of the string. It was like a red cherry in the sun. It was like a round ball of vital energy. It gave her a feeling that she had not had since she was a child at grange fairs, when someone paid out the money for a balloon which she had carried around all day like a badge of optimism among all those dour Vermont faces. A red balloon, today, seemed to her especially gay and pleasant. She wondered what it was that the sight of a balloon evoked; one felt a kind of extra sense operating — not mere sight, nor taste, nor smell, but another sensation, of a mysterious nature.

She turned into the elephant house. One small-sized elephant stood there, and, on the opposite side of the passageway, a pair of hippopotamuses, planted at the brink of a tank of water. One hippopotamus stood with its back to

Abby, fat heels close together, pinkish behind voluminously displayed. He made her think of Mrs. Howe, and Mrs. Howe made her think of Andrew; and now she was in for it. She would have to make up her mind. Gone was the solace of the red balloon. She walked on, trying to think out the consequences of the courses of action open to her.

It would undoubtedly be the finer thing, she thought, to refuse to dine with Andrew, basing her refusal on her wish to remain Edith's friend. He would be disgusted with her, but she had weathered disgust before. Then she and Edith would be free to become intimates. They would discuss Proust for hours. They would drink innumerable cups of tea. They would exchange their most sensitive insights into literature, their most whimsical fancies. With so much about Edith that was civilized and distinguished, she would be bound to prove a rewarding friend. The relationship was sure to be a profound one, and even to think of it, Abby found, depressed her.

She could, on the other hand, go to dinner with Andrew, and be one more of the women of whom Edith had said that day after lunch, "they are attracted principally by Andrew; they keep their eye on him." It was hard for Abby to contemplate such a role; it did not seem a nice way to be. If she went to dinner with Andrew, she thought, he had made it fairly obvious that soon thereafter he would make love to her. Or was it only that she hoped he would? The prospect was of an affair, an affair with an Englishman, a man of the world, someone from whom she could learn what the great world was like; they were unlikely, she felt, to do much talking about literature. Dinners with Andrew, while not at all acceptable and rather frightening, seemed much more attractive than teas with Edith.

Andrew had said to Abby that day, "But why choose? Why not both of us?" Abby looked blindly at a giraffe she happened to be facing and considered the possibilities of that remark. It involved being two things at once. She felt in her bones that she could not go out with Andrew without his making love to her, and she felt in her bones that Edith would not want to be her friend if such a situation were known to her. Therefore a relationship like that Andrew had suggested would have to be compartmentalized, one side not knowing what the other side did. Such a relationship, Abby suddenly felt, would be absolutely ideal, from the point of view of getting everything one wanted.

Of course it was out of the question. It would be dishonorable, disloyal, two-faced, cynical, unfeeling, and selfish. I *promise* I would never do a thing like that, Abby found herself in the act of vowing.

But to whom? It dawned upon her, as she inspected a small fawn with white spots, that there was nobody on earth to whom she need any longer make such a vow. The realization came as a most uncomfortable discovery. She had, all at once, the sensation of carrying around a small, unpleasant parcel that she would like to get off her hands but could find no place to lay down. The parcel, containing the awareness that it would be nice to have Andrew and Edith in their separate ways and without the slightest compunction, weighed heavily on her hands; it adhered to her fingers.

The fawn with white spots offered no solution. Animals seemed all at once to have failed her. With a pang of nostalgia she thought of Starkeyville. There, unappreciated as she had been, no such problem had arisen as having to make up her own mind about what was right and what was wrong. She had simply done what Boogher said, what Miss Grace Starkey said, and what anyone else who was around said. She had been loyal, unselfish, selfless — in fact, no doubt, a worm; but a worm with an untroubled mind.

Her problem was moreover becoming twice compounded. Not only could she not make up her mind what was right to do about Andrew and Edith; she could not make up her mind what to do about making up her mind, either. It seemed necessary first to investigate the identity of that presence to whom she had found herself vowing, "I promise I would never do that . . ." Was it only the specter of Boogher? Was it the Vermont conscience? Was it what the people at the cocktail parties called the superego? Was it, conceivably, God? And what was the correct attitude to assume toward it? The people at the cocktail parties, if she understood them correctly, said their analysts advised them against letting the superego push them around. But suppose it was not the superego, or Boogher, but God? And who was God?

Overwhelmed by her difficulties, Abby turned and fled back toward Fifty-seventh Street. It was true that the telephone was there, waiting, and that she had not been able to make up her mind what was right to say to Andrew. But the Humes were there too. They might be able to tell her what to do. Any people at all, she felt, would be an improvement over going round and round in her thoughts alone. As she stood on the sidewalk bordering the Park, waiting for the light on Fifth Avenue to change, she looked longingly up at the sunshine gilding the tops of the millionaire apartment houses, and thought how lovely it would be if she could simply be Abigail Woodbury Daniel, that talented and distinguished artist, and never have to do anything at all.

When she walked into the studio, Elsa was poking with a sculptor's tool at the prelate's head on the stand, and Tommy was sitting on the sofa with his legs hanging over the arm, smoking and reading the paper. In the strong morning light Elsa looked magnificent, wearing a man's white shirt with the sleeves rolled up on her strong arms and the collar open around her columnar throat. She walked backward and forward, to and from the stand, adding and subtracting morsels of clay. Abby stood just inside the doorway watching her.

Tommy looked up over the pages of the *Tribune*. "How's tricks?" he asked Abby. "You been somewhere?"

"Yes," Abby said. "I've been over at the Zoo again. Looking at the animals seems to do me as much good as a night's sleep."

"I wish it did me," Tommy said. Elsa, smiling quietly, continued to back up and then walk forward. "I can get just as exhausted as the next man, but animals only seem to make me nervous."

Abby hesitated. She felt she needed to make a little more inconsequent conversation before broaching her moral problem concerning the Felloweses. "I do feel amazingly rested," she remarked brightly. "All fresh, and ready for our next party."

Tommy let the newspaper crash beneath the weight of both his arms. "Jesus God!" he said. "You really are insatiable! 'The daughter of the horse-leech, crying "Give, Give." ' "

In her consternation Abby sat right down on a chair. "I'm

terribly sorry," she gabbled. "What — what have I done?"

Elsa looked quickly from one of them to the other. She moved up close to her sculptured head and began working on a minute point in it.

"Oh, quit being pitiful," Tommy retorted. "Quit apologizing. I'm not your ex-husband, I'm not going to hit you. I'm just dead on my feet from so many parties."

"But don't you always —"

"What do *you* think? Do you imagine any human being goes to parties every God-damned day in the week? I've done my best for you, Abby. God knows I've introduced you to every human being of note I ever met. And I trust I've weaned you off that preposterous bully back home. But still you don't get the hell off your can and start working. Or get the hell into some place of your own. I don't think you're ever going to," he said, his face like a petulant boy's. "I think you're a one-book author."

Out of her devastation Abby said, "If I'd only known you didn't always live this way —"

"Known! You didn't know because you didn't think, I know that. Don't imagine there's anything I don't know by this time about the artist ego. Completely, utterly, totally bound up in itself." Tommy got up off the sofa and began to walk around the room making small, jerky gestures. "It's not a normal ego, that makes plans to do things and puts them into execution and succeeds or fails. It's a God-damned child's ego, immersed in ridiculous daydreams. You're an artist, all right, Abby, I spotted you at once. But I never thought you'd turn out to be quite so insatiable about attention, I really never did. I suppose I should have. Artists are either crazy about attention or they're sure as hell not. Artists aren't really human, did you know that?

232

Any more than little children are. The communion of immature saints, God damn it. In any case, my feet hurt and I've got a headache and a sour stomach, and if anyone comes to this apartment this afternoon I'm going to bed."

Tommy sat down and picked up the paper. Abby could hear her heart pounding.

"I'm going to lunch with Mr. Jason today," she faltered. "Would you like me to move out when I go?"

"Oh, for God's sake," Tommy said behind the paper. "No. No. No. Of course not."

"But I thought —"

"You thought I was created in order to wet-nurse artists. And so I am," he said.

Elsa crossed the room swiftly to Abby's chair and put her arms around Abby, leaning over her. "Darling Abby," she said. "Don't be upset. We love you dearly. Tommy's just tired. He loves you."

"Oh, love!" Tommy said, still from behind the paper. "We make a profession out of loving everyone."

"You've been so wonderful to me," Abby said. She hardly knew what words were coming out of her mouth.

"We love you," Elsa repeated.

"I'll go to a hotel this evening. As soon as I get back," Abby said. "Or perhaps I had better move on my way to Mr. Jason's . . ."

"No, no," Elsa said soothingly. "Of course you must not."

"Tomorrow morning, then." Nobody spoke. Abby went on, "If you had only *told* me you were getting sick of so many parties! And of having me here! How could I know?"

"I can't imagine," Tommy said. "I just can't think."

233

"How could I have told that you don't always live this way?"

"Not possibly," he said.

"I feel horrible," Abby said.

"Please don't," Elsa said. "We love you."

"I feel like a monster," Abby continued, slowly.

"Darling. Don't be absurd," Elsa said.

8

At twelve-thirty Abby stepped into the rickety old elevator which conveyed passengers to the editorial offices of Jason & Terhune. Everything about the atmosphere of her publisher's office emphasized the down-at-heel, the Dickensian. The furnishings of the reception room where she waited while the old maid who presided behind an oak desk went, on foot, to notify Mr. Jason of Mrs. Daniel's presence, were three bleak office chairs and an oak bookcase displaying copies of Jason & Terhune's newest publications. Comfortlessness was the note. To the uninitiated there might well have seemed an air about the whole premises of being about to go into bankruptcy. But any such impression would have been opposed to reality; Jason & Terhune did rather better than the average publisher.

The old maid returned, followed closely by Mr. Jason himself, tall, gray-haired, soft-skinned, with long sensitive hands, wearing a gray suit. He came forward smiling. "Welcome, dear Abby!" he said. "How splendid to see you again and how exceedingly well you look!"

Abby rose. After shaking hands, she took a step in the direction of the hall where the elevator was.

"There are some matters I think we should discuss before going out," Mr. Jason said, checking her. "The German rights, and the payment from Paramount . . . Shall we go back to my office for a few moments, dear Abby?"

She followed him down the familiar corridor leading between glass-partitioned offices, where the lesser lights of Jason & Terhune worked at desks crowded together. It seemed a very long time since she, too, had sat at a desk in one of those cheerless cubicles, typing the letters Mr. Jason dictated. That day was more recent when, on first arriving in New York, she had been led in triumph along the corridor, and all the subeditors had come to their doors to speak to Abigail Woodbury Daniel.

When they reached the door of Mr. Jason's office, he stood back to let Abby enter, followed her in, and closed the door after him. He held out a padded leather chair for her, and then seated himself at his large, imposing, mahogany desk. He picked up the thin red Chinese lacquer ruler with which he always played while talking to authors; tapping his cheek with it, he began, "What I really want to talk to you about, dear Abby, is writing your new novel. It will not do to let your reputation die aborning . . ."

She leaned back, only half attending. Her eyes strayed around the large, square room with its black leather chairs, black horsehair sofa, crimson rug, and framed photographs of the deceased editors of Jason and Terhune. The firm had been founded a hundred years before by Mr. Jason's grandfather, in partnership with Mr. Terhune, a gentleman with flowing mutton-chop whiskers, who had left no heirs.

Abby's eyes returned from Mr. Terhune's picture to Mr. Jason's well-bred face, with its soft pink cheeks sagging slightly over an old-fashioned starched white collar. Should she move to the Gotham, tomorrow morning? Or telephone the Felloweses and ask them to recommend another hotel? The Gotham had been across the street from the room where she lived, long ago; in those days she had often imagined that it would be pleasant to be able to afford to lodge within those dignified and conservative portals. Now she could. If she were to telephone the Felloweses to ask their advice, she would first have to come to some decision about them . . .

Her mind thus encountered Tommy's outburst this morning. She flushed burning hot, and said out loud, interrupting Mr. Jason, "I'm going to have to find an apartment. I can't stay with the Humes any longer."

The Chinese ruler was suspended in mid-air. Mr. Jason glanced at Abby sharply. "Nothing wrong, I hope?" he said. "Simply feel it's time to have a place of your own?"

"Well . . . As a matter of fact . . . Everything's wrong!"

The publisher crossed his long thin legs and prepared to sympathize with an author. "Tell me, dear Abby," he said. His refined features expressed real distress. Abby gazed imploringly at him, as her troubles burst from her in a torrent.

". . . I don't see how they expected me to know, that they don't usually live that way! People dropped in for drinks every single afternoon, and I just assumed . . . I don't see how I could help assuming people always did drop in. I thought I was just fitting into the way they lived!" she cried. She got up and began to walk about the room, dis-

237

tracted. "Now I feel I can never face them again! Apparently they got other people to give parties for me, too. Apparently they put themselves out tremendously, to give me a good time and make me, well . . . make me realize that people know who I am, here. That I am, well, somebody. But to have Tommy suddenly tell me I'm insatiable . . . I can't tell you how it makes me feel! As if I were a monster! I mean, my husband always used to tell me I was a monster of selfishness, and now to have the very person who took me away from all that tell me I'm insatiable for attention — the same thing Boogher said! Maybe I *am* a monster," said Abby, her small face strained with anxiety.

"Abby," Horace Jason said warmly, "I assure you, you are not. Far from it, dear girl. I know. I tell you I see authors constantly, day after day, and never have I seen an author — moreover a talented author — so devoid of self-interest. So unaware, actually, of her own interest. You seem to me selfless to a fault, dear Abby."

Abby sat down on the edge of the black horsehair sofa and clasped her hands together tightly. "I *try* not to be selfish," she said earnestly. "I *try* to do what's right."

"You do indeed," Jason said. "I don't think you realize how different you are from your contemporaries. Your retirement from the world has been good for your art, it seems to me, but it has kept you innocent of the simplest expediencies. By the way, if I may inject an anxious note, I do hope this unfortunate episode does not mean that you are considering returning South? I do hope you have left that man for good? — Don't think me impertinent," he added with old-fashioned courtliness.

"Oh, no," she said abstractedly. "I shan't go back . . .

But how could I have guessed the Humes were crazy to get rid of me?" she burst out afresh. "They never told me! How can anybody know what nobody tells them? It never occurred to me the Humes were doing anything special for me, in that life we've been leading. They never even hinted they were. When I think how I might have gone on staying even longer! Getting on their nerves more and more!"

"If I may say so, it was hypocritical of them to pretend eagerness to entertain you if the entertainment was in fact becoming a burden," Horace Jason suggested. With the tips of his fingers he formed a spire. "I think perhaps you've been somewhat put upon, dear Abby. In your innocence you accepted their hospitality on its face value."

A word he had used seemed to strike a nerve in Abby. She stared wildly at Mr. Jason. *"You* haven't been making a terrible effort to entertain me, too, have you?" she demanded. "All those lunches with Malcolm Bentley and Lilian Howard and all those people — were they a terrible effort for you?"

"Certainly not," Jason replied. "You forget. You are one of Jason & Terhune's most valued authors."

Abby burst into tears.

Horace Jason got up from his desk and crossed to the sofa. He sat down beside Abby and patted her shaking shoulders.

"Dear Abby," he said. "Poor child."

"I thought it would be all different up here!" she wailed. "Tommy told me it was all different! I thought it was only down in Starkeyville that people were hypocritical. Pretending to be what they weren't. But they are here too!" She paused, sobbed, and hiccoughed. "Underneath all the enthusiasm and the praise, it's all just —" She hesitated and tried again. "It's just —" But she could not say it. She began to cry again.

"Dearest Abby," Horace Jason said. "Let me assure you that my own feeling for you has been, and remains, deeply sincere."

She peered up at him through bleary eyes. His arm was solidly around her. She sighed, and lifted her face for his kiss — that expression of what seemed to lie at the bottom of everything, here in New York. She reflected upon what their relationship would be like. Since there was a Mrs. Jason, out in Smithtown, Long Island, Horace Jason would set Abby up in an establishment in town. He would spend the late afternoons with her, and perhaps two evenings a week. He would probably feel it appropriate to pay for the dresses she would buy at Carnegie's. How did a demimondaine dress? Something chic in black, Abby felt . . .

Her meditations were disturbed by the withdrawal of Horace Jason's arm. Astonished, she let her chin, which she had kept tipped up, drop.

"I hope you will always feel free to turn to me, as a shield and support," Mr. Jason said without altering the cordiality of his tone. "As if I were, perhaps, *in loco parentis;* or your own brother . . ."

The telephone on Mr. Jason's desk rang, a thing it was seldom allowed to do when an author was closeted with him. The publisher rose and went to answer it.

"Yes, Miss Doby?" he said into the instrument. "Oh? . . . Well, put him on."

Abby was drying her eyes. If Mr. Jason had not wanted what she had supposed he wanted, she was thinking, then had Andrew wanted it, either?

"Yes," Horace Jason was saying. "Yes, she's here. I'll see if she'll speak to you. Abby," he said, putting his hand over the mouthpiece, "Mr. Hume is on the wire. Don't talk to him if you had rather not."

"I will," she said, rising. She avoided Jason's eyes. "Hello, Tommy," she said drearily into the telephone.

"Baby, I could shoot myself," Tommy's voice said. "I'm sorry as all hell. You know me, or I hope you do. I just seem to get these awful blow-offs, and before I know it I've insulted someone . . . Abby, come on home. All is forgiven or so I fervently hope. We miss you bad."

"It really is time I found a place of my own," Abby said.

"We'll discuss that when you get back . . . Listen, the other reason I called you is that some old horror in Starkeyville seems to be trying to get you on the telephone. She's called twice since you left, although I kept telling the operator you wouldn't be back for hours. I could hear the old horror's voice at the other end, saying, 'It's *real* urgent.' So I'm afraid, darling, you better call her back. Operator Three in Starkeyville; it was an eye-opener to me that they had that many . . . On the other hand, maybe you better wait till you get home, so Elsa and I can hold your hand while you talk, by turns. I just thought that seeing the old horror had such ants in her pants I better let you know about it, in case you were planning to stay out for dinner or anything."

"All right. I'll call her back."

"You aren't mad at me, are you? Please don't be mad at me! I am well aware I am a louse gleaming fresh from the louse factory, but I love you. I wish to devote the remainder of my life to glorifying you."

"All right," she said, and hung up. "There's an impor-

241

tant call for me from Starkeyville," she told Mr. Jason. "Could I put it in from here?"

"I'll have Miss Doby give you an empty office," he said, and pressed the buzzer under the rim of his desk. In a moment his secretary, an elderly woman with hair dyed black, who had worked at Jason & Terhune since the days when Abby was an employee, knocked and came in. She nodded to Abby with a look full of recognition, respect, and dislike.

"Show Mrs. Daniel to Mr. Hobhouse's office," Horace Jason directed. "She must make a long-distance call. And Miss Doby. I will need you for a moment after you return. Dear Abby," Jason added, "do not be prevailed upon, whatever this call may prove to be. I feel sure it is your husband. Do not yield to whatever may be his pretext. I have no wish to seem interfering, but someone must keep your welfare at heart."

Abby threw him an abstracted smile. Once inside the glass-walled office of an absent editor, with the door shut, she put the call through Jason & Terhune's switchboard.

As she waited, her thoughts went back to Starkeyville. She walked through the old apartment on the third floor of Miss Clara Harrison's house. Even as her real, physical eyes stared out at the high buildings on the other side of Madison Avenue, her inner being moved through the familiar Starkeyville sitting room and bedroom, into Boogher's study, and out into the kitchen. It stood, hesitant, before the sink, and pulled out a drawer. There seemed to be something that it was searching for.

The Virginia operator was ringing the number in Starkeyville. It rang, and rang again, sounding incredibly far away; sounding as if whole oceans intervened. Somebody answered at last.

"Miz Starkey," the Virginia operator said, her voice hardly more than a whisper from across the billows. "Here's New York for you, ma'am."

"Thank you, Miss Justine," Miss Grace Starkey's booming voice, much reduced, was heard to reply. "Hello? Abby? Ha yew, child? Been trying to get you all this live-long day. Boogher's —" But Abby could not catch what Boogher was.

"I can't hear you, Miss Grace!" she shouted. "This awful connection!"

"I'm hollering all I *can* holler," Miss Grace replied. ". . . Dying. He says he's dying."

"*Who* says he's dying, Miss Grace? Dr. Ramsdell?"

"Listen to me, child. I'm trying to tell you. *Boogher* thinks he's dying. You better come straight on home, child." Miss Grace's top-sergeant voice faded away into a kind of limbo, where it could be still heard but not comprehended. Then another voice, totally unconnected with the call, suddenly spoke up. A tiny gabble forever unidentifiable, it said, "I just tole him, 'Pinky, she's not goin' to have them dishes and that's flat. Pinky,' I said, 'now you listen here to me.' " Like the piping of an angry doll the voice chattered away off in nowhere.

"Miss Grace! Can you hear me?" Abby called. She had stiffened; *they're all just trying to get me back,* she thought. "What's the *matter* with Boogher? Can't you tell me?"

Miss Grace's voice returned from limbo, suddenly strong. ". . . Poisoning," she said perfectly clearly. "He thinks he's poisoned because of the Augustines and their history of . . ." A word was lost. Her voice faded out again, like a dissolve in a movie. Then it returned, stronger than ever. "I tell him just have faith. Why, Lord have mercy —"

Abby did not reply. Like a stroke, like a blast of lightning, memory had struck her with the object her inner being had been looking for.

". . . Dr. Ramsdell tells him wait. What did *you* say?" But Abby had not spoken. "I can't hear one solitary syllable, child," Miss Grace said. "Come on home now, hear?" The connection, such as it was, was broken.

Abby set the instrument back in its cradle on the oak desk and stared blindly out of the window that looked down over Madison Avenue. Throughout the conversation with Mrs. Starkey, that inner being had kept searching unceasingly through the drawers, the cabinets in the kitchen in Starkey Street, hunting, hunting. Then in the middle of what Miss Grace was saying it had stood up, holding the quarry in its hand — the bottle it had found in the left-hand lower cabinet under the sink, with a label marked Listerine that contained Clorox. Poison.

A crimson wave spread over Abby's body. She thought, Underneath I wanted to kill Boogher, and I have; and now he's dying.

I've done it. *Now* I've done it, her mind kept repeating, even after she had got to her feet and started out of the vacant office to go ask Mr. Jason to help her get back to Starkeyville in a hurry.

Part Four

1

THE train from Washington to Starkeyville was an anachronism among the streamlined aluminum Diesel trains speeding by it down the tracks; it could not be long for this world. On this one branch line, known in the timetables as the Washington, Starkeyville, and Fredericksburg, the Southern Railway Served The South almost as of yore. It meandered along a roadbed lined with honeysuckle banks, that in summer sent waves of overwhelming sweetness through the open windows of the un-airconditioned, unswept, uncomfortable coaches. The train stopped at every wayside shelter — Gainesburg, Happysburg, Mount Aureole, Buggsville Courthouse.

In former days, Abby remembered being told by Boogher, grave-faced colored women had issued forth from the brick hotel overhanging the tracks at Mount Aureole, bearing trays of fried chicken on their heads, to hawk among the passengers. Meanwhile the conductor, Mr. Parabel, standing up near the engine by Mr. Lovegrove the engineer, would write down on a slip of paper the errands that the residents of Mount Aureole came or sent their maids to commission him with, for execution when the train got to Fredericksburg that afternoon and turned around to come back: one spool of sewing silk to match a sample of taffeta with which Mr. Parabel was entrusted; two packages of the special troches that were all that would keep old Mr. Howes Massie from coughing in the night until Mrs. Howes Massie felt sure she was about to expire — Mr. Parabel knew the kind desired, square, silver and teeny; sometimes a real emergency, like a pair of white cotton gloves, size 5½, for Miss Johnny Jo Patton to wear to the Dowling wedding that very evening. Sometimes, just at the last moment, after Mr. Parabel and Mr. Lovegrove had said good-by to everybody and the engine had made its first forward lurch, a colored man in a white shirt would be seen running down the hill waving and calling. Then Mr. Lovegrove would stop the engine again, and all the passengers would peer, while the colored man, panting, called out what Mr. Parabel and Mr. Lovegrove realized he was going to call out as soon as they had seen him coming: that Miss Sidney Delaunay of Mount Aureole — the house that gave the station its name — had been delayed, but wanted to go to Fredericksburg. Would Mr. Lovegrove mind holding the train, just the least little bit? Mr. Lovegrove never minded, and Miss Sidney would presently come driving down the hill in an old buckboard behind a piebald mare, wearing a pink dress and carrying a parasol, dimpling and smiling and looking so sweetly pretty that no engineer worthy the name of Southern gentleman could have been otherwise than proud to wait for her.

Those days, Boogher had lamented, were gone forever. Mr. Parabel had long ago been gathered to his fathers —

the same fathers as those of the Richmond Parabels and the Loudoun County Parabels, certain branches of the family having fallen upon evil days after the War; it would have been right mean to hold it up against them when the only single solitary crime they had committed was to make a living as best they could, in Parabel's Shoe Store in Buggsville Courthouse, or conducting the Washington, Starkeyville and Fredericksburg. Conducting it just beautifully, too; there was fifteen carriages at Mr. Parabel's funeral. The conductor nowadays was a Mr. Grimes, who came from very plain people.

Miss Sidney Delaunay was still alive, Boogher had told Abby, but very old; but crossed in love and still maiden; but a little touched. She kept white mice in the Sheraton sideboard in the dining room at Mount Aureole, and gave them each a name — Catullus and Horace and Mephisto, and Beatrice pronounced with the Italian *c*. No longer did she descend the hill, dimpling, to take trains specially held for her. It was not that the personnel — if such a brisk term could be applied to them — of the Washington, Starkeyville and Fredericksburg had ever explicitly refused to execute shopping commissions or to be obliging about stretching train schedules. It was, Boogher had explained, that the passengers themselves, infected with the virus of a newer age, would have felt silly, poky, to ask the present engineer — from West Virginia, it was said; nobody knew his name — to hold the train. One didn't do that sort of thing, these days. It didn't fit with the times. It had become instead part of the canon, a fragment of the legend, and worked fine into stories about the old days when there wasn't all this bustle and commotion and everybody was much happier.

Abby thought of the story Boogher had been fond of telling, about when his Uncle Peter Mark Hammond was alive and used always to have his toddy, rain or shine, at half past four in the afternoon. "Seems Mr. Parabel was supposed to bring Uncle Peter Mark's wife, that would be Aunt Virgie," Boogher would relate, leaning back in his chair, "— bring her back a yard of yeller dimity from Fredericksburg, to piece out a dress she was making. Well, sir, Uncle Peter Mark never could abide the color yeller. Said it made him think of puke, and of his deceased old Cousin Hattie Blythe from Roanoke, who smelled. So Uncle Peter Mark, he instructed Mr. Parabel via Mose the yardman not to buy that yeller dimity — to tell Aunt Virgie the store said it was fresh out of yeller dimity. That yardman, Mose, was a no-count niggra if there ever was one. Couldn't keep a secret. So Aunt Virgie got hold of what had transpired. Mad? Aunt Virgie was fit to be tied. What she did, she up and hid the drinkin' whisky, so Uncle Peter Mark couldn't fix his half past four in the afternoon toddy, just to spite him. Well, sir, Uncle Peter Mark went poking all over that big old house — *you* remember that house," Boogher would interpolate at this point to whatever old friend was handy, "we used to play hide-and-go-seek in it, remember? — he went poking and rummaging around looking for his whisky. He looked in the sideboard, and he looked in the china cupboard back of the china, and he looked in the hiding place behind the molding in the highboy, and 'fore God if he didn't look in the commode . . ."

The days when the train from Washington was like a member of the family might be gone forever, but it was still a very odd mode of locomotion indeed. It still lurched when starting, and proceeded down the track, from one shed of a station to the next, in a series of violent jerks, as though each forward propulsion were born of the dying effort of the last. It was still without any form of air-cooling system, and, as one of the last branch lines in the country to use a steam locomotive, extremely dirty. Grit and smuts flew in the open windows to smear the sweaty faces of the passengers, of whom Abby made one. Beside her sat the usual fat woman with a monstrous bunch of chrysanthemums she was taking down the line to where she was visiting kin for supper. Four teen-age girls in cotton dresses, which had been fresh when they got on the train, giggled in turned-over red plush seats just ahead. The usual elderly man with a gray face, wearing a limp gray suit, sat reading the Washington *Star*.

Having made a dozen halts at way stations the train now began once more to jerk to a stop. Mr. Grimes, in his shirt sleeves, threw open the door at the end of the car and called apathetically, "Sta'*ville!* Sta'ville!" A few passengers rose and struggled down the aisle, battling the train's increasingly violent spasms.

Abby had taken an afternoon plane from New York to Washington; but short of wiring somebody in Starkeyville to meet her at the airport in a car — something she felt too guilty to consider — the only means of transportation from Washington onward had been the train; it had felt somewhat like traveling by jet to the moon only to be met there by a barouche. A fat man and a thin man stood on the Starkeyville platform in front of two taxicabs. "Cab?" they said. "Take you up the hill?" Other passengers trotted by without even looking up. Abby stopped and gave her suitcase to the fat man. "One Twenty-two Starkey Street," she directed, after getting into the back seat, which smelled of hot, sweet chewing gum.

The fat man climbed into the driver's seat. "Well, turned out a pretty day," he offered. But Abby did not reply. The taxi started off.

In order to distract her mind from the terrible spectacle that might await her at home, Abby turned her attention to the familiar buildings they were passing: the courthouse, dominating the early evening scene with its classic pink-brick distinction; the law offices that had housed lawyers, she told herself politely like a tour guide, for a hundred and fifty years. Would Boogher be lying dead on his bed when she walked into the apartment? Would they have already taken his body away to Bell & Hargrave's, the undertaker that the nice people patronized?

The taxi took the route up Main Street, with its rows of stores that looked, in the early October sunset, as if exhausted after a long hot summer of serving the public — windows dirty, awnings drooping. Mr. Wilson was standing out in front of Wilson's Shoe Store, as usual, and Mr. Jewell was standing out in front of Jewell's. Abby's impulse was to lean forward and bow to them out of the window of the taxi, in the role of local lady returning from her travels. But what if that would only make them say, *Saw Miz Daniel this evenin, gettin back from up North. Nodded and smiled, she did; an' old Boogher Daniel lyin' there in his grave twenty-four hours. Never could understand Yankees.* Abby leaned back again. The taxi swung around the corner into Bolling Avenue, past the Rumsey house with its round turrets in the four corners, past the Nashes' and the Whitings' and the Parabel Greenes'; the Harry Scott Greenes', to whom the other Greenes did not speak, was the next house. Now they were turning into Starkey Street.

Abby gathered her purse, her gloves, her suitcase and her fears together and prepared to alight. Then she had to put them all down again while she found a dollar with which to pay the driver. The ride was seventy cents, and she did not tip the man, remembering that in Starkeyville tipping in taxis was considered one of the things only Yankees did, thus ruining the pay scale just as they did when they raised servants' wages.

She stood still in front of the Robert E. Lee Apartments, where she had lived, married to Boogher, for all those years. The building looked completely different to her. It was as if, in the past, she had been wholly merged with it. The house had been a part of her; was her; had been almost, in a sense, her only outer covering. Now she was looking for the first time *at* it, from outside it. For the first time she noticed the line of white mortar running between all the bricks of which it was constructed. Where the combined English ivy and Virginia creeper hugged the walls, a smooth green surface rippled in the light autumn wind. The vines had almost obliterated one of General Larrimore's windows. Perhaps it was his bathroom window, in which case how convenient! He need never pull his shade down at night . . . Abby snatched her thoughts to her like a pack of children who were evading a just punishment. She turned and faced the front door; then she walked in and began to climb the two flights of stairs.

2

Boogher was sitting in a deep red corduroy chair before the fireplace, staring into an unlit fire. A copy of Publilius Syrus lay open on his lap. At the sound of the front door opening and closing to one side of him, he glanced up and saw Abby, and a variety of expressions crossed his face. As Abby stood still, overcome by her relief at finding Boogher alive instead of in bed or a coffin, he registered surprise, satisfaction, and anger, in rapid succession. Then he settled down to more deliberate shows of amazement, reserve, and offended withdrawal; ending up with an expression of cynical amusement.

"Well?" he remarked rising.

"Oh, Boogher," Abby cried. "I'm so glad to see you're all right! You don't know what terror I've been in, ever since Miss Grace called me!"

"Oh, she called you? I might have spared myself the moment's fancy that concern for me on your own part had brought you home." Boogher stood sidewise to Abby, his head, with its smoothly brushed orange hair, turned to face her. With some care he laid his volume down on the end-table by the sofa.

"Boogher, don't let's get into a fight, please. I came home because — because Miss Grace told me you were dying. Naturally, I threw everything up and rushed down. I flew as far as I could."

"Fight?" Boogher inquired. "Who said anything about fighting? It is true that I have come very close to the final precipice. But I am distressed," he added with irony, "that you should have had to lay aside your no doubt pressing engagements, to come home on account of what must seem to you very small potatoes indeed — your husband's life or death."

"Oh, Boogher," Abby said. "Please don't talk that way. That fancy way. You don't have to. You can talk perfectly simply when you want to."

"Indeed?" he replied. "I presume your new acquaintances in New York speak in far more streamlined fashion? Alas, I must content myself with my native idiom — the English of my Virginia forebears; the English of the King." He ran a hand over his red hair.

"This is all beside the point," Abby said. "I *must* know what happened to you. Are you all right now? The telephone connection with Miss Grace was so terrible I never found out exactly what was the matter." She stopped. There was no point in confessing about the Clorox bottle, she reflected; since here Boogher was, alive. "Did you eat bad seafood?" she suggested.

Boogher stared. "No," he said. "What gave you the idea my affliction had anything to do with my stomach?"

"Miss Grace said . . . It was one of the things I did hear, perfectly distinctly. She used the word poisoned."

"Poisoned?" Boogher repeated. "Poisoned? I may have expressed myself that the fate I feared was poisoning my system. Possibly she quoted me as saying so. I regret to say that it is like you, Abby, to mistake the whole nature of your husband's illness, and to assume, with considerable blitheness, it was no more than a stomach-ache."

"But what *did* you have?"

"I beg," he said, "that you do not assume a concern for me which you do not, with sincerity, feel."

"Oh, Boogher!" Helpless exasperation rose in her. He was so awful; so elaborate, so arch. How could you deal with such a man? "Would you rather have me go away, now that I know you're all right, after all?"

"No, don't go," he said hastily. "If you're really interested, I will tell you the history of what I had feared was to be my final illness. There are some fascinating details."

Abby had not moved from the doorway since her arrival. Now she left her suitcase standing there and came over to the fireplace. She sat down in the other of the red corduroy chairs, which had been at Danielstown in Boogher's childhood. She slipped off the light coat she had worn traveling and threw it over the arm of the chair, assuming an intelligent expression and an attentive pose. She reflected uneasily that, in spite of her reprieve from finding herself a murderess, there was no getting away from the fact she certainly put Clorox in that Listerine bottle. It was something that was going to take an awful lot of expiating. Desire to kill your husband, even unconscious desire, wasn't anything very nice.

"Tell me," she prompted.

"It all began," Boogher said, stretching his long legs and settling his shoulders in his coat, "with the mole, or perhaps

I should call it a wart, on the side of my neck. Of course you remember it."

Abby shook her head.

"You don't?" he said. "I should have thought it rather conspicuous. However, I never entertained any qualms about its constitution until one morning — it must have been a week or so after you took your departure in that unceremonious manner." Boogher lifted his eyebrows for a moment. "By mischance, I sliced the top of it off with my razor, in shaving. These things happen, to a man," he explained parenthetically. "A man does not, as a rule, give them any attention nor, in fact, do they usually cause untoward results. However this mole, or wart, was apparently of a different order. It bled profusely. As usual, I merely applied a bit of paper to the wound and paid it no particular mind. I was trained as a child," he said, "to ignore such affairs. A man does not get in a state of agitation over every little cut and bruise he may incur in the day's work. So, after the bleeding had stopped — I say, after the bleeding finally stopped," he said, falling into that rhythm of Southern storytelling which requires sentences to be repeated for purposes of cadence, "I put the matter completely aside and proceeded with the business at hand as if nothing had happened.

"*In so far*," he continued with emphasis, "as it has been possible to proceed as if nothing had happened! I fear that in your giddy whirl in New York — which city, I grant you, can provide the greatest of plenty in the way of slightly tawdry gaiety for those so easily satisfied — you gave little or no thought to the difficulties inherent in the position you left me in. Of the questions which were, inevitably, asked. Of the innuendos. Of the curled lips. It was all very well for you to have said — as you did say when you left this flat — that it was your intention eventually to return. But was I supposed to have been able to publish this laudable intention, like a sort of advertisement in the window of the shop? 'Mrs. Daniel Will Be Back in Her Own Good Time.' Is that what you assumed it would be easy for me to do?" he asked. Abby shook her head.

"Well, sir," Boogher continued. "It was right difficult for me, those first days after you ran off, Abby; right difficult. Oh, I took your part! 'Gone to New York,' I'd say. 'For a little fling.' 'Her publishers are giving her a tea,' I'd tell them when they inquired for you. But that sort of thing can't go on forever. On the contrary. Soon they began to say, 'I suppose Mrs. Daniel has returned?' or 'Bring Abby over for a drink, soon's she gets home.' What was I to reply? I ask you that. On second thoughts, I retract the question, rhetorical as it may have been. For when have you ever been interested in making things easy and pleasant for me? The answer is, quite simply, never. Frankly, you haven't given a Continental, Abby. Admit it."

"Yes, I have, too," Abby protested. "I felt because — *you* know why I left. You were reading my private journal, and after all the preaching you'd done about Southern honor, I just thought it was the most hypocritical —"

"Stop right there," Boogher said, raising a hand. "Let us sift this thing down to its logical basis before proceeding any further. I read your diary, or journal; agreed. As to whether the act was a dishonorable one, I fear our dissimilar backgrounds make our views on that point quite incompatible. Quite opposed. Perhaps it would do you no harm to listen to my view, Abby. It is that a gentleman transgresses no code of honor whatsoever in reading his wife's diary, if he sees fit so to do. He is on the contrary fulfilling his duty as mentor of her intellectual welfare. He reads it, if he does read it, out of devotion to what is in his charge; out of concern for what is dear to him."

"I don't think people feel that way any more," Abby said. "I'm practically sure nobody does."

"I do," Boogher said. "My father read my mother's diary as a matter of obligation. He reviewed her use of the language, improved her acquaintance with syntax, and she was grateful to him for it, we may be sure of that, Abby. My dear mother bore my father a devoted and unswerving love. They raised seven children, a token of the love there was between them. I remember," he said, and his voice took on a richer tone, a more pronounced accent, "yes, sir, I remember like it was yesterday, my Daddy comin' into my mother's room, when I'd be there with my brother Henry Davis, sayin' good night and kneelin' side of her bed like we used to, sayin' our prayers. There we'd be, us little tads in our white jersey shirts we slept in, and there would come my Daddy, in through the door from his dressin' room. My Daddy was a big man; big and tall and strong. He'd walk into the room in his ridin' breeches — been out ridin' the place, most likely, and taken his boots off with that big old bootjack he kept in his dressin' room, there. His breeches ends would be hangin' down round his bare calves, I remember, an' he'd give the two of us little tads a swat on our bottoms as we knelt there. He'd say, 'Now we're going to hear your lesson, Boogher, sir.' So, kneelin' right there by Daddy's and Mother's gret big bed I'd start prayin' hard, out loud, hopin' to gracious I wouldn't forget anythin' —

'*O gentes omnes undique, laudate dominum; Illum laudate, populi, per orbis ambitum.*' An' if I forgot a word, or if I got my cases wrong, why, I can tell you my Daddy would whip me good," Boogher said with pride.

"He seems always to have been whipping you," Abby remarked. "Didn't your mother ever protect you?"

"What's that?" Boogher said, not attending. "So then my Daddy'd set Henry Davis to sayin' his prayer, in Greek maybe, or maybe just some little old English prayer. How Henry Davis did holler when he was the one got thrashed! I can hear him now: 'Daddy, please Daddy, don't wallop me so *hard!*' Like a real little siss. Henry Davis was always a softy, pore soul; like as not he was softenin' up already for his untimely death of TB . . . Well, like I was tellin' you, my Daddy used often to say, 'Now seems as good a time as any to give my family here a little instruction. I propose to instruct y'all.' Often's the time he'd begin with those words. So, after he'd tended to Henry Davis an' me, heard us our prayers an' all, why, he'd have Mother bring out her diary from where she kept it in the drawer her side of the bed. It was a pretty diary, I recall, violets and pansies painted all over the front. 'Let's see, let's see,' my Daddy would say as he turned over the pages. 'Let's see now — Lucy, honey, this won't do at all,' he'd say. 'Don't ever use any such phrase as "common as pig-tracks" when writing the English language, honey, no matter what you might say in conversation. Use some word like "vulgar." Erase it, dear; substitute a more elegant expression.' So Mother would take out her little real silver pencil and pull the end off where there was an eraser inside, an' go to work patchin' up what she'd done wrong. And when she'd finish, why, my Daddy would go on correctin' and refinin'. Because my Daddy graduated from the University top of his class, and knew the English language like he knew the front end of a horse.

"Henry Davis an' me, we'd be gawpin' like a couple of little hound puppies, until my Daddy'd see us an' say, 'What the hell you boys doin' in here? Said your prayers, haven't you? Well, go on to bed and mind you live up to what you asked the good Lord to make you be.' I tell you we'd scamper; and tuck our little bottoms under us as we ran. Because my Daddy had a hard hand, Abby," Boogher said. "A big, hard hand." Boogher glanced down sightlessly at his own hands.

"You were going to tell me about the place on your neck," Abby suggested.

"Oh. But I was telling you, first, about how a Southern gentleman behaves with his wife. A couple happily married, as were my own dear father and mother, share everything; and that's a lot when the couple is as richly endowed as were my parents. Mother was just as sweet and pretty! And as gentle as a dove; she would no more have thought of bein' hard and secretive, critical and withholdin', with my father than she would have thought of flyin' to the moon. Because he wouldn't have stood for it, that's why!" Boogher said. "Not that I ever saw my father raise his hand against a woman. He had other ways of governin'. Boss, that's what my father was at Danielstown. Boss to the niggras — took no nonsense. Boss of us boys; I'm grateful for my Daddy showin' me the right way to do, because how in the world would I ever know, without my Daddy taught me to respect him, long ago? An' he bossed my mother too, I can tell you that — oh, he was kind an' courtly, chivalrous and all that. But you could see from the way her eyes follered him, and the way she'd answer him quick — 'Yes,

261

Hubert' — you could see she knew who to respect. He was a real man, my Daddy was, an' my mother was a real woman. She was all woman, like he was all man."

"That isn't supposed to be possible," Abby said.

Boogher turned the eyes of a sleep walker on her. "What do you mean, it's not possible? Of course it's possible. An' it's right, too. I have no use for an effeminate man, any more'n I have for a mannish woman, one that tries to go against nature an' use faculties God didn't endow her with, like ratiocination, an' pittin' her mind against her husband's. I got no use for a woman like that."

"I know," she said. Gradually, and as inexorably as the evening fog stealing up wisp by wisp to envelop the land, the old spell of Boogher's childhood memories was overtaking her.

"So I was reading your diary more as a favor to you, Abby," Boogher continued. "If you were a more feminine kind of woman, you'd be grateful to me for it, too; I remember once hearin' Amelie Nash remark she didn't think a lady kept a secret diary, once her courtin' days were over. There's a lot I could have told you about the use of the English language if you'd ever been interested. I may not be one of your slick New York advertising copy writers, but I had a better education than any of them, Abby. If you'd ever cared to avail yourself of the benefit of it, which you never have done."

"I'm sorry," she said. "I know you have a wonderful education, Boogher."

"It seems a shame and a pity," he said, "that all the treasures of learning, and the storehouses of recorded wisdom — I say, the masterpieces of philosophy, history, and literature — should be shut away for no other reason than that modern so-called authors won't take the time to study. The whole trouble with modern literature is, it's uneducated. Take this feller Jones —"

"But you were telling me about your neck," she said.

"I am coming to my neck," he said. "This feller Jones sets out to give us a picture of life today — tough; primitive. Supposed to be realer that way. Well, sir, what I say is, it ain't real to me, all that loose and undignified behavior before ladies. I thank my stars I was born in a part of the country where the amenities still obtain an' where manners are still cultivated. You hurled some mighty uncivil epithets at me when you departed, Abby," Boogher said. "But I tell you this, I think it is a finer thing to try to be courteous and maybe fail, than not to even try. An' how you ever goin' to have even any violence, Abby," he asked urgently, "if it's violence all the time, like those writers have it? Like if you were to go to bed every time you felt tired, where would you have left to go if you got sick? I thank my stars my Greek has never left me, nor my Latin neither. And it is a matter of self-respect with me to use the King's English. How would I ever know how to speak real rough and mean, on occasion, Abby, if I didn't have somethin' higher from which to descend? As a matter of fact it was while I was readin' a Horatian ode that the realization first struck me of the cross my Cousin Dorothy Ann Augustine bore."

"Who was *she?*" Abby asked. "I just want to know what was wrong with your neck."

"That's precisely what I'm tellin' you, if you would do me the kindness to be still," he said. "Cousin Dorothy Ann Augustine was one of the Tidewater Augustines, the ones at Beauport on the James. Many's the time I've watched Cousin Dorothy Ann, in the days when I was knee-high, and before the cross of her illness came upon her, walkin' down the grass slope from the house to the river with her flat basket on her arm, gatherin' roses for the table from the old rosebushes that were all that was left of the original gyarden at Beauport. Have I ever shown you Beauport, Abby? — Yankees occupy it now."

"Yes, you have," Abby replied.

Boogher gave no sign of having heard. "It is situated just below Westover, and above Berkeley," he said. "And was at that time the property of my Cousins Harry and Dorothy Ann Augustine, she who bore the cross of the Augustine history of cancer."

"Oh!" Abby exclaimed. "Miss Grace did say something on the telephone about the Augustines and their history, but I didn't get the connection! You mean you thought your mole might turn out to be malignant? Oh, Boogher! I didn't realize. You must have been worried sick. Oh — but is everything all right now?"

"Permit me to tell my story in my own way, and stop jumping to conclusions." Boogher lifted a hand to smooth his hair. "I was, as I was saying before, sitting in this chair, reading an ode of Horace — the VIIth. I had just sat down again after having a rather lengthy telephone conversation with Amelie Nash," he added, and paused.

Abby became aware that something was expected of her. "Have you been seeing much of Amelie?" she asked vaguely.

Boogher raised his brows. "A gentleman does not see what you call 'much' of any married lady," he replied. "But yes; Amelie is very charmin', gracious, agreeable company. And no: I have not spent the entire period of your absence

264

clothed in sackcloth and ashes. I'm a man, Abby; a normal, natural man, with a man's normal, natural instincts. You ought not to want your husband to be other than normal and natural."

"Oh, no," Abby said.

He looked at her, dissatisfied. "Picture the routine of my life after my wife had gone off and left me, and without a cause," he continued. "I'd get up in the morning to a cold, cheerless kitchen. Clifford did come in and clean up most every day, but Clifford couldn't be depended on to get here in time for breakfast. He used to get me my dinner."

Abby cast an involuntary glance around. No broken objects at once met her eye, but she could imagine the carnage in the kitchen.

"Then I would go down to the shop," Boogher said. "There customers would ask me — entirely out of the kindness of their hearts — when you were returning. What could I say? How could I reply? I varied my responses. At one time, you were being detained on account of interviews; at another, you were being feted at a series of entertainments. In no case could my heart be other than heavy; my pride other than mortified." Boogher ran his hand over his hair again. "I had no precedent! I can by no stretch of the imagination see my mother going away and leaving my father for more than a night except to visit kin. Nor can I see my Cousin May Beth Richardson going away and leaving old Tad Richardson, or my Auntie Ruth . . . In any case. By the end of the average day I would be very, very tired. Understandably enough under the extraordinary circumstances, I fell into the custom of dropping in at Amelie's, for a little tetch and for the balm that only a womanly woman can apply to a man's wounds. For it *was* a wound you dealt me, Abby," he said gravely. "A real wound. To my pride and to my sensibilities."

"I'm sorry," Abby said.

"I do not feel you have the right to reproach me for any comfort I may have sought in the company of Amelie Nash," he continued, eying her. "It was no more than normal and natural on my part."

"I suppose so," she said, remembering with a flick of self-castigation the night after the party at the Blue Rooster with Tommy Hume.

Boogher snatched a cigarette from the pack lying on the table beside him, and tapped it irritably several times. "To continue. I was telling you about the moment when, seated in the very chair I now occupy, reading Horace, my hand strayed absently to my neck and to the mole I had irritated. A flash of pure horror shot through me. I realized! The association of ideas was obvious: Cousin Dorothy Ann Augustine, moles, the irritation of a mole by a blow or wound, the Augustine susceptibility to cancer. You can perhaps imagine that within two minutes I had telephoned Ernest Weston and made an appointment for the following day."

"— And Ernest was able to relieve your mind," Abby supplied.

"By no means! On the contrary!" Boogher retorted. "I spent a good half an hour in Ernest's waiting room — time that I could ill spare from the shop — waiting in mingled trepidation and the hope that my fears might prove groundless. Finally I was shown into an examining room. I've known Ernest Weston all my life. He was a couple of years behind me at the University. Ernest is a good feller, but a great one for his own importance. It has more than once

266

occurred to me, in the course of my many visits to Ernest's office —"

"Oh, you had to keep going? It wasn't all right after all?" Abby asked.

Boogher looked at her. "Try, if you will, to realize that you are being told the story," he said. "Try to appreciate that you will not know what the outcome was until it is divulged to you. I was saying that it has more than once occurred to me Ernest's office is so organized, with its rabbit warren of separate examining rooms and consultation offices, that a patient might well be kept waiting regardless of whether there were, in actuality, a press of appointments. I may be oversuspicious, but I very much doubt the necessity for the delays I myself experienced. Be that as it may. When I was at length shown into Ernest's *sanctum sanctorum*, I was tense. Very tense indeed. To make a long story short, Ernest examined my neck. 'Boogher,' he said to me, 'I don't like this. It's a right suspicious-looking place. We've got to wait on this.'"

"Oh, darling!" Abby cried spontaneously. "How awful!"

"It was awful indeed. That was only the first of my visits. Ernest insisted it was necessary to wait so that he could observe the progress of the irritated spot — whether or not it did what he called 'regress.' That is to say, in lay terms, whether the very definite lump that had formed did or did not reduce in size."

"Why didn't you write me?" Abby said. "I would have come straight home. This was something real."

"Real?" Boogher said. "Real? Am I to gather you do not consider my pride real? Or my honor real? Or the relation between us as man and wife real? Those deepest, most profound of realities? Is it only a lump on the neck — a mere

267

physical condition which a man should be expected to sustain without whining — that is real to you?"

"Just it's awful to think of you sustaining it," she said. "Go on."

"It was, I think, on my fourth visit that Ernest took the step. 'Boogher,' he said. 'We must have a biopsy of this.' No doubt you don't know the meaning of that technical term. A bit of the tissue involved is examined under the microscope in a pathology laboratory for malignant cells. Meant sendin' it down to the Medical School in Charlottesville, course. 'Come back Friday,' Ernest said. 'We ought to have heard by then.' Well, sir, I walked on out of that doctor's office like I was facin' my death sentence. I was due at one of Miss Grace Starkey's parties, one of those where she and a few of the ladies talk matters out before we gentlemen put in an appearance. I had agreed," Boogher added delicately, "to meet Amelie there."

"Oh," Abby said. She could tell that more was expected of her. But she could not think of what to say. "I expect that was when Miss Grace learned about your trouble."

"Very probably," Boogher said coldly. "Perhaps you can guess how much gaiety I was able to summon to greet my friends with at the party. It would certainly have been the most natural thing in the world if I confided in Miss Grace — an old and valued friend of my family's and a motherly woman. You understand, I hope, the chances were heavily weighted on the side of my inheriting the Augustine susceptibility. The most probable outcome of the whole affair was that I would undergo surgery on the lump on my neck. This would, however, be only a temporary measure. Sooner or later metastasis would set in. A series of operations would follow — first on one, then on another section of my body.

Optimism was a silly, an unrealistic attitude. I had to accept that I was doomed to the identical end so many of my family have met."

"But surely you weren't doomed, darling?" Abby cried. "Surely you're all right now?"

"I do not expect nor wish to transcend the tendencies of my family," Boogher said. "The deaths that they sustained, I also can sustain. 'I have a rendezvous with death,'" he quoted. "'At midnight in some flaming town. And I to my pledged word am true—'"

"If you mean we're all going to die sometime," Abby said, "I suppose you're right. But you can't know how you'll die."

"*I* can," Boogher said. "I am a Daniel and an Augustine. And partly a Harrison."

"You still don't know how you'll die," Abby protested. "You might be hit by a truck."

"I see your absence has not changed you," Boogher said. "Not that I imagined it would. You are still the same critical, argumentative Yankee."

"I'm sorry," Abby said.

"I suppose you can't help it," Boogher said. "If I may continue. The hours until Friday — today, that is — passed on leaden feet. You have never suffered, you can't know what it is to try to find thoughts, any thoughts, to fill the ghastly interstices between the minutes of a dread-filled day. What I would have given for one calm and cheering reflection! But what happy thought was there for me to think?" he asked, bending his gaze on Abby.

"You make me feel dreadfully," she said.

"Dear Abby," he said. "I seem to remember that you were always a little late with your sympathy and your attentions. I will spare you a detailed description of the days I passed until I was to hear my verdict. Suffice it to say that this morning I appeared for my appointment with Ernest and was kept waiting a long time. Doctors appear not to be the most sensitive of men. It may be the agonies they are forced to witness render them callous. At all events, 'Be the day short or be it long, At length it cometh to evensong.' "

"My God!" Abby cried. "You mean he kept you waiting all day?"

"No, no. That was a quotation, Abby dear. My name was eventually called, and the little ceremony which Ernest seems to have devised duly enacted: a nurse conducts me to an examining room, where she leaves me and I unbutton the collar of my shirt. The nurse reappears, heralding the approach of the great man himself. Finally there is the entry into the examining room of old Ernest, lookin' like he thought he was the Lord God of Israel. Well, sir, I was scared clean down to the bottom of my fundament; I can tell you that. All I could do was just sit there on that cold enamel stool, waitin' for what he was goin' to tell me. Seemed hours. 'Boogher,' he said at last, 'seems we got no cause for alarm,' said. 'Seems the test shows the slight cyst that has formed,' said, pokin' around in my neck, 'is benign. An' I'm glad to inform you,' said, 'that the swellin' has reduced significantly.' Well, sir, I want to tell you I busted out of that old doctor's office like a bat straight out of hell. If I hadn't been who I am I would have skipped. Gret day in the mornin', I was ready to jump right top of the cars parked alongside of the street, or kiss every girl I met, or either turn handsprings down Bolling Avenue, one."

"What *did* you do?" Abby said, smiling.

"I went to see Amelie," he said, throwing her a sidelong glance.

"Well, I'm just delighted at the outcome of your troubles," Abby said. "It's all simply wonderful."

Boogher's face fell. Abby became aware that Boogher had not only had a love affair of more or less extent with Amelie during her absence, but was perishing to tell her so and to boast that he, too, had been up to no good. The code debarring him from doing so was almost tangible. Boogher had got into an inarguable situation where self had no choice but to frustrate self.

Abby did the kind thing. "I'm glad you had Amelie to go to," she said. "She's always been mad for you. I used to notice her at parties, following you with her eyes. It must have been a big thrill for her, when I went away and left her free to make a play for you. Armistead must have been fearfully jealous."

A gratified look stole over Boogher's features. He did not reply directly; he would never be able to refer by word or deed to whatever had transpired between Amelie and himself. But he did not contradict Abby. "I see that your vocabulary has been affected by your visit to New York," he contented himself with saying. "And not for the better. 'Mad for you,' 'make a play for you,' indeed!"

Abby tried to imagine this afternoon, when a reprieved and joyful Boogher had paid a call on Amelie. Did they embrace? Did they kiss? Or did they only talk, as Boogher was continuing to talk now, in a mixture of colloquialisms and high-flown verbiage?

"Old Ernest Weston, I knew him when he was no bigger than a mayfly down yonder at the University, and now he's settin' up to *be* somebody. I consider the medical profession to have exceeded all bounds in its pretensions, and to be vying with God himself for the right to dispose of man's hopes and fears. Who's old Ernest Weston to keep me on tenterhooks nigh on a month? Why didn't he go on have that old test made before, so he could tell me nothin' in the world ails me, long ago? I consider his dilatory tactics self-important and offensive to a degree."

There ensued a silence. Abby became aware that Boogher was staring fixedly at her. "I presume," he said, "that residence in the metropolis may have rendered you more or less impervious to more simple — if more heartfelt — attentions."

"Oh, darling," Abby said helplessly, "if you want to make love to me, why not say so?"

"It seems to me you have acquired a definite veneer of sophistication," Boogher said huffily.

"Darling, I'm not repulsing you," she said. "You *are* my husband."

"But not the type of husband to assert marital rights by force," he replied. "Simply I had become aware of the promptings of the Cyprian."

Abby came and sat on the arm of Boogher's chair. "Darling," she said, stroking his red hair, "you're the boss."

"Why do you always have to pronounce it bahss?" he asked. "The word is bawss."

"You are the bawss, bawss," she said, kissing his cheek.

There was a silence.

"Let's go to bed," Abby said in desperation.

"If you are fatigued, you must of course retire," he said. He jerked his head away from her, and his hand went up to smooth his hair.

"I didn't mean that," she said.

"What did you mean?" he asked. "If I may presume to inquire."

"I'm trying to show you," she said, kissing him.

"Why must you always be so damned calm about it?" he said.

"Why do you always have to get so angry?" she said.

"But I'm a Daniel!" he began, outraged. Then he gave a groan at the incommunicability of human needs, and pulled Abby off the arm of the chair into his lap.

3

I'm sorry," she said, "I guess I'm tired."

In the darkness of the bedroom they lay, not seeing each other; only imagining the other's wishes, preferences, abhorrences; lost in a wider darkness than the bedroom's.

"You're such a cold woman," he complained. "Critical. Unyielding."

"I'm really not," her voice said. "Really."

What they said made little difference.

"You seem to expect me to be some sort of hero," he went on. "God knows what a woman like you does expect. Something went on, up there in New York. Did somebody spoil you for normal, natural relations with your husband?"

"No," she said, "I promise you I was true to you."

"Then what *is* the matter?" He spoke to the woman in the darkness with him; Circe perhaps; a vast alarming female creature. "Why . . ."

"Perhaps I'm just tired," she repeated helplessly into the dark, to the invisible representative of that which despoils,

274

which brings down change and suffering. They were silent. Then she said, "Boogher. Maybe . . ."

"Maybe what?" he whispered. *Maybe some night in the dark the one password would be happened upon, the one keynote struck . . .*

"Boogher, what do you suppose your father and mother used to do?"

There was a silence in the dark bedroom. They lay, little and speechless, in this heroic crucible, waiting, minds filled with self-doubt. Gradually night overtook them and their doubts were, not resolved, but mounted over. Now they could be anybody, anywhere; beautiful or great. Old models possessed them, and they existed not now but always. Shadows sang to them, images strode for them and led them in the wild enormous paths.

Back in herself at last, Abby wondered, as she settled herself for the night, whether anything might come of this; whether she might have a child.

But she never had become pregnant. And what kind of a child could possibly be conceived — her thoughts, becoming sleepily crazy, wandered on — by a woman who was not just Abby and her own mother, but Boogher's mother too, and other myths and goddesses? By a man not only Boogher but his father too, and all the other fathers? What real child could possibly be born, she thought going to sleep, of what was only the past; nothing, nothing, but the past?

4

I FORGOT to pass on to you last night, in the heat of this and of that," Boogher said at breakfast, lifting his eyebrows archly at Abby, "Miss Grace said to tell you she wants you to help out this afternoon. She's entertaining the Tuesday Club. They've got an authoress down from New York to speak, Eulalie Hobson Howe. I ordered twenty-five copies of her new novel for the shop, and I b'lieve I'm liable to sell them all. *Peregrine Place.*"

"I met her when I was up North," Abby said. With a sudden yearning for something undefinable, she took a large helping of marmalade.

"You say you did? My little wife moved in exalted circles, didn't she?" Boogher commented comfortably. His ruddy cheeks shone from the razor, his red hair was wet and sleek, and he was wearing his best dressing gown over his trousers and shirt. "Roll the rolls down and quit muffin around," he chuckled. It was his favorite pun.

"There isn't anything very exalted about *her*," Abby said. "She writes trash."

"Ah, ah!" Boogher shook a forefinger at her. "Mustn't give way to jealousy! We can't all sell a million copies of our latest novel!"

"I'm *not* jealous," Abby said; but without hope of being believed. She had certainly come home. All was as it always had been. She had, it was true, found that in New York her name was highly thought of, but she had been reasonably sure of that before she went away. She had furthermore found that, out in the world, all was not beer, skittles, and a literary reputation. Involved, in addition, was the making of certain types of decision — highly distressing types — which back in Starkeyville, at least, one need never give a thought to. But this discovery, too, she might have figured out for herself without expense of time and money, and with no change of scene.

At the moment, fatigued as she was in the early morning, she could not call to mind any point whatever in her having gone to New York. She would far better have remained here at home where people might be hypocritical, but no more hypocritical than people proved to be in other places. What she was experiencing, she reflected, must be what was called disillusionment. She appeared to be undergoing it rather late in life, like most things. I am immature, she thought drearily.

"Miss Grace said to tell you to be there at two sharp," Boogher said. "The lecture is to begin at three, to be followed by tea."

It dawned on Abby that of course Boogher must have known perfectly well all along she was coming home. Miss Grace must have told him about the long-distance telephone conversation. That brown study, before an empty grate, Greek author in hand, that Abby had discovered him in had been the sheerest posturing. What a fake! Abby exclaimed inwardly, remembering the succession of astonished expressions which had crossed Boogher's face at sight of his returned prodigal.

Yet there was no point in repining. Boogher would never change. Suddenly she experienced a wild impulse to run away. She had an impulse to write a book against Boogher. She had a third impulse, to put prussic acid in his food.

There it was: her sin. She pounced upon it with a self-castigatory severity that was, at least, reassuringly familiar. With her New York education in psychological motivations, she was able to tell herself that her unconscious attempt in the past to kill Boogher had not been a joke or an irritated impulse or a figure of speech. There existed the terrible and incontrovertible evidence of the Listerine bottle that she had put Clorox in. The fact that he had not, in fact, drunk the Clorox had no bearing on the case. Nothing Abby could ever do to make amends for her sin would be too much.

In an access of horror she sprang from the table and hurried into the kitchen. Imagine lolling sybaritically in bed all night with the poison still out there! Boogher might quite as well have gargled with it this morning as at any time during her absence.

With shaking hands she opened the cabinet to the left under the sink. There the Listerine bottle stood, next to a newer, a legitimate Clorox bottle; innocent-looking, lethal as a gun. Abby took the cap off and smelled it. Sure enough: Clorox. Hurriedly she poured the contents down the drain.

She snatched the remaining rolls from the oven where they had been keeping hot and took them in to Boogher.

As she handed them to him, she felt like Judas, and touched his hair in penitent caress. He looked up at her, smiling.

"Whose little fuzzy-wuzzy wish-wash are you?" he inquired, with a trace of the W. C. Fields imitation.

"Yours," she replied obediently. "I'm *so* glad everything is all right and there's nothing the matter with your neck."

He rubbed his chin against her arm.

"Just, I wish you could have told me so last night, right away," she continued. "That everything is all right. I was worried sick. Why did you have to make such a long story of it?"

Boogher looked up at her. His shining face bore an expression of faintly shamefaced trust. He blinked. "Because I wanted you to sympathize with me," he said.

Abby sat down and opened a fresh roll. Her heart smote her. Perhaps the reason she had been capable of committing such an enormity as the attempt to kill her own husband had been that she had never really tried to understand him. She had never sympathized with him. She had been so wrapped up in her own frustrations in Starkeyville that she had overlooked Boogher's own problems, which seemed to her now — in the light of last night's recitation together with this morning's simple confession — heartbreakingly important.

Poor Boogher. She could not say it out loud without offending him, but she could say it in her heart. Poor, timid, uncertain Boogher, forever in the shadow of an overpoweringly punitive father; yearning for the soft breast of a forbidden mother; driven to self-justifications to still the gnawing doubt lashing at him like the switches of his boyhood. No wonder he was so awful, she reflected; no wonder he talked in that absurd fashion. His tradition required him to be at the same time obedient son, masterful husband, loyal Southerner, and polished classicist.

"Oh, darling," she said earnestly, leaning across the table and laying her hand on his, "I really will be a good wife to you." At the moment she was sure this was a resolve that she had never before made.

"Good," he said. He wiped his mouth with his napkin, cast the napkin into his plate, and rose. "See that you are. I put my foot down," he said, raising his eyebrows roguishly as he put on the jacket he had hung over the back of a chair, "on any more trips away without me. And on any more clandestine novel writing. Next time I will assist you!" He shook his forefinger at her.

"Of course," Abby cried, practicing selflessness and the new conviction that Boogher's mannerisms were not his own fault. "I intend to devote myself to making up to you for all the things I've done in the past."

Nevertheless, as she cleared the breakfast table after Boogher had left, Abby could not avoid a sudden vision of how nice it would be if, this afternoon, Mrs. Howe should call Starkeyville's attention to the jewel within its breast. "It is a rare pleasure," Abby could hear her beginning her lecture, "to find myself in a city which can claim among its proudest boasts that distinguished young writer, Abigail Woodbury Daniel."

5

WHEN white Starkeyville had a celebrity to entertain, it spared no efforts to entertain him. (Brownsville was different. Its celebrities were all jazz artists, and entertaining was mutual, amid cries of "Go, man, go!") A celebrity of the stature of Eulalie Hobson Howe — author of the sweet stories so in demand at the Library that new copies had constantly to be bought to replace the old, velvety ones — called for the utmost in hospitality that Starkeyville could summon.

When Abby reached Mrs. Starkey's house its rooms were already a-flutter with ladies who had come to put finishing touches on the floral arrangements and to set up the folding chairs from Bell & Hargrave's in drawing room, dining room, and hall against the forthcoming lecture.

"Ha, Abby!" cried Relia Fenn, hustling through the hall with Miss Grace's best silver water pitcher, which had been buried out in the garden at Azalea during the War, to put on the card table that the speaker would stand behind. "Ha yew?"

Mrs. Starkey came hustling right in after Mrs. Fenn.

"Relia, honey, you know we don't want that old pitcher in yere yet. Take it on out to the pantry, hear? Till time to bring it in filled with water case Miz Howe is taken with a coughing spell," she directed. Then she spied Abby. "Or, no. Here's Abby Daniel, let her do it. Abby, child, make it your sacred responsibility to see that pitcher is on the speaker's table, filled with the coldest of ice water, when the time comes. Abby," she went on, lowering her tones from their customary heights of command, "certainly am glad you came on back, child. Never did see a man need a woman like Boogher's been needing you. I'll hand it to you," she declared. "You always did know how to manage the Daniel disposition."

It appeared that at the moment Mrs. Howe was being entertained at luncheon by Lady Barbara Parkinson, at Azalea. Abby chided herself for her own instant reaction of feeling left out. After all, nobody had known she was home.

On the other hand, she could not help reflecting as she mopped up water that somebody had spilled in carrying a vase full of russet chrysanthemums, nobody seemed to realize she had been away, either. "Abby Daniel," Miss Lilybud Carter scolded as she hurried up with a clean embroidered cloth to put on the speaker's table, "where you are, you're right square in my walkway."

Abby found herself wondering where Amelie Nash was. Perhaps out at the Azalea luncheon party. "Miss Grace," she asked, cornering her hostess as she stood leaning to rest from the labors of command against the newel of the stairs in the front hall, "who's at the lunch for Mrs. Howe, do you know?"

"Certainly I know, child," Miss Grace replied. "Havin' told Lady Barbara who to ask. Men. Men can't come to meetings of the Tuesday Club, course, and it was felt Miz Howe might enjoy mingling in mixed company in the middle of the day. I sat down and drew up a list of those I thought Miz Howe might be expected to enjoy talking with; our most interesting and representative Starkeyvillians. Fred and Lucy Whiting, Rushton and Annette Barr, Armistead and Amelie. As for myself," she added without false modesty, "I felt the need more pressing for me to stay home and fix everything nice."

"I met Mrs. Howe when I was in New York," Abby said. "At a party that was given for me," she felt impelled to add.

"Mercy, honey, that's just wonderful!" Mrs. Starkey exclaimed. "— But I reckon you may have got to meet right many celebrities, didn't you, one way and another?"

"Well, I did, yes," Abby said furiously. "Because I am a celebrity myself."

"Honey, I know," Miss Grace said. "But down here we think of you more as just plain old Abby Daniel."

Unaccustomed bit in teeth, Abby said, "I know you do." She drew a quivering breath. "You've never given me the slightest recognition. That's why I had to go away to New York — to get recognition."

"Why, Abby Daniel," Miss Grace said, laughing heartily. "Honey, you're just as crazy! You never said boo-turkey to anybody about any writing you ever did. You didn't even sign that old book when you *did* write it. You veiled your literary endeavors in the deepest of secrecy, so naturally we assumed you didn't want to talk about them."

"And then the news that I wrote *The Rose That Died* came out," Abby plunged on, "and still nobody paid any attention to me. Nobody ever lionized *me*," she said bitterly. "Nobody ever asked *me* to lecture to the Tuesday Club!"

"Why should they, honey? You *come* from here!" Miss Grace exclaimed. She hesitated, and trimmed her sails. "I've gone to endless trouble, keeping everybody from talking to you about your book; you showed us, plainly and evidently, that you didn't want to discuss it. If it was praise you wanted, concealing the fact you wrote the book for so long was a mighty funny way of showing it! I told every single separate member of the Tuesday Club, I said, 'Don't you go plaguing Abby Daniel about that old book of hers,' I said, 'because she just don't want to discuss it with us. Let her have her peace and privacy,' " I said.

Abby was still riding the crest. "All you ever wanted," she raged, "was to use me as your slavey at parties. All you wanted from me was a willing hand. You just wanted plain old Abby Daniel to be there when you needed her."

"But child," Miss Grace said, staring. "Didn't you like to help? You always *said* you liked being one of us. You always declared you were crazy about it down here. If you didn't want to help out at parties, why didn't you say so? If you just wanted to be some little old literary celebrity or other, why didn't you just come on out with it? — I think it was right hypocritical of you not to, Abby Daniel," Miss Grace Starkey said. "*Right* hypocritical."

"None of you ever showed me any attention," Abby continued. But the torrent's drive had broken.

"Why, child, we showed you love," Miss Grace said. "What you reckon love is, hm? It ain't adulation, that's one thing certain sure. I declare, I never will understand Yankees."

"You mean *I* was hypocritical?" Abby asked slowly.

But Relia Fenn was plucking at Miss Grace's sleeve asking what was to be done with the tea sandwiches for later

— put them on plates, or leave them where they were in the refrigerator?

"Put them on the Delaunay Canton platters, Relia," Miss Grace said, reassuming command. "Cover them with clean tea towels wrung out in cold water. Wrung out tight, honey!"

Miss Lilybud Carter was waving a frantic hand from the now filling drawing room, where one of the undertaker's chairs had collapsed under a chubby member of the Tuesday Club. Miss Grace marched away to deal with the situation, as imposing-looking as an army with banners.

High-pitched sweet voices were raised in concerted excitement at the front door as Lady Barbara's scream heralded the approach of the afternoon's lioness. "But how fright-ful!" Lady Barbara cried. "I *don't* see how you endure such grueling la-bor!" From the living room Mrs. Starkey, brushing aside those who came in her way, swam forward toward the front door as within its frame appeared the majestic lavender-clad bulk of Eulalie Hobson Howe.

"Certainly am glad to welcome you to my home, Miz Howe!" she cried. The two women, both elderly, both vast, shook hands. "Come right on in! Looking forward *so* much to hearing you talk about your writing! So charming and delightful! We're all devoted readers." Miss Grace's hostess eye fell on Abby, still standing, motionless, by the newel post. "Come yere, child," she commanded; to Mrs. Howe she said, "Let me present to you our own little aspirant to literary fame. Would the name Abigail Woodbury Daniel mean anything to you, Miz Howe?"

"It would indeed," Mrs. Howe replied, extending a plump, ringed hand. "And so we meet again," she went on. "I remember well our first encounter when, all interest

285

and eagerness, I asked you how you had ever come to publish a novel anonymously. I must confess I felt my friendliness dashed when you refused to reply candidly. I had been feeling so waggy-tailed toward you," Mrs. Howe said. Her eyes gazed sadly at Abby over the mounds, as of delicately rose-tinted marshmallow, that were her cheeks.

"But you didn't understand!" Abby said.

Miss Grace Starkey looked from Abby to Mrs. Howe and back; she was trying with all her might to size up and deal with the social situation. "We always felt Abby was reluctant to put the Daniel name on public view," she began. Then possible implications of her remark as they affected Mrs. Howe occurred to her. "Abby has always been a reticent, selfless child," she started afresh. That, too, seemed now to strike a false note. "— Or so we had always thought," she added. She turned from Mrs. Howe to Abby, a maneuver resembling the wheeling of a battalion. "Why *did* you write your novel anonymously, child?" she demanded.

Abby looked into the two large, self-assured old faces turned upon her. Her mind struggled to grasp its own significance; to put into communicable form what felt so real. "Because I couldn't commit myself," she essayed. It was not what she meant. "Because I hadn't any self to commit."

"Stuff," said Eulalie Hobson Howe; Miss Grace Starkey merely looked her scornful incredulity.

All around them ladies were thronging in, to attend the lecture and to partake of one of Mrs. B. D. Starkey's teas — dressed in their best getups for the coming winter season, if possible from Montaldo's in Richmond or Garfinkel's in Washington, if not possible, then reincarnated by virtue of a new hat, a scarf, a pair of red shoes, or Aunt

May-May Gordon's real diamond pin. "Ha, Miss Grace," they piped, eying the speaker with healthy curiosity. They did not linger. The great thing now was to secure a good seat, preferably one in the drawing room where Mrs. Howe would be, instead of stuck out in the hall or back in the dining room along with the cups and saucers. Their turn would come to meet Eulalie Hobson Howe, they knew. Entertaining for the visiting celebrity was by no means over with the approaching tea. There would be the cocktail party given by the Fred Whitings, and the Nashes' dinner at the Country Club, to be followed by a large soirée. They would all have an opportunity to meet her and to produce whatever remark they had been polishing for the moment. Now they pushed, bosom against bosom, thigh against pneumatic thigh, into the rows of Bell & Hargrave's chairs.

"I should like to withdraw," Mrs. Howe said to Mrs. Starkey. "Is there a small chamber, somewhat apart, where I could be alone? I always precede my public appearances with a few moments of quiet meditation."

"Yes indeed," Miss Grace replied. "I'm afraid the drawing room and the dining room and the hall are right jammed this minute, and the kitchen wouldn't do because Mattie's out there, but you could go upstairs." Then she threw the comprehending glance of one very stout woman at another. "Or would the downstairs toilet serve?"

"I shall make it serve," Mrs. Howe declared.

As she followed her hostess down the hall between two blocks of chairs, she could be observed drawing from her large, black pin-seal handbag copies of *Epictetus*, the *Spiritual Exercises of St. Ignatius*, and the *Bhagavad-Gita*. Mrs. Starkey opened the door on a large closet that had been

287

equipped with the usual conveniences when Miss Grace got too heavy to go up and down stairs with ease. She assisted her guest into this space with a friendly and understanding shove from behind, and closed the door after her.

"Right spiritual," she observed to Lucy Whiting, who had followed along behind. "Right dedicated. We may expect an inspiring lecture." She cast a wrathful glance toward Abby Daniel, still hanging around the newel post like some old mayfly, being of no use or inspiration to anybody, doubtless just getting up steam to say something else pert, saucy, and difficult to squirm out of to her elders, and hurried off to deal with whatever required dealing with in the living room.

As the moments passed, the high-pitched babel of the Tuesday Club in session, which Fred Whiting always swore he could hear clear down to Courthouse Square, dropped several decibels and the sort of expectant hush which precedes the opening bars of "Lohengrin" at a wedding began to settle. Abby Daniel slipped down the side of the rows of seats in the living room and perched on one of the deep window sills, sharing it with a potted fern.

Everywhere glances were being thrown backwards, to the entrance. Too tightly buttoned jackets were being loosened; handkerchiefs were being waved to cool heated brows and bosoms. All at once there was a definite catch in the psychic atmosphere, and down between the banks of chairs marched, first, dimpling and scared to death, Amelie Nash, whose election as this year's president of the Tuesday Club represented a compromise between the old guard and too drastically new blood like Annette Barr; then Eulalie Hobson Howe, a juggernaut in lavender; and, bringing up the rear like a sort of subsidiary juggernaut sent along to clean up the victims, Mrs. B. D. Starkey in her gun-metal. Miss Grace had no particular function to fulfill up at the speaker's table, but it had been felt that this was, after all, her own house, and she did so love marching up.

The ladies settled themselves in the three chairs that had been placed behind the card table, Amelie in the middle, the two monoliths flanking her. As close to a silence as could fall at a meeting of the Tuesday Club fell.

Amelie, in a blue wool dress with a square-cut neck that showed where her collarbones would have been if plump pretty flesh had not covered them, coughed and glanced from Mrs. Howe to Mrs. Starkey. But they were both staring magnificently ahead. She stood up, hesitantly. "Will the meetin' please come to order," she said in the tiny voice of a very little girl. She cleared her throat. "Will the meetin' please come to order," she said somewhat louder.

She had only accepted this old presidency because she had allowed herself to be advised that it was her civic duty to. "Y'all need no introduction to this afternoon's speaker. I mean, our speaker this afternoon needs no introduction," she said. She heaved a long, quivering sigh. With visibly shaking fingers she drew from her little bead bag some remarks her adviser had written down for her in case she got stuck. She *had* got stuck.

"Suffice it to say," she began to read from her slip of paper. The timbre of her voice altered completely, became confident and oratorical. "We are about to have the pleasure of listening to one who may, with justice, be called one of America's beloved storytellers; nay, its best-beloved. The millions of readers of her novels, both in serialized and in book form, bear witness that in the field of romance she plucks the very heartstrings of the country.

"She was born in Callaway County, Missouri, and thus claims with us her audience a common Southern heritage. As the wife of the late Perkin B. Howe, of New York, she carried out for many years the combined duties of hostess, mother, and civic leader with unfailing distinction and graciousness. But deep in her heart shone always the lodestar of literary aspiration, and even before her three children were born she had set her mark on American letters with such early works as *My Spirit's a Rainbow Cloud* and *Hush the Hot Heart*. It was with the publication in 1932 of *Gracious Lady*, however, that she attracted the national attention which, at the time, was rivaled only by that accorded the closing of the banks."

Amelie paused. She had been led to believe that this was a joke. But nobody laughed. For what was there funny about the banks closing? The reference recalled only Franklin D. Roosevelt and that unladylike wife of his who precipitated this whole racial mess. Amelie continued.

"Indefatigable —" she stumbled over the long word, "traveler, internationally known hostess, citizen of the world, the prestige of her private personality rivals that of her public fame. It may be confidently asserted that no American author even approaches her for popular, appealing, wholesome artistry."

At this point Amelie's notes ran out, and with them her platform manner. Speaking once more in that tiny little girl's voice, she continued. "So it gives me the greatest of pleasure to introduce to y'all —" she looked frantically back at her piece of paper, and by it was saved "— Eulalie Hobson Howe . . . At this time," she concluded, beaming. The addition was an inspiration of her own. She sat down amid applause.

Abby Daniel, in her window niche, had the sensation of coming to after a dream. The voice she had been listening to was Amelie Nash's, but the words seemed to her to have been unmistakably Boogher's. No one else in Starkeyville could have composed just that introduction — ornate, rotund in its periods, complete with crack about no other American author even approaching Mrs. Howe, which Abby took to be aimed directly at herself.

But instead of resentment she felt only worried pity. For how perfectly matched they were, Boogher and Amelie; he with his elaborate education that dovetailed with Amelie's lack of any information whatsoever; he with his need for self-justification, she with her instinct to justify anybody in trousers; he conditioned to accept in himself nothing short of complete masculinity, she unequipped for anything but utter femininity. Together they seemed to make a whole. Abby experienced a pang that, instead, things should be as they were: Amelie married to chilly Armistead, Boogher to herself in an imperfect, jangling, make-do relationship. Abby felt another such wave of acute self-reproach coming on as the one this morning at breakfast. The wave was stemmed by the voice of Eulalie Hobson Howe, who had gotten to her feet and stood before the assembled ladies. If her bulk seemed to loom startlingly large, her voice boomed out even more startlingly strong.

"Thank you from my heart, Mrs. Nash, for your gracious introduction," she said, in the authoritative and faintly reproving tones which had given audiences all over the country such a feeling of confidence in her. "Naturally it is a joy to find myself once more in our beloved Southland. My dear mother was a Virginian," she said, and paused for the inevitable patter of pleased whisperings. "I myself, as a bride, came with my bridegroom on our honeymoon, to lave us in the cool wave at Virginia Beach. Too, throughout my life I have carried in memory those lovely lines, doubtless familiar to you all, that begin, 'The sunshine nowhere beams so bright, As in Virginia . . .' "

She paused. So much for the South.

"Just how do I compose my works? — I know that is what you are all waiting to hear," she continued. "What breeze wafted to me the first whisper of a theme for *Peregrine Place?* What manna did Heaven drop down to nourish me as I sat penning *Land of Magnolia?* Let me say at once that I sense a sacred responsibility to bring to birth no literary offspring not conceived in purity and beauty. Long ago I swore that never would I indite one line I would not be willing and eager to show my own daughter, my Deborah — now herself the mother of four in Short Hills, New Jersey. I think I may say in all honesty that my flag has never been struck, in the face of the indecency, the filth, the moral squalor that threaten us from the pages of so-called literature today. I may say with St. Paul, that I have kept the faith."

A sympathetic coo answered her from the audience. Abby prepared to stop paying the slightest attention and to leave Mrs. Howe to clean literature and St. Paul. She experienced the melancholy satisfaction of realizing that she was probably the only person in the room who considered Mrs. Howe a perfectly horrible writer. But she had a great deal on her mind of a worrying nature, and now she leaned back against the curtains and set herself to worry about it.

Not only had she nurtured murder in her heart; it turned out that she was a hypocrite as well. After all her outrage at the Southerners' claims to perfection, after all her hurt at the Humes for not telling her they had wearied of giving her a good time, it appeared that she herself was the greatest hypocrite of all. A nightmare vision flashed across her fancy, of going from one place to another, from one group of friends to another, rejecting all of them in turn for their hypocrisy, when all the time the vice was resident in her own breast.

It was obvious to her now that she had always wanted recognition, passionately. Andrew had been right, everybody wanted recognition; but she, Abby, had been so filled with false modesty, so cowardly, that she had never asked for what she wanted. Ask and it shall be given unto you, Abby repeated reproachfully to herself. Then she was struck by the ghastly suspicion that her mind might be working like that of Eulalie Hobson Howe.

Having failed to insist on recognition, she had nonetheless been furious with the Starkeyvillians for not giving it to her. Miss Grace had said, just now in the hall, "But you always said you liked being one of us." She *had* said it, too. What could have been more hypocritical, if she wanted to be something quite different? But it had never seemed, to Abby, quite nice not to admire people. One pushed one's negative sentiments down and behaved as though — as though one were all goodness and love, Abby realized with a shock; without dislikes, prejudices, or aversions. One acted as though one were perfect. Suddenly Tommy Hume's voice came back to her, raised in exasperation: "You're not really human, did you know that?"

It dawned upon Abby, cradled in her window niche, that it *had* been only adulation she had craved, just as Miss Grace suggested. It was as if she had wanted to inspire the same fear and awe that she herself once felt for the self-assured, the aristocratic Starkeyvillians. But they were not really to be feared, she saw. Poor souls, they made themselves an identity out of such bits and pieces as citizenship of a state, membership in a family, haughtiness about Yankees, finickiness about birthplaces. They deserved not awe but compassion. And no doubt they, too, might enjoy getting a little recognition, not as gods but as human beings. Abby felt herself bathed in the old familiar sensation of pity — a vast sea of pity for everybody on earth.

Her reflections were suddenly broken into by Mrs. Howe's basso voice saying, "As I begin to draw the curtain across the peep I have given you into my inner world of faerie, I would like to make some recognition in passing of the presence in your midst of one of our younger authoresses. To such as she, perhaps, my failing hands must one day pass the oriflamme that I have held so high."

Mrs. Howe paused before administering the chastisement she contemplated. Andrew Fellowes had been right when he said Mrs. Howe's real creative talent lay in the invention of fictions about those who offended her. To do her justice, in the present case she had managed to confuse two young women, both of whom had, she felt, been rude to her at the Walters' party. The two had become so integrated in Mrs. Howe's mind that now they were the same. This one brash young woman had just now compounded her original discourtesy by being insufferably impertinent out in the hall before the lecture.

While wedged into the downstairs toilet, Mrs. Howe had meditated upon what would be the most telling way to deal out the correction she felt it as much her duty to inflict as she had long ago felt it a duty personally to whip her little daughter Deborah. In a spiritual sense, indeed, and in the line of literary succession, the present erring young female could be viewed in the light of a daughter. "Om," she had repeated in the privacy of the toilet, experiencing a sense of close harmony with the Absolute. "Om. Peace. Peace. Peace." It was revealed unto her that what might do the saucy child the most good would be to let her good, kind friends here at home know what she had been up to, of late.

"It is my fond hope," she resumed, "now that this budding scrivener has returned from Dominica, where, Dame Rumor has it, she was the constant companion of the expatriate author, Harrington, she will soon favor us with another of her charming romances. Be that as it may," Mrs. Howe said, shifting back into omniscient gear, "here is the thought with which I would leave you. When you peruse my works, think of me as one standing fast for the finest in literature, who will give America only what is good for it."

How do you go about suing somebody? was Abby's first thought. The question collapsed in her mind like a bubble pricked by the pin of futility. She knew her Starkeyville. All the lawyers in Courthouse Square, all the suits conceivable, could not clean up that little nest of gossip.

Annette Barr came hurrying by the window niche. "Why, Abby Daniel!" she cried. "I swear! And I thought all that time you were in New York!"

"I was," Abby began, but Annette hurried on. This is what I get for wishing Mrs. Howe would recognize me publicly, Abby reflected. Pride goeth before a fall, and a haughty spirit before destruction. Maybe I really am going to turn into a Bible-quoting author like Mrs. Howe, she thought; maybe she really did just hand me that oriflamme.

6

Bᴀᴄᴋ in the apartment, Abby waited with growing trepidation for Boogher to come home. It got to be six, then six-thirty. The store closed at five, and Boogher usually reached Starkey Street within a quarter of an hour. Where was he? What was happening? Where was Abby supposed to be? This morning, when Boogher had told her that her services were needed at Miss Grace's, he had not mentioned the remainder of the entertaining for Mrs. Howe: the cocktail party, Amelie's dinner, the soirée. It was more than probable that Boogher was invited to all of them. Abby had escaped from Miss Grace's as soon as possible after the nightmare lecture, not even pausing to take tea. No one would have had the opportunity to come up to her with an invitation, even if it were not likely everyone had assumed Boogher would simply bring Abby along to the parties, now she had got home again.

Got home again from where? Questions jumped at her as though out of dark corners. Had someone hurried away from the tea and down to the bookstore to notify Boogher of his wife's interesting recent whereabouts? Was a large delegation even now calling upon him to impart the glad tidings? What, direful thought, would be his reaction? Was he seeing a lawyer at this moment? Buying a gun? Or had he moved already to the Hotel General Starkey without more ado, intending to send for his clothes?

Oh dear, Abby thought gazing anxiously out of the window; the trouble with having an imagination for writing novels with was that you continued to have an imagination on less appropriate occasions. He that lives by the fancy must die by the fancy, she reflected. The ideas thronging her mind were most improbable; on the other hand, what could be keeping Boogher? It was no fancy that he was absolutely sure to hear the preposterous canard about Abby which Mrs. Howe had set afloat on the babbling waters of Starkeyville society. Another fact was that he was going to be furious; unimaginably furious.

A third fact was that it was going to be difficult to persuade him that the rumor he had heard was sheerest invention. Nobody from Starkeyville had seen Abby in New York in the weeks that she was there. Why should she not have been in Dominica all that time, keeping a convenience address in New York?

This time she really was in for trouble, Abby reflected, and at that moment saw Boogher coming down the sidewalk from the corner of Bolling Avenue with Fred Whiting. Her heart sank. She had braced herself for the impending storm, and now she would have to wait for it to break until old Fred went away. She turned from the window. It was amazing how guilty one could feel about something one had not done.

"Ah, there!" Boogher said, entering the apartment after

Fred. He threw his hat over onto the bookcase and kissed Abby. His breath smelled of liquor.

"Well, charming lady!" Fred declaimed, bowing over Abby's hand. "A real pleasure to welcome you back!"

Charming lady; was it a cynical euphemism? Abby could think of nothing to say but, lamely to Boogher, "I was wondering where you were."

"Detained, my dear; detained," Boogher said. And now Abby was almost positive he had heard the news. He seldom called her "my dear" except when he was in a rage. Her heart began to pound painfully. "There has been a slight change in social schedule," Boogher added.

"Bunch of us boys are whooping it up at the Malamute Saloon," Fred contributed. He, too, seemed to have had a few drinks.

"Which, being interpreted," Boogher said, "is to say that a number of alumni are foregathering here in a minute or two. Since the dinner party planned for the evening is unexpectedly kaput, its guests have been reorganized on other lines. The gentlemen involved decided they would like to get in training for the Homecoming Game at Charlottesville tomorrow, and the ladies proved to feel not only complaisant but very hungry."

"But Mrs. Howe —" Abby began.

"Ah, Mrs. Howe." Boogher looked wise. "A remarkable breed, the genus literary lady."

Abby waited. She was unable to see how whatever had happened could be her fault, but in the state she was in it seemed more than probable that she was responsible for any calamity.

"Miz Howe bitched us," Fred said. "Apol'gize for my language."

298

"It happened thusly," Boogher said, sitting down in one of the corduroy armchairs and leaning back; his manner appeared more than usually ornate. "As you have no doubt learned, the ladies had planned a number of fetes for her who addressed you this afternoon. Simple, rustic entertainments they would no doubt have seemed, after the type of sophisticated revelry to which one from the metropolis may be accustomed. Nonetheless they were planned with the pleasure of the honoree as their sole object." Boogher paused. "Be that as it may," he continued. "Directly after partaking of a single cup of tea at Miss Grace Starkey's, Mrs. Howe informed her hostess that she intended leaving Starkeyville in a matter of moments. A car, she said, was being sent to fetch her."

"Poor old Lucy," Fred said, referring to his wife. "Fit to be tied."

"They were all fit to be, in your phrase, tied," Boogher agreed. "But you may imagine they did not hesitate to expostulate. They laid before the lady the plans that had been made for her. Plans which she had of course been informed of earlier, in the letter, note, or whatever missive had been dispatched giving the details of her impending visit. Representations were now made to her that whoever was calling for her would be made welcome at the merrymaking. But Mrs. Howe was adamant. One is forced to assume that, once she had collected the check handed her at the close of her lecture, she took no further interest in the proceedings. She wrote finis to her Starkeyville venture."

"Said, 'To hell with you!' " Fred suggested.

"In spirit, if not in so many words," Boogher agreed. "Shortly thereafter, while the ladies, in great distress, were still attempting to persuade Mrs. Howe to change her mind, a large automobile of expensive make drew up at the front entrance to Mrs. Starkey's residence, and a chauffeur came to the door with the message that it awaited Mrs. Howe. On being so informed, that lady forthwith took her departure in classic Yankee style — with more speed than graciousness. Perhaps the most shocking part of all —"

"The real stinger," Fred interpolated.

"— was that when the lady made her, I am assured, somewhat elephantine progress down the front walk, a presence was seen to alight, allowing the lady to precede him into the back seat. A presence that conveyed a particularly disturbing significance to many of our good and agitated ladies. A presence, in short, whose collar was dog and whose shirt front purple."

"God-damned bishop," Fred said.

"She did seem very religious," Abby observed.

"A pity, then," Boogher said, "that such Christian principles as the Golden Rule have not affected Mrs. Howe's idea of behavior. I am sure she would not herself enjoy the anguish she caused her hostesses today."

"They *will* overentertain celebrities," Abby heard herself say.

"Oh?" Boogher enquired, glacially.

"Seems like to me you're runnin' a temperance meetin' here, bwah," Fred said. "Somebody say somethin' about a drink?"

"Right away," Boogher said, jumping up. "Abby, ice!"

"How in the world can we ever beat old Vanderbilt tomorrer if we don't do a little preliminary warmin' up, bwah?" Fred continued.

"We sure as hell can't, boy," Boogher said, going toward the liquor cabinet in the sitting room.

As Abby was filling the ice bucket at the sink, Boogher came out to the kitchen. "What do you want to do about dinner?" Abby asked him in a low voice. The pounding of her heart had somewhat subsided. Boogher's indignation at Mrs. Howe and her behavior, his mellowed condition, had produced in her the hope that by some miracle he might not yet have heard the Dominica story; or that, having heard it, he was by another miracle not convinced. Perhaps he was too mad at Mrs. Howe to be mad at anybody else. Perhaps he was so mad at Mrs. Howe he wouldn't believe anything she said. "Do you want me to get something to eat together?" Abby added.

"If so, of the simplest," Boogher replied. "Put yourself to no great inconvenience, since the taste of the evening will incline, I fancy, more to liquid than to solid refreshment — A few sandwiches," he said, on inspiration. "Cut us a few sandwiches. Nothing at all elaborate."

Abby could not but reflect, after Boogher had gone back to the sitting room carrying the ice, that it was lucky she had stocked up on bread when she marketed this morning. She drew a long breath. Now was as good a time as any to begin practicing the good resolutions of the morning, to be a good wife. Perhaps if she were a good enough wife, Heaven would reward her by so arranging it that Boogher viewed the Dominica business with other than an angry eye. Perhaps if she had been a better wife in the past, he would not have been angry with her so often, she told herself; though without conviction.

The front door could be heard opening and shutting several times. Abby recognized the voices of Armistead Nash, of Rushton Barr, of Robbie Fenn; loyal sons of the University whose voices were shortly raised in song:

> Come, fill your glasses up
> For Tilka, for Tilka, for Tilka . . .

Rebellion in other factions of the ranks seemed to develop, and in a few moments the song of the rival society arose:

> Eli Banana, Eli Banana . . .
> It's not the first time, nor yet the last time,
> That we go on a hell of a bum, bum, bum . . .

Shortly before nine o'clock Abby carried a big platter of sandwiches in to them. Rushton Barr was sitting in one of the corduroy chairs, his glass held out at arm's length, talking to Armistead Nash with great intensity, accompanied by gestures. "What kind a team you gon' have," he was saying, "under those kind circumstances? Hm? Ever since the God-damn Gooch Report . . ." He waved his arm in emphasis and a gout of whisky sprang up from the glass and plopped onto the rug.

Boogher, Robbie Fenn, and old Fred Whiting stood in front of the fireplace in a huddle, heads together, listening to their own close harmony. "Ba . . . Ba . . . black-bird . . ." they sang softly.

Somebody saw Abby putting the sandwiches on the table, and a momentary pall fell. The song stopped. Those seated rose.

"Ha, Abby," Armistead Nash said, coming forward and shaking hands. "Glad to see you back." The others stood, smiling politely, looking toward her with abstracted eyes. They were waiting till she went away to go back to contemplation of days past, the great days at the University; to making a reality out of memory; a present out of what was over and grew lovelier, dearer, the further away it got. In alma mater they were one. Animosities — dislikes as of Boogher Daniel — were forgotten. They came from old Virginia where all was bright and gay.

When Abby returned at half-past-ten to get the sandwich platter, the fraternal bond had strengthened to a point where excerpts from an almost mythical record called "Two Black Crows" were being recited. Fred Whiting and Army Nash, the two oldest, were the only ones who had ever heard the actual record. The rest had only had it quoted to them by upperclassmen when they were at the University, or used, as now, for a sort of litany during such evenings as they were currently creating.

"You wouldn't *be* broke if you'd go to work," Rushton Barr was saying to Robbie Fenn. Rushton's necktie was loosened and its knot had worked around to the side. He gazed earnestly at Robbie and spoke with a thick Negro accent.

"Ah would work if Ah could find any plai-sure in it," Robbie replied. The richest man in Starkeyville lay back, coatless, in his deep chair, stomach protruding.

"Look at all that black smoke! Bet that old *fire*man's busy," Fred Whiting interjected, for the ritual did not require sticking to the original sequence of the dialogue.

No one got up as Abby entered this time, nor did she disturb the atmosphere of unity that flowed between them all.

"Ah-ha!" Boogher exclaimed, spying her as she picked up some ashtrays to carry out to the kitchen. "My little fuzzy-wuzzy wish-wash!" The endearment was not really directed at Abby, it was another bit of the ritual — the famous W. C. Fields imitation. Boogher had cocked an imaginary derby over one eye, and worked an imaginary cigar around in his mouth.

Armistead Nash sat somewhat apart. His chin rested on his chest; he seemed to have dropped out of the order of service. "Wonder could I have lil soda?" he said as Abby passed him. "Settle my stomach."

His host caught his words and reinforced them. "Soda, my little fuzzy-wuzzy wish-wash!" he commanded. Suddenly the imaginary derby disappeared, to be replaced by an imaginary boater hat. The imaginary cigar dropped from an under lip which was instead thrust out. "Not tomorrow, not next veek, but rrrrright-now!" Boogher declared, moving without the slightest hitch into his other famous imitation, the Maurice Chevalier one.

Abby brought a teaspoonful of soda dissolved in half a glass of water to Armistead, and went back to the kitchen to wash the sandwich platter and put it away. She wiped the ashtrays with a damp cloth and took them into the sitting room. A huddle had been formed once more, before the fireplace, that included Armistead. They were singing:

> When the red, red robin comes bob, bob, bobbin'
> Along . . . along . . .
> There'll be no more sobbin' when he starts throbbin'
> His old . . . sweet song . . .

There would be no more sobbing; no more regrets; no more shrill and incommodious reality. Their arms were around each other's shoulders, their heads were bowed in harmony. "Live . . . Laugh . . . Love and be happy," they sang, meaning every word of it. Abby did not need to tiptoe; in the dear land where they were, she had no existence. As she was leaving the room the song ended and

Robbie Fenn raised his head from the huddle. He looked up at the ceiling, his flabby face wearing a blind and dedicated look. "You take peas, and soak them in vinegar, and when they swell up, they is olives," he declared ecstatically. The others looked their Amen.

Abby went into the bedroom and lay down. She tried for a time to continue reading *Mrs. Dalloway*. As she dropped asleep, she heard from the sitting room the voices singing, deep, soft, and harmonious, "Sweet Sue . . . It's you . . ."

She was awakened some time later by Boogher moving around the bedroom. The light was on; she had never turned it off. Boogher was hanging his jacket over the back of a chair.

"What time is it?" Abby asked, rolling over on the bed. She still had her dress on.

"Go to sleep," Boogher said.

Abby sat up. "I have to get undressed first."

Boogher groaned. "Oh, God," he said. "It's so dismal to come back here and find *you*. Can't you just go on to sleep?" He did not sound drunk, only depressed; only bitter.

The sharp pounding of Abby's heart brought her awake. "What's the matter?" she asked.

"Nothing's the matter. Everything's the matter. Don't let's discuss it."

Abby jumped off the bed. "We must discuss it," she said feverishly. "Is it that absurd story Mrs. Howe put about, that I was in Dominica?"

Boogher gave a heavy sigh and sat down in front of the dressing table. He put his head in his hands. "Don't let's discuss it," he repeated. "I'm so tired."

"We must discuss it! Don't you realize it's perfectly preposterous? I've never been to Dominica in my life! I could telephone, right now, to all sorts of people who could tell you I was in New York the whole time I was away."

"No doubt," he said.

"I never even met Harrington," she said, "until the day before I came home."

"I should like to go to bed now. If I may," Boogher said.

"Please don't be nasty! Listen to me!" she cried.

"I thought I was being very polite," he said. "Considerably in excess of what the situation demands, in fact."

"As far as I can see, you really did have some kind of affair with Amelie while I was away," she said. "Whereas, I tell you, I've only just *met* Harrington . . ."

"Any more accusations you would like to dredge up to level against me?" he asked. "If not, may I again apply for permission to retire? On second thoughts, I prefer to sleep in the sitting room, I think. It is more attractive to me — or shall we say, less unattractive — than here."

"But I didn't go to Dominica!" she cried. "I don't know Harrington! Why don't you believe me? It's the truth!"

Boogher groaned again. "You force me into a situation which is distasteful to me; which is not of my own choosing. Why should I believe you have been true to me? Why should I expect to find you changed? You have never before thought of anybody but yourself."

"I know," she said impatiently.

"You have always craved publicity, attention. To be the center of the stage."

"Yes, I know," she said.

Boogher was warming up. Fatigue had left his face and he stared at Abby with burning intensity. "Notoriety is what you have always sought," he continued. "It hasn't been enough for you to be married. Mere love hasn't satisfied you."

"That's right," she began.

Boogher raised his hand for silence. "It's all very easy to agree, but the fact is you have always put your personal success above my happiness, above modesty, above every other consideration."

"I know, I know," she said.

"— Displaying complete egotism," he said.

"Yes," she said. "Isn't it funny, I used to feel thinking badly of yourself wasn't thinking of yourself . . ."

But Boogher was not listening. A glaze had settled over his eyes. It came to Abby that he was comparing her with some dream of his mother.

"You've been tough," he said. "Hard."

She nodded.

"Unfeeling. Selfish."

"I'm anything you say," she agreed.

His eyes, lit by fanatic fires, stared through her. "You never even loved me!" he exclaimed. "You said you loved me! You told me and told me that you loved me. But you never did."

Abby stared back.

"And yet you dare bring up *my* behavior!" Boogher cried. "You dare deny what appears to be common knowledge — that you have been consorting with a notorious character like Harrington!"

"But I *didn't* consort with him," Abby said.

Boogher groaned; his face was dark and heavy.

"I just didn't," she said again.

"You've always been ruthless," he muttered. "Ruthless!"

307

She shrugged her shoulders.

"Oh, well," he said.

"Just this morning, at breakfast," she said, "I was thinking how much I want to be a good wife to you. I want to make up for the things I didn't realize."

"Charming," Boogher said.

"Can't you just believe this one thing? I hardly know Harrington, and I've never been to Dominica."

There was a long silence.

Boogher rose from the dressing-table bench and walked over to the bed where Abby sat. "I am what is known as the complaisant husband, it seems," he said. "I find myself not averse to the promptings of the Cyprian."

"How can you think of such a thing!" Abby cried, staring back at his unseeing eyes. "How can you?"

"Why not?" he said. His hand went up to smooth his red hair. "I have always affirmed you have many charms."

"But it's impossible," she said.

"Ah, but it's very possible!" he said. "You were just now asserting a most laudable and to-be-encouraged wish to be a good wife to me; I am affording you an opportunity."

"But it would be hypocritical," she said. "If I don't love you."

7

I FIGURED I'd take off and go to the game today," Boogher remarked after a subdued breakfast.

Abby's first impulse was to ask if he wanted her to go with him. She suppressed it with some relief, reminding herself that the duties of the loving wife — that goal she was so far from achieving — included refraining from, as well as making, self-sacrifices. Boogher was sure to prefer to go alone, or rather with the men with whom he had shared last evening's mystique. She contented herself with saying, "That will be nice. Have you got a ride to Charlottesville?"

"I do not propose to walk the fifty-odd miles thither, no," he replied, smoothing his red hair. "Rushton Barr has offered to drive me."

Abby looked at his arched and haughty eyebrows, and concentrated hard upon her Aunt Ernestine Brewster, of Brattleboro, Vermont, who had often been heard to say, in Abby's childhood, that though she had married Uncle Cal without love, she was rewarded when the respect and esteem she bore him blossomed into a more tender sentiment. Perhaps the capacity ran in the family. A radiant future might possibly be in store for the Daniels, also, Abby sighed and began to gather up the coffee things.

"It would be nice, though quite unheard of," Boogher observed, rising from the table, "if some day you should volunteer to take over the duties of the shop when I plan, as today, to be out of town."

"Oh, Boogher!" Abby said; she sat the coffee cups down again with a clatter. "It's never occurred to me!"

"Obviously," he said. He wiped his lips with his napkin and cast it into his plate.

"But I'll do it!" she cried, anxious to atone for anything and everything. "I'll wash up and go down right now."

"Too late, I'm afraid," Boogher replied briskly. "Mrs. Harmon is in charge although usually, as you know, she doesn't work Saturdays."

"We could telephone her; I could," Abby said feverishly. "And tell her she could take today off."

"My dear," Boogher said, "I'm afraid that the wheel of business, in which my own concern is a tiny cog, cannot suddenly be reversed to satisfy the sudden whims to be of service of every impulsive wife."

Abby subsided.

"Doing the work of others is not the same thing as thinking of others," Boogher continued.

He had never said a truer word, Abby thought after he had gone. Boogher had always been full of true words. In a momentary clearing of the mists befogging memory, she remembered the day at lunch at Reidecker's when Boogher had made that remark to Tommy, "If we waited till what's

worthy of our love came along, our love would rust away."
At its wisdom, Abby, standing over the kitchen sink, felt
moved almost to tears. Boogher was filled with wisdom and
truth and good things; it was just that on top he was so awful.

And, she assured herself, as she washed the dishes and
dried them, more and more she was coming to understand
the reasons for his awfulness. There was a cause behind
every one of his mannerisms. At the bottom of them all
shrank Boogher's tiny, suffering self, nearly strangled by
its own efforts to pull esteem in after it. Boogher was awful
but human; someone locked up within the traditions he
had been raised to admire. Often at parties Abby had
thought of Boogher as being like a child showing off — unable to moderate his behavior for sheer excitement; now,
however, as her self-reproach waxed, it seemed to her that
he was actually more mature than she. She was only beginning to find her identity; he already had one. She was
like one lying at the bottom of a well only dreaming of the
future, she reflected as she poured some of the new Clorox
into the rinse water to whiten the dishtowels. It seemed to
her that Boogher, angry with her as he had often been, was
coming closer to thinking about her then, however nega-
tively, than she had ever come to thinking about him.

Tout comprendre, c'est tout pardonner, she thought
with considerable exaltation, wiping off the tops of the
table and the stove with a damp dishcloth. Maybe if she
could just come to appreciate Boogher's latent superiority,
love would burst, in her loveless heart, like a bomb.

The ring of the doorbell punctured her meditations. It
was Clifford Joy, standing outside the front door.

"Mownin'," he said, ambling in and stuffing his moldy

311

green felt hat into the pocket of his old jacket. It seemed impossible the elastic band which apparently connected his limbs still had any stretch in it; feet, hands, elbows, knees fell here and there without discernible central control. "Mister Boogher, he say for me to come wash he's dishes," Clifford said. "Mus' I do it now, Miz Daniel?"

"No, Clifford," Abby said patiently. "I have come home, you see. I have washed the dishes. There is, however, plenty of work for you to do. I see the windows need washing again. I would like you to take the whole day to it, and wash as many as you can get done."

"I done washed them all, that time," Clifford said wistfully.

"But that was a long while ago, wasn't it, Clifford?" she asked.

"Yes, ma'am," Clifford said obediently. "Reckon so."

"Well, then, let's get started. I'll help you get the vinegar and water."

"Yes, ma'am," Clifford said. He took his old hat out of his pocket. The hand holding it approached, in an approximate way, his head. "I be back."

"But Clifford!" Abby cried. "You mustn't go! You already intended to stay and get Mr. Boogher's dishes done," she reminded him.

"I wasn't studyin' bout washin' no winders," he explained. "I be back. I got me a regagement on Parson's Hill. I fixin' to come right back an' wash the winders," he added; conciliatory, anxious to please.

"But when, Clifford?" Abby pressed. "Promise you'll come back today."

He grinned, and scratched an armpit. Promises were jailhouses. The only safe regagements were on Parson's

Hill. The sole freedom the Negro possessed here, Abby thought as she had thought so many times before, was the freedom to slide out from under, to refuse to be pinned down. He had the freedom not to commit himself in any way. But I am not a poor Negro, Abby's mind continued mysteriously, striking out into unexplored territory; I can commit myself.

"I fixin' to come back real soon," Clifford assured her.

"On second thought, Clifford," Abby said, "you needn't come back after all. I won't be needing you. I've decided I'll wash the windows myself, or get somebody more responsible."

"Yes ma'am, Miz Daniel," he said. He was willing to agree with anybody; even with a Yankee lady who would wash a window herself. "I be seein' y'all." He turned and began the disjointed performance of ambling out again.

"Don't bother to come back," she called after him. Even as the words left her lips she knew they were wasted. Clifford would be back. He would come back to see Mr. Boogher, who understood him. Clifford had never paid too much mind to what white folks told him, anyway.

But if Clifford came back she could just send him away again, Abby said to herself. She drew a deep breath of freedom as she went back to the kitchen; freedom from having to be paternalistic to Clifford. Inefficient, slow, certain to break fifty per cent of what he touched, he was just not worth employing. She felt an exhilarating sense of sailing contrary to the prevailing wind. I am the master of my fate, she thought; I am the captain of my soul. She wrung the dish towels out of their rinse water, hung them on the rack by the window to dry, picked up the big Clorox bottle she had left beside the sink, saw that most of it had been used up during her absence, looked about for something smaller to put the remainder in, and took from the trash can on her right a discarded Lavoris bottle.

Then she set both bottles on the work surface and sat down heavily in a kitchen chair. I'm trying to kill him again, Abby thought. All I seem to be interested in is killing poor, pathetic, long-suffering, tortured Boogher. She waited for the familiar answering pang of remorse.

Instead the cold realization filled her mind, If I don't love him, and if I want to kill him, I'd better go away. All that about my understanding everything and forgiving everything is all very well, but Boogher isn't safe in the house with me.

She got to her feet and went sadly to pack the bag she had so lately unpacked. The apartment had never looked so sunny and pretty. The suit which Boogher had worn yesterday was thrown over the back of a chair in the bedroom. Abby could not forbear clucking, for a last time, at Boogher's inability to keep his clothes in any sort of order. She wrapped the trousers up within the jacket to take along with her when she went to the station.

Abby paced up and down the platform of the Southern Railway Station waiting for the northbound 12:50 train. She had bought a ticket to Washington, for she supposed she might as well go back to New York, in spite of the insoluble problems which appeared to exist in what Boogher would call the metropolis, and the decisions that they would inevitably thrust upon her. Recoiling from that prospect, her mind reverted to the note she had left in the apartment, pinned in the classic location on a pillow of the bed. It had ended, as handsomely as she could make it, "I

314

realize that my going off constitutes one more way in which I have failed you as a wife." But she had not been able to resist adding, "However, I have never been to Dominica."

Her meditations were disturbed by the approach of Miss Lilybud Carter, who came scuttling down the platform like a busy mouse, carrying a number of packages in a string bag. Miss Lilybud must have business in Washington. Perhaps she was taking one of her famous illuminated family trees to present to some favored friend.

"Good afternoon, Miss Lilybud," Abby said as the mouse came abreast. But Miss Lilybud cast one horrified glance at her and scurried past. In the position in life she occupied, born as she had been in the Valley of Virginia, it had always been somewhat of a social risk to be seen talking to a Yankee like Abby Daniel. Now that scandal had touched the picture, Abby realized, there was even less question of it. I am in bad odor in Starkeyville, she reflected; and all because of something that never happened.

With a steady tooting of the whistle and a cloud of smoke, the earlier train, the southbound 12:44, steamed slowly into the station. Brakes screamed, the engine wheezed as if expiring, and the train came to a shuddering halt. Mr. Grimes the conductor stepped down from one of the three old coaches and turned to give a hand to the passengers alighting, some of whom had reached their destination, other of whom would take the air, while the 12:44 stood, for three minutes, taking on mail. Abby stood watching them get off: the perennial stout motherly woman with the perennial bunch of flowers; the giggling teen-age girls with their freshly washed hair; the man one never saw anywhere but on this train — gray all over, born to be anonymous, without hope, born to travel on trains. These were followed after a moment by a man in a brown suit; rather small; unimpressive physically except for a black beard. It was Harrington.

Abby looked away. But as he walked in her direction recognition came into Harrington's face and he lifted his brown hat. "Evenin'," he said. "Aren't you Abigail Woodbury Daniel?"

"Yes," she said. "How did you remember my name? It's so long."

"It is," he said. "But I read your book, other night."

She could think of nothing to reply, yet, looking into his eyes, lit by the wicked light of intelligence, she felt entirely at ease.

"It ain't bad," he continued. "Only don't let's us talk about books. Where you goin'?"

"New York, I guess," she said. "I don't feel very sure where — I'm running away," she felt impelled to add.

The wicked light in the brown eyes strengthened. "So'm I," Harrington said.

"Where are *you* going?" she enquired.

Harrington turned to buy a paper from the colored boy hawking the William and Mary *Messenger* up and down the platform.

"I'm goin' clear to New Awlans," he said. "Aimin' to go the hard way. Takin' trains an' boats. I do despise an airplane, of all things." Harrington hesitated. "Come on go," he said.

"But I've bought my ticket to Washington," she said. Harrington did not even reply. He went on looking at her intelligently. "All right," she said.

Up in the engine the engineer whose name nobody knew pulled the string and the whistle blew with fretful urgency. "Bo-ard!" called Mr. Grimes. Among those strolling up and down to enjoy the cool October weather, there was a scramble for the steps. Harrington let everybody else go first, then helped Abby up into his coach.

As he was turning over the back of a seat to make a double space for them to sit in, Abby stood in the aisle, scooching down to catch a last glimpse of Starkeyville spread over its temple-crowned hill, radiant in the autumn sunshine. "I just love Starkeyville," she remarked as she took her seat beside Harrington. "Starkeyville's not what I was ever mad at, really."

Harrington settled his small, neat person against the gritty plush seat back. "This is right snug," he said. Opening a leather bag he had placed on the seat opposite them, he drew forth a leather-covered flask and several Hershey bars. He laid the candy out, invitingly, on the opposite seat. "Just a jiffy," he said, getting up. He went down to the back of the car where a tube of paper cups hung lopsidedly beside a sorry-looking water cooler, and returned with a number of cups. He unscrewed the top from the flask, poured drinks into two cups held in one hand, and handed one to Abby. "This is the first sip of the day, for me," he said.

"Me too."

They tasted the strong, living ichor gravely and looked approvingly at each other.

"Who you runnin' away from?" he enquired.

"My husband. It wasn't safe for me to stay with him. Who are you?" she said.

"Not exactly my wife," he replied. "Man, that's what I mean! When you get out of somethin', you know you want to stay out."

They drew long sighs and leaned back comfortably. After

a moment Abby said, not raising her head, "But I thought you were an expatriate."

"My native land ain't what I need to get shed of, right this moment," Harrington explained.

Another silence fell.

"S'pose I while away the time readin' to you," Harrington suggested. Abby sipped at her drink as he began to report the local news which was all the *Messenger* carried. "You'll be glad to hear the bond issue for the new bridge was floated," he said. "Man named Taliaferro's been made cashier of the bank. Word has reached the *Messenger*, it says here, that Miss May Gunn has landed in New York after an extended tour of the Continent. Man named Nash dropped dead in his office with a coronary occlusion."

"He did?" Abby said. "Then I guess I won't be needed at home."

"Good," Harrington said. "Board of Supervisors voted to supply a new school bus for children in Buggsville, wherever in the wide world that is." He turned over the page. "Well, now, it says here Mrs. B. D. Starkey is entertaining a few friends on Monday afternoon at tea, to be followed by cocktails."

Abby wriggled uneasily in her seat. "I hope she'll manage all right," she said, "with me not there to help her."

"You'll be somewhere round about Rocky Mount, North Carolina, way I figure our i-tinerary," Harrington said. "Course, you understand that ain't the direct route to New Awlans."

"I suppose not."

"You ready for another drink? Or would a Hershey bar sit well?"

"A drink, please."

318

"First sip may taste the best," Harrington said as he filled their cups again. "But the second is more warmin' to the heart. An' the third drink gets to movin' in toward the soul.' The train gave one of its uncalled for, racking lurches, and Harrington's pouring hand shook. "Pshaw," he said. "We can't afford to spill a damned drop."

Up from the seat in front of them shot, like a jack-in-the-box, Miss Lilybud Carter, whose diminutive stature had hitherto concealed from them the top of her head; the next stop the train would make was Oat Hill, where Miss Lilybud was spending the night with kin. She drew her possessions to her. "Good day, Miz Daniel," she said with awful distinctness. "Good day, *Mister* Harrington." She swept down to the end of the car with a loud sniff.

Abby thought of the gossip at Miss Grace's next Monday afternoon, after this. The truth would be lost irretrievably; it had probably just now gone down for the third time. The doors of Starkeyville had just shut against her with a loud clang.

As usual, Abby reacted in rejection of the inevitable. "Oh dear," she said. "Maybe I ought to go back and explain."

Harrington shook his head, and took a sip from the cup he held. With the other hand he made an expressive gesture as if to recall Abby to the whisky, the Hershey bars, the newspaper, and other present joys. "Man, when there's a choice," he said, "like the psy-chologists say, between fight an' flight, I fly."

"I don't think *I* do," Abby said worriedly. "I think I more fight."

Harrington viewed the meager form and small, triangular white face beside him. "I don't know your weight," he said, "but you look mighty unpugilistic to me. Take the

319

lady to whom I had reference a while back. She was a nasty infighter, I mean to say. Ever'body's got the urge to kill *one* time or another, but she and I — man, that was bad! Like old G.B.S. said, ain't no struggle so treacherous and relentless as the struggle between the artist man and the mother woman. I was gettin' right involved with a mother woman, there, for a while," he said reflectively.

Abby was frantically squirming into her coat and reaching for her suitcase. "I've got to go back," she said, breathless. "I don't know what I've been thinking of! I never wanted to kill anybody. I never even tried to. I've *always* put old Clorox in old bottles, all my life. Good-by."

"What in the world you talkin' about, child?" Harrington said. He put out a hand to detain her, but she had gone. The train was shuddering to its Oat Hill stop.

Abby climbed down the steps in the rear of Miss Lilybud. When they had attained the platform, Miss Lilybud threw her one look and scurried off; but the look had been full of perplexity. It was possible that Miss Lilybud would always believe it had been her implied reproof that had in the nick of time saved Abby from a life of shame.

Abby walked down the platform toward a bench where she could sit down and wait for the next train back. Ahead, men were loading gray canvas sacks of mail onto the train.

"You don't make a particle of sense to me," Harrington's voice said, just above her. He had opened the window and put his head out.

"I'll write and explain," she called up to him. "Where will you be?" The train gave a racking jerk and began to move again.

"Double-Seven Hotel. . . ." his voice floated back to her. ". . . Good Children Street."

8

W HEN Abby, breathless from hurrying, opened the door of the Starkey Street apartment, it was upon chaos. Boogher stood in the middle of the sitting room peeling off his trousers, which seemed to be sopping wet. His topcoat was thrown into one corner, his jacket in another, and there was mud all over the rug. His shoes, caked with red mud, were placed side by side in front of the fireplace.

"Well!" Boogher began when he saw Abby. He faced her in singlet and shorts — tall, red-haired, skinny-shanked. "About time."

"Wait a moment," Abby said.

She went into the bedroom. To her relief, the note was still pinned to the pillow; she unpinned it, tore it up, and threw it into the wastebasket. Only afterwards she realized it might have been better to let Boogher find it and realize how close he had come to losing her.

She went slowly back into the sitting room. "What on earth happened?" she said as she began automatically to pick up Boogher's clothes.

"Would you be so kind as to fetch me a dressing gown?" he asked with some asperity. "Or would you prefer that I stand here catching my death of cold while you satisfy your curiosity as to my condition?"

"Condition?" Abby began; then she saw his cheek. Dried blood streaked down from a cut and the cheek was beginning to swell. It was so dirty that it was impossible to see whether it was bruised or not. "But you're hurt!" she cried.

"A sympathy which expressed itself in acts would be more welcome," Boogher replied.

When Abby returned with his flannel bathrobe Boogher was lighting the fire.

"Here, put this on," she said. "Heavens! I never saw such a mess in my life!"

"By all means re-establish order, if that is your wish. I shall warm myself by the fire, if I am not in your way, and presently I shall take a bath." Boogher ran one shaking hand over his roughened hair.

"Oh, darling," Abby said helplessly. She drew a long breath. "Tell me what happened to you."

A smile penetrated Boogher's hauteur. "Well, sir," he began, crouching down on the hearth rug before the fire, which had begun to roar. "My day has been a right curious one. Not at all what I anticipated when, this morning, I left Starkeyville full of innocent anticipation of the athletic contest between my alma mater and Vanderbilt, the odds on ultimate victory being, moreover, with the University."

"The University of Virginia, you mean," Abby amplified.

"That's what I said," Boogher replied. "As I was saying, by no stretch of the imagination could I have prophesied the hazards I was in fact to encounter. A ten-mile walk through the wilds of the Ragged Mountains; a wild ride with a drunken stranger in an out-of-date automobile; the misadventure of being stuck in a Ford miles from human habitation; getting wet to the skin in a charitable attempt to assist in dislodging the vehicle; an entrance into Starkey-ville seated in a trailer truck —"

"But what happened to your face?" Abby interrupted.

Boogher made a small, exasperated sound. "Must you be so importunate? Try, if you will, to listen to the story which you insisted upon being told. I set off, as I was saying, in sanguine mood. The countryside was fair, never fairer; the air brisk; every prospect favorable. It was upsetting, to say the least, to find myself an hour later standing at a cross-roads, forty miles from home, instead of approaching the sounds of revelry and cheering which invariably attend a homecoming game at Charlottesville. Nevertheless, my Daddy raised me to b'lieve a man doesn't whimper or run about in circles; he deals with the situation as it may re-quire. Now, it chanced that I recalled a short cut through the Ragged Mountains, known first to me when, as an un-dergraduate, I used to make forays, more picaresque than legitimate, back to Woolwalk's Hollow in search of that life-giving commodity known as corn. Without more ado, I set off at a brisk pace —"

"You mean you never got to the game?" Abby exclaimed. "What happened? Did Rushton's car break down?"

"Well," Boogher said. "Not to say break down. Thing is, I wasn't goin' to shake that bastard's hand nor ride in his car either, for all his protestations about forgive and forget. He can purely go to hell. No one's goin' to insult me an' then come weaselin' round with forgives and forgets." Boogher ran his hand over his hair. "So, like I was sayin', I struck off into those big old mountains, havin' the i-dea I'd come out round about Elvira, and so thumb my way back home on Route 43. Tell you the truth," Boogher said. "I had some i-dea of revisitin' the scenes of my youth. Hadn't been back up past Woolwalk's Holler since I was knee-high. So —"

"You mean you fought with Rushton Barr?" Abby interrupted. "But Boogher! He's twice as heavy as you are! And he's younger, too."

"Aw, most of that weight's flab," Boogher said. "Like I was sayin' —"

"And that's how your cheek got cut? Oh, Boogher!" Abby cried, marveling at his courage.

"Please." Boogher raised his hand for silence. "Like I was sayin', I went on up that mountain road fast as I could sprint. Time went by an' I began suspectin' I was on the wrong track. One road looks mighty like another back up there in those old Ragged Mountains. The trees I passed didn't look like any trees I ever saw; but I said to myself they might have grown some since I was at the University. Then I saw a shack, sittin' up on a knoll, had two chimneys, one each end, and I knew I hadn't ever seen any mountain shack got two chimneys. One's all —"

"Boogher. Listen. You didn't fight Rushton on account of me, did you? Because of anything he said about Dominica?"

"Abby, for God's sake," Boogher said, "Credit me with some modicum of the manly virtues. — Like I said, I figured I was just as lost as hell when I saw that old —"

"And you hadn't even believed me, either," Abby said. Tears sprang to her eyes. She got up and went over to

324

stare hard out of the back window at the afternoon sunshine bathing Bolling Avenue.

"Right about then an old Model T came tremblin' and bucketin' down the road toward me, and I figured I better catch me a ride, even though it *did* look like it couldn't make it more'n about a mile further. So when I climbed up there side of the old drunk man drivin', name of Woodbine, course — ever'body that part of the country's named Woodbine or Woolwalk, one — I mean to tell you —"

Against the continuing sound of Boogher's voice raised in narrative, Abby stared on at the scene outside the window. She had never even dreamed he would stand up for her in anything; yet now he had fought an outsider for her, without so much as belief in the truth of what he was fighting for; out of that quality, known here as chivalry, which back in Vermont they called cussedness. Now that he had, she could with curious ease imagine him out there in the broad Virginia country, fighting Rushton Barr by the side of some October road, climbing the lonely hills toward home on his long legs like a man striding on stilts. It seemed that he could always surprise her; she could never quite catch up to Boogher. He was, in the end, inscrutable.

From far down on the other side of Starkeyville's hill Abby heard the 5:02 train whistling as it steamed into the Southern Station on its way to Washington and the world. Her mind, all at once released, ranged far out, glancing off what it touched: Andrew and Edith, Tommy and Elsa; her friends, with all of whom she shared some common trait or other, and who, she felt, would all seem different to her now, when she saw them next. Her feeling, gradually withdrawing its range, moved to rest upon the stocky figure of Mr. Parabel Greene, stumping up Bolling Avenue

325

with the newspaper under his arm, on the way home from his law office.

Out of a window in one of the turrets of the Rumsey house, two feminine heads were suddenly thrust like the two nubs of a forked stick. They looked up the street and then down — for whom? for what? — and were as suddenly withdrawn. Across the street Mrs. Harry Scott Greene sat rocking on her front porch; her enormous girth was said to be partly accounted for by the presence under her skirt of four petticoats, a chamois-leather money purse, and a Smith-Wesson revolver. Further up Bolling Avenue near the corner of Starkey Street, somebody had hung a bunch of purple chrysanthemums tied with a black crape bow outside the Nashes' house. Amelie might be visualized inside weeping, surrounded by condolatory layer cakes. Next door to her was the old Barr place, Rushton's mother's, which had a ghost, a beautiful mulatto slave sometimes seen at midnight rushing out of the front door with hair streaming. Beyond lived Annette and Rushton, Miss Grace Starkey, old Fred and Lucy Whiting; all the Daniels' friends. Here in Starkeyville is the wide and various world, too, Abby thought; mysteriously rich and true, and she a part of it.

"Well, sir, I climbed down out of that old Model T and dog if the water didn't come clear up to my knees, just about," Boogher was saying. His recounting voice dwindled off, uncertain. "But perhaps I bore you, with my admittedly unprofessional storytelling?"

Abby turned from the scene outside. She went and crouched down on the hearth rug before the fire next to Boogher. "I get *all* my ideas from you," she declared with a rush of emotion.

"I trust not," Boogher said. "I trust you retain some suitable core of originality." He gave her arm three rapid pats. "It is not my wish to pry into the nature of your, no doubt, pressing engagements," he said. "But may one ask you to tell where you have been, this afternoon?"

Abby gazed for a moment before replying, back at his lifted eyebrows and curled lip; he was so arch, so elaborate, so awful. There was hardly a word he ever spoke, a thing he did, she could herself subscribe to. Her feeling left him and moved still further in, to feeling's source, where there were no names, no New York or Starkeyville, and no words for things.

Then it moved out again. They had not married each other, she reflected, because of being alike. And if she loved him, it was less because he had been loyal and courageous, or foolish and in need of her, or even because she understood him better or found him more lovable, than simply because he was her husband, and she just did.

"No," she replied. "Or not now."